A HEART OF ICE

THE HEARTFORGED DESTINIES

BOOK 1

K. WRIGHT

Published by K Dub Publishing

Cover Design by JoAnna Howard

Ebook ISBN: 979-8-9985824-1-7

Paperback ISBN: 979-8-9985824-0-0

For Daysy,
We miss you more than you know

AUTHOR'S NOTE

A Heart of Ice is an adult fantasy romance that contains content that may upset some readers. It is intended for readers over the age of 18.

Content warnings include cursing, sexual themes throughout, explicit sexual scenes, digital monitoring / light stalking, mentions of violence and kidnapping, death (off page), burns.

If you found out about this through my mother or my sister without context. I ask you again, to please read the content warnings. If the word "dick" gets you upset - you will see words such as that and acts including said appendage in at minimum:

- Chapter 3
- Chapter 21
- Chapter 25
- Chapter 49

To my grandmother, I love you... just... if you read chapter 49, please don't tell me.

PROLOGUE

THE FATES

The door to our little house creaks open before the sound of boots stomping across the wood floors greets our ears.

"We are in the living room," one of my sisters sighs. Jaeson has been coming by more and more often. Begging us to meddle in the affairs of the mortal world.

We have kept a close eye on Summer Chase since the time of her birth. Only once have we struck the chord of her life to try to steer her in a different direction. That was ten years ago, and Jaeson has been a thorn in our side ever since.

She is his long awaited heir, here to finally bring balance back between the human and Fae. And he is clearly beginning to lose his patience. We cannot begin to understand why. He's only been here just shy of a thousand years. Ten years, thirty-seven years for that matter, should feel like a drop in the bucket at this point.

"What can we help you with today, Jaeson?" My sister asks, concealing our collective premonition of what he is about to ask.

"Sisters, thank you for having me." Jaeson is about to begin a monologue.

"Oh now he has manners," I huff out a laugh. "Just get to the point young man."

"It is time for Summer to come into her full powers. I need Dune to return to her back in Lyra to finish what was started."

"We've told you many times, we are unsure of what the repercussions of this will be."

"I understand, but it has to be done. We can wait no longer for her to understand what her powers truly mean."

My sisters and I look to each other. "Which thread is the safest to tug on do you think?"

"You aren't going to fight me on this?" Jaeson stutters.

"No dear, I tire of your presence and would like to spend the next millennia without having to hear your voice."

My sisters and I gather around the dais. We raise our hands, and though six hands hover over the silver water we still only expected one strand of fate. To our surprise, six strands float to the surface.

"I told you it was time," Jaeson whispers. Not many have seen this process, but he knows to show it the respect it is due. "Who are they?"

Who are they indeed? Koda and Summer's lines have continued their entanglement even after Dune removed himself from their three strand braid. Dune's line has not been cut from Summer's though. The other three are more intriguing. We are unsure of how this young woman's line, Emily Turner, will affect Summer. Emily has her own set of chords running across her own.

The final two are the reason Jaeson is here. Ashryn and Aaron. "You do understand with Ashryn and Aaron's fate lines risen, any ripple in the dais will have effects on their decisions as well? It could speed up any of the actions you fear are happening."

Jaeson nods. "It must be done."

Each sister presses their right index finger into the liquid. "May the wheel of time turn once more. The human must lose themself. Only then can the heir rise."

CHAPTER 1
QUEEN ASHRYN

I sit at the table in my private garden, waiting on my cousin. As the Queen of this Fates forsaken country, I should not have to wait for anything. It proves that my powers are truly waning, if my own cousin cannot heed my order to show up on time. I tap my foot, trying not to look bored. The garden is well-kept, beautiful even. I would spend more time here if beauty was something to be admired. Right now, I just want the power to maintain my own beauty.

These days, I only ever use the garden for private conversations which should not be accidentally overheard. The glass in the windows and doors that face this garden are enhanced with sound proofing materials that make it impossible to hear anything from inside or outside. Which is why I am taken by surprise when I don't hear Aaron until he is swaggering through the door to meet me.

"You are late."

"Your security guards would not let me pass without going through the metal detector seven times." He raises his blonde eyebrows at me, waiting for an explanation. My staff has been finding surveillance bugs throughout the palace and federal buildings. No one has been able to catch the culprit, despite the fact they are on high alert.

"New security protocol," I wave it off.

Aaron pulls the chair out from the other side of the table, "Well you called me all the way across the country, dear cousin. Do tell me what was so urgent."

I always forget just how different we are from each other. He's six foot four, with the build of a tree. Blonde hair, blue eyes. Compared to my five foot two, tiny build with red hair and green eyes. He is ten years my junior at thirty-five, but you would think we would have some tiny similarity seeing as we are cousins. The only similarity is our pointed Fae ears.

"Have you found the leak in your program?"

"I have told you over and over, there is no leak."

"Then how come you have a rebel group blowing up buildings in your region and kidnapping people? Humans that - should I remind you - your technology is supposed to be finding!" I rub my hands along the black skirt of my dress reminding myself to have outbursts like that. It is unbecoming of a Queen, after all.

"Ashryn, you know that …"

"I don't want excuses, Aaron. I want answers. We need a human power wielder. Do you not feel your powers waning? It is as if the more they use their powers, the more they steal from us."

"I am still the governor of Alnitak, Ashryn. I cannot just disappear someone without cause. The paperwork and due process is quite excessive."

"Fuck the paperwork, then."

"You know I cannot do that."

"You can. And you will. We need to start running labs to see what the source of their power is. You do not test your power levels as regularly as I do, since you know… your mother did not help you there. My labs are showing a steady decrease. It is getting worse."

Aaron chews on his lip.

"I will do what I can."

"You will do more than that. I will be sending my federal level approval of your program to the government officials here in Lyra. You will negotiate a contract with FaeTech. Despite all of the background checks, someone on the team at Star Technologies is a mole. Get a contract and a team going at FaeTech. Find. The. Leak."

Aaron gets a nefarious gleam in his eye. "No. I know you are obsessed with that little brunette human that works at FaeTech. You absolutely will not build the team under her."

Aaron smiles wide now, as if I did not just give him an order. "Summer Chase is the best in the damn business, Ashryn. If even just for women's rights, you can't let me give this to a man less qualified."

"If she was Fae, sure. She is *human*. I am not about to risk the powers of our people being lost just because of your little crush on this human."

Aaron waves me off, but his smile remains planted on his face. "Maybe by expanding with FaeTech and capturing data in Lyra we may finally find the fire wielder." Aaron mocks. He doesn't believe the myth about the chosen one. I don't know when the scroll opened, but sometime in the last decade it did. No one outside of myself and a few historians have seen it. Those historians did not live long enough to tell the tale to anyone else.

The Scroll of Peace laid open on its pedestal. Words prophesying the chosen one of the humans to help restore balance and peace between the Fae and humans. A chosen one, a sole human gifted with the power to wield flames.

"No need to make jabs at my expense. Go do your duty to this country now."

Aaron stands and gives a mocking bow before turning to leave.

I don't trust that he will not at least try to enlist Summer

Chase. Once the contract is written up, I will give their CEO a call. No need to leave it up to chance. Knowing that Aaron would want to hire her, I preemptively gathered some intel of my own on Summer Chase. I grab the burner phone from my purse and open to the only number I saved in it.

It takes a few rings for the other line to answer. "This is Dune Raydn."

"Mr. Raydn, this is Your Royal Highness, Ashryn of Elinder." I hear him cough, most likely choking on a drink not realizing who exactly was calling.

"Your- your highness. Why, uh, what can I do for you?"

"I'd like to talk to you about a job opening up soon in my federal technology office."

CHAPTER 2
SUMMER

Sweat is dripping into my eyeballs. At this point it may actually be my eyeballs that are sweating. My caramel hair is braided and off to the side, but even the tips are slicked together with sweat. If it isn't the scarring on the ruddy brick walls, the bullet-sized holes in the punching bags, scarecrows, and other various targets are all evidence that this task is more challenging than I initially thought it would be.

The goal was set a couple weeks ago. Over the years, Jackie and I would add new training "goals" to a jar. We have also started gathering ideas from the trainees. We always say it is a goal. This wouldn't explain the chalkboard filled with tally marks in the surveillance room, though. Once one "goal" is done, the first person to finish it between Jackie, Jackie's wife Kyria, and myself gets the tally on the board under their name and pulls the next goal. Jackie and Kyria then will take it to the trainees to let them have their fun.

I sure didn't put this monstrosity in the jar. I stare around at the ten targets in a circle around me. Each of them is eighteen inches from the wall with the exception of one. Somehow we are supposed to essentially shoot one target - any target, then redirect that "bullet" into the only target that is flush with the wall.

I've been at this for two hours today. Any minute now Jackie or Kyria is going to walk in and interrupt the very little progress that's been made.

Based on the fact Jackie hasn't tried it in the last week, I have to guess she has all but given up. She's great at making large balls of wind, cyclones, and even walls of air that can be used as a shield or a cage. Creating a tiny bullet size ball of wind and directing it has not been a success.

Kyria has gotten a little closer. This has been a great refresher on… dirt clods. And sticks. All the non-flowery parts of her powers basically. She hates it. She did also shoot a stake so hard at a target that it went through and splintered into a thousand pieces on impact. Thankfully Jackie was so entertained she cleaned them up… after chasing us out of the room with a wall of tiny shards.

Kyria's latest iteration has been trying to rope off her stake with a vine, but she hasn't been able to get the same speed and momentum. The instructions on the goal explicitly call out that it is a singular, *non-connected* projectile anyways. So the move would only be a stepping stone.

In that same vein, I have tried using a stream of fire connected to my hands. I can direct it around the room. As soon as I disconnect it from my hands, it follows a straight path.

My final target sits to my back, a punching bag hanging in front of me. Contemplating the intent of the goal, I flip the idea over in my head. We've each been in more of an offensive stance. Would a slower approach work? Could I create more of a tie to the projectile in order to pull it back? It seems so… simple. So comic book like. When I think back to building the foundations of our training it does almost make sense. We have people start with stances you would see in a superhero movie. So maybe this move can also start with an exaggeration. *Just pull it back.*

I mean, I do shoot fire bullets with finger guns. Here goes nothing.

With the idea to "pull" the fire bullet back to me I form a small fireball, no bigger than a grape in my right hand. Raising my hand so the hot orb faces the target ahead of me, I force myself to embellish my movements. I pull my arm back as if to pitch, then rocket the fireball out of my hand with the momentum.

As if waiting for the end of a rope, I leave my hand out. I wait until *just* the right moment to "grab" the air and pull the bullet back through the far target. What do I do if the sphere turned missile actually turns back my way? Sling my arm like a whip back? Turn and push it?

The fire does a quick reverse, which is great. Thinking too hard about how to keep the momentum going, I forgot one tiny detail.

To move out of the way.

The bullet of fire pummels straight into my stomach, singing a hole into my shirt as it fizzles out. It doesn't hurt outside of knocking the wind out of me. The laughter bubbling up is just a side effect.

I take a moment to catch my breath before setting up again. Along with moving out of the way, I swing my arm downwards on my pull motion. The small blaze of heat bolts past me into the target and wall behind me.

I gape at the wall, finally having done it.

Now on a high and feeling cocky, the next bullet is formed in my hand. This time the intended goal will be met - swing the single fireball through every target. There is a bit more mental geometry this round. Slinging the fireball across the room, it hits a target. I pull it back to hit the one opposite side of the circle. Then back to the target next to the first one. If my flames left a trail, a beautiful multi-pointed star would be drawn.

I hear the door click shut at my back. It is most likely Kyria coming to grab me for class. Knowing she can be a sore loser, I throw up a wall of fire with my left hand. The sizzle of something being incinerated fills my ears. She probably shot an avalanche of flowers to distract me. The fireball hits the final target as I release all of my flames.

I face her and my main target with a smirk.

"I always knew you were a little shit." Kyria laughs as she inspects the singed hole in the target closest to her. The scarecrow almost meets her five foot four frame.

"You been out gardening today? Didn't Jackie say no more wildflowers in the community garden? That people were beginning to question where they were coming from?"

She looks at her pink arms that are on their way to matching her waist long red hair. Kyria's green eyes slant towards me before she retorts, "For calling me out like that, you can tell Jackie you figured this horrid goal out."

"Hopefully we never have to use it. It's slower than just flicking new conjurings at each target. Why do I have to tell her this? Don't I have class to go teach?"

"True. If I tell her, I'm going to lie. Tell her you think we should time trial this and set new personal records for the next month."

I shiver at the thought. Jackie totally would if we thought it was a viable skill. The viable skills are solved. Then we time them. Next, we attempt to beat that time over and over and over. And we document *everything*.

"I will tell her. We can decide then if it's something you two want to teach the rest of the group."

Kyria gives me that look I am all too familiar with by now. She and I both know that this is one of those moves that would only be useful for me. Sure, Jackie and Kyria may tweak it a bit to make it work for the other power wielders. This one will go in the "Summer Show Off" jar. A jar that will never be used.

Changing the subject, "I need to change my shirt before class."

Kyria shakes her head before commenting with a small smile,

"I won't forget to pull that part of the recording. I can't wait to see how that happened."

Unlike the top floor of training rooms, this room thankfully has windows. It is about the size of a normal school classroom. While there are individual desks, they are not orderly. Instead, they are scattered around the room depending on the number of new folks each week. Regretfully I pull down the blinds so that people aren't baking from the heat.

Once everyone has filed in, I introduce myself and start my spiel. A spiel that has been repeated dozens of times over.

"Hello everyone! My name is Summer. Jackie and Kyria, who you have already met will be overseeing your training and accommodations. My job is to oversee and assist with your transition back into the general public should you choose that path. This will take into account mostly technological changes with a sprinkle of lifestyle changes. The intent of our program is not to hold you captive or in exile. We want to empower you over the next month while you are here. This way, if you want to go home or go live somewhere else you can do so feeling safe."

I survey the room of new faces. Luckily, most look refreshed. We give them a few days to get settled in after their trip before hitting them with the heavy things. The unfortunate reality is we have to get them to take this seriously enough to be safe out in society. They obviously felt enough fear - not only to leave Arcalis - but to also find our specific travel escort group. Every so often someone pops in and catches the caravan along the route from Arcalis to Lyra, but it is rare.

Over the years we've gone from the caravan arriving once a quarter to once every two weeks. We've told the team in Arcalis that we cannot take groups any faster than that. Not unless it is some sort of tier one emergency. We haven't seen one of those yet thank the Fates.

A brawny man raises his hand tentatively. I nod at him, knowing what question he is probably about to ask. There is always one.

"You said technology … Will we be given any cool weapons to protect ourselves? Are you preparing for a civil war?"

It is a question we get with every new group. It is getting harder and harder to answer with gusto. Kyria's unspoken commentary lingers in my mind, flared back to life by this question.

"I can definitely understand the desire for cool technology. We don't know each other well, yet. I can imagine you have been frightened enough for this lifetime and the next. Wanting a defense is only natural. Luckily, Kyria and Jackie are going to help you hone in on your natural weapons. They also trained me. I can attest that what they will teach you will be better than any weapon we would scrounge together."

I hesitate before continuing. It is always about the phrasing. "We are not asking you to hide once you leave here. Our operation does not have the funds or reach to be able to start any sort of conflict. We do have advantages with that. Bear with me as I start with our bit of history lesson before we get to the fun stuff."

I smile, the seven faces give me tentative smiles or nods back. "Outside of Arcalis, our kind have generally stayed under the radar. We generally look like humans, and we don't have any physical tells outside our powers themselves. This gives us an advantage that the first generation of Fae did not have."

Addressing the grimaces, I proceed, "Yes, we all learned in grade school about the immaculate conception of the Fae kind. Thousands of children spontaneously being born on the seventeenth day of every month. Born with pointed ears, this was the only physical tell upon birth. This was odd, but nothing to be concerned about. As they started to age, their magic started to shine through. Only then did they go from being an oddity, to a threat to the established power system. The Fae were rounded up year after year after this. For twenty years they were poked and prodded, seen as scientific experiments, or treated as lesser beings.

One day, before anyone could comprehend the impact of their actions, thousands of Fae children were now millions of angry Fae adults. A fifty year rebellion was started, and with their magic they came out on top. According to the history books, the Fae have 'ruled fairly and equally across all species for over a thousand years.' Don't we just love how the victor gets to write their own history?"

I keep eye contact with the man who asked the initial question. "When the victor writes the history books, they sometimes like to leave out the pieces that could expose them to another rebellion. *That* is what we are all digging for. What is the key information that is buried? What are those critical movements on the chessboard that tip the advantage one way or the other?

"Any major country or world wide event opens the doors for a lot of political oversight. Personal privacy laws end up going out the window first, with the roaring applause of societal approval. Any inklings of war put people on edge. They will give up their privacy saying 'I have nothing to hide' with the expectation that the invasion is temporary. It never is.

"I won't start my smart home technology soapbox yet. We have advances in technology that have opened the door for corporations to sell your habits to the highest bidder, and government entities to create a pseudo surveillance state with that information. All of that said, it is astounding that our kind has not been revealed to the rest of the world. This gives us a large advantage the Fae did not have."

Despite my cynicism, I still know when to give a good theatrical pause. Only once a few heads cock to the side in anticipation do I continue.

"So long as this government does not give us a name, they

cannot use us to generate fear across the nation. If there isn't enough fear, there isn't an excuse to cut further into our privacy rights. Fear is the motivator for the general population to give up those rights. The current privacy laws have stood for the last fifty or so years. We have a general idea of where government officials can legally obtain data about our lives. Extensive research has been conducted on which technology companies, ads companies, manufacturing companies have contracts with the larger government entities. Additionally, our network has grown to ten thousand people. Some who have come through here, others we simply met in the field. No one in our network has the resources to start another rebellion - not one with the hope of being successful. Until then, my job here is to help us all live our lives invisible to the ever watching eye."

The man doesn't want to let this go though. "Why don't you just send all of the fire wielders out to government bodies and do a purge? Why do we have to hide ourselves away in fear?"

This man ran from his home in fear and now wants other people to go fight for him. What a fantastic rebellion. I resist the urge to pinch the bridge of my nose.

"Anyone here a fire wielder?" I ask, already knowing the answer. Every person in the room shakes their head.

"Can I ask your name?"

"Caleb." He sighs.

"Caleb, I appreciate and fully understand your frustration. My powers appeared about ten years ago. I was frightened, nervous, questioning everything. The last thing any of us need to do is rush into a war without any connections. Any weapons. Or frankly a unified cause. We also don't need a fight on both fronts - Fae and human. We all thought we were human until we found that we weren't. The rest of the world doesn't know that. We are just another power hungry race that hides among them. They didn't see us scared shitless when flowers or wind or water suddenly surged out of us. We can't afford to be brazen and encourage humans and Fae to work together to stamp us out."

"And the fire wielders?"

The lie comes so easy. "Haven't met one. I am not here to theorize or philosophize on the lack of fire wielders. I'm here to help you live a life with a healthy respect for technology, but living nonetheless. At least until the next Jaeson the Bold arrives. Fair?"

"Yes ma'am."

"Oh please don't 'ma'am' me." Clasping my hands together, I look at the seven faces once more. "Let's get started."

Tugging the blinds open again, I bask in the sun for a moment now that class is done. The heat of the sun warms me as my eyes, trying and failing to not to think about Caleb's question about fire wielders.

A fire wielder *would* be a great leader. At least, that is what I am told. It's the symbolism of being able to burn something to ash and allow for rebirth. New growth. New life.

There is a great power in being able to control fire.

Jackie, Kyria, and I put on an equal and united leadership front for anyone that walks through our doors. The two of them have always wanted me to take a more prominent role, though. The memory bubbles up through my brain as if the sun calmed me down enough to let it through.

"You already lead a team of people at your job. You have the skill set to motivate people to be more. You shouldn't squander that." Jackie *says.*

"People are scared," Kyria adds. "They can look to you for inspiration. Hope. A lot of people are running because all they see are people like them disappearing. Whether by the government or a government funded terrorist organization, they are scared. They need to see someone like them leading. "

"You both are already doing a great job. We do a great job as a trio."

"Wind and flowers aren't exactly the most impressive of powers, Summer."

"Let's pretend the government of Alnitak is behind the swath of missing humans. Based on the collateral damage, they are going after more dangerous or by your words 'impressive'. Fire specifically. What happens if we put my powers out front and center for our refugees? Maybe they are ready to start a rebellion. A rebellion that we don't have the resources to actually start. Maybe they are just confident enough to live their lives with the technological prowess I can give them.

"Maybe the whispers of a prominent fire wielder get back to that terrorist group. That group decides to expand their reach to our side of the country. Aaron Dubois is fucking related to the Queen. If he is behind it all, he could probably simply ask her to start allowing it.

"Do we risk our safe haven? Do we risk being able to live our lives and provide refuge? You are asking me to give up my life! For what? To light the fuse of a rebellion that would get promptly stamped out."

They stay silent.

"I'll throw some more marketing funds for my security webinars into those regions, yeah? I'll track attendance. See if I can start doing more in the Arcalis region. Travel there to do some in person ones. Do not ask me to lead this group. Even if I am special, even if I am the only one with this power... that is already lonely enough. Leading this group - whatever that would entail - would just make life that much lonelier. I do not want to do this alone. We are better as a team."

That was the end of the discussion. I was only twenty seven at that time and had only known of my powers for a couple of years. Shortly after that, we decided to let my power remain a secret from that point onwards. We've known each other for nine years and have not met another fire wielder. Nor had they met one before I dropped into their lives.

I am a party of one.

Am I constantly surrounded by people? Yes. Our powers are fed through emotion, which means I chose to live behind a mask. Before my power surged, I lived life so that I could feel every emotion I was gifted. I leaned into those feelings, whether it was sadness, joy, love, anger. Those feelings meant I was alive, it gave me humanity. It was the sort of liveliness that could start a fire - burning you or lighting your way. Now, it could literally start a fire. A surge of love caused a pain that will never leave me, no matter how dull it becomes. So I wear my mask. I can smile, laugh, and be friendly. Those closer to me see the kindness, the respect, the friendly love I can give. Outside of that circle, they see the steady, emotionless Summer.

So, I go home to myself and my books.

Sometimes I go home to Koda. Koda isn't "mine". He only knows half of my life. Going home to him helps fill a void rather than to draw comfort.

It is enough.

It has to be.

Being the leader of this group would just add another layer of solitude. More death to my desire to fully live. Kyria and Jackie have each other. At least if we are equal in our leadership, I still have them too.

No. I am not going to create another lonely circle.

"You look at peace for once."

I peel open an eye to find Jackie leaning up against the wall in front of me. I sigh, sitting up. "Then why did you disturb me?"

"To make sure you are okay."

I look back at my friend. Concern lines her dark face. Her silver hair is braided and hanging off one shoulder. After nine years of friendship she knows most things about me. Jackie and Koda share the ability of catching my bluffs. They can tell when my mood has changed and which direction it has gone. They are both so intimately close, and yet Jackie is the only one with the full context of my life.

In the early years, I did wonder how Koda would react to finding out about my powers. Scared after what happened with Dune, I wasn't ready to lose another friend. As the years went by, my two parallel lives stabilized. While Koda could have been told at any time, I just chose not to. It has simply been easier that way.

"Who are you thinking about?" Jackie pulls me from my thoughts.

"Who?"

"Yeah, I always thought that look was when you were thinking about Dune. At least, when we first met. Now, I don't have any reason to think this has anything to do with him."

I'm not exactly sure why I hesitate to tell her the truth. Maybe it is the fear she may actually encourage me to tell Koda. Or make a bigger deal of my thoughts than necessary. It will be safer to change the subject.

"I solved the latest goal this morning. Want to go watch the recording and make the decision to just leave that one in my jar?" I am already up and walking to the door now.

Giving me a knowing smirk, Jackie lays an arm on my shoulder as we walk out, "Oh yes. Kyria said we should watch the full recording based on a hole in your shirt?"

CHAPTER 3
SUMMER

I let myself into Koda's apartment, but my mind is still whirring. The little fan is constantly trying to keep my brain from overloading. Jackie did not make any comment about the training activity. Other than about my shirt, of course. We dropped the piece of paper into the "Summer" jar. A jar that has been growing taller month over month.

I toe off my shoes at the door, but before I shuffle down the short hallway there are new pictures on the wall. Koda goes to concerts pretty regularly as bands rotate through. He has two posters on his wall at any point in time. Between those, he has eight frames that house photos he takes at those concerts. It is the only time I ever see him take out the expensive camera. Although, depending on his seat, he has taken some incredible shots from his cell phone. The poster on the right has changed. "The Iron Bloom presents for the first time live: Girl with a Heart of Fire!" Maybe that can be my theme song. I chuckle to myself to cover the twinge of sadness at not having been there with Koda.

Speaking of, looking into the living room from here, I don't spot his scruffy hair at the couch. Turning to my right, I find him in the kitchen. Finally, my brain pulls all my strands of thought into one singular focus. That tapered line from Koda's shoulders to his ass in those damn gray sweats. He is fussing with the pizza box on the counter, unaware of my presence. I take advantage of my moment and admire my view.

Shirtless, I can see every line of muscle in his toned shoulders. Fates bless whoever told him about functional fitness. His shoulders are broad enough that he could be mistaken for a swimmer. The thing that gives it away is the strip of oblique muscles that fill the tapered abs. My mouth goes dry thinking about licking them again. His sweats sit low on his hips… Most people see Koda in jeans and a collared shirt and imagine he has a nice runner's body under it all. My mind slips to thoughts of squeezing those thighs, that ass.

"I knew I was just a piece of meat to you," Koda halts my scouring.

When I meet his blue eyes, his lips are tilted up toward the small earring in his right ear. His beard and mustache matches his black hair only in color. It is the type of black that when you look close enough, you find streaks of barely there reds and caramels. The beard is clean, trimmed and seemingly groomed in comparison to the strands of hair that look like he's been pulling on throughout the day. He turns around and leans back against the counter. I can't help but watch his hands clutch the counter, flexing his forearms to keep him rooted. The bulge in his pants growing as I eat him up with my eyes.

One hand reaches behind him and closes the pizza box.

"How long has it been since we last fucked, Summer?" There's the slightest growl in there.

Seven months, three weeks, and a day. "Seven months or so."

His eyes inspect my face as he takes three strides to reach me. He takes my purse out of my hand and drops it in the closest chair before grabbing me by the thighs and wrapping my legs around him.

"We both know it was closer to eight. How long has it been since someone last worshipped you?"

My eyes must blow out at the question. Koda is the last person I slept with. Have I really not found any sort of release from anyone since the last time? Koda starts walking somewhere, pulling my shirt off as he goes, while I sort through my thoughts.

He is kissing down my chest as he purrs, "Poor girl. Am I ruining you for others?" He pulls down the cup of my bra, taking one of my nipples into his mouth as he sets me down on the edge of his bed. The leggings are easily slid off before Koda leans over me, crawling us farther into bed. "You didn't answer my question."

His eyes are glittering with mischief, poking at one of the unspoken boundaries. The only time we ever bring up other one-night stands is if it is recent enough to need testing. I never interfere if he is dating someone. He never asks about my sex life. Koda hasn't been on any dates in at least a year. Apparently, I have not slept with anyone else in a similar time frame.

Not ready to think about any of the reasons why, I bite back a response. "I think you should quit talking and start doing better things with your mouth."

Quicker than I can react, Koda flips us. I am straddling him, but he kept himself close, his nose nuzzling mine. "Make me," he orders. Our breaths mingle together, his hand holding us together by the back of my neck.

After all my thoughts this afternoon about living fully, I forget myself. To taste Koda, to know what his lips felt like on my own… that would be living. I haven't been kissed in ages. While kissing a stranger is nice, it means nothing. Kissing Koda… that could be electrifying. The gravity of that idea pulls me closer. Koda's eyes go wide just slightly, but it is enough to remind me that kissing Koda could cost me my world. I bring a trembling hand to the crook of his neck to give him a nudge. He leans back so I'm laying fully on top of him now. There is still just miniscule amount of space between us.

"Make you do something better with your mouth?"

Koda's grip on the back of my neck tightens as he breathes out, "Please."

"Your wish is my command." I try to ignore that small lift of his head as I scoot myself up and away. His eyes show just the smallest shade of sadness, before they go feral with my knees straddling his face now.

It is easier this way, is my last thought before I sink into the pleasure.

CHAPTER 4
KODA

My phone buzzes me out of sleep. Before I open my eyes though, I breathe in the lingering scent of Summer's perfume from my pillow. The memories from last night bubble to the top of my mind. She almost kissed me. Multiple times. I've replayed the moment she left over and over wondering what I could have done differently. How I could have convinced her to stay the night.

Summer hops back into her pants as I lean against the doorway to my bedroom. She looks at peace, despite her hair being mussed up, strands going in random directions. She unfortunately catches me staring. "What? Do I have something in my hair?" She pats at her hair as she asks.

"You sure you don't just want to stay the night?" I ask, attempting to not sound needy.

"Nah, I need to get home and finish up some work. Thank you for the offer, though." She strides over to me, pushes up her toes, and kisses me on the cheek before promptly walking out the door.

I groan as I roll out of bed. There is no use in reliving that moment. I can't get it back. The clock flashes a red seven am. Sundays are our lazy days together. My phone should not be going off for at least another thirty minutes.

Turning my phone over, I see multiple texts from Dune. If it is an emergency he would call. My morning routine and stretches take over, albeit less rushed. Once dressed I call him on my way out. He answers on the first ring.

"Isn't it before eight am?" Dune answers instead of a "Hi."

"Oh, I was beginning to think you forgot you are three hours ahead of me with your incessant texting, asshole. Good morning to you, too."

"Yeah, yeah, yeah. Not like you had a long night last night. Otherwise you wouldn't be up now anyways."

A flash of Summer's body arched beneath me last night flashes to the front of my mind. No need to open that can of worms. "Whatever you say buddy. So what has you so twisted up on this Sunday morning, Dune?"

"I either need you to push me over a ledge or away from it."

"Okay…I've got like ten minutes. Hit me with it."

"I'm thinking about leaving my job at Star," Dune blurts out.

"Wow, that's …"

"Huge. I know. We are those oddballs that have stayed at our companies just climbing the ranks for a decade now."

"So what is the job?"

"It would be for a Chief Technical Officer role at a new division being created in the Office of the Royal Cabinet."

"Damn."

"Yeah, it is a pretty quiet creation."

The Royal Cabinet falls under full country, federal jurisdictions. Federal offices are all here in Lyra…where Summer and I are. Dune has spent the last decade a whole country away from us. Something feral urges me to push him away from taking this job. We've maintained our friendship. Although it has generally just been in the form of yearly trips out to Arcalis. This year was going to be my last. He hasn't set foot in Lyra in ten years, and I am tired of hiding my friendship with Summer from him.

"How did you find out about it? Sounds pretty sketchy if it's a federal job. Aren't they required to actually post new openings? To be fair and equitable and all that?"

"I know a lot of people in that space due to some of our contracts. I trust the contact that told me about it."

"And you are willing to change career paths for this mystery job? What if you take it and it isn't what you think it is?"

"I have some personal reasons to take on the challenge." Dune pauses before trying to distract away from that comment. Laughing he continues, "Star would take me back if I needed to go back. It almost sounds like you would not enjoy me being back in Lyra."

"Nah, man, it's just…"

"Summer." I can hear the grimace through the phone.

Waving to the object of his ire, I cross the street to meet her. The Fae that pass her with their pointed ears look more ethereal, but she glows brighter than anyone around her. She is putting her brown hair up in a ponytail as I approach. She's in black leggings and an ice blue tank top that hugs her curves. Fates above, she is beautiful. What would have happened if I hadn't let her leave? Grabbed her by the back of the neck and pulled her lips back to mine? Would she have stayed or ran? We started this friends-with-sometimes-benefits eight years ago. Sometimes we go a year without sleeping with each other. Other times, it could be every weekend in a month. With it, though, the small, playful touches that came with our friendship stopped. Would she want that back? I miss her playfulness. Fates, if I miss her touch so much what will happen if I feel her lips on my own? Would I be able to just stay friends? What is going on? Maybe I am just confused. The last time we had unplanned sex was the first time we ever slept together. All other times have at minimum had some sort of booty call text ahead of time. Maybe that is why I am discombobulated.

"Dude, are you even listening?"

"Nope." I pop as I finally walk across the street. "Sorry,

Dune. You know my mind stops functioning when a beautiful woman walks by."

Summer nods and smirks before using my shoulder for balance as she stretches out her hamstrings.

"What I was saying - It's not like I would meet you at your office after work or anything. Although we totally could just to fuck with her. It's a big city. I should be able to steer clear of Summer Chase."

Unlikely.

"Uh huh."

"The next step will be to convince you to come work for me. Then we can both steer clear. Summer will probably be pissed once she finds out I am back in town. You don't need to be in the firing range of that."

Now it is my turn to laugh. "You know I like my boss too much to come work for you." Summer ... I am not sure how Summer would react. She wouldn't take it out on me, I know. Would she simply be disinterested? Or would his presence break that careful mask she keeps up for everyone else?

"I need to figure out what this guy is putting in your water at work."

"If you ever meet them, you can ask. Look, I gotta go man. Keep me posted."

"Tell your running buddy he needs to get laid so you can sleep in."

I laugh and look at Summer, "Hey. My friend wants me to tell you to get laid."

She wiggles her eyebrows at me. "Bye, man."

As soon as I hang up, Summer scoffs. "I still cannot believe he has no idea we are on talking terms, let alone friends."

I shrug, really unsure of what to say. Our triangle of friendship died ten years ago. Summer did try to hold us all together for a few years despite Dune's action. He left her broken in pieces in her apartment ten years ago and never looked back. I've never gotten the story of what happened out of either of them. I figured someone would tell me eventually. Because of this, I came to realize over the years that it was never Dune tying me to Summer. It was Summer tying us together.

Have I told Dune that I never cut contact with Summer? No. Has he asked? Also no.

"He never calls you this early. Or at least if he does, the conversation doesn't last this long."

"I think that is the first actual comment you've made about Dune in like eight years, Summer. "

She shrugs. "Let's call it growth, or something. What was so important?"

I eye her shrewdly before she puts her hands up.

"I'm not planning anything. Really it is just pure curiosity. You will remember that I was never the one attacking him in interviews."

"True, true. Eh, he is contemplating leaving Star. Looking at a couple other jobs."

"No shit? Wow."

"Yeah. Will also try to get me to jump ship if he does. You heard me though. I like my boss too much." I pull her into me with my arm around her neck. My height over her brings her head right under my chin. She still smells like whatever perfume she wore yesterday. "You owe me a hug, boss lady." I say to cover the fact I am trying to breathe in the smell of her.

Pushing me off her, she shuffles a hand through my black shaggy hair. I set it back somewhat straight before we start our run winding down the streets.

Sundays we diverge from our normal five mile loop. We still run past my apartment complex, but instead of heading north we turn south. It is not a direct path to the farmer's market, rather, a path that still gives us a five mile run..

It must have been five years ago when Summer discovered this market. Unwilling to give up her morning run with me, Summer insisted we find a way to run down there and still get five miles in.

Once we figured out a path that worked, we have run it liter-ally every Sunday since. It is a day I can claim as my own with her. A day no one else gets to see. No Jackie. No work colleagues. No Dune. Just me. It is the only time Summer removes her mask in public. She is wholly herself, at least this older, tamer version of herself. If there is ever a time and place where her younger, exuberant self ever comes out, it is here.

Fates, she even found these little collapsible bags that she clips onto her running belt just for Sundays so we could meander around and grab things. You would think she would actually buy food at this thing. But you can hardly find anything fresh in her apartment. Outside of maybe a loaf of bread.

Fifty minutes later we are at our Sunday sanctuary.

Summer does a little twirl and pulls to uncollapse one of those bags.

"I see we are *very* ready for the farmer's market today."

Summer hums as she twists around people as we mosey through the tents. She is practically buzzing as I pull her in close to keep her from forgetting that I exist.

"You are extra excited this morning. You practically jumped me last night. Anything fun you want to share with the class?"

I keep my hand on her back. It doesn't feel wrong or weird.

This feels right.

"I don't know what you are talking about. Are we conve-niently forgetting that you specifically had on gray sweatpants and no shirt on when I got there. It is like you were begging for me to."

"Oh come on. If you don't tell me, I am just going to assume you have some weird mental competition. That you have been secretly staying at FaeTech just to outlast Dune at Star. Oh my goodness! you aren't planning on quitting on me now are you?" Getting more obnoxious to make her spill her secrets, I keep going. "Is this you breaking up with me? I will have you know I am following you wherever you go. You don't just get to leave me Summer Chase!"

"FATES ABOVE STOP. Okay, okay." Summer scowls. "I am *not* going to leave FaeTech so stop worrying about that. I stopped living my life around Dune Raydn a long time ago. You should know that."

"Then *what* aren't you telling me?"

Summer huffs out a breath. "It's a little stupid. I don't really talk about my self defense class I take with Jackie. We have been practicing this one move for a month or so. Yesterday, I finally got it figured out. That's all."

I turn her by the chin to face me with my thumb and index finger. "That isn't stupid. I know I don't ask you much about that class… which is strange now that I think about it. You are my best friend. *Obviously* I am your best friend - despite whatever Jackie says. So I want to hear those things. You want to show me one day?"

Something that almost looks like sadness crosses her eyes before Summer cups my cheek with a small pat. "I wouldn't want to hurt you, dear."

Her hand feels too nice there. It is sending me straight back to that missed opportunity to kiss her last night. Before doing anything stupid, I peel her hand away and kiss her palm. "I am not *that* fragile. But keep your secrets then. I will just make sure to never accidentally mug you."

Our hands stay clasped together until we split up. I grab my fresh lemons, strawberries, and herbs while Summer peruses the stacks from the Prison Library Project stand. She always buys one. Everything she buys here is intentional. Whether for the item itself, or which stand she buys it from.

She has never said anything about it, but Summer will only stop at stands where there are both humans and Fae working the stand. Every bit of her life is given to empowering others that don't have the same advantages as the Fae. The same advantages I have had. Whether it's by shopping at local small or independently run businesses, or just ensuring she has a diverse hiring pool.

That is how she carries so much respect from her various teams, no matter what any outside critics have to say about her. It is why FaeTech will never let her leave. Whether it is because they actually value her views or just the impact she has. Her influence carries a solid weight through the ecosystem.

Our second to last stop is grabbing some coffee at the end of the street. Starstruck always puts out a stand and Summer, ever the regular, makes sure to stop.

Kristyn, our favorite barista, is manning the booth today. She gives me a big, toothy grin which I return with a look of confusion. She pointedly looks down between me and Summer. Somewhere between filling our bags and getting to the coffee stand we found our way back to each other, hands twined together.

How did I not realize that?

I shake my head, letting go of Summer's hand and giving her a small nudge forward. Summer looks back and forth as a silent conversation continues between Kristyn and I. Kristyn's poker face leaves much to be desired.

"Everything good?" Summer asks.

"YUP!" Kristyn says way too loudly. "Summer, you want a chai today? It's warm out. Iced? I'll grab it. Koda will stay and pay after he tells me whatever monstrosity of a drink he wants today."

All three of us stare at each other. Summer looks unsure of what is happening. Kristyn clearly knows something.

"SCOOTCH." She waves Summer off before turning to me. "You are going to tell me that was nothing?"

"Could you say that any louder?" I hush her, putting my body between her and where Summer went to go stand.

"Dude, I just wanna know if I have finally won my bet with the rest of the staff."

"Whaaaaat are you talking about?"

"Koda. You and Summer are best friends. I get that. Best friends don't hold hands."

The anvil that has been hanging in my chest since last night finally drops in my stomach. Why can't I say anything? Why is my mouth parched?

"I ... "

"Fates," She curses. "Okay. Reset your brain. Tell me what drink you want today. Then please tell me when you figure out your hand holding situation."

I pick up the Sunday paper for Summer as we head to our last stop.

"Everything okay?"

"Yeah…" I mumble. *I think?*

I am desperately scrolling through memory after memory in my mind as we wind our way back north on the next street over. I've held Summer's hand before… right? Neither one of us shrugged out of it. It did not feel strange or out of place. The reel of time in my head is not bringing anything up where we have held hands before. Even in our early years, it was only ever linked arms.

Then how did it feel so normal? So right?

Summer did not shrug out of my hold at all today. *She* kissed me yesterday. I mean a peck on the cheek, but still. Things would get really weird. Summer has not dated anyone seriously… ever. Not since Dune left, and they never even dated. Our friends-with-sometimes-benefits works for us. Neither one of us has ever asked for more from the other. Random booty calls when lonely can be hidden from jobs, friends. But a whole relationship?

Dune would kill me. Despite his hatred of her.

Do you care what Dune thinks anymore? Really?

I would have to quit my job. Summer would never go for it while I still worked for her.

You can find another job easily.

Okay… okay… slowdown. No one is quitting jobs. We've had twenty years to flush this out if it was going to happen. I catch myself staring at her as if by staring it could let me see inside of her brain.

My focus is pulled back to the present as we arrive at the

flower shop. Summer keeps giving me questioning looks. "I'm fine. Go buy your lilies."

By the time Summer gets her lilies, my head is back on straight. Mostly. I don't want to mess up our friendship. Perhaps this is just a fluke. A slip in the multiverse.

We walk back to her place as we normally do. Sipping on our drinks as we chatter about what the next week would bring. Every time her arm brushes mine feels like a lightning bolt skittering across it. My body is going into hyperdrive with every touch, every brush. This is just nerves. From what? Anything. Dune suggesting he may come back to Lyra. Kristyn's comment about holding hands. That damn peck on my cheek. That's all this is.

It has to be.

I'm just being proactively overprotective of my best friend from my other best friend that hurt her in a way neither have told me.

That's all this is.

CHAPTER 5
EMILY TURNER
TWO MONTHS LATER

*C**alm down.*

Calm down.

Calm down.

How could I have been so stupid?

After feeling the explosion behind me, it's as if the shock-wave pushes me along as I run back to my apartment. Normally I would stay under the radar, but my gut tells me to throw caution into the wind. I fumble with my keys, shaking with the events of just the last thirty minutes.

I should have taken Teivel with me.

I shouldn't have gone at all.

Finally, my keys power through the shaking of my hand, allowing me into my apartment. Trying to breathe, I look around my apartment. So many flowers and plants.

So much evidence of my powers.

I press my thumb and index finger to the closest flower, grounding myself in the feel of the petal. All of this beautiful life that's been created over the years in this apartment. A blaring noise comes from my phone in my pocket.

It is the sound you would generally associate with a missing child alert. This time though, it is my name and face staring back at me with "SUSPECT" in big bold flashing letters.

Although I never thought they would be needed, plans have been in place for an event where leaving is required. Sprinting to my bedroom, I toss bags and shoes out of my closet until my grip finds the handle of my bug out bag. There is a nondescript plain white hat and a hooded sweatshirt in the closet that I throw on.

There is no time to leave Sarah a note. Instead, I turn off my phone and leave it on top of a picture of the two of us in her underwear drawer. Hopefully, whoever comes looking for me will not go looking that hard for the phone. Even if they do find it, they won't be able to track me.

As soon as I am on the fire escape staircases, my burner phone is in my hand. Only one number is programmed into it. This is what the masked men didn't realize. I wanted to hear them out, see what they were doing. I did not anticipate them trying to coerce me into leaving with them right then and there. My choice was made for me, but I am unwilling to give them full autonomy of how I leave now.

The receiver clicks as the call connects.

"Hey Teival, I need your help."

CHAPTER 6
SUMMER

*"**ummer! Koda wants us to all be great friends. And his roommate has been struggling to make friends...", she pauses without saying "like you".*

"We are going to have a game night next weekend and Koda is going to bring him along. We won't make it weird I promise!"

"You will love him." Koda says.

"Okay...but don't expect me to date him just because he is your friend."

The freshman dorm dissipates as reality and the waking world starts to interfere. Almost as if narrated from the cloudy sky above a booming voice in her dream drums.

The human must lose themself. Only then can the heir rise.

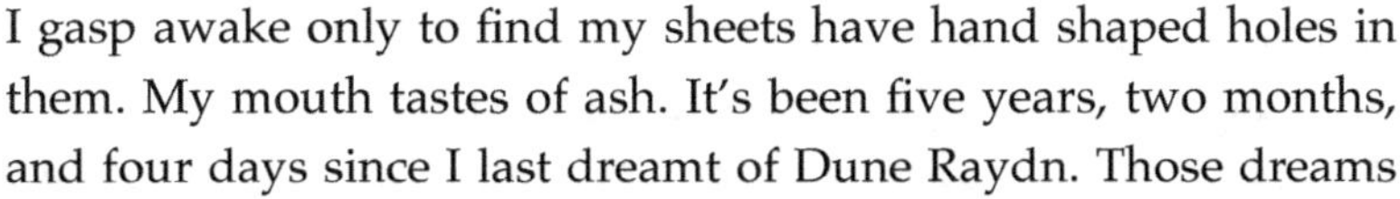

I gasp awake only to find my sheets have hand shaped holes in them. My mouth tastes of ash. It's been five years, two months, and four days since I last dreamt of Dune Raydn. Those dreams had never spun the tail of our lives together like this one though.

If my dream last night didn't set me on edge, the news coming out of Arcalis certainly has. My fingers are tingling in a dance with the flies in my stomach. Starstruck is conveniently located in my direct route between home and the office. Kristyn gives me a nod from behind the counter upon my entrance. There is only one other person in the beige covered coffee shop. I drop my bag in a chair in the back corner of the shop before heading to the line.

My chai is ready by the time I get to the register, placing today's paper next to the till.

"It is a different take on the missing persons this morning." Kristyn nods at the paper.

"Oh yeah?"

"Yeah. Just read it." Her face is pensive as she says it. I thought that would be the end of our conversation until Kristyn placed a hand on the paper. "Hey, I haven't seen Koda in a bit. How is he doing?"

Ah… yes. Koda.

"He's fine."

Kristyn arches her eyebrows before she remembers she is at work, not out at brunch with a friend. I am sure we are both thinking back to the farmer's market where we skipped merrily into an alternate universe without realizing it.

"You see a lot more than most, Kristyn."

"I'm … really sorry if I spooked him, Summer. I -"

"Kristyn." I lay my hand over the counter. "He and I have been friends for a very, very long time. He's seen the best of me. And the worst, frankly. If he needs a bit of space right now then I will happily give it to him. He probably just needs to sort through some feelings. So don't worry yourself over it."

"Have you sorted through your feelings?"

The question stops me short. I carefully tuck her tip into the jar as she hands me my drink and breakfast sandwich.

"That is a great question."

Kristyn gives me a small smile.

"Let me know if you need anything while you are here."

I simply nod at her before walking back to my table. Looking at the bits and bobs on the walls gives me a little bit of a distraction. Unlike the Fae owned chained with its minimalist greens and browns, Starstruck would use paintings and pictures as wall paper if they could. Pictures of celebrities that have come in, obnoxious wall art with quippy quotes you can find at hobby stores, paintings of hairy cows. I know Kristyn framed that Fates forsaken magazine article and it is probably hanging up in the kitchen or office since I refused to sign it.

Unfortunately, my eyes hyperfocus on a sign that reads "Live your dream. Love well. Stay strong." With my eyes so focused there, my mind wanders. It wanders straight back to that morning at the farmer's market. It's been on a constant cycle in my head. Koda had cupped my chin as he spoke about wanting to know about my training. I almost spilled all of my secrets to him right there. Some switch got flipped in my mind; maybe his mind too. I short circuited enough that when he took my hand as we wound our way to our goods, I did not pull away.

We were always touchy until we started occasionally sleeping with each other. Neither of us really mentioned the change. Turns out it was the right call. One unplanned booty call and we started walking around with all of our lines blurred. Holding his hand never felt wrong in that moment. It never felt like a big *thing*. Maybe that is why neither of us unclasped our hands that day.

It has only been seven weeks and three days… not that I'm counting. On the surface, everything looks fine. Where he would normally push me ahead of him, or steal food off my plate I can see the hesitation. Now if he does brush against me, every fiber of my body turns its attention to that spot, even if it was just for a millisecond.

Should we just talk like adults and get all the strange tension out?

Totally.

Have I been putting it off?

Definitely.

That would require me to actually sort through my feelings. He is the one person who has truly seen me at my worst. He stuck around to help hold me as I put the pieces of myself back together. I came out a bit fragmented in the end, but he still stayed. He did more than stay. Koda helped me start living again.

If I let myself, I could fall so deeply for Koda. I would probably end up falling harder than I ever have before. That scares the shit out of me. I don't want to break myself for someone who wouldn't do the same for me. I've done it once. I cannot go through that pain again. If I lose Koda… Our friendship is part of the glue holding so many fragments of my soul together. Like little golden tendrils wrapped throughout. Recovering from the gaping hole in my chest he would leave me with would be impossible.

A white shirt blocks the "Love well" sign, breaking my hyperfocus. As Jackie sits down in the seat in front of me I try for the thousandth time to close down these thoughts. He leaves for his annual trip to Arcalis next week. That gives me a little more time to sort through my feelings. Koda time for his. We can talk once he comes back.

"You good?" Jackie scrunches her eyebrows as her head tilts to the side.

"Yeah. Yeah I am fine." I shake my shoulders out and look down at the paper between us.

"Have you read it yet?"

"No, I was waiting on you." I huff.

"Yes, well I was impatient. Something about this one felt off." She sits, bouncing her heels trying to patiently wait for me to catch up. Emily Turner's face staring up from the front page of the newspaper on the table.

Emily Turner, age 20, until further notice is a suspect at large in the recent bombing of the former meat packing warehouse in Arcalis on the corner of Washington and Morris streets.

Turner was seen entering the building via the north entrance at 1:36pm on Tuesday afternoon. Cameras see her leave thirteen minutes later through the same door she entered.

At 1:51, the explosion destroyed the north facing wall, cutting out power and cameras on the building.

Aaron Dubois, Governor of Alnitak, commends the surveillance systems and the partnership between the Star Technology and the Alnitak government. The video footage of Emily Turner was reported and reviewed by local authorities by 2:00pm. "In under ten minutes - a record time - our teams were able to mount a search for Ms. Turner in hopes of apprehending her."

Numerous missing persons and explosions have become more frequent through the years. When asked if authorities believe that Turner is responsible for those disappearances, Dubois could not say.

"We cannot remove the possibility. Personally I do not think she is the leader. These events would have started when she was merely fifteen. But I do suspect she is associated with the group in some way. I only hope we are able to find her and understand the motive behind all of the harm caused."

Turner's parents are distraught, saying ...

"That is different." I murmur, looking away from the paper. "Do you think a 20 year old could be behind it all?"

I scoff. "No, I actually agree with Dubois on this one. I don't think so."

Jackie and Kyria asked me to lead our little rag tag group at twenty-seven. Imagining this pretty well organized group being led by a twenty year old is absurd. It would be chaos.

"No, it does not fit. Let's pretend she *is* the leader of this group. She would not let herself be caught on camera unless she absolutely wanted to be seen. If Emily Turner wanted to be seen…"

"Why not just stick around and let the authorities nab her in record time?" Jackie finishes my thought.

"Exactly. At least come out with a statement."

"Do you think you could hack some servers to see the camera footage?"

"Probably, but it could take some time."

"It is a good thing I control your calendar then," Jackie smirks.

"Okay, I'll work on that later then. Your people in Arcalis have not heard from anyone?"

"Not a peep. Teivel just mentioned he wanted to come all the way back to Lyra this rotation. Which was strange, but nothing other than that."

"Shall we go do our normal day jobs then?"

It takes us ten minutes to walk to the office. I don't tell her about my dream. It has been almost ten years since I last burned through a set of sheets. Giving the dream an interpretation gives it more foreboding power. It is nothing more than that. Just a dream. The elevator opens up right at that moment to let someone out on the same floor that Koda works on.

He is there, laughing with a colleague over a shared office mug filled with what I assume is shitty office coffee. I can't actually hear his laugh from here, but my brain fills in the gap. My longing turns to anger then sadness over the chosen coffee. Why get good sugary, flavored coffee with Summer when you can have piss black coffee from the office? Koda *hates* black coffee.

"Everything okay?" Jackie asks quietly. Quickly, my mask drains my face of any remaining emotions.

I nod as the elevator lets us out on our floor. Jackie excuses herself with a "if you say so". Luckily, her desk is around the corner from my office. Even so, I frost the glass that makes up three out of four of the walls of my menagerie of an office. Checking my calendar, there is thirty minutes or so to make sure my corporate mask doesn't slip again for my first few meetings.

After these meetings, the rest of my day is a clean slate. Jackie should add "calendar magician" to her resume. We don't normally push meetings around for non-work related things, but this will take more time than finishing up my reports at home.

Would it look more or less suspicious if I locked the door? I stare at my door for far too long contemplating this. In the end, I lower the frosting to the lowest setting and lock the door. At least then if I am deep in concentration, anyone looking to enter my office will see and have to knock to jolt me from it. No need to risk someone unintentionally sneaking up on me as I am heavily focused on hacking a government server.

Two hours go by and I have nothing to show for it except some slightly pulled hair and a grumbling stomach. Instead of torturing myself more, I head down a couple floors to the cafeteria.

There is a gaggle of college students on their building tour right by the door. I hear one girl whisper to another, "Is that Summer Chase?"

"Don't forget to try out the new cookie station." I comment to them, their eyes rounding as I scan my badge and let myself through the barrier. The recruiting team likes to bring in students from neighboring universities to show them what working at FaeTech would be like.

You used to be able to recruit based on a company's values and mission. Now, though, you would think the fresh grads just live at the office. Nap pods, ping pong tables, microkitchens with hidden snacks throughout the building, cafeterias full of chefs of various culinary backgrounds. Don't get me wrong. I *love* this new cookie station. Like the soda machines that let you mix flavors with your base drink, I can pick any base flavor of cookie and add any toppings or goodies I want. Do you want a chocolate chip cookie with a sprinkling of sea salt? Coming right up. Adding in some sprinkles? Why not? There are little mini ovens where your uniquely made single serving cookie dough is baked to perfection in ten to twelve minutes.

I settle on a freshly made sub sandwich, then make my cookie order. Once seated at a table, I take a moment to be grateful. While I love these great perks, I made it through my early years here without them. I also have never felt that it was okay to stay here eighteen hours a day. Before I can philosophize too hard on the harm these benefits can wreak on someone's work life balance I am interrupted by a quiet "Hi."

I look up to a brunette girl with pointed ears twisting her hands, trying to find the courage to say more. She looks like one of the college students. I smile up at her, "Hello. Are you on one of the college tours?"

As if she finally took a breath, she stopped wringing her hands and a large smile spreads across her face. "Yes! Oh, sorry. I am just excited. And nervous. My name is Kelsey. You spoke at one of our college seminars my freshman year. I just think you are so awesome. And I wanted to say hi. And, like, could I ask you some questions?"

"Hi Kelsey. It is nice to meet you. Did you grab any food yet?" She shakes her head. "You go grab some food. My cookie should be almost done and I will grab that. Then we can sit down and you can ask me all the questions you want."

"Wow, really?! Okay. Okay. Cool. I … will go get some food."

Kelsey spends most of the next forty minutes peppering me with questions about working here. Being a woman in technology. Being the only *almost* executive woman. Is it okay to have friends at work? How do you maintain a work life balance?

She allows me to sprinkle in my own questions about her, her schooling, her goals.

Feeling rejuvenated by the conversation, I am about to let her know I need to head out when she asks a question out of left field. "This is going to be random, but I am curious about your thoughts since you specialize more in the security of devices. Did you hear about the most recent building explosion in Arcalis?"

"Yes, I was reading about it this morning." I try not to look too curious at the direction this conversation has gone.

"Me too! Which is what got me thinking. Most of the street cameras or CCTV are either outdated or brand new but from Star Technologies. Those cameras are cheaper priced, which for most companies, they will jump at since they don't want to spend more than they need to on security."

I nod at her to continue as I am not quite sure where she is going with this.

"Well, the old cameras, you could place the security on the fact that more than likely the recordings are sitting on a server in a closet of that building. The newer cameras come with cloud back up right? So if someone buys a camera from FaeTech, the footage is backed up to FaeTech cloud servers right? Same at Star Technologies?"

"Yeeeees," I drawl out.

"So why is there no footage from the other explosions? Someone would have had to wipe the footage right? Couldn't you use that in your security whitepapers or battlecards when competing for business? If people can get into Star Technologies servers and wipe data at will, that is not secure and people should be aware of that when making buying decisions."

I gape at her before remembering I am supposed to be the professional at the table. Dominos in my head start to fall into each other with the ramifications of Kelsey's theories. Trying not to rush her away, I stutter, "That would be difficult to actually prove it, unfortunately. But you make a solid point." I stand, grabbing both of our plates to take to the dish drop. "Keep up those creative thinking skills, Kelsey. Fates know we need more of that in this space."

Kelsey smiles and doesn't notice that I am itching to get back to my office now. One of her classmates hurries to her side at that point, whispering that it is time to go. We snap a quick picture together and I thank her for the conversation. I watch the two girls leave the cafeteria before I do everything not to sprint back to my office.

Trying to hack into a police database is cumbersome. You know exactly where you are trying to go, you tend to just hit literal firewall after firewall in an attempt to get in. Most would do this with a phishing email asking someone to log in. I don't have the time or energy to create a twin website for the Arcalis PD secure login page in order to code in a keylogger and steal some poor officer's password.

The street camera search is just as taxing, but at least feels more productive. Without being able to walk to this corner and searching to find the available wifi networks there, this search is all virtual and hit or miss.

Find the corner.

Check public city records for any cameras on that corner.

Find the owners of those cameras.

Find a way into each of those cameras.

As if the Fates planned it, there is only one camera on this corner and it is an extremely old model. No attempting to hack into Star Technologies servers today!

I spend another thirty minutes tracking down a computer inside of the company for an easy hop into other servers on the same network. Once I find a computer, everything happens quickly. Mentally thanking Kelsey for her divine conversation, I rewind the footage to the right time frame where Emily Turner would be entering the building on Washington. I try not to think about my dream rewinding my own life as I do it.

Why this property was chosen I cannot guess. It is right next to a brand new redesigned building that headlined the architectural world for a good six months. It stands out above all of the other pure brick buildings in the area. The tower added to the original building is a twisted, steel exoskeleton that contains a curtain wall of tall, mullioned windows. With it being so new, and glass-filled, the city put cameras on every corner possible. Why anyone would risk their work exploding in that city is beyond me. Yet, there are three other Star Tech cameras along the path Emily would have taken from that building to this specific camera. Why did none of the others have footage of her? Emily Turner walks nervously past the architectural marvel and into the brick building next to it. On the way out through that same door… she looks frantic, scared. But this is not the fear from something she is guilty of, of running away from something she made. This is a fear caused by someone else.

No, Emily Turner is not part of this terrorist group. One point that Kelsey didn't realize she had made - there has been no footage to this point, which means someone has been wiping the footage. This means the people in this group are beginning to slip up.

Good.

CHAPTER 7
RUNE DARREN

"Welcome to the first class in your Security for *the normal citizen*. Hopefully you read the description. This class is not intended to cut you off from the world of technology, but rather give you the knowledge to empower you to make the changes you feel most comfortable with. I would guess a solid thirty percent of you signed up for this class and said to yourself 'I have nothing to hide. I don't know why I am taking this."

A few laughing face emojis get dropped into the chat agreeing with the sentiment. There are always a few. Summer's voice echoes around my unofficial office space, bouncing off the bare gray walls. I am leaning back in my chair, tilting back a little farther than probably safe. Normally I would take these webinars from the comfort of my own home. In my own comfortable computer chair. But no, not today. Probably not next week or the week after based on recent events.

"I read all my post class surveys." Summer smirks to herself, pulling me back out of my spiral. "But it is also why I do these courses at an extremely low rate."

Twenty five dollars. This is all it costs me to join these classes to get a direct view of the course material. To get a direct view of Summer Chase…

"I don't record these so please feel free to come off mute, ask questions as you feel comfortable. There is also a chat feature where you can chat anonymously if you want to go that route." Summer goes through the rest of the preflight checklist of virtual meetings. It isn't like we as a society haven't been conducting video conferences for hundreds of years. The fact that she is not jaded by this does make me smile.

Running a hand through my unwashed blonde hair, I sigh. I really should try to go home at a more decent time. I need a shower. And more than a few hours of sleep. Instead, I start noting down the names of the other attendees. When I first began doing this five years ago, it was mostly out of curiosity. My team doesn't really understand my fascination. They still investigate any name I hand over to them. I used to give them the name of every attendee. Ninety-five percent of the time, anyone who put their full names in the name box had nothing to hide. Well, rather nothing so salacious it warranted myself or my team to acknowledge it.

The other five percent gave us some solid gossip or rumors. Usually this was due to a connection with other people in power. It is certainly helpful but not the information I am looking for.

It is the humans who don't put in their full name. Perhaps it's only their first name or first name and last initial. Those are the ones that we have found the most interest in. Finding them though is a literal race against time.

Summer Chase is teaching these attendees how to shut out as much surveillance as they want in this very short four week course. This also means not asking too many prying questions. She maintains her attendees' privacy. Never asks for locations or personal questions like a normal host. "How was everyone's weekend? Do anything fun?"

No, she always keeps everything solidly impersonal.

The few people we have been able to match up are exactly the people I am looking for. Humans with Fae powers.

Emily Turner is the most recent find. She did everything right in Summer's monthly webinars. She attended this course a year ago. She popped into a webinar and left her camera on *one time* a month ago. It was just for a few moments, but I was still able to snag a screenshot of her face and put her in my repository. To her credit, it took a full month to finally locate her. We picked her up on facial recognition scans from a brand new park camera. A park where she had been planting flowers.

It is unfortunate that she has caused such a ruckus. Based on her profile we were never expecting her to say no to our offer. Now she has truly disappeared. No one has found even a small clip of her. What was a victory has become a race to find her before anyone else.

"Why haven't you just hacked Summer's system to get the information? You send us on these goose hunts that don't have a great return on investment. She has all of that information in her registration sheets. You would know. You fill it out every four weeks." My associate asks when he sees me still here.

"You don't think I have tried that?" I roll my eyes. That pot of information is the bane of my existence. Luckily he is spared my snark.

"Does anyone have any questions before we get started?"

Every few courses I like to pop in a question. In good fun this round, I decided to make my name very specific. I am trying to find a crack to exploit. Could Dune Raydn be my way into Summer Chase's mind?

"Rune has asked, 'Don't you work for FaeTech? How do we know this is not just a sales pitch to buy your company's products?'" Her face scrunches at my chosen name. It is just enough that someone who has watched every class for five years would notice, but she recovers quickly enough.

"That is a great question, Rune. While FaeTech technologies, in my opinion, are more transparent and easy to navigate the privacy policies, it is not full proof or perfect. The intent of the class is to make every person knowledgeable on the opportunities to protect your habits and your personal information while being device agnostic."

Summer pauses to see if there are any other questions.

"Okay let's start out with a poll, shall we? Take a few minutes to read through all these and answer. It is okay if you do not know. We are going to define 'smart' as anything that you can connect to with your phone or voice activated."

Multiple polls pop into the chat box.

Do you have a Smartphone? "Yes", "No", "I don't know" are the choices *She does. It is locked down.*

Do you have a Smart TV? *Yep. Locked down.*

Do you have a Smart Thermostat? *Yeah. Infuriatingly locked down. I couldn't even tell you what her average temperature is. She is the only person I have ever seen be able to lock it down. She must be breaking terms of service on it somewhere.*

The list goes on and on...

Smart Home Hub? *Surprisingly not that I can find.*

Smart Refrigerator? *No. Or if she does, locked down.*

Smart Coffee Maker? *Nope.*

Smart Microwave? *Nada*

Smart Oven? *Nope .*

Smart Lightbulbs? *Yes... and still locked down*

Smart Curtain Motors? *No... but I recently found an installation permit for frosting windows.*

Doorbells? *Yes. Locked down.*

Smartplugs? *Yes. Again. Locked out.*

"Great, We are starting to get a lot of answers. So I will ask a few more questions. Anyone want to take a guess how long it would take you to read the privacy agreements and terms of service on your typical smart thermostat? Including any links to other documents? Because let's be real, none of us read those."

She lifts her lips to the side again in a smarmy smile. We are only seven minutes into this seminar and I am still getting hooked. I've literally heard this spiel fifty times. The few people on camera are physically leaning closer to their computers.

"Three days," a man named Brian comes off mute.

"Five days", "Twelve days." "The limit doesn't exist!" someone types.

"Seventy two days." Summer proclaims.

The faces I can see in those small squares go slackjaw.

"Now. Any of you with one of those smart ovens. Do you typically cook your meals around the same time?"

A smattering of answers come in.

"Great. For those that cook on a regular schedule. Do you also tend to be on social media scrolling through videos or podcasts before that?"

One person comes off mute and answers with a tentative yes. She scrunches her face questioningly.

"Have you ever gotten an ad for delivery or takeout during that scrolling?"

The blonde girl's eyes go wide. "Ye – yes. A couple days ago actually."

If we were in a room together you could probably hear a pin drop.

"The misconception people tend to focus on is that it is *just* the microphone access that sends you targeted ads. It definitely is a culprit, but you can turn off microphone access to every device in your living space. You would still be subject to these ads. We willingly and freely give over information about our everyday life. And don't kid yourself - that information is valuable. You scan your member card every time you shop. You get a discount on your groceries. Great! Now that store takes all that data and sells it to ad companies in bulk to make up the difference. That ad company then sells the insights to say the various food delivery platform apps. Their analytics programs send out a couple of well timed texts or coupons.

Then there you are ordering dinner instead of grocery shopping. Some people have looked at this like philosophers would debate over gods or the Fates. Do we still maintain free will if some big 'other' can take our data, manipulate it, and put something in front of you to take you down that decision over another?"

The pause she gives takes its effect across the screen.

"The Smart Home or Aware Home technology set was built in a technological utopia where greed for information did not exist. It was built with the best intention to help us live an effective and efficient life. The technology in itself isn't inherently the problem. Anytime you add humanity to the mix, our hubris will muddy the intentions.

"So just remember that this class is not here to make you feel that it will be inevitable for you to escape this oversight. I am here to help you find the scale that you want. Take back your right to be forgotten by corporations or the rest of the world. Or find a happy medium between inevitability and a fully anonymous life in the technological dark. Are you ready? Let's get started."

I lean back in my chair again. She begins her lesson while I take in her movements, expressions, tones. Some have called me a bit obsessive. I could let others take these classes, watch the webinars, and take down the attendance. She is an enigma I want to unravel. I can't very well do that by reading notes about her behavior after the fact.

She has a very public life, at least in her career field.

Yet, every bit of her personality, the crux of who she is, is locked down behind a strong wall. Summer knows her shit. She's done the research. She knows exactly how much data about her own life and habits she gives out. It is carefully crafted so that just the right amount of information is out there.

Almost like me.

What is it that you are hiding, Summer Chase? What is it that made you learn all of this? What made you so uncrackable?

Would you see right through me if we ever had the opportunity to meet?

My phone starts buzzing next to me and my eyes can't help but roll. Muting the speaker on my computer, I pick up. Staring at the ceiling, my laugh escapes me. "What can I help you with, dearest cousin?"

CHAPTER 8
SUMMER

une's eyes have been haunting my sleep. Those three words, "You'll love him" repeating through the night refuse to let me rest, physically or mentally. It keeps recurring as if reminding me of a thread of my life lost. Hopefully the dreams will stop after today. What other reason could they have other than counting me down to today? One could argue that somewhere in the last year marked the milestone, but today will cement it. The ten year anniversary of Dune Raydn walking out of my life. Dune has now been out of my life longer than he was in it. In the ways that matter, at least. He has certainly tried to make my life difficult in the last decade with his work antics.

Trudging into the bathroom, I splash some cold water on my face, staring at the reflection. The mirror reflects the changes since that fateful day. Thirty-six is just a mere couple months away now. This is a fuller face from my younger self. Really it is just a face I learned how to take care of over time. My golden brown hair still kept a few inches below my shoulder, though now streaks of lighter caramel and ruby mixed in. My matching amber eyes have learned how to go cold and distant when space is needed. They used to at least. Now they are simply exhausted.

Enough.

This date has transformed over the years, going from extremely difficult to a weight finally lifting off my chest, to complacent acknowledgement. The itching anxiety this year must be solely from the significance of the number. My twenty-five year old self was filled with unabating optimism and positivity. Ten years later it is all still there, just a bit tamed, muted.

The locket necklace Dune gave me that final night glares at me through the drawer it collects dust in. The air in the bathroom stills as I open the drawer and pull it out. My fingers clasp the silver oval locket. I rub my thumb across the surface, removing the light film settling on it. It has kept its shine despite the years. My thumb lifts slightly as it slides over the burnt orange inlay to the enamel tiara cameo.

I never wear it. I also refuse to let myself get rid of it. I wouldn't even put it in storage with the rest of the memories Dune left me. So, anytime I would clean my jewelry, the token did make its way into the pile. My jeweler later confirmed it is a refurbished vintage piece. Even if I am not wearing it, I should respect the "simple, yet ornate piece that someone worked hard to create." Not to mention the person who found it "must have taken great care to get it back to this state." The words had stabbed me at the time. There is a twinge in my chest. Whether we realized it or not, this locket turned the trajectory of both of our lives that night.

Dune had been so tentative that night, almost nervous. All of his touches were light. My immediate reaction when he showed me was to assure him that I liked it. That was just the beginning of the end. We had our soft moment. Then in the blink of an eye he was gone. My heartbreak was only at its precipice.

I realized a few days later there was a latch that would let me open the locket. I told myself to wait. Open it once I see Dune again. Once I could explain what I had no words for before. The hopeful optimism turned into hopeless waiting. My calls went unanswered, unreturned. His locket stayed closed. My fingers linger on the clasp, now. A spark of curiosity pushing me closer to the edge.

Maybe one day.

I tug open a drawer and lower it back in, my palm forcing it to the surface as harsh as the drawer would allow me.

One day I will put that away for good.

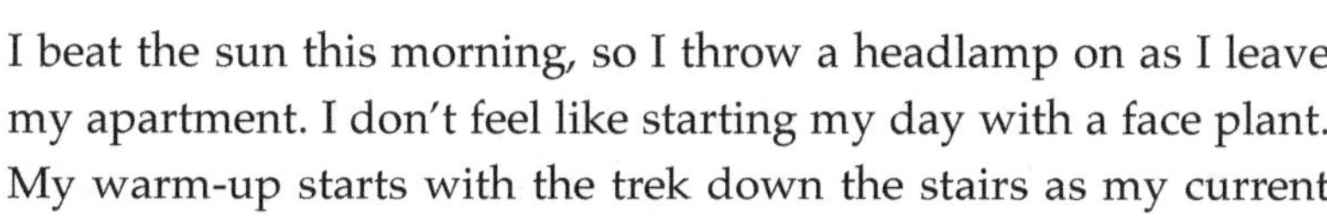

I beat the sun this morning, so I throw a headlamp on as I leave my apartment. I don't feel like starting my day with a face plant. My warm-up starts with the trek down the stairs as my current audiobook in queue starts up.

Normally, my five mile route is sprinkled with people as I wind my way through various streets filled with apartments and condos. Young college grads tend to be walking like zombies as they attempt to keep to their gym routines or try to get an extra few hours in at the new job. Koda poking at me to run faster or slower.

This early the streets are empty, leaving no distractions from my book or my thoughts. The narrator drones like a nest of bees until I finally give up after rewinding the same scene three times. Running to the sounds of the empty streets leaves my mind to wander.

Thump, thump.

Thump, thump.

Thump, thump.

Better to listen to the drum of my feet than my thoughts as I veer off, entering the park where my five mile loops used to be run. Halfway along the trail, between the second and third turns I pause. This spot filled with trees on either side of the trail, you would never imagine you were in a major city, buildings scraping at the sky mere miles from here. The bench is the only one on the trail. Sitting here now, I wonder if the installer knew that this was a spot for contemplation.

For reflection.

For forgiveness.

For forgetting.

I cannot tell if the weird pull in my gut is a sense of foreboding or just general anxiety. It certainly isn't longing I tell myself, preventing my palm from touching the tree in front of me. Touching the spot where are initials are grooved in. Initials carved on a day long gone when we promised to be friends for all time. Nothing would ever come between us. A promise made before anything tested its strength.

The last time I was here - five years ago - bubbles to the top of my thoughts. It was the last time I had any dreams or thoughts on Dune until now.

Pulling the small strip of paper from my pocket, I stare at his name. Five years. Five years of waking up on this day from nightmares or dreams of a different future. Five years of wishing, of hoping. And now it is time to forgive myself for my own part in it. He has made it abundantly clear he will not.

I have heard in some cultures, they write down their secrets and then burn them. Letting it burn to ash to be kept between them and their gods. He had kept my secrets, and I have kept his. the man who walked into my apartment that night was lost to the man who walked out. And I am tired of holding on to the secret of who he used to be. I am tired of holding on to a love for a man who no longer exists.

Lighting the strip of paper, I watch as the edges blacken in my hand. The burning boundary curling over his name. There are no tears. No, there have not been any to shed for him in many years. For myself, I grant forgiveness, I hope for no more nights like tonight. I made a mistake. It cost me a friendship, a love. Though it did bring me new friendships, new loves.

And with that final thought, ash is all that is left.

CHAPTER 9
SUMMER

call out sick today. Why bother pretending to work while my mind is elsewhere? I already told Koda I wasn't feeling well instead of admitting I ran early without him. I doubt he will truly realize what day it is. Toweling my freshly washed hair, my thoughts wander. The "guest room" across from my own has gone unused for a few months now. It honestly just holds spare clothes for when Koda happens to stay the night.

The living room by itself could fit my first apartment in it. I pay a solid sum of money to have a large open space to be alone in. While the idea of an open floor plan is awesome, I did not realize how the size and shape of your couch could impact the view. The large, white oversized couch can hold ten people. It is far away from the gently used tan fabric post college couch in both size and color. It barely fit two people on it. I was so proud of myself when I bought it, though.

I can still remember the intricate weavings of the upholstery. Browns, tans, blacks, greys interconnecting and blurring together.

Why had the colors started blurring together? One strand going over two, under two, over two, under two. I keep my eyes trained on those strands. There is a finger following the path of the current strand. Somewhere a door clicked. My door?

I don't look up as soft footsteps pad closer and closer to me. In fact, I would rather close my eyes. I know it is not Dune. Which means it is Koda. Koda who would have just come from getting Dune packed into his car and starting his three thousand mile drive to his new home. His new home away from me.

One hand slips under my knees, another under my right arm that has been slowly losing circulation as I laid on it. I am lifted vertical, before being set on a lap, still on this Fates-forsaken couch.

A hand pushes my hair behind my ears before rubbing along the top of my cheek. So the blurring was actually from my tears. Finally I open my eyes to Koda's blue ones staring back at me.

"Is he gone?" I whisper.

"Yes," is all Koda says.

I start to tremble, lips wobbling and Koda pulls me in. Holding my head to his shoulder he just whispers, "It will all be okay," over and over as I finally release my tears.

My present white couch comes back into focus and I shake the memories off. Striding across the open space, I set about cleaning my kitchen. An audiobook is turned on again to keep any other memories from boiling up.

After sweeping the floors, a quick clean of all the unused appliances, removing old takeout from the fridge, I haven't passed enough time yet. I grab the big guns - the mop, the toilet cleaner, the duster. The audiobook finishes and surely I have cleaned my way through the day.

It is only ten thirty in the morning. Shit.

I could go to the gym for a bit.

But then I would have to actually talk to Jackie or Kyria.

They know what today is. I don't want or need them hovering. Instead, I lug my computer onto the high top breakfast bar that is used as a dining room table. I suppose I can upload my recent registrations into our database.

My monthly security webinars are a great cover. We are able

to reach people without exposing my fire wielding powers. Most people see this as building my personal brand, which does give more influence across the industry. Why would anyone think it was anything other than that?

For the sake of my own time and sanity, I conduct a monthly webinar and start a new four week course within a week of each other. I attempt to empty out my brain before transposing names, regions, and other pertinent information into our secured database. Despite the blank mind, the acid still creeps through my stomach. This part of the process has never gotten easier.

As Jackie and Kyria hate to remind me, it was either this or be a fucking "chosen one". So I hand over the information despite that gnawing. We have a team of people who then keep tabs on any of the registrants in the Alnitak region specifically. Everyone assures me it is done tactfully enough. No one suspects the connection. Or if they have, it is only after they have run away to Lyra. I have yet to decide if that makes me feel better or worse.

Every so often I look at the counts of people who technically I have helped through this outlet. Kyria will always cross reference the list of incoming members to this ever growing database. Every few months she will give me the heads up that someone from a webinar has walked through our doors. So the names continue to be handed over. Even if I feel a little gross about it every time.

Kyria and Jackie have always focused on the good. It isn't like she is proactively checking names. I wrote the damn app for it. She types in a name in her list, and a notification tells her if it matches someone in the webinar database.

Have we ever checked if …

firstName:Emily&lastName:Turner

The cursor in the database filter blinks at me. I close my eyes, take a deep breath. My thumb hovers for just a moment before pressing the enter key.

What good will come from knowing if Emily had attended any of my classes? My breath hitches before I force my eyes open.

Fourteen results.

Fourteen.

The database filters down to just those results. Cross referencing the police reports, the address matches. It is her. Every time. She came to all of my webinars in the last year and took my full four week course.

Now she is missing.

Not presumed dead like all the rest, but still missing.

All the rest…

My apartment suddenly starts to close in on me. "If you are talking you are breathing," I repeat to myself as I pace around the perimeter, following the walls. My eyes hone in on the closet that holds my heartbreak. The dread isn't enough to stop my feet from finding a step ladder, climbing it, and reaching for the top shelf where two unlabeled boxes hide. These two boxes can only be distinguished by the color.

I pull down the grey box and place it next to my laptop. My heart prepares itself - either for pain or relief. Grabbing the closest notebook and a pen, I write down Emily Turner's name on the first blank page.

Placing my hands on both sides of the box, I lift the lid. A pile of newspaper clippings sit neatly inside. The article for Emily Turner sits on top. I gently pull it out and place it face down next to the box. One by one, each article for a missing person is pulled out and cross referenced against my database.

Maria Kover went missing a month ago.

Maria Kover attended a webinar six months ago.

Naja Gunther. Missing for two months.

Enrolled in a course a year ago.

Ferko Boelen. Missing for three months.

Enrolled in a webinar five months ago.

And on…

And on…

And on…

With each name found, the need to punch something gets stronger. Wilder. I breathe in through my nose. Out through my mouth. Count down from ten. The tingling in my fingertips starts to recede.

The only missing humans not in my database are those that went missing before I started marketing to that region.

At least I am not one hundred percent at fault.

I did not *know* them. I *had* interacted with them at some point. Am I the reason they are no longer here? They came to my webinars searching for a way to keep them safe. Is their capture my fault?

Names with mostly checkboxes are scribbled through multiple pages of the notebook. Some names are smudged by dried tears. I don't dare risk touching any of the newspapers just yet, not with my fire sitting so close to the surface.

Staring at my computer, as if it could tell me, I ponder where the leak is. It is *not* the database. That is under every secure protocol, locked down tight. Every log in pings my phone to be let in. It is a tight fucking ship. The registration page is completely quarantined. It gets wiped once I have transposed the information into the database.

Then *how* did someone crack it?

My pacing transforms my sorrow into problem solving. Simmering down my fire waiting to be let loose.

Look at the facts. What can I know for sure?

If someone could get in, they would have addresses, full information. It would not take three to twelve months to kidnap people. Every single attendee of my classes or webinars would have been found or looked into quickly.

The only way to be one hundred percent positive about that is to check the perimeter. I comb every piece of code, firewall, and protective system attached to the database and the intake form. After another hour I am finally satisfied that no one has hacked the system.

It would have to be social engineering. They would have to sign up for the webinars and blend in. Join and take note of all the names. Screenshot any faces to use for facial recognition software.

Fuck.

I should have thought of that.

My fingers thrum across the keyboard. "Alright asshole. Who the fuck are you?" I start the search wide and narrow it with each filter.

Twenty minutes later, I have them. I will pat myself on the back later. It took splitting out the street from the building number and sorting them by street and then by number. And right there taking up a whole screen.

Tom Smith, 12345 Elm Street, Phone Number: 123-456-7890

Jane Smith, 12346 Elm Street, Phone Number: 123-456-7891

Todd Tom, 12347 Elm Street, Phone Number: 123-456-7892

The most recent registration:

Rune Darren, 12344 Elm Street, Phone Number 123-456-7899

This fucker has not only been joining my classes but also participating.

Twenty minutes of speed walking later, I am storming into the warehouse. Jackie and Kyria stare at me as if smoke is creeping out of my nose. I am surprised there isn't.

"Summer, what are you -"

I slam my notebook down on the desk in front of them. "You are going to give me a surveillance team member to watch my course this week. They are going to track down the IP address of this fucker …" Shuffling to the page with his name angrily and largely scribbled, I stab it with my finger. "Rune Darren. Even if it takes the next two weeks to get in. I want this fucker flushed out. And I want to go after everything they have."

I charge out, flinging the door open and continue towards my training room before they can stop me.

As soon as the door clicks shut behind me, my anger and sadness find their release. I send a pillar of fire at the wall directly in front of me. There are no targets set up. There is no need. I just need to get this power out. The sadness, the guilt. I let the screams out. Let the cameras record it. Let Jackie and Kyria see what the guilt will force me to become. Screaming that maybe this would finally release me from this responsibility. Screaming to avenge. Screaming to run. Screaming just to scream because how could life ever just *be*.

The initial strength of power wavers. Wavers but never runs dry. I stare at the perfect, crisp black circle on the wall before hanging up a punching bag.

Ten minutes later, the door clicks open and shuts behind me. I refuse to stop hitting the punching bag. Singe-ing it with each slam of my knuckles. Soft footsteps trek across the room waiting for acknowledgement.

"I guess that is a different use for it than the usual target practice." Jackie states.

"Leave me alone, Jackie. I don't want to talk."

Out of nowhere, she shoves me into the bag with a gust of wind.

In response, I sling a fireball at her without turning around to face her. I hear it explode against the wall to my right.

"Don't talk. But you better look at me if you are going to throw shit at me." She then dumps another gust of wind right at my head.

That gets me to turn around.

The anger finally explodes through me again. "This. Is. Why. I. Did. Not. Want. To. Lead." I punctuate each word with a ball or stream of fire aimed at her.

Jackie is pure defense. She lets me cry profanities and hateful words as I send flame after flame in her direction. She redirects everything towards walls or other flammable things in the room. All I see are swirls of oranges, reds, and yellows. Finally Jackie puts up a wall to protect against the final constant stream I hurl in her direction.

Once my throat is raw, I sink onto the floor. There are no more tears. They've all been dried up with the fire in my blood. Jackie sits down next to me and pulls my head onto her shoulder.

"Everything I do, even if for the good of others, is always tainted. That was a stupid mistake. Something I should have foreseen. Now, it is my fault they are missing. It is my fault they are gone." Jackie is only a few years older than me, but holds me as if she were my mother. "Please don't ask me to lead again. Everything I do leads to pain for those around me." I whisper.

"You listen here, and you listen good. Those people going missing are *not* your fault. You are not the reason someone else chose to go after them and kidnap them. This group in Alnitak is making their own choice. We will make them regret it. I promise you. Every person we have in the region is looking for Emily. And hopefully… hopefully she can help us with some answers." Jackie pauses, although I hear the *"if we find her"* that she doesn't speak aloud. "I know what day it is. The significance of it. He had so many options, Summer. Your *accident* did not force him to do anything. It is not your fault he left without hearing your story. Every choice he made from that moment was his own. And not your fault."

CHAPTER 10
DUNE

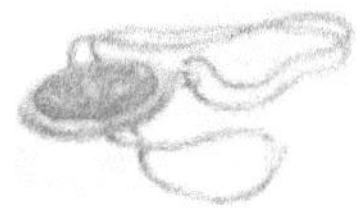

My phone starts buzzing. Seeing the number, I am not surprised. During the application process months ago I was informed about the final part of the interview process. They called it "political navigation competency". Could it be seen as labor on a private company dime, rather than federal? Definitely. The trickiest part - it requires me to move back to Lyra. I've been slowly packing up or donating my things, but I did not expect it to take this long.

"You've stayed out here for long enough," my boss informs me. Steve is stern, but with the tone that he knows he is going back on a commitment made years ago by someone else. He does not know that this was orchestrated by powers beyond both of our controls. "All of the other Vice Presidents and above in the company are based in Lyra. We can help with your apartment and those logistics. When do you think you can commit to moving?"

"I'll make the move at the end of next week. I'll send you any logistics I need covered. Including my airfare." He audibly sighs and then stutters his agreement. Probably shocked that I am not making a fuss about this, Steve isn't about to give me time to change my mind by arguing my demand.

Referencing Koda's itinerary, I book a seat on the same flight home. "End of next week" makes the period of time feel longer. Koda arrives tomorrow and leaves six days later on Friday morning. With such a last minute booking, I screenshot the cost difference between business class and economy to give to Steve. Then book the more expensive ticket.

I dig out my "moving at the last minute" planning list and start churning through it.

Plane ticket, done. Moving pod, scheduled. Give notice to my apartment building, done. Find a place to live.

The list of ten pre-furnished apartment complexes that are walking distance to the office was recently updated. Despite this, nine out of ten of these complexes do not have an open place. Three months is the soonest possible vacancy. The final uncrossed name seems to glare up at me. It has remained last on the list for a reason. Those bricks witnessed life altering events that can't be taken back now.

Could I just live with Koda for three months? Does Koda even have an extra room? *Why don't I know that?* Rather than dive into that question, I start dialing the number for Summer's old apartment complex. If my luck keeps its current run, it will also be booked out for the next three years.

My dialing is interrupted by an incoming call. My future boss.

"Dune Raydn." I answer as professionally as possible.

"Mister Raydn. Lovely to talk to you again." Queen Ashryn responds cooly.

"You as well, ma'am."

"You understand why I am calling you?"

"Based on the call from my boss earlier, I assume there has been some movement between Aaron Dubois and FaeTech?"

"Yes, you are correct there. But ..."

In all of the briefings we've had about this job, Queen Ashryn has never once hesitated when disclosing information. This is a job that needs utter but discrete transparency. What could give her pause?

"There is an interesting twist to it. When I spoke to the CEO at FaeTech he mentioned the best place for a new department would be within Summer Chases' org. While I was a bit taken aback by Ed's respect for the human so I attempted to redirect him to put this team elsewhere for a time. Due to the nature of Aaron's program with Star Technologies, a human being in charge of it isn't going to go well."

My body immediately reacts, wanting to defend Summer. Summer is one step away from being the Chief Technology Officer at FaeTech. This new department would oversee the partnership with the Alnitak government. If it becomes anything like the department at Star Technologies, it will be the largest governmental revenue stream at FaeTech. Alnitak officials spend a lot of money to have a full time team inside of Star. Whichever VP takes this department will have a shoe-in for the CTO role if it ever opens up.

Summer would be more than capable of both roles. She won't shy away from taking this, nor should she have to fight for it. Her accolades speak for her. I only have the list from three years ago when she had a five page magazine spread. Nevermind that she was awarded Elinder's Most Eligible Executive. The rest of the article laid out all of her work accomplishments at that time.

She successfully moved the entire development platform to the latest and more secure programming language.

The new OS features in their phones increased sales by 40% year over year after that.

She made it on to Fae Magazine's 40 under 40 lists. That is in addition to her addition to the 30 under 30 earned a couple of years after I left FaeTech.

She has built the most diverse development team... Anywhere.

You have been quiet for too long.

"When are you moving back?" Queen Ashryn asks curtly.

I must have zoned out of any additional commentary if my silence went unnoticed. *Thank the Fates.*

"End of next week."

"Great. I understand you have a mutual friend visiting. See what information he can give you about Summer Chase while he is there. You need to find a way to monitor her once you have moved to Lyra. Learn what she knows. Report back what you find."

"I - well -"

"I understand you don't have the best of relationships with that human any more. Thank goodness. But you need to find a way. The success of this program depends on it. You need to know if you can trust her to work together to bring the program nationwide. Knowing my cousin, Aaron will find a way to put her in charge no matter what I do."

She does not need to voice the implication on my own job as well. There is no use fighting a direct order like that.

"Yes ma'am."

Her only response is the silence of hanging up the phone. I thread my hands into my black hair.

This is karma. Yes, I may have made Summer's work life a living hell for a few years. Whatever Aaron Dubois is doing in his region is not something she should be subjected to. Frankly, I am still not sure what Ashryn is going to do with any information she receives from me.

Six months ago or so, after losing the CTO job to Steve, I was informed that Steve was basically a shoe-in. He ran the team that partnered with Alnitak which showed "political savviness and confidentiality that no one else has been able to replicate." So I interviewed to laterally move and take over Steve's former role. After a few months of interviews and processes I was informed that Aaron Dubois personally rejected my application.

Trying to figure out my next career move, I received a call from a blocked number. Queen Ashryn wanted a meeting in two week's time to discuss a potential opportunity. They would cover airfare and accommodations. I was too curious to say no.

Queen Ashryn had been notified of my interest in taking over the Alnitak team and offered me something bigger. She needs to expand the "Safety via Survellience" program with Star Technologies and Alnitak nationwide. This requires FaeTech and other smaller device companies to be involved and informed of technology changes, product updates. There will be a CTO office opening at the federal level that would oversee this expansion and maintenance.

I have to prove my ability to gain access to technology that her cousin - Aaron Dubois - will not give over without a fight. He is hiding something from her. My job is to figure out what Aaron is hiding

Two months ago, I had thought maybe it was that Aaron was misusing the technology and kidnapping citizens. Maybe he was hiding the fact an actual terrorist group is kidnapping citizens using his technology.

Now though…

I've come to terms with the fact that going into this role at a federal level is a risk. I could be helping implement this same technology across the nation. Unifying it. Whether it is the government or domestic terrorists, the technology is being used - not to keep people safe - but to kidnap humans.

Based on some of the explosions, my fear is that the humans are like Summer. Humans that wield extraordinary powers.

Over the past two months, my thoughts have shifted from wanting to make this next move to questioning the morality of it. Ultimately, Summer is the reason I made the choice. It is my final apology that I never thought she would hear. I will dismantle it from the inside if the information I find would put Summer at risk.

That was the plan at least. Now that I know Aaron Dubois personally asked for Summer to lead up his team at FaeTech the plan will have to change. It means, more than likely, I am on the wrong side. This will have to be a game of deception. How do I deceive a Fae Queen though?

Luckily, nothing in Queen Ashryn's order would warrant me handing over information *about* Summer. I cannot let Queen Ashryn become suspicious. Directly asking Summer to help is out of the question. Every part of this needs to look real in the eyes of our queen.

Will I have the heart to deceive Summer? Try to befriend her again, look her in the eyes knowing the secrets I know, and lie. There will need to be a balance between the amount of groveling she deserves versus what I can give her while being watched.

I spent the better part of those first few years apart trying to tear her down. It was subtle... for the most part. But people figured it out. Even technology companies have their own gossip apps. "Fishbowls." One app has a whole subpage dedicated to our rivalry. People will dissect a conference talk or a video blog where I made a targeted comment about Summer. For every comment or remark I would make, she would never sling anything back in my direction.

Those subpages turned into a pretty toxic place after a while. Even if one of my comments wasn't even about Summer, someone would misinterpret it and start the whole cycle over again. The misogynist Fae men would go on a sexist and elitist rampage and talk shit about Summer and all she stands for. Which in their eyes is basically just that humans and women are coming after their jobs.

Then you have the Summer fans who march in with a break-down of every accomplishment that she's ever done. This is simply to fight the men saying she doesn't deserve to be in the technology space.

This is the mound of shit of my own making that I am going to have to climb through in order to rebuild a friendship with Summer. Imagine what gossip that app will churn out if anyone ever found out. We could probably break the app.

The levity of that thought does not alleviate the pull in my gut. Building that trust back is going to require breaking down walls that Summer has put up. I know she has them, they probably match my own in some ways. This will most likely end with me destroying whatever foundation is rebuilt between us. It will be worse than anything she ever did to me.

That right there is the kicker. She was the villain in my story for many years until I realized my mistake. Five years ago I found myself in a conversation at a bar over the most recent explosion in the city. A human had been announced missing right after. One Fae man swore he saw someone freeze the building where "that human" just went missing from. The explosion was to cover up the fact that a human - let alone anyone - had enough power to do that. The rumor was that Aaron Dubois probably had an underground bunker where he was kidnapping these humans and running tests on them.

I drank more that night than I had in my whole life. At home, in such a trashed state, the walls of my mind cracked, and memories of Summer flooded me. The events of that night ran on repeat in my mind. I thought about all of the people who have gone missing. She would not have flaunted her power on purpose. In the time since I left Lyra, she had never once shown any indication of the power she showed me that night. I knew then. I knew what happened was an accident. I should have known by the look of shock on her face as she looked quickly between her fingers and my face. There should have been trust in the woman I had known for almost a decade. Instead, I left the woman I loved without another word. Over an accident.

A wave of regret led me to her social media profile and typed *"I'm sorry"* in a direct message. Thankfully I didn't press send. She deserved more than that. I owed her the time and energy to tell me her side of the story. Tell me what I wouldn't hear before.

At that point, the bridge had already been burned. Our connection destroyed. Any closure between us would be near impossible. That day I stopped any foul commentary about her.

Blinded by my early anger, I did not realize the trajectory I set for myself would never bring me peace. So I continue putting on a mask of my distaste for Summer Chase. The mask is so well ingrained that even Koda anticipates it. He stopped bringing up Summer in our conversations long ago. So I wear the mask, and never bring her up either.

I stare at the television. A protest is happening right down the street. Friends and family of the late Emily Turner cry on the streets. They seek justice that they will never receive. If that was Summer's face on those posters, what would my reaction be?

There is a loud thumping in my chest. An ache I haven't felt in ten years. Is it fear? Anticipation? I pour more cement into any cracks in the wall around my soul that is rattling to get out.

As the Fates would have it, the final complex has a furnished apartment currently vacant. So this is how my story starts over, in the place where the story of us ended. With this new beginning, filled with regret, I will become the villain in her story.

CHAPTER 11
RUNE DARREN

ummer Chase has not gone off script in this class, but something is off. I can't quite put my finger on it. She seems distracted. Yet her focus has not strayed. Has she heard about Dune Raydn's new job offer? Has the reality of that man moving back to Lyra sunk in yet? Surely not. That secret hasn't been let out yet..

Once again, I am watching her class in my unofficial office. Not in my own damn home in sweats. There are literally not enough hours in the day.

Emily Turner was supposed to be an easy pickup. Nothing in our research indicated that she may reject us. We *could* have dealt with the rejection. The camera footage of her using her powers had already been wiped. We would have just kept an eye on her.

That was not what the Fates had in store though.

Someone missed a camera. Anytime we have a meeting with a potential wielder, camera locations are checked. Somehow this one camera, conveniently located on the street Emily walked in from, did not get programmed with a loop.

The Chief of Police, in his ecstasy of having any lead, released the video footage before we ever realized we missed it. He did not even wait for the warrant to be approved. We got the alert about the warrant request right after the news was released. Police could not legally go to her apartment for another hour. An hour window which we could have wiped the footage without too much suspicion.

In his haste, Emily Turner's face was plastered everywhere. She had an hour. The Chief of Police did not take a moment to think that she may have been prepped to disappear. Emily Turner disappeared. Cameras show her walking into her apartment complex. The police arrive to find the apartment empty. The only indication she was ever there was the strewn out clothes on her bed. If I had to guess she had a bug out bag buried in her closet. Summer trained her well.

There is not a camera pointed to the fire escape on the back side of the building. No human matched her clothes or description on the footage on either corner she would have gone down so the trail ran cold quickly. We have teams of men and women scouring any and every bit of camera footage across the country. Any slight match to Emily Turner's description has been looked into.

Protests have been ongoing in pockets across the region demanding justice for Emily Turner. Rightfully, character witnesses for Emily have vehemently denied her involvement in a terrorist group.

I have been fucking livid. Glass tables have been shattered, mugs thrown across rooms. Books as well. Every person I have spoken too has been on the receiving end of poison dripping from my voice.

My only spot of joy was seeing the Chief of Police fired. According to the filing, he was fired with prejudice for "not doing due diligence and providing woefully ill-prepared information to the regional officials prior to a press conference."

It can only bring me so much joy though. This is *exactly* what I have been trying to avoid. We have gone to such lengths to keep our operation under wraps. Whoever was on duty to cover cameras in the area that day was promptly removed.

It is great that the public is starting to rouse their anger. The risk right now is ensuring it does not fade. Legend foretold that the human power wielders would have a single fire wielder among them. That person is meant to lead them to victory. We haven't found that person. This leaves us with too many unknowns. This country - neither Fae or human - is not ready for an uprising. I have to maintain hope we will find the fire wielder before these tentative beginnings of a rebellion flare out.

Summer Chase has the new department at FaeTech that essentially extends the reach of the program in Star Technology devices. Will she just be a pawn or the key that everything hinges upon. The role this new technology has in her world is the exact opposite of what she stands for from a surveillance point of view. Will she fight it? Will she start making her own moves?

Bugs continue to be planted in the palace and federal buildings anytime I visit Lyra. They have paid off in more ways than one. Various chess pieces are starting to move now.

Our dear Queen has a burner phone that she makes calls from while hiding in a cute little private garden. Many of the calls are cryptic. She uses a predefined code that means nothing to me. Two major things have come out of this though.

First, she adamantly argued for the FaeTech extension to live outside of Summer Chase's org. Second, she orchestrated Dune Raydn into moving back to Lyra. I suspect this move is a distraction tactic, to ensure Summer does not look too closely at her newest employees. Dune Raydn has been kept out of the ranks of this technology team at Star. Perhaps this is also some sort of "comradery" act to get more information on what that team does. There is an information leak from that software. I am not sure what Summer will do when she finds it. I have an idea of what Dune might do though.

So outside of trying to keep tabs on Summer, finding Emily Turner, and keeping a rebellion steadily fed, I've been filling my free time trying to find out what else Ashryn and Dune are up to.

A knock brings me out of my thoughts. I scrub my face with a hand as the knock comes again. I sigh. "Yes?"

One of my surveillance guys, Jeff, tentatively peeks his head around the corner. "Boss, you've got to see this."

"Did you find someone off the list in record time? Or Emily Turner perhaps?" I follow him out of my room towards the surveillance office.

"No, but someone is looking for us."

"That's not possible."

We walk past a few empty desks. The trash cans filled with empty take out and chocolate wrappers remind me that I am here late. Again.

I lean on my elbows and watch as our IP address scattering program is lighting up on his screen. We have hundreds of misdirections so I am not concerned about anyone finding the right one. This has always been a contingency plan though. In the seven years or so we've been doing this, no one has located any of our public IP addresses.

A brick plummets through my gut at the thought that not only has someone found one entry point but also were not deterred at the maze of IP addresses. Could this be why Ashryn has started moving players around the field? Watching the pings and numbers streaming up the screen, I start a checklist of every possible hole that could be exploited that needs triple checking.

"Which device did they start at?" I attempt to keep the concern from my tone. Jeff must not buy it though.When the man doesn't answer immediately I turn to look at him. The color drains from Jeff's face.

"Just spit it out already."

"It's… they jumped on via your laptop's IP address."

"Mine?"

Jeff falters, "Yes, uh yes sir."

It's as if a lightning bolt just hit the worry off my shoulders.

The weight of it immediately shattered. A maniacal smile spreads across my face. Jeff takes a step back. I try and fail to reign it in. He is newer to this post, and after the last couple weeks, my behavior has been less than ideal. Ornery and short. But this… this news is the best I've received in weeks. Now I know exactly what she is distracted by.

"Let me know once she gets close."

"She?"

"Yes, she. It seems that Summer Chase has figured out that someone is using her classes and webinars for their own purposes. I imagine she will only let me continue to attend her classes until either she tracks me down, or until this class ends."

I go back to my office with just the slightest of skips in my step. Deep in my soul, there has always been a hunch that she would eventually find my registrations. Some might argue I wanted her to find them. If not, I would have taken more care in randomizing my actions. Then she may never have found me. She never could have shown her cards - she is looking for something.

This is my favorite type of race. I only have two weeks left watching her with anonymity. Two weeks to figure out how to find a way to get in front of her. Such a limited time to find out why she would be looking into my registration? What would prompt her to research it? Does she know about the power wielding humans? What is making her tick?

I start planning ways to get in front of her as she stares into her camera and into my soul.

"I can't wait to finally meet you, Summer Chase."

CHAPTER 12
EMILY TURNER

"You said these windows are tinted?"

Teival looks up from the computer in front of him and nods. I barely see his green eyes before they are back on the computer, confirming our travel plans and routes for the thousandth time. His dark brown hair keeps falling into his view, forcing his olive hands to take turns brushing it out of the way. We've only known each other for a little over a month, but my chest aches when I watch him. It has only gotten worse as we have been practically living with each other for the last two weeks.

Attempting a distraction for myself, I drag a chair up to the window and stare down at the masses filling the street. We are on the fourth floor of a brick building that blends in to all the other brick buildings in the area. This is Teival's private residence when he is in Arcalis. Residence is a loose word for it though. The whole building is vacant. Outside of a few rooms carved out on each floor, the space is huge, bare, and lonely.

Teival told me it is rare that people need to leave their homes in the same rush that I did, so the space is hardly ever used. Due to the high visibility of my disappearance we are waiting until the safe houses along the way are cleared out. There is a network of buildings just like this one - although with a few more rooms - all across the country. Although this is a well oiled process, sometimes caravans overlap so there is an actual booking system set up. Yes you may be smuggling yourself across the country, but at least you can do it and have your own bed.

Arcalis and Lyra are the end points. With most people trying to leave Arcalis, it has been easy enough to lay low here. Looking at the schedule, Teival has set us up to leave tomorrow. Once we leave we will be on a strict driving and sleeping schedule. Rather than take a van, we are taking Teival's little sedan. We will be able to get farther distance in a day, sometimes opting for the next safe house rather than the closest.

The drumming outside the window pulls my attention back. I had been watching protests grow in size day by day from the television. Today's protest fills the streets by this building. The intersection was blocked off for a quick podium to be set up. From this vantage point I can see the whole street right outside my window is filled with thousands of people. Across the intersection is the same. People are chanting through megaphones to the beat of the drums.

Testing the latch, I am able to slide the window just a smidge to the side to let the sound in. Teivel looks to the window. Seemingly satisfied with the amount I crack it, he looks back down to his computer.

The noises and voices, no longer muffled, reverberate around our space.

"JUSTICE!"

Crack-crack.

The drums match the pace of the two long syllables. There must be drums on every street, all meeting at this central apex.

JUSTICE! Crack-crack. JUSTICE! Crack-crack.The drums and the voices are echoing and bouncing off the buildings, intermingling as they go. I soon hear the drums from other streets matching the voices closest to us.

Sirens wail from the intersection. The traffic lights blinking above the podium. My breath catches as I see my best friend and roommate, Sarah Pranler, as the source of the sirens. She stands there, triumphant. Her dark hands holding a megaphone in each, sirens blaring as she looks to the sky. Her brown curls bounce in the wind. There is a sad smile on her face as she turns to look at the crowds around her.

Now I understand why the protests have grown. She knew about the note that had been left for me. Sarah had taken a picture of it, "for collateral". I don't know what happened to the physical copy in my rush to vacate my apartment. Sarah had apparently made sure that not only did the police know about it, but also the entire city of Arcalis.

I take a closer look at some of the signs on the street. "Right to privacy!" "We are not data!"

The crowd goes as quiet as it can, filled to the perimeter. Sarah enchants the masses. I had always been the quiet one of our duo. Sarah was not only the social one, but the more charismatic one. She is a fighter. She could woo you into giving your life savings and all of your free time into a cause you didn't have a clue about before you talked to her. And I just became her beacon to bring people together. Both of us as humans had been victims to small cuts of classism. It could be as small as getting into a club one night, or a class we needed to graduate.

I refocus on her words. "Why was she being watched by our government? Why was she tagged for kidnapping? A woman who has no criminal record. A woman whose greatest gift to this world was to help nurture life. Now that gift is gone! We should not be in constant fear of doing something arbitrarily wrong in the eyes of the government! They may not have taken my friend, but they did not fail to take her away from me. From her family. I vow to keep fighting to break down this system. You should too! NO JUSTICE!"

"NO PEACE!" The crowd booms in response. It is so loud, so unifying I almost back away from the window.

Sarah continues the chant, tinny as she yells into the amplifier.

"NO JUSTICE!"

"NO PEACE!"

The crowd is starting to shuffle, small pockets of space starting to crop up. Suddenly, the streets explode. Literally.

Fireworks scream up from the vacated pockets. The fireworks are not shot with any rhyme or reason. The sounds of them ricochet as they take off and sizzle. Reds, greens, yellows, purples filling the space between buildings.

"Those are too low." Teival stands next to me now, watching outside. My skin prickles with how close he is.

They aren't meant as a celebration of power. They are covering the vision of cameras on the corners. People are climbing to them, up poles or walls. Others are keeping two feet firmly on the ground and shooting bottle rockets directly at them. I look back at the podium in time to see Sarah smile - obviously at a plan being successful - before pulling a plain white mask over her face. She steps off the podium and into the crowd. A crowd I now realize is filled with plain white masks. Sarah will immediately be lost in the chaos as they start to disperse.

Confetti bombs start going off, obscuring the visibility further. I don't know how, I don't care what I did to deserve the goodness of the Fates. I see her - the lone fish swimming upstream against a tide of humans. And she is heading this direction.

Sarah knows going up on that podium, her voice now lighting up a city, that the government will come down hard on her. Putting on the mask will get her out of this crowd, but I would not be surprised if there is someone waiting for her at our door even now.

Abruptly I stand from my chair and grab one of Teival's giant hooded sweatshirts and my hat for good measure. With all the cameras on this street now shattered, we need to move fast.

"What - where are you going?!" Teival jolts.

"Pack up what's left. All of those carefully laid plans just went out the window. This street is going to be crawling with repair crews for the next week. If we don't get out tonight, we aren't getting out until they leave. I just need to see Sarah one last time."

I run down the stairs rather than waiting on the elevator, hoping she doesn't pass the building quickly. Hoping she is not walking on the other side of the street. After I unlock the seven locks and deadbolts to the door, I slowly open it. She's ten yards away. I can tell by the curls of her hair. Her confident gait that only someone who grew up with her would know. Keeping my head down, I speedwalk to intercept her. I loop my arms through hers to turn her towards the building. She struggles against me before I say, "Stop struggling. Don't speak."

Sarah gasps. As we walk back to the building I am distracted by the confetti we are stepping on. As we step up to the door, I crouch down to pick up a handful of the confetti before letting ourselves in.

As soon as the door closes behind us, Sarah rips my hat off, choking back a sob as she confirms it is me. She pulls me into a hard hug, refusing to let go. Teival finds us there a few moments later, breathless and scolding.

"What in the world are you doing?! What if someone had seen you? What if - " He stops short at the two of us crying.

As we go back up to the fourth floor, I fill in Sarah with all the details she is missing - how I met Teival, what has transpired since, and the plan to leave. Tonight.

Before she can protest, I interject. "I need to find more people like me. Teival says that most power wielders have been moving out of this region. His organization is based in Lyra and gets people there. If there is any hope of being able to live freely, I need to meet them, understand why we are all hiding - other than the obvious reasons." I pause and look at Teival now.

"Can she stay here? She isn't going to be able to go back to our apartment now."

"Emily - I will do the time, they may not even put me in jail because of the outrage."

"Or they will throw you in jail, keep pushing the hearing back, until you are forgotten." I take her hand. "You need to keep this momentum going. Maybe I will be able to come back with a bunch of power wielders ready to enact change."

Teival sighs. "I will let HQ know that this space will be occupied until further notice. I'll wait til we get to Lyra to tell them why. Please don't bring a bunch of trash in here. Why did you bring in a pile of petals? Ja - They won't like it if this place is left a mess."

Petals?

I look at the pile he is pointing at. The confetti I had grabbed. He is right though. It is why I was so thrown off by it. What I thought had been multi-colored strips of paper dancing through the air had been flower petals. Petals of all shapes and colors.

I look at Sarah now. "I... did not arrange that. Just asked people to bring things that would obscure the cameras - like confetti."

We look out the windows and find the petals are still floating, swinging, spinning through the air. There is no clear spot where they are coming from but they are starting to pile up like fallen leaves as summer turns to autumn.

A spark lights within me.

"Maybe I will find the fire wielder there. Stay here, use this space. Lets get ready to give Aaron Dubois a scare, yeah?"

CHAPTER 13
SUMMER

onday morning is dreary. Not the weather, just knowing that Koda is in Arcalis with Dune. Protests are apparently still going on in the area. We have to look incredibly deep to find footage of them though. There is a knock at my door and Jackie swings her head in.

"Why didn't you tell me you had a new hire?"

"A new hire?"

"Uh, yeah. HR was pinging me. They were freaking out that there wasn't a one on one already scheduled."

"I…" Why would I have a direct new employee? They only require first day one on ones for direct managers. I have not interviewed anyone. Nor did I have any job openings. *That I knew of.* "Were you able to get time on the calendar?"

"Yep. I am great at my job."

"Can you perform two more scheduling miracles then? Grab some time with Abhi from bizops. And Ed, please."

Jackie stops short at the mention of Ed, our CTO, also known as my boss. "You really do want me to earn my living today, I see. I will do what I can."

Keeping my calendar up on one screen, I open our HR portal

to learn my new hire's name. Geremy Kann. Senior Director, Department of Government Relations. *Government Relations?*

Another knock is followed by the friendly smile of Abhi Shekar. "Hello Summer. It has been too long. I hear congratulations are in order!"

Abhi from our Business Operations team became a fast friend as I moved into my managerial roles. His literal job is to know all the business metrics and how things - like a new department or employee - could affect them.

"It has been far too long, Abhi. Please sit." I gesture to a chair at my desk. He tugs at his brown pointed ears as he enters. With his laptop at the ready, we sit side by side so he can walk me through all of the facts.

"You are the first VP in quite some time to gain a whole new department, Summer. Great job." Abhi remarks as if I had campaigned for it for months. "Jackie mentioned having a meeting. I have the next hour free so I can talk through whatever you need."

"Can you tell me about the metrics you have documented?" Abhi looks at me with concern. Why wouldn't the VP know the makeup and metrics set for a team that she lobbied to create? "I want to make sure nothing is amiss."

This seems to settle him. He pulls up a screen while I grab a notepad and pen. Then he goes over the key performance metrics as if he is checking off a grocery list.

Open headcount. Three individual contributors by next month.

Budget for salary.

Budget for travel.

Revenue by the end of this fiscal year. One million dollars.

Expected year over year growth. Sixty percent.

I nearly choke on all of these numbers. These are nearly unattainable without a contract already signed, ready to go. Geremy also basically needs to know exactly who he is hiring if he is going to fill his headcount in the next month.

"So what is the new team going to do?" Abhi pulls me from my downward spiral. I stare at him for a moment, my brain buffering on the question. Abhi wouldn't spread rumors purposefully, I do not want to admit that I have no clue what this team is doing. As the only woman and human employee that reports into the executive team, there's no reason to let anyone think I have lost my marbles.

"It's, uh, confidential at this time. Only on a need to know basis."

Abhi doesn't seem phased by this answer in the slightest.

I have time before my meeting with Geremy to review his resume, previous roles, and newly available interview notes. The audit trail shows that Ed opened the role, interviewed only Geremy and then sent an offer out. Rummaging through the notes I see comments about his ability to partner with others, lead effectively and maintain discretion. The interview was ninety minutes. A quick check shows that Geremy does in fact have three job openings. Ed's assistant opened those and recruiters are already screening applicants. I keep coming back to a sentence that is incredibly vague. *AD has run background check and okayed him.*

When I finally get to meet Geremy, he is dressed like a typical Fae man. Black dress slacks and a white button down shirt. Brown hair, pale skin, pointed ears. a personality that will fade into the masses. No one is going to notice Geremy. No one will go out of their way to say hello, ask him his role.

"I just want to make sure we are in alignment on your role and department. Can you tell me your understanding of it?"

"The role is to make and maintain contractual relationships with various government entities. Then to ensure the contracts are also fulfilled." Geremy states this with exact precision. It's as if he knows that I did not know this job existed until three hours ago. He memorized a bland answer and knows there isn't much I can say in response.

"You know there are three open headcounts for next month?"

"Yes. I have interviews starting at the end of the week."

This goes on for a few more minutes. He continues to evade my questions, knowing I am digging for answers that have not been provided to me already. The answers are not a lie. But they are certainly not the full truth. I excuse him, knowing I won't get any real answers from him.

CHAPTER 14
KODA

"Hey Koda," Dune calls my attention from the morning news cycle. "I have a couple of time sensitive errands I need to run. Feel free to chill or go explore the city." He's got his black hair in that loose bun that the girls go wild for. I yawn and give him a thumbs up.

After an hour of lounging and slowly waking, I grab a jacket and the spare key Dune left me. No need to sit with my thoughts in his apartment. The city blocks are actually square here, compared to the winding curves that make up Lyra - even in the downtown district. So I wander. The leaves on the trees are already starting to turn over for fall here.

I keep my hands in my pockets and try not to look too much like a tourist as I sneak peeks into shop windows. Arcalis has always been a great city to visit. Every year it seems we can find a new shop that hasn't been visited. Dune has taken me to quite a few hole-in-the-wall shops that have had some of the best sandwiches or baked goods I've eaten. This year it seems like every few windows has a flyer with Emily Turner's face. *Justice for Emily Turner! Emily is innocent! Humans can have power too!*

That flyer stops me. It is printed on black paper, the block lettering white. Under the photo of Emily Turner is a white circle with the silhouette of a flame of fire. Rumors were stirring about the humans that had gone missing in the recent years. Discussion boards had all sorts of theories on why buildings were exploding across the region. The deeper you go, the more outlandish the theories get - including humans with the power of the old Fae. Not the watered down ounce of power we Fae have today. Enough power to bring a building to ash in seconds. To freeze a building into a giant block of ice. Implode it with hurricane strength gales of wind.

What is stopping a group of humans with power that strong from rebelling? I continue my walk, but I am reminded of that subtle passion Summer has for human rights. Whenever she has a new idea to help further equality, even within our technology stacks, she will find a way to get it done. Many times she is raising up the most educated or experienced human on the subject. Or it is as simple as where she spends her money. Are these people fighting to keep their rights, or looking to be the new power in this world?

My thoughts are interrupted as I pass a small flower shop. Did the shop remind me of my Sundays with Summer? Perhaps. Did the cute, rotund old lady pull at my heartstrings? Sure. Could Dune's place use some vibrancy? Definitely. Whatever the reason I turn back and go in.

The small graying lady eyes my pointed ears wearily as I look around. Trying to put her at ease, I say, "My best friend back home loves shopping for flowers every Sunday. I missed this past weekend with her, to be on a plane coming here. She loves lilies." I wave a hand in the direction I am heading. "Plus my friend's place here is so bland. He could use some color."

The woman smiles, "And you could use a reminder of her?"

I sigh, "Yeah."

She hobbles over to me. As she nears, she is much shorter than anticipated and I just see the top of her gray head and her blunt ears. Did she look anxious solely because I am Fae? Or is there backlash from the Fae right now over the protests happening here? "You didn't have to come over."

"Nonsense boy. I am going to show you how to pick and make a bouquet for your woman."

Your woman. My mind sticks on those two little words as the shopkeeper continues talking like she didn't just slice my brain in two. I used to tell Dune that, jabbing him to make a move. She's not wrong.

Summer has been through hell many times over. Hopefully all of that is behind her. We've been there for each other through our highs and lows. My mind rakes over memories of Summer flinging herself onto me in joy. How easy it could have been to just tip her face up to me and kiss her. Every moment since *that day* we have measured our movements. It's as if every cell in me is attuned to that measured distance. My body burns to be closer. To hold her hand. To hold her by the waist or gently on the back. I'd even buy a damn car if that meant my hand could rest on her thigh while driving to nowhere.

I have to tell her. I am going to get off that plane, take a taxi straight to her building. Straight to her. Nudged out of my thoughts, my eyes refocus on this room of flowers.

"Just a friend, eh?" She laughs. "You didn't hear a word I said did you?"

I shake my head guiltily. "No ma'am."

"Helpless. How long have you been friends with this girl?"

"Nineteen years."

"Nineteen years?! Boy are you stupid?"

"Honestly?"

She chuckles. "When did you realize you wanted to be not just friends?"

"A couple months ago."

I finally read her name tag, Gerba. Gerba weighs this answer with her head swaying. "Maybe there is hope for you yet, boy. Now *listen* this time. Depending on where you go, they may have bouquets pre-bundled, but you should make them yourself.

So don't go rushing to her with damn airport flowers, you hear me?"

Gerba then proceeds to show me again the process of picking out the right flowers to last the longest. That you cannot just have the flowers, you need garnishes or something. You mix those sprig things in with and around the main showpiece. And voila - you have a beautiful bouquet.

Gerba puts the flowers in a vase and I take a picture with her, the flowers in front of us. She hands me a card and points at her email address. "You send me pictures of your progress on making her flowers. Send me a picture of the two of you once you figure things out. Let an old woman live a little."

Back at the apartment I snap a picture of just the vase of flowers on Dune's kitchen island. The flower arrangement is quite beautiful. There is a mix of orange and yellow lilies. When I wanted to add red lilies in as well, Gerba had lightly smacked my hand and pointed at the peach carnations and unbloomed rosebuds.

I texted the picture of the flowers to Summer and dip my toes into the water.

KODA

Missing you. Had to get a reminder of you.
Made it myself!

I send it before I can regret it and not a moment too soon. Dune walks in the door and I try to not flip my phone over on the table like I was doing something wrong.

"Those are... nice." Dune says it like a question. His eyebrows are scrunched together as he looks between the flowers and my phone like he knows exactly what I was doing.

"Yeah a nice lady named Gerba helped me make them."

We sit there awkwardly looking at each other and the flowers between us. Dune looks at the flowers like they hold the answers to every question the universe could hold. My phone buzzes us out of our strange silence. I realize my mistake of changing my background to be a picture of Summer and myself. I cover Summer's face before looking down to fumble with the phone.

SUMMER

Those are beautiful! Maybe I should let you pick out my flowers this weekend.

KODA

Anything for you.

I promised Gerba I would send updates on my new found bouquet making talents

SUMMER

Gerba, eh?

I send her the picture with Gerba and realize Dune is just staring at my phone.

"Shit, sorry man. I am trying to woo a lady back home with my newly acquired bouquet skills. You don't have to keep the flowers. Your apartment is empty if I am being frank. Feel free to woo your own lady with my skills."

"I ..." There is a war of emotions on his face. Suddenly I am churning through memories of college. Did Dune ever buy Summer flowers? When did Summer start having fresh lilies in her apartment? Shit. I am about to get punched in the face.

I get out of the stool and take one step back, "Look, Dune -"

"The apartment is bland because I am moving back to Lyra." Dune doesn't look at me as he says it. He moves towards the flowers, eyes only on them. Dune is mindlessly rubbing a flower petal between his thumb and forefinger as though he had not just dropped a landmine between us. He hasn't set foot in Lyra since he left ten years ago.

"You... why?"

Dune looks at me now. The petal is still between his fingers. "All of the other VPs are based at the Lyra office. I've been told to move, or find a new job. So I am moving back."

Trying to ask questions in more than one word, I ask "When are you moving?"

"Friday. I am on your flight. Maybe you could, I don't know, show me a couple places to eat Saturday. While I get food and stuff. I haven't been back in … a long time. I am sure it has changed a lot."

His boss tells him to move back and he doesn't even fight it? He just says yes. Then nonchalantly tells me two days before I leave that he is coming home with me. That he would love my help getting reacquainted with the city. No big deal. Who wouldn't be happy their friend is moving back to the same city as them? What else would I be doing right as I got home after a week away?

Is my eye twitching?

It is.

Stop. Twitching.

The slight movement is the only thing holding back the tidal wave of full chalant I want to fill this room with.

My phone buzzes in my hand. Reminding me of home. Reminding me of what this man did to Summer. He can't see the memories of Summer broken on her living room floor after *he* left. The years of her trying to shut me out, only for me to pry her walls back open. He doesn't know the flashes of her smiles and laughter after she put herself back together. He doesn't feel the rage of protectiveness. The fury that he would dare come back right as I finally realized that I wanted her all to myself.

Dune crosses to the fridge and pulls out a couple bottles of beer. Snapping them open, he slides one in front of me.

"You are worried about Summer aren't you?"

I stare at him, not sure which direction he is going with this.

"No - it's just -"

"It's fine, Koda. I won't try to grab lunch with you at your office or anything like that. I'm not even sure I would be allowed into your building anyways unless I was interviewing. She won't even know I am in town."

An alternate universe flashes before my eyes where I stop by Summer's office. *"We are going to lunch, want to join?"* *She looks up from her desk, smiles at both Dune and I. She wraps an arm around each of our backs and she slips between us and we walk out thick as thieves. A universe that erased ten years of heartbreak and yearning. A universe where neither Dune or I would get to have Summer. Dune never making a move, and me staring longingly at the girl I could never have because Dune wanted her first.*

I shake the false memory free from my mind.

"No, of course not. It's… it's not that I am unhappy you are moving back. Yes, Summer will cause a wrinkle for you. You just like to come and go from our lives with a jolt don't you?" I laugh. "Leave on a whim, come back on a whim. Not on a whim, I guess. I guess it is your turn to reorient your life around mine."

"I hadn't thought about that. I thought you would be happy. It could be like old times."

I bore holes into him, unable to hide my anger at his selfishness. "This week I spend with you every year is a vacation. A single week to make up for a year's worth of time we don't see each other. I have a life and routines that were rebuilt after you left. You think the only person affected when you left was Summer. Just because I am still friends with you doesn't mean it didn't affect me too!"

I take a breath. "Wow, I didn't realize how much I needed to say that." Dune rubs at the back of his neck, looking sheepish.

"I… wow. I am sorry. Obviously, I don't want to monopolize your life. I shouldn't have downplayed it. Part of me has been expecting this call for a while so I have been prepared for it. I didn't want to tell you and it end up being delayed or not happening." Dune threads his hands through his hair, pulling it out of the loose bun it was in.

"May as well go back to the other elephant in the room. I don't expect you to play referee between Summer and I. I should probably try to reach out to her though. Knowing our luck, we would run into each other at a coffee shop or something despite being in a big city. Based on your reaction to me coming back, I should at least give her a heads up. It will probably be the only thing I will ask of you when it comes to Summer."

Do I even let him near her? He may be apologizing for throwing a curveball at my face, but I doubt he would blink an eye at doing the same to Summer but in a public place. He must expect me to coordinate a coffee date between the three of us, with Summer unaware that Dune would be there. No, that is not happening. She will be informed as soon as I see her. Changing the subject I state, "Moving to Lyra should make it easier to get that federal job you were looking into though. Did you ever hear back about that?"

Dune goes still with the beer bottle close to his mouth. He puts the bottle down. "I am surprised you remember that."

I simply shrug, waiting to see if he says more.

"It will help. Definitely." Sirens blast through the empty space. Dune moves to turn on the television and mutters, "It will be nice to not live in a city that is constantly in a state of chaos, too."

CHAPTER 15
SUMMER

I knock on Ed's door to alert him of my presence.

"Come in Summer. Close the door behind you please." Unlike my office, Ed likes to keep his perpetually frosted over. Most of my time in his office is spent when I am on the go. Ed isalways running around from one meeting to the next. He has been my boss for five years now, and we have a pretty decent working relationship. Leaving him a bottle of Bocelli's wine every year for the holidays, or just dropping in to check on his family. I hardly ever need real meetings with him, leaving most of the work talk for our group reporting meetings. Today he looks like a defeated man. Ed's hands rest on his pale, bald head, pointed ears especially prominent. His elbows sit on his desk propping him up.

"I should have more meetings with you, if you are going to look like that. Or do I need to go strangle a coworker?" I cock my head at him, trying to make light of this situation. Although I am pissed off I also know I will get more from him with sweet honey and direct conversation than yelling. The little bit of sarcasm physically softens the stiffness in Ed's posture. Good. I just need to keep my own feelings in check long enough to lure the information I want out of him.

Ed sighs, leaning back into his chair. He flops his head side to side and asks, "How mad are you?"

"I am not here to yell at you, Ed. You should know better than that after all this time."

He smirks. "You didn't answer the question."

"It doesn't matter. I came here to ask if you could give me any idea of what is happening."

"I do not owe you that." He says sternly. He puts a finger to his mouth to silence any reaction I might have. He slides his chair far enough along his desk to reach for the buttons I know are under the desk. One to control the frosting, one to control the sound proofing. Then, in a surprise move, he palms a square box on the edge of the desk. It blended in with the pens and papers strewn across the desk.

At this point, Ed finally crumples. "Thank you for not yelling at me. This is not recording, and the jammer is on for good measure."

"When did you get a jammer?" I am so astounded, the question simply slipped out.

"I may be your boss, but you teach me enough." He sighs. "After I was approached about starting your newest department, I thought it couldn't hurt to have it."

"What is going on Ed?" Every well laid plan of this conversation is now out the window.

"Let me tell you what I know, and save your questions please. I am sure someone is going to pass along the timestamps of the soundproofing along with the fact it is you that walked in my office. I don't want to have to start a rumor of an illicit relationship. My wife would be quite unhappy."

"Okay. Mouth shut."

"There was a lot of drama over the placement of this department. There is a similar one over at StarTech. It sits as an org all on its own, not integrated with any other teams. The org reports straight into their CTO over there. The issue is that StarTech runs off fear and politics and bureaucracy. People know that the department exists, but any employee who speaks about it there would get slapped with a lawsuit so large the employee may as well just start digging their own grave."

An ominous feeling crawls through the room filling every crevice.

"For better or worse, *you*, Summer, broke us of that sort of culture over the last five years. You also are simply the best in the business at what you do. All it would take is one new hire looking at the org chart and asking about this nondescript organization that has a direct line to me. Chaos would ensue, gossip would spread, and people would spend more time trying to find Geremy instead of working."

At the mention of that, I try to remember where Geremy's desk is, but my mind comes up blank.

"No one would blink an eye if I put a couple new hires under you. Why wouldn't I? I've been prepping you to take over my job whenever I decide to retire. Everyone knows that. If they don't, they are just blind."

Ed pauses for a moment as I grapple with what he is saying. He looks at me, then flicks his eyes to my ears for the smallest second. If I hadn't been watching him closely, I would have missed it.

"The issue ... the department is sponsored by two government officials. The ..." Ed stares up at the ceiling, closing his eyes. "The jammer is on," he whispers to himself before returning his gaze to me.

"I tell you this with full confidence that you will understand the gravity of this ever getting out. The contract was signed without my prior knowledge. I was simply handed the responsibility, just like I am doing to you. I fought where I could - which is where you come in." My heart thumps loudly in my ears. It is a drum beat building with anticipation.

"The Governor of Alnitak approved of my decision. He had actually advocated for you to run the team. That would have caused more visibility into the department and contract. Ultimately it would have been a demotion for you. Governor Dubois was strangely understanding. But… Her Majesty, the Queen, did not approve. There was no justification that would appeal to her. She…"

I finish the sentence that he can't. "Based on the rumors about the contract Aaron Dubois has with Star Tech that he uses their devices to spy on humans she did not want a human in charge of the department set to fulfill that contract here?"

He lightly knocks a fist on to his desk. Without words telling me I nailed it on the head.

"Is that what it does, truly?"

"I don't know. It is the weirdest contract I have ever seen. It is forty five pages of nothing. It is basically a giant description of all the legal ways we are not allowed to ask about the work being contracted."

He spins in his chair, unlocking a drawer, to pull out a manilla folder with a thick stack of papers in it. "I printed this out for you as soon as Jackie put this event on my calendar. Take it home, do *not* leave it in your office."

He stares at me now, with a look of sadness or empathy. I cannot tell which. "I know how much you disagree with the surveillance tech that Star Tech does. I am in agreement with you there. I have never told you that. Do with this information what you can, as I have not been able to figure out what goes on over there. All I know is … no matter what you find, you tell no one unless you trust them implicitly. Do not even tell me. I fear by sticking my neck out for you, it will bring extra scrutiny. Governor Dubois is probably going to be more intrigued by you but the Queen sounded like she will be watching you to make sure you do not suspect anything."

Some puzzle pieces start to come together. The "AD" comments in the hiring process. The need for secrecy. There are still so many blank spots.

"I am supposed to simply tell you this - Geremy will send me his reporting directly, there is no need for you to include anything about the department in your upwards reporting. This part I am not supposed to tell you. Since you are in the reporting tree of this department, your computer has extra security protocols that were installed on Monday without your knowledge. Everything you download, every chat, every email will be processed and reviewed if flagged for suspicious activity. That contract - literally printed once - I told security it was so I could reference it without being flagged every time. Then I took it to the local office supply store to make a copy for you. You have a separate phone for work?"

I simply nod, taking in everything.

"Good. Do *not* log in to anything work related on your personal devices, the program does not discriminate between personal or work related web traffic. Know that you are being watched." He checks his watch, seeing that ten minutes have passed since he pressed the jammer. He picks it up, putting it in his pocket as he presses it. He stands, pressing the sound-proofing button on his desk again to turn it off.

"I am glad we understand each other, Summer. Have a great weekend."

Ed leads me towards the door slowly. Allowing me to regain my composure after the whiplash of the conversation before reaching the door. My head is still spinning when I get back to my own office. Almost as soon as I sit down, Jackie is swinging in through my door.

Out of breath as if she ran here she simply says, "We need to go."

We must both be sheet white because her eyes widen at the sight of me. I raise a hand, hit the soundproofing button before turning to my bag to pull out a jammer. Seeing my actions Jackie closes my door but is pacing around my office. I frost the windows.

"Why do *you* look like you've seen a ghost?" Jackie asks quickly.

"You said we need to go? Why?"

Jackie notices the diversion but allows it. "Teival's back."

Teival was supposed to return three days ago. He was already being extremely tight-lipped about the reason he was returning without the caravan. Then he went dark and no one could reach him.

"Did he give a reason why he was so delayed?"

"*That* is why we need to go. Kyria called a code orange. The whole building is on lockdown."

Hazardous materials? "What?"

"I don't know! She sounded really freaked out though and demanded both of us."

"Okay… okay. Ed will not care if I take the rest of the day. Let's pack up."

CHAPTER 16
SUMMER

Kyria meets us at the front entrance. As soon as the door is closed, her anxious rambling starts. "They showed up via the back door. Teival did not give me any warning. I just walked in and there she was!"

"Who, Kyria?" We reach the surveillance room on the second floor, where most of the training rooms are. The room is empty, amplifying the anticipation building in my gut. There's normally someone in here, watching to make sure no one has knocked themselves out. Who is so serious that Kyria wouldn't let anyone stay?

Kyria clips on the monitor that always shows the water training room feed. There is a "dead" blonde girl on the video live stream.

"Emily Turner in the flesh. Very alive! I didn't want to ask her what had happened without you two here."

We watch as Teival splashes Emily with drops of water as she attempts to block with flowers and vines.

"She looks…" Jackie tries to find the word.

"Happy? Healthy?" I offer.

"I was going to say 'like a girl in love' and not someone who has been on the run from a government entity for three weeks."

All three of us nod in agreement at that. Teival is also… smiling. It isn't like he is a statue of a man, but I don't think I've seen him show this much emotion in the five or so years we've known him.

A heaviness drops in my gut. I had kept some hope that she was a fire wielder. My face must drop because Kyria rubs my back and just murmurs, "I know…"

I've already been hit with one set of strange news today, what is a little more? At least it probably can't get much worse.

"Let's go talk to them."

When we get to the room, Emily has Teival pinned to the wall with a thick trunk of vines. He is looking at her with fondness, happy to be trapped by her. "Kyria can teach you how to tie him up with vines if you stay long enough." Jackie says as an opening statement.

Kyria coughs. I shake my head. Teival looks strangely turned on by that before realizing how many of us just walked into the room. Emily squeals. "SUMMER CHASE?!" Concentration lost, Teival drops to the floor. "You didn't tell me Summer Chase would be here!" Emily points a finger into his chest before speed walking to meet the three of us.

"Holy shit. I have been to so many of your webinars and classes! You are an idol of mine."

Taken slightly aback by the sheer amount of energy, I struggle to find a response. "I know. It is nice to meet you in person, Emily. You met Kyria earlier? This is her wife, Jackie. We co-run this space, if that's what you want to call it."

"This is so cool. I love what you all have done with the various rooms."

All three of us are stunned into silence. The level of energy Emily brings punches me in the chest. She is a reminder of my past self. This curiosity, this energy, this willingness to feel everything persists after everything she's been through in the last month is inspiring. I push down the bubble of regret filling me.

"I - wow - okay. Can I just say, if I ever imagined meeting

you, it would not have been this… positive? Energetic? I personally need a second to reset myself."

"That's fair. My face is all over an entire city. My best friend is holed up in one of your safe houses as she keeps leading protests. I am here in front of you, not a hot mess."

"Exactly." I say slowly.

She laughs.

She laughs.

Teival has reappeared with chairs from somewhere. He grabs the energetic blonde by the waist and sets her on his lap, kissing her forehead as he does. There is a domesticity that pulls at my soul. Kyria shrugs. Jackie is gaping. I have no idea how to proceed. Sitting is a great start.

"I feel like you are going to take anything I ask you in stride. So I will just come out with it. Can you tell us anything about the people you met in the building?"

"Fates. I was so stupid. I had not necessarily been trying to hide anything. Why would anyone care about little ole me? It isn't like my abilities were hurting anything. Yet, they still found me. Well someone did at least. I think they saw me planting flowers."

"The people that left you the note. Where did you find it?"

"They must have been following me. I found it in one of my school books after class that Tuesday. I debated on going. My roommate, Sarah, told me not to go. In the end, my curiosity won, and I decided to hear them out. They have been sending buildings up in flames once a month for the last year. Why would the fire wielder do that? I did not pack anything. Just walked right out of my dorm. I figured I would be back in time for dinner."

Something in her statement makes me flinch. Kyria must catch something too as she cocks her head next to me.

"The person who met you at the building. Did you recognize them?" I ask.

Emily continues, "Yes and no. There were four men. They all

kept their faces covered with scarves or balaclavas. One of them looked really familiar. He had dirty blonde hair. He sticks out in my memory the most. He hardly spoke, but I still get this feeling like I had seen him around campus or something. I cannot place him though."

"What did they tell you?"

"Um, oh. Yeah… basically what the note said. That they had hacked some of the government systems. Harmless as my actions were, the powers that be had named me their next target. The government would just kidnap me when it was least expected. They offered me a new identity, safety, a new home. The only catch was I needed to leave with them right then and there."

"What made you say no?" Kyria probes.

"I need lists. My parents are saddled with debt from getting me into university. I had obligations to square up. I couldn't just up and leave. I would take the risk, and start putting my affairs in order. I had clients out of town. Who would have taken care of the pets if I just disappeared?"

The confusion dissipates as I remember the recent news cycles where her pet sitting and walking clients made pleas with the public.

"I didn't even make it back to my apartment before the first news cycle started reporting on the exploded building. And me. All of my options went up in smoke. Literally. If those people were willing to take away my choice, I would not trust them with my future. I had met Teival a couple weeks prior. I grabbed my bug-out bag, called him. Now here I am."

Pieces of this puzzle are trying to click together. There are too many things that aren't fitting. Then a piece snapped in place. We had assumed Emily was also a fire wielder, based on how the building exploded. She clearly is not.

"You said you wanted to talk to their fire wielder. Did they say anything about why they keep exploding the buildings?" I ask.

"Oh that was also strange. The fire wielder wasn't there!"

Confusion must skitter across my face. Kyria is looking between me and Emily now. Jackie has her eyes scrunched at Kyria.

"They… didn't have a fire wielder?" Jackie presses, tasting each word as it is spoken.

"Strange right? As I left I saw a wind wielder starting to spin up a ball of air. Another man had a box of matches. I think I remember someone pouring gasoline on the walls. My guess is they threw the match in the airball, and tossed it where the building would burn fast. That may have been the most bizarre part of the whole interaction honestly."

Yeah, no kidding.

"Wait…" I get up to pace the room. "I always assumed the buildings being destroyed in Alnitak were out of self-defense. Why would this group *want* to leave a trail? They didn't try to … trap you in the building or something? Force you to go with them?"

"No, they let me walk right out."

"Why did they come prepared with equipment to set a building on fire?" I ask, more to myself

"They must be desperate for a fire wielder. A show of force maybe? They wanted to make it look like they have fire wielders ready to go?" Jackie finishes my thought track, pushing my brainstorming along.

"There are easier ways to destroy a building. I mean even a wind wielder could have just gotten on the roof and demolished the building making it look like a cave in. Why go through the hassle?" I ramble. Kyria is staring at Emily now.

"Do you think they are trying to flush out fire wielders? Trying to add some, any to their ranks?" Jackie murmurs.

"I think they are looking for the fire wielder. Yes." Emily interjects. "For any rebellion like this to work they need to find the fire wielder. There is a unique power in holding a flame. That person has the power of destruction and rebirth. Just like a wildfire helps forests clear decay for new growth, the symbolism the fire wielder could have on a country could tip the scales."

Kyria is staring at me. Finally, the word clangs through my head. It bulldozes through me. Jackie and Kyria watch me now as Emily and Teival snuggle up on each other like she did not just drop a bomb in this room. She is even leaking plants now as she allows in the feeling of joy, of being adored.

"How do you know they are looking for one person?" Admittedly, my voice cracks like a pubescent boy at this.

Playing moss and flowers across her hands, Emily never looks away from the life she has brought to the room. Orchids, ferns, and succulents are starting to attach and hang themselves to the walls surrounding us. "I am - was - am? - a Computer Science major. I do credit my abilities in technology to the fact I regularly use both sides of my brain. When I was not trying to subtly add a new plant to my collection, Sarah would find me in the library at school. If there was a mythology book available, I read it. I was so intrigued, hungry to know everything possible about these powers. How to control them, where they came from, why we have them. The librarian at school even gave me access to the restricted archives. This room had digital scans, paper copies, scrolls that weren't catalogued anywhere else. In those stories, no matter which philosopher or ancient civilian wrote it down, whether the human wielders of power were good or evil in their foretellings- there was always only one major theme. There is only one who kept the power of fire."

"That…I mean… certainly they did not provide counts." I sputter, avoiding Jackie and Kyria's eyes.

"Only to call out the single fire wielder. Even the imagery had groupings and pairings of various power wielders. Every rebellion needs a Chosen One to lead the charge, right? I agree with your theory - that they are trying to flush out the fire wielder. I just think no one realizes they are searching for one person."

Do not hyperventilate.

Do not freak out.

Hold. It. Together.

I *almost* release my grip on the chair. I *almost* excuse myself in time. "Myths are usually diminished to just that. Myths. But everything I read about mating bonds seems mostly accurate so who knows."

It is Kyria's turn to stutter. "I am sorry. What now?"

Teival blushes. "Yeah that is why we were delayed. Sorry. We were just testing out our powers together at the last safe house. Then we felt something like a bolt just snap together between us. And … uh. Please don't make me go into further details."

Emily picks up the conversation, but with more of the research she's done. "I never thought that was real! Or real outside of the Fae. Maybe since we have enough powers we have mates too! The history books say that a mating bond can help deepen the well of power each person can have. Is the fire wielder here? Do they have a mate?"

Emily continues her exciting tale of Queen Nyara's mating bond as buzzing fills my ears, fills the room. My breathing feels too loud, too heavy. My eyes focus on the closest drain on the floor.

Inhale. Ten.

There is a unique power in holding a flame. The power of destruction and rebirth all in one.

Exhale. Nine.

Mates. Chosen One. The. The. The. The

Inhale. Eight.

Not plural. Singular. Alone.

Exhale. Seven

Jackie, Kyria, creating this place. Creating security. Together.

Inhale. Six.

Chosen one. One.

Exhale. Five.

Dune smiling at me over ice cream. A rumbling in my chest.

Inhale. Four.

Dune, scared. Leaving. Alone.
Inhale. Three.
Koda cupping my chin. Holding my hand.
Inhale. Two.
Koda. Missing you.
Inhale. One.
To lead is to be alone. Lonely in a crowded room.
Inhale. Darkness overflows my vision.
Inhale. Try to find the oxygen in the air I am breathing in.

"Summer," Jackie is next to me, whispering. I see her feet in front of me now, her hands taking hold of my arms. "Exhale." I lift my eyes to her. Before I can stop it, a tear drops as I do as she commands. Every single person in that room sees it. The gasp from Emily barely registers in my mind.

No one stops me as I turn and walk straight out of the room without another word. The stairs and hall are a blur, until my room is before me.

A room specifically built just for fire wielders.

Fire *wielder*.

Jackie is calling my name behind me, but I cannot stop. I don't bother locking the door behind me. She will not follow me in until my meltdown is done.

CHAPTER 17
THE FATES

After ten years, she finally understands.

The room is charred on every surface outside of the small circle where the Chosen One now sits.

We, the Fates, felt all of her emotions push through the flames that exploded from her chest. The imminent loss of the life she chose to live this last decade will impact every decision she makes from here on.

This is the nature of humans who love. We attempt to not intervene often because of this nature to love, this desire to be loved. The consequences can never be fully known until they occur.

Hopefully, we chose correctly, plucking the chord of her destiny early all those years ago.

Hopefully, her memories will build the flame in her soul up, rather than dampen it.

Now the chord is plucked once more, the wheel on its next turn. The Chosen One must bear this weight of what happens next.

Tears burned up with her flames, but the path they had made streaked through the ash on her face. Determination and anger fill her eyes, but sadness and exhaustion reflect through her hunched figure.

The paper sits on the floor of the training rooms, singed black on the edges.

The End of the Fae-Human wars.

> **Image:** A sealed parchment scroll in a reinforced glass box.
> **Location:** Elinder Museum of History, Alnitak
> **Description:** The Scroll of Peace, sealed in 1536.

There is no written record of what the treaty actually says due to the lore behind the seals. One of the few records found with the scrolls from Geoffry of Myrddin gives the most insight into why no one has dared to open the scrolls:

Jaeson the Bold, now to be known as Jaeson the Peacemaker, signs the treaty forever allowing humans and the Fae to coexist in harmony for the rest of eternity.

But what a reader will not see in the treaty is the oath stamped onto its seal from both Jaeson and King Haruna. Haruna's queen places her hands over the two men as they press their thumbs to the paper.

"In order to ensure this treaty holds, the Fae shall give this promise, honored and held through the blood of Jaeson the Peacemaker and King Haruna. The gift of fire, used to destroy so much of human life with no reservations, shall forever more be removed from the wells of magic available to the Fae.

"Should a day ever arrive where the Fae forgets this tragic war and wishes to use their powers to suppress the humans once more, the gift of fire shall return. But the fire shall return to a purely human ancestor

of Jaeson. Fire will be gifted to only one. To be used as a signal of unification, not for mass casualties or damage.

"If an heir of Jaeson is granted this gift, other humans shall begin to manifest powers. Earthly magic shall be granted as a means for protection."

Gold threads wrap around the human and Fae King's hands as a stream of fire crawls from the Fae Queen to the human before her. As the fire wraps around both arms from shoulder to shoulder. Then, the fire starts to feed into Jaeson's chest, pulling away from the Fae Queen's shoulder.

The room filled with Fae and humans watch with astonishment as the fire disappears entirely from the connected arms. With a woosh all of the torches lit with magic extinguished themselves. Starlight emanates from the Fae Queen now, illuminating the three figures.

No longer connected to each other or the treaty, the parchment has formed its seal with the blood and transfer of magic.

King Haruna proclaims, "Jaeson, Peacemaker, human, now has a heart of fire. A gift that shall be passed to his human kin. Not to manifest into magic until the day that the seal on this treaty is broken. May this day never come to pass. Go to all your peoples, proclaim peace across the lands. And may we never know the pain of fiery deaths again."

Due to the ambiguity of whether the seal being broken would cause Jaeson's heir to manifest his powers, no historian has been willing to break the seal. The human line of Jaeson Peacemaker was lost to the records centuries ago. As the world forgot the promise behind the scrolls, lineage records started to record only those of mixed or full Fae heritage.

CHAPTER 18
SUMMER

F*uck.*

CHAPTER 19
RUNE DARREN

Today is my final class. My final opportunity to watch Summer's mannerisms anonymously. What role will she play in the coming weeks and months? Based on the surveillance of her office, she is at least aware of having a new department. It is too bad Ed wouldn't let her own the department completely.

My best hackers have been working overtime to get into her systems. They have yet to be successful. After tonight we will have to start over from scratch. Every class she has gotten a little closer to finding us though.

She looks… pale. Unnaturally pale. Is she sick? I doubt this is nervousness. Does she know that Dune Raydn is twelve hours away from being on a plane back to Lyra? Could it have anything to do with her absence from any surveillance?

She left work early yesterday. We never clocked her leaving the FaeTech building. She then disappears for ten hours before suddenly triggering a CCTV camera two blocks from her building. She hasn't left the building since. Her email activity shows that she is working from home. The frustration has simply grown the more time I spend trying to figure out how she keeps circumventing our technologies.

Ten minutes before the end of this class, we dump her into a sandbox virtual machine. The change in her expression is so subtle, but I see the moment that she realizes that her program stopped running. Now, instead of IP addresses and code filling the screen, she should simply see a cursor blinking at her. I type the first message so she knows I am also watching.

>> RD: HELLO SUMMER CHASE.

She is flawless. As she pauses in between my classmates making their final remarks she types back.

>> SC: WE FOUND YOU.

I smile to myself.

>> RD: BUT DID YOU REALLY?

>> RD: OR DID I LET YOU STOP SEARCHING?

>>

>> SC: I WOULD HAVE FOUND YOU EVENTUALLY

>>

>> RD: AH. BUT YOU RAN OUT OF TIME.

>> RD: THIS COURSE IS DONE.

>> RD: EVEN IF YOU LET ME INTO YOUR NEXT COURSE, YOU WOULD NOT MAKE THE SAME MISTAKE AGAIN, WOULD YOU?

>> RD: SO I WOULD JOIN AND FIND NO GAIN OTHER THAN WATCHING YOU PING PONG THROUGH MY MAZE TRYING TO FIND ME.

>> RD: ENTERTAINING. BUT WE BOTH HAVE BETTER THINGS TO DO.

Class has ended. Summer and I the final two left on the call. She is staring into her camera with purpose. I'm just a black screen to her. But there is a ferocity to her at this moment.

"Whoever you are, I will find you. I won't let you get away with what you have done."

>> RD: I LOOK FORWARD TO THE DAY YOU FIND ME SUMMER CHASE.

>> RD: UNTIL THEN...

I sign off the video call and dump Summer out of my network.

CHAPTER 20
KODA

I'm going to skip out tonight. You probably
need the rest anyways.

Okay

I have a surprise for you that I need to pick up
in the morning. I'll just meet you at the market?

Yeah that's fine.

Determined and nervous to continue my practice with the flower arrangements, I almost miss the lack of push back. Was her week as strange as my own? The flowers will hopefully lessen the blow of finding out about Dune in the open air of the farmer's market

At Summer's favorite flower shop, I fumble through picking out a combination of red and orange lilies with some of the extra bits. As I start laying them on the counter the florist wordlessly sidles up next to me, watching. She looks so similar to Gerba from the top, graying black hair, it gives me deja vu. About halfway done, she places her wrinkled hand on mine and simply says, "Hold on, I'll bring you something better to add."

She disappears in the back for just a moment. She returns with three pink flowers she calls dahlias. They are giant flowers that sprawl on their stem. I understand why she only brought three out. She helps me tuck them into different edges of the piles of flowers. They look very nice if I do say so myself.

While checking out, something compels me to let the florist know that I was buying these for Summer. I don't want her upset if Summer only comes in to say hello. The little lady gives a soft smile. "It is good someone is buying her flowers for once."

Step one of my mission complete, I weave through the crowds, going against the flow of people. As if waiting for me to show up, the group in front of the book stall clears a path that leads straight to Summer. She is perusing the books, her fingers tapping across the spines. I sidle up just behind her, not touching her. Wrapping my free hand around her right side, I point at a book that is face up on top.

"*The Maiden and the Orc* wasn't appealing to you?" I whisper into her ear with a smirk.

Her posture loosens knowing it is me. Turning her head to face me she simply says, "I've read it already."

"Was it good? Maybe I will read it." Now that she knows it is me, my body leans into her now to reach the book. As I do, she turns around to face me. There is the tiniest flicker of something that looks like shock before she attempts to move out from my arms. Instead of letting her, I simply say, "Don't crush the flowers, I worked hard on them."

She looks down to my left hand while I flag down the stall attendant to pay the three dollars for this book. I do my best not to look at her while paying. The weight of her staring bores into me. I can feel my restraint leaking. It would be so easy to cup her cheek and lift her lips to meet mine. After three breaths, and finally paying the attendant, I risk looking at her. It may have taken me a few months to get my shit together. But now I am ready to win her, whatever it takes. Even if what it takes is a little self-control in order to not scare her off.

"Did you pick a book for yourself?"

"I … uh. No." She coughs before turning back around. Testing my luck, I rest my chin on her shoulder as she combs through books again. Her breath stutters just slightly but eventually calms back to match the steady beat of her heart. Fates above she smells so good. How have I never taken giant whiffs of her hair? I want to just nuzzle into her. Fuck, how did I never realize just how bad I have it for her? It's as if the moment I gave myself permission to really want her, decades worth of longing and dreaming pummel into me.

My vision is overtaken with dreams of every touch. She's going to say she hates the public displays of affection, but will secretly love it. Holding her close as we shop here every weekend. Stretching my arm around her as we get coffee at Starstruck in the mornings before work. Waking up to her perfectly slotted into my body every morning. The beating of my heart is erratic, frantic, causing me to almost kiss the crook of her neck when she suddenly jolts out of my arms. Lost in my daydreams, I didn't see Summer trying to flag down the attendant.

A few steps away from the stall, I gather up the remnants of my common sense, trying to calm my heart. Summer pinches me in the side when she finds her way back to me.

"Well, are you going to give me my flowers or not?" She has a smirk and cocked her hip out, just enough to show she is putting on a show of being petulant. I cup her cheek with my free hand before pulling her into a hug.

"Hi." I croak out.

Summer chuckles a bit and just says, "Hi," back into my neck. The brush of her lips is electrifying as she voices the simple word. My body shivers as it tries to release every desire I had just shoved into a box. Taking one step back I lift the flowers between us.

"Wow, Koda. This is beautiful. You arranged this yourself?" Summer scans the flowers, smiling softly.

"I did a good job?"

"I would certainly say so!"

"Perfect. Obviously these are for you, but we now need to take a selfie so I can send it to Gerba." Summer rolls her eyes playfully and pulls us further out of the main walkway.

"Made quite an impression, did she?"

"Wanted to help me woo my woman. I fear she may actually just appear at my door one day if I don't update her on my progress."

"Woo - what?" Summer's face is clouded with confusion.

Not letting her focus too much on that comment yet, I swing her around in front of me. I stand behind her, lifting my arms around her, phone at the ready. Summer turns her head to me right as I am about to rest it on her shoulder. Her breath mingles with mine, her lips mere centimeters from mine.

"What… what is this, Koda?" It is the smallest of whispers.

She's so close. The compulsion surges through me to take her by the face and consume her. To let her overtake my soul. Tucking a windblown caramel lock of hair behind her ear, I try not to let my hand tremble too visibly.

Then I pinch her chin, turning her back towards the phone. My voice refuses to release my confession while looking at her. Barely above a whisper, "Wooing. And hoping to the Fates that I didn't wait too long to realize I wanted to."

From the phone screen I see Summer's eyes widen slightly. "Smile, honey." I whisper.

Testing out the endearment brings us both back to reality. The word tastes funny, and Summer's small scowl before smiling gives away her feelings on it also. That one is out.

We take a few pictures, ensuring the flowers are clearly visible. Once done, Summer turns and opens her mouth to say something. I don't find out what, though, because she is interrupted by a very booming "SUMMER!" from behind her.

I look over her shoulder to see a short, stout woman waving both hands as high over her head as she can. The little brunette human woman is jumping up and down in small spurts like an excited child. I am confused about how such a loud yell could have come from this small woman, but then my gaze falls on the man next to her. This man must be six foot six and built like a lumberjack. The small woman's hands barely reach the man's head as she waves them about. There is a teenage boy with sandy blonde hair on her other side, laughing but shrugging away embarrassed at the scene being created. Who are these people? How do they know Summer?

"Shit." Summer murmurs. "Don't… fuck. No matter how much I prep you, they are going to be nosey and intrusive. But I love them so … I'll explain how I know them after."

Summer grabs my hand reluctantly to pull me to this new trio. I take advantage and intertwine my fingers with hers. Summer turns to scowl at me quickly before we reach them. She drops my hand, leaving me staring at our hands as she hugs the small woman in front of us. When I look up, the lumberjack man is inspecting me.

"Uh, hi, my name is Koda." Lumberjack takes my hand to shake while still staring me down. It's as if I still haven't passed a test that I have no idea I am even taking.

"Roy," he finally huffs out. "This is my wife Berta, and our son Henry. It's nice to meet you, Koda. Tell us how do you know our dear Summer?"

Summer puts her hand over my mouth to stop me from answering. "We are friends."

The woman, Berta, huffs out a sigh. "When are you going to bring us a boyfriend to meet, Summer?"

Summer looks to the sky, as if asking for help from the Fates. Henry, the teenager, is the one to comment, "He definitely doesn't look like he's just your friend."

A maniacal smile crosses my face as I wrap my arm around Summer's shoulder, trying to pull her in at the neck.

"That is exactly what I am aiming for, thank you Henry."

Roy's chuckle is deep and strangely calming. This comforting feature lessens the blow of his next words.

"I like him, Summer. At least he is upfront about his intentions, unlike Dune."

Summer stiffens under me, and my body mirrors hers, trying to understand the connection.

"You knew Dune?" Berta asks with a cock of her head, noticing my reaction.

"We all went to college together." I manage to say.

Roy frowns, but stops himself from saying anything when Berta presses her hand to his arm.

"Summer, dear, it has been far past time for you to share. Shake up that routine. You don't need to come see us alone just because your original ice cream partner is no longer here."

Summer smiles softly at this and mouths a silent, "Thank you."

"Come on, Roy. Let's let these two finish their shopping. Hopefully we will see you again soon, Koda."

With that the jubilant lady leads her husband and teenager off through the crowd. I tuck Summer's hand into my elbow and weave us back into the crowd.

"Do you need to get anything else?"

"Nah, let's just get our coffee and head home."

She says it without realizing the yearning for that. To call us home. To go back to a place we both call home. We order our coffee - no Kristyn to ogle us - and start our journey home. I can practically hear Summer leaking. She is trying so hard to figure out how to start this conversation. I had already put most of the pieces together. There is no reason to be mad or upset.

"Roy and Berta own an ice cream shop?"

"Yes. It is called Bert and Rocky's." Summer answers matter of factly.

"It's where you and Dune would disappear to on Friday

nights. You would leave me to go on my dates, and you two would go get ice cream together."

"How did you know?" She looks at me bewildered.

"It wasn't hard to put together based on what Berta mentioned. But can I ask you a question?"

"Sure?"

"Why didn't you ever take me there? After Dune left I mean." Summer takes the question like I slapped her. I move in front of her, grasping her elbow, to show her my eyes are truthful. "I am not angry, just curious."

Summer sighs. "It… I don't know. It never really felt fair to bring anyone else into that space. I think any person would have had an expectation to be Dune's replacement in their eyes. They clearly are invested in my dating life. That is a heavy burden to bear, but I never wanted to stop going."

"It has nothing to do with keeping a memory with Dune alive?"

Summer scowls at my bluntness. "How dare you? No. It does not. Maybe in the first year or so. But not in ages. Now I go for the fucking change in scenary and company." She rips her elbow out of my grasp and makes to move around me.

I put an arm out to stop her before she gets far. "Shit. I - Summer - I am sorry. Fuck, I…" I look down at my shoes, willing myself to tell her. "I am asking for a couple of reasons." Walking back in front of her, her arms are crossed and she refuses to look at me. Softly, two fingers pull her chin back in my direction. "I am being selfish. I want to block any holes where old feelings for him might seep through."

"What in the Fates' names are you talking about, Koda?"

Just spit it out, Koda. It will all be okay.

"Dune moved back to Lyra."

Summer's only tell is that she takes one step back. She scrutinizes my face, trying to find the lie. Slowly, as if tasting every word as she speaks them, "He… Dune. Moved back to Lyra?

And you thought… I guess there's no good way to tell me that." She sighs at the realization.

"He sprung it on me in the last couple days I was in Arcalis. He even had a ticket on my same flight and everything. I didn't want to tell you over the phone or via text. That would have been shitty."

She takes another step back. "Is that why you are being…" Summer waves her hand up and down as if that describes how I've been acting.

"Absolutely not." Close the space between us, my hands grasp both sides of her face. "I may be an idiot, but one that would *never* try to keep you from happiness. If he is who you wanted, I wouldn't interfere.You can take care of yourself plenty fine, so don't think this is a protection ploy."

"You aren't an idiot." She whispers.

"I am. How else is there to explain why I haven't done this sooner? Before you could question if it had anything to do with Dune. I will prove to you that me being this…" I wave my hands up and down imitating her. Her light laughter loosens the tension in my chest. "This is about you and me. Not Dune. I'll break down those pesky excuses that are going to get in my way."

She pushes me away laughing. I flick her nose, before pulling her back to me to walk arm in arm again. Summer asks, "Did Dune move for that federal job? Or is he still at Star?"

This is not the time to make a sarcastic comment about her being curious about Dune. She needs to feel safe to ask questions. I don't want to accidentally push her away over a relationship between them possibly reforming. Because it won't.

"No, he is staying at Star. I asked him about that actually. Sounds like he is still interviewing for whatever job it is. But he was very secretive about it."

"Hmmm." I look at her, finding her face scrutinizing something in her mind. Thinking through some scenarios I can't see in her head.

"What are you thinking about?"

This seems to shake Summer out of her thoughts. "Just… work. Guessing what that job is. Wondering if I should be the asshole this go round."

"Color me intrigued. How do you want to be the asshole?"

"I have to assume Dune did not expect you to tell me he moved? Maybe he would ask you to set something up, but not actually tell me? Try to gauge my reaction to running into him in the wild. What if I turned the tables. Stage running into him somewhere of my own choosing?"

We grin at each other. I ignore the pain that she still knows him well enough. "I like this scheming side of you, dear."

At this endearment neither of us flinch as much as "honey".

"Better than honey," is all Summer mutters as we continue walking, scheming about how to stage a run in with Dune.

CHAPTER 21
SUMMER

've been pretty successful at warding off Koda's flirtations all week. Mostly. Our morning runs are the most alone time we have, which helps. I can't let myself give into these flirtations until he knows my powers. I cannot string him along. I won't. It is the only secret I have kept from him for ten years. I probably won't have a choice on this *chosen one* thing, but that one can be held off for a little bit longer.

My stomach twists at the thought that time is running low to do any of that. Especially since it seems Koda is no longer waiting. Normally, as I pass his apartment he is outside ready to just jump in and go. We just keep going. This morning he yanks me back to him. My eyes go wide, but he pulls me into a hug and coos, "Sorry, you were going faster than I expected. Didn't mean to give you whiplash."

His hug turns into roaming hands. His fingers spread wide across my back, caressing every inch he can get. One hand holds my arms as the other travels to my ass cheek. It almost distracts from his mouth tracing down my collarbone.

"Koda! I am already sweaty!" I push him off me, determined to finish this run.

His eyes are glossed over as he smirks. Turning me around, he smacks my ass and says, "Lead the way, then."

I ramp up my pace to try to wear him out. It keeps him quiet, and his hands to himself. We make it through the four miles he does with me, and sooner than I expected we are back at his apartment. I slow down to say goodbye, failing to cover up my heavy breathing. Koda keeps running past me and his apartment building. He turns, jogging backwards. "You coming?"

As soon as I pick up my pace again, Koda smiles, turns, and runs even faster than I had earlier. If we weren't in running attire, a random passerby might think I was chasing him down.

He doesn't slow until we reach my own apartment building. By the time we make it, there is absolutely zero chance of hiding my huffing. I bend over with my hands on my knees, sucking air into my lungs before yelling at Koda. As soon as I look up, I find him bent over next to me. I mistake it for him also being out of breath. Instead, he leans in, wraps his arms around my hips and lifts me over his shoulder. He carries me like this all the way into my bathroom. He doesn't set me down until he has turned the shower on.

Wide eyed, I lean back against the counter. "What are you doing?"

"I want to take a shower with you. Since you conveniently gave us a personal record run this morning, I have time to do that."

He pulls his shirt off before closing the two steps between us. His fingers leave a trail of heat on my skin as he drags my shirt over my head. Before I can stop him, Koda crouches, kissing my hips and my curves as he pulls my leggings down. His tongue traces a path back up my stomach and ribs before his fingers sneak under my sports bra, pulling it up over my head.

"Shower." Koda says gruffly.

I groan with need as his shorts come off, freeing his erection. His hand on my back pushes me lightly ahead of him into the shower. My shower isn't small, but it isn't exactly meant for two.

If I wanted to get away, I'd have to get out of the shower entirely. But I don't. It has been months since we last slept with each other. Months filled with confused emotions and feelings. Maybe we can just once before…

Koda playfully slaps my hands away from his cock before distracting me further. Massaging shampoo into my hair. I hadn't even noticed him grab it. Resting my head on his shoulder, I let him continue to rub scalp.

"I just wanted to be with you a little longer. You've been running away all week. Avoiding me. So this is me simply reminding you that I'll be here when you are ready." He pushes us under the water stream to rinse the suds from my hair. My back close enough to the wall, I use it as leverage to wrap a leg around him, grinding him to temptation.

Koda huffs out a strangled laugh before grabbing my loofah and body wash. He disentangles me before turning me around chest flush against the wall. His hands are everywhere, one with a loofah, his other with fingernails scraping along my body, sparking every sensation.

"Maybe taking a shower with you was a bad idea." His erection slides between my legs and he groans. His ministrations done, he lets go just long enough to turn me around, raise my hands over my head and clasp them to the wall. I scour over his body as he cleans himself, wishing my hands were the ones holding the loofah. I squirm, trying to get closer.

"I know, baby. I know. But if I let you touch me we aren't leaving this apartment today. We have scheming to do, or did you forget?"

I pout, but he doesn't relent. Rinsing off, he leans over, gives me a peck on the cheek and then pops out of the shower. "See you at Starstruck in a bit." It takes all of me to not collapse onto the floor of my shower.

Koda is already waiting with my drink sitting on the table when we walk through the door to Starstruck forty-five minutes later. As Jackie and I walk over, a small smile creeps up my face.

Koda's hair is still a little damp from a fresh shower, but it is swept to the side. Leaning back casually, he has an arm slung over the chair that my drink sits in front of. His eyes light up when he sees me walking to him, as if he didn't just have his hands all over me less than an hour ago.

"Oh, I see you didn't want to get my drink. Thanks, Koda." Jackie grumbles, ripping me out of my dreams being what our shower time could have been..

"Summer's drink is easy! It is a hot chai latte when it is cold, or an iced chai when it is not cold." I am sitting down, taking a sip of my iced chai as he says this. Then he leans into my side and whispers, "Isn't that right, pumpkin."

I promptly snort chai all over the table.

"What the fuck?" This could have been either Jackie or Kristyn from behind the counter. Probably both. I skitter out of my chair to make sure nothing drips off the table onto my clothes. Kristyn is laughing as she comes over with a towel. I am scowling at Koda before I notice Jackie's gaze flicking between Koda and myself. I can see her trying to piece together what actually just happened.

This is why I've been attempting to keep some distance. He's been doing this all week. Resting a hand nonchalantly on my thigh as Jackie and I talk over coffee. Leaning closer to say something. Buying my drinks. Testing out pet names. Pumpkin is better than *Gummie Bear*. But Fates above it is still bad.

Babe, love, dear seem to be sticking better. But then Koda has to go and test out baby doll, or buttercup, or kitten. I purposefully tried to trip him on our run the morning he called me kitten. Then he countered it with "See you do have claws!"

I have held myself back from testing out any nicknames for him, just like I've held back on touching, on flirting. That dam is starting to crack though if this morning's events are any indication.

Jackie sits back down at our freshly clean table with her vanilla cold brew. Before she can ask about what happened, I ask. "Hey, want to go dancing Saturday night? This one is hanging out with Dune." I point a thumb at Koda as relaxed as I can.

Koda's thumb rubbing circles on the inside of my knee is making that hard. Jackie seems to be sufficiently distracted by the question though.

"Wow. Aren't your Saturday nights sacred? We never hang out on Saturdays. This will be strange."

"Please? We haven't gone dancing in forever. I could definitely use an opportunity to get scandalously sexy and dance the night away."

Koda's thumb stalls mid-circle. Clearly he had not thought about that little tidbit, but it is too late to change plans now. This is the last bit to make our meeting with Dune not look staged. If it gets him back for this morning, even better.

"Ha, yes, let's go. Anywhere you were thinking?"

"The Aster?"

"Oh we are going big! Kyria will definitely be down now."

"Sweet I have this lovely black dress I haven't worn yet. It has this great slit in the side. I am going to need you to check if it is too much or not."

Koda's grip on my thigh goes tight as he groans. He then scoots his chair back to leave before he lets loose any other commentary. Jackie is staring at him with eyes wide, she starts to make a comment when he stops her.

"I'm going to let you continue your plan making without me. Plans with Dune are going to be so boring in comparison to little black dresses and a night out on the town. Plus I like to beat my boss into the office sometimes. We all know she can be a hardass about that when she wants to be."

He pokes me on the nose with a "boop" noise before leaving. Jackie and I both gape at him as he leaves the cafe. A little bit of overcompensation there, but he will figure it out.

"He's been acting weirder and weirder ever since Dune moved back," Jackie mentions.

"There is so much going on, I don't know if it is him or me. Or both of us."

"Fair enough. You still haven't told him about your newest department?" I shake my head in response. Every morning after Koda leaves us, Jackie and I have been parsing through our findings of anything we could find about the agreement Star Technologies and the Alnitak government has. Today I brought research focused solely on Aaron Dubois.

"You do remember our best path to getting intel on Star Technologies is going to be through Dune, right?"

"Yes, Jackie."

"Are you just going to keep Koda out of the loop as you try to fake a friendship with Dune?"

I sigh, "No, it's just …"

"You are stalling."

"Of course I am. How am I supposed to tell my best friend of almost twenty years that I have been holding a secret from him for about half of that time?" I cut her off. She doesn't know half of the plan is already in motion for Saturday. I can't tell Koda about what I need from Dune until he also knows about my powers. As soon as I tell Koda about my powers I could also lose another love. Frankly, I am just not ready for that moment, despite me kicking off the events that will lead up to it.

"I don't want a lecture. What did you find?"

"Absolutely nothing." She laughs. "It almost reminds me of when we have the team do a test search on you."

Looking at the lack of information I also brought to the table, it makes sense. I always had an interest in keeping tabs on Aaron Dubois. It helps that it isn't that hard to do at a surface level. Dubois is a fit, blonde haired, blue eyed Fae male that looks like he could have come from a mold. He almost has an ethereal glow when you see him. His pointed ears are the only part of him that is dull. Maybe that is just my bias.

Outside of news articles and pictures from the media, information you would expect to find simply does not exist for Aaron

Dubois. Things like where he grew up, primary schooling, or sports during higher education cannot be found.

Even all of his social media accounts are bland. Social media accounts for many government officials have at least some pictures of family, pets, hobbies. The things outside of managing their region that makes them seem more personable to their constituents. Dubois has none of that. Sunrises and cityscapes mostly. The more recent photos are of sunsets on a beach. I cross reference the dates on the sunsets and locations, Dubois must come to Lyra at least once a month.

I hand the paper with dates to Jackie. We can have our research team look into those. Maybe there is a chance of a correlation between events in his region.

But no matter what I found or didn't, there is one question that keeps creeping up. *What are you trying to hide?*

I know this is an internet wipe. He wiped most of the information about himself off the internet, and has put out the bare amount of information ever since. There is one piece of public information that hasn't been hidden yet. Either Dubois doesn't have the power to erase it from the history books or it is still too soon to wipe it.

Aaron Dubois' father, Queen Ashryn's Fae uncle, married a *human* woman. Queen Ashryn's father, king at the time, almost denounced the entire family. The humans of Elinder fought back. Nothing in House Law explicitly said that members of the Royal House could not marry humans. "A flaw that should have been rectified" was the King's only comment before never speaking on it again. It was an attempt to pacify an agitated population.

Maybe that is why his ears look dull compared to the rest of him. Is it because he is part Fae, part human? Did he get shunned for his human side?

After perusing this information, Jackie whispered. "This is interesting. I went looking through some of the gossip rags. There had been a rumor right before Dubois was born that his mother had been having an affair with a human man. A servant within the castle. The servant in question was never heard from again. As soon as Aaron was born with the defining pointed ears of the Fae, the rumor died."

"Hmmm… He doesn't make any sense. He is full of contradictions."

"It also makes me wonder what Ashryn has to do with any of this. We already know she is trying to expand the program at Star Technologies through FaeTech. That should cover most of the country. Then you have the new mystery role that you said Dune was looking into."

With that, we decide a refresher on our dear queen is necessary.

"We never have outings like this together anymore!" Kyria exclaims as she walks in my door. Rather she is swishing her hips as she walks past me. "You always go dancing with *Koooooda* and leave us behind."

Jackie gives me a peck on the cheek as she walks in behind her wife, carrying both of their dress bags and make up bags. "She pregamed." The simple explanation to Kyria's languid walking and speech.

I look at the pile of research on Ashryn sitting on the living room table. "Just leave your stuff here tonight. Pick it up tomorrow after the farmers market and we can go through what we found."

"Sounds good. You want to catch up to her?"

We grin at each other as I pull a bottle of vodka out of my liquor cabinet. Shots are poured and drunk, the preparations begin. We have finished the vodka bottle before our makeup is even done. I burn off some of the alcohol to keep enough of a level head tonight. Since I appear to be the most sober of us, Jackie holds Kyria as I apply her eyeliner.

All of our faces done, we split up to get dressed. Jackie and Kyria go into my guest room. As I slip into this piece of cloth that can barely be called a dress, I hear Jackie tell Kyria to stop snooping.

I stand in my doorway, putting on my heels as I wait for the door across from me to open. Curious what Kyria is doing, I don't have to wait long. She marches out, "SUMMER ARE YOU HIDING A MAN FROM US?"

My eyes go wide as she throws one of Koda's black t-shirts at me. Shit. The last thing I need is for Kyria to drunkenly tell Dune that Koda and I sleep with each other every so often. Jackie is watching me as I scan my brain for an excuse that will work.

"No, Kyria. No. That's just spare clothes in case Koda needs to crash here or our run went long in the morning. Nothing nefarious."

Jackie squints her eyes at me, but Kyria seems to buy it. It is literally the only secret I have kept from them, solely because I didn't want them to make it a huge deal.

"Now can either of you tell me if this slit is too high?" I twirl in my dress which provides enough of a redirection. Kyria walks up and slides her hand up my right leg.

"I forget how touchy you are when you drink, Kyria." I whisper.

"Just doing what half the men at the club are going to attempt to do, dear. The slit seems fine. They aren't going to get to your goodies without giving everyone on the dance floor a show."

"I'll call a car," Jackie huffs out a laugh.

CHAPTER 22

DUNE

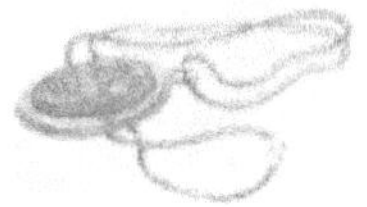

Throughout the week, Koda's been helping me get settled and reacquainted with this city. Tonight he has promised me the best of the night life this part of Lyra will offer. The club is much nicer than I expected. Koda made sure to send me the website in advance to check out the dress code. The Aster is a bougie hotel in the middle of downtown. The club is on the top floor. The dress code dictates that we have to wear blazers. I throw on some jeans and a tight black button down shirt under the blazer. This is a look that should be able to pull some company for the night if someone catches my eye.

The thought of a woman's company reminds me that I still haven't found a way to ask Koda about Summer without it being suspicious.

Honestly, the last time I could remember Koda explicitly talking about Summer was at least seven years ago. Queen Ashryn did make that vague comment about Koda being a mutual friend between us, but I had brushed it aside as misinformation. Or old information. Koda still works at FaeTech. Though, I can't see him hanging out with her. Surely, not often enough to warrant labeling them as friends. Knowing her, she would have iced him out after I left.

Something nudges me from the back of my mind, as if trying to bring up memories from the past. As if trying to tell me I've missed something. I wave away the feeling, knowing either way I'll have to bring her up soon. Even if it is only to show Queen Ashryn there is no purposeful delaying of her direct order. Monday. I'll do it on Monday.

Tonight will clear the air in my head. There is nothing a night on the town, alcohol, and beautiful women could do better than empty your mind of any other distractions.

Koda's place is conveniently on the way to the club so we meet there.While Koda is distracted trying to find his blazer in his room. I place a bug in one of the planters around his apartment. Hopefully it will stay hidden by the leaves. That would be a really awkward conversation. *"Oh yes, sorry. I just needed to make sure you are telling me the whole truth about Summer. Just making sure you didn't call her to let her know I was asking about you."*

I just place the one before reverting back to normal snooping. You know, looking at photos or books around the living room. Koda always has some photos or posters up on his walls. The wall leading in from the front door is surprisingly bare. Though there are nails and nail holes there. There's a stack of frames turned face down on the coffee table. Before I can flip one over to see what is going up next, Koda pops back out of his room.

"Okay, let's go."

The spring air is brisk enough to walk there without ruining our clothes with sweat. As we walk I try to make light conversation. This week has been a reminder that we have not hung out this long in ten years. During Koda's trips out to Arcalis we have a year of events to talk about in more detail than texts allow. Realization dawns about how right he was last week - I will need to reorient myself around his life.

"So you go running every morning?"

"Yeah, six am every day."

I can't help my groan at the thought. Koda just smiles.

"Don't worry, I am not inviting you to join, seeing as you don't run."

"I mean I could start," I mention.

"My running partner would eat you alive." He chuckles as if it's some inside joke.

He grabs coffee on the way in to work with a woman named Jackie. Just a friend, he adds. Maybe he will let me meet her.

Saturdays are also usually booked up but he made an exception this week for me. Sundays he goes to a farmer's market. Correction, he runs to the farmer's market, so again, cannot join there.

This is the schedule I have to work around.

Twenty minutes pass, and we reach the Aster Hotel. As we walk up, the bouncer gives us a quick nod and waves us to the elevator attendant to key in the top floor. "There will be a coat check upstairs should you want to relieve yourselves of your jackets."

"Do you come here often?" I ask to fill the empty space of the elevator ride up.

"Yeah, I try to come here once a month or so. I like the people here."

"What's the deal with the coat check if that is part of the dress code? Not going to complain but it is curious."

"Honestly, I think it is more to maintain the image for the hotel than the club itself."

The elevator lets out right into a main throughway of people. Booths and tables line the walls to the left of the elevator. Some tables are roped off for special table service. There is an ebb and flow of people to get to the bar that lines the wall to the left.

"Coat check is over here," Koda nudges me to the right. He has already removed his blazer and is rolling up the sleeves on his black button down. We both must think the same thing - we are basically twins in our outfits. We burst out laughing, which seems to alleviate the strange tension growing between us. "Well, we may just have to split up tonight."

Turning, I take in the rest of the room as we start walking into the main pathway to the bar. The dance floor takes up most of the space not already taken over by tables. With good reason - it is filled. There is enough space between groups for a single river of movement to make their way across it. The lights flash across the room matching the beat of the DJ.

With any luck both of us would be getting laid. At least that is my plan. From the look of the room there will be plenty of choices. Anything, anything to finally get Summer and reality off my brain and -

Summer.

The path to her breathed open as soon as I bid her to the back of my mind. Did someone shine a spotlight on her? Summer is there, surrounded by bodies, dancing with and around others. Blending in and yet completely separate. Summer looks wholly in place here. Unrestrained, blissful, happy. One hundred percent the opposite of what I imagined her to be. Had I ever created this scenario in my head? Nothing close.

Every imagined scene was in a conference room, an office. Summer in some sort of power suit or a blazer or jeans. Or Fates, anything that covered up… everything.

Suddenly I am twenty-one again, trying to keep my jaw off the floor. Koda and I had taken her out for her birthday. She walked out of her room in a short silver dress that shined like a damn disco ball. It had been so hard to keep my hands off her that night. Then every day after that. But tonight she did not need the glittering lights bouncing off her.

Summer has the tiniest black dress that only barely covers her ass. Her thighs and calves honed, straining only from the various dips in her dancing. Her signature one spot of color is not present today. Her heels are a matching glittering black, giving her an extra three inches. Her hair is in just that move-ment where everyone knows she styled it in some capacity, but the dancing has left it a little dizzying. She is glowing. *She is perfect.* The thought spikes through my brain before I can stop it.

There is one very large miscalculation in my plan. When I agreed to come back to Lyra, my mind kept seeing the girl from my early twenties, just mixed with the ice queen front she gives the world today. Ten years had changed not just me, but also Summer.

She is a fucking woman now.

A sexy, fucking woman.

I cannot help but watch every curve of her in that skin tight dress, the dress sparkling when the light hits it. It takes every bit of me to not rub at the new ache in my chest.

Koda breaks my thoughts with a hand on my shoulder. Have I even taken a breath since the moment I saw her? "Well, this will be fun. She will leave you alone as long as you do the same."

A brown skinned woman with silver hair dancing with Summer notices us staring and swirls Summer a few times. There is a look of recognition as she looks between Koda and myself. She whispers something in the red head woman's ear, before beelining it in our direction.

"All I have to say to you two is please do not ruin my night. Specifically you." This woman must be six or seven inches shorter than me, yet stares into me with hard eyes while poking my chest. She may be small, but there is a strength to that little finger pushing on me.

"Dune meet Jackie. Jackie meet Dune. Jackie, he won't cause any problems," Koda states.

"Good." She takes a step closer towards me. "You stay away and she will too. Asshole." She mutters the curse before looking at Koda. She squints her eyes at him as Koda gives her a soft smile. "Don't make me dislike you, Koda."

The woman named Jackie spins on her heels and swishes her pink dress as she struts away. Why does her name ring a bell? Didn't Koda say he gets coffee in the morning with a woman named Jackie?

"Ha. Here she is telling us to not cause issues." Koda chuckles. "Besides the fact that she is married to Kyria over there, she is also one of Summer's closest friends. Also her executive assistant. So don't try anything with her."

When we look back in the direction she headed, Summer has clearly seen us. Her eyes are hot coals on us. She does a small curtsy with her arm outstretched as she bows, hand twirling in the air. This is going to be a night to remember, that is for sure. When Summer comes up from her bow, she has almost a feral grin that reaches her eyes.

"Is that the Jackie who you get coffee with in the morning?" I ask Koda, not taking my eyes off Summer even as this Jackie woman pulls her away to a table.

When Koda doesn't answer, I finally turn to look at him. He is eyeing me curiously.

"What?" I spit out defensively, failing to cover up the fact I was staring at Summer's ass.

"It is, but let's grab a drink and go talk at one of those patio tables while I tell you it is actually Summer and sometimes Jackie that I get coffee with."

CHAPTER 23
DUNE

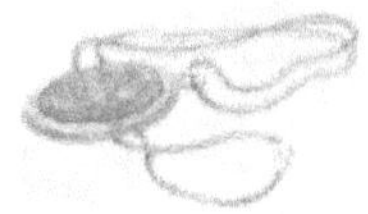

Even though Koda and I have no problem finding plenty of willing dance partners, my eyes always find their way back to Summer. How can they not? Every part of my self control is fried. Summer keeps gradually dancing her way closer. Dance after dance, she weaves her way towards us, building her web to trap me. Finally, when she has pulled herself too close, I escape her web, heading to the bar. If she wants to play games, I will have more alcohol in me to play along.

Maybe the alcohol will dull down the spiraling in my head. Making it past the crowd of people, I wait for the bartender. This gives me a few minutes to churn through all of the information dumped on me tonight. Details of life that have been simply quietly left out over the passage of time, were exposed over a beer.

First, Queen Ashryn was not wrong. Koda, *my best friend*, is still friends with Summer. My guess is the two of them are still thick as thieves. Just like we all were back in our university days.

They've replaced me with Jackie, the silver haired spitfire.

Summer is Koda's boss. We've had so many conversations about all the ways his boss has empowered him, and made him do great things. I don't know how I was ignorant enough to think Koda had been talking about anyone other than Summer. What had he said just a few months ago? *You know I like my boss too much to come work for you.*

Sunday mornings are spent with Summer at a farmer's market. No exceptions.

The running partner... Summer. She would eat me alive if I tried to join their runs.

There is a sudden clarity about why I have had so many open questions about Koda's life. Koda's life is so intertwined with Summer's that the small nuggets he shared were the only ones he could.

My mind continues thrumming through memories. Trying to put together the pieces of some of Koda's more memorable stories, wondering if one of the companions was Summer. Trying to find a story that would piss me off, make me dislike her. But all I find are positives. All that optimism and hope from our youth is still there. Now it's been forged into a confident, strong, sexy woman with fire running through her veins.

If I hated her, walking into the trap she's set for me here would be easier.

It would be easier to hate her if she was not amazing.

If she was not ... *herself.*

I risk searching for her on the dance floor, to see where she's ended up.

Time falters as my eyes find her sidled up behind Koda. Her chin sits on his shoulder, her hands on his waist, fingers twined within his belt loops as if swaying him from there. My brain has finally caught up and the only thing keeping it from exploding is that Koda seems extremely uncomfortable.

Good.

Stay friends with her.

Fine.

But what if ...

Why would that matter to me?

It definitely does not.

Then why am I clenching my fists so hard?

Unclench your fists.

The bartender finally interrupts my downward spiral, "What can I get ya man?"

Jealousy wrapped in anger and confusion answers for me. "Six shots of your best tequila." His eyes widen, and then widen further as I point at the dance floor. "And put them on Summer Chase's tab."

The bartender, Stan, according to his nametag, scrunches his face with intrigue. Why does he look familiar? His mouth quirks to the side, his tongue poking out thinking on my request. "It'll take me a second to grab that. Feel free to wait over there. I'll be right over."

When he returns with the tequila and six shot glasses my lungs remind me to breathe. As he sets up the shots Stan asks, "So, tequila man. Who are you?"

"Excuse me?"

"Most guys would give me their left kidney to know Summer's drink of choice. Though none of them could probably afford it. She tips me extremely well to expressly forbid me from pouring drinks for her without her presence. That means they had the balls to talk to her first. You, though," Stan pauses from pouring and looks up. "You already know her drink of choice. She also okayed it. Yes. I texted her to ask. So spill it. Who are you?"

"Just an old friend from college. Recently moved back." Looking back at the dance floor, Summer and Koda are now dancing, Koda clearly loosened up a bit. His hands on her waist sends another flare of anger through my stomach. What the hell do they put in the drinks here?

"Are her tips enough to keep you from pouring drinks that others want to buy her? Can I bother you for an extra shot? You can put that one on my tab. "

Is she still the person that could earn the respect of a random bartender? Everyone else has been getting her smiles, her kind-ness, her touches. She used to give those to me. Now all we have is this distance. She used to be my everything. I lost her and now she is toying with me. I shake that thought out of my head. She probably doesn't even realize I am watching.

No, Stan made sure she knew that I knew exactly where she was.

Stan once again pulls me from the torrent of thoughts.

"Yes and yes. It is worth it. Summer's a good person. She has helped me out of a few binds in the past years. You would know of course."

You should know...

He continues as he pours, "So one night a couple years ago maybe, a guy drugs her drink. Somehow she was able to detect it, got away from the guy. Koda immediately took her home. That man was banned from the club. In her words, 'If a man doesn't have the nerve to come talk to me before getting me a drink, he doesn't deserve to give me one.' So after that, if anyone asks what her drink of choice is, every bartender in here knows the answer is 'Ask her yourself.' You circumvented that by actu-ally knowing the drink, and her name."

"Stan, man to man..." When did my throat become a desert?

You are just gathering info.

You do not care.

You just want to know how much shit to give Koda.

I finally grit out, "I have been gone for ... a while. They are ... were... are my best friends..."

"Yes, yes. I -" He halts himself while waving me on to continue.

"Do you know if they ever ..."

Stan turns to look in the direction I am in. Summer is pulled into Koda's front, his fingers tight on her waist. He leans into her ear, but I jerk back to Stan when he says, "Well I'll be damned."

"I ... don't know how to take that."

Stan returns his gaze to me. It is a calculated look, as if he is trying to piece some puzzle together in his mind. I try not to look over eager, or like a hurt animal, hopefully my face settles some-where in the middle.

"No, man. I have actually never seen them dance together, like, ever. Not si- No. They always only ever wingman for each other. I suppose that's why she came with those other women tonight. She will need a new wingman."

"For real? They never went home together?"

"Outside of the night she got drugged, I have never seen them leave this club together. I've seen them both leave alone. They always only ever helped the other find a dance partner for the night. It is somewhat believable that the two of them would wingman for each other. Especially when no one to this day has ever seen Koda place a hand on her. Throw you in the mix, no man is going to go near her. I imagine this is the first and last time either of us will ever see this scene."

They didn't come near her when I was around…

"Thank the Fates."

"Ha, interesting. Here is your shot." I chug it back before grabbing the other six. "I will, uh, wish you luck? You can carry all those?"

Three shots to a hand, I give Stan a nod of thanks. For the shots, the info, and easing a little bit of jealousy that I really should not even be allowing myself to have.

CHAPTER 24
KODA

Summer creeps up behind me causing my whole body to go stock still. My stiffness allows her to pull me away from the high top table I've been nursing my drinks at.

"You do know that Dune has been trailing your every move across this club, right? I would rather not be caught with your hands this close to my dick."

She sways behind me, "My hands are on your belt loop *dear*, he can't get his panties in a twist over that." Then Summer nips the point of my ear which has me twisting around to hold her in place. Oh we are using pet names are we?

"How drunk are you, love?"

"Not drunk enough to lose control. Enough to loosen me up to have a little fun while trying to get into Dune's mind." The grin on her face is huge and I can already feel her hands trailing south to grab my ass. I twist her around so that her back is to the bar. Clearly showing that my hands are not on her ass. As much as I would *really* like them to be.

"How pissed is Jackie?'

"Incredibly. She's coming over tomorrow morning anyway to pick up stuff she left at my place. I'll explain then. I didn't want her to lose her anger. I supplied her with a lot of alcohol on my own tab, so hopefully that will help. How much did he freak out on you?"

"He kind of just… absorbed it. I imagine once he has some time to flip back through some of our trips and dissect everything I have ever said to him in the last ten years he will freak out. Or he will just stop talking to me." I take her hand and put it north of my ass cheeks. "I specifically did not tell him we've fucked around. I have no idea how he would react to that. So please, just for right now, stop grabbing my ass, love." Not to mention the fact I want to be dating her.

"Well he's talking to Stan. Stan truly thinks we have never done anything more than wingman for each other. We should be safe for one more night."

"How do you know that?"

"I'm really interested to hear what questions he asks…" She murmurs.

She pulls out her phone from the front of her dress, turning it toward me. Through the web of texts all I know is the Dune is coming back with six shots of tequila.

"Wait, since when do you have Stan's number? How does Stan know who Dune is?"

Summer twirls around and starts twisting her hips in front of me. Is she… fucking… flirting? I wouldn't say she's been against my wooing. She certainly hasn't been actively participating in it… or egging it on. "Don't you remember that one morning senior year?"

"What are you talking about?" I grit out pulling her back into me. I grip her chin, forcing her to keep looking at me.

"Oh, you know, I went out with the girls one night. You and Dune came to check on me the next morning… walked in on me getting some great head?"

"THAT WAS STAN? THAT STAN?" I point at the bar.

Summer twirls out of my arms and just smirks at me. She wants to play? Game on.

Or… she's now thinking about taking Stan home.

Nope.

Fuck it.

Dune can punch me in the face for all I care right now. I grab her hips and pull her ass into me. My hands skate down the outside of her thighs every so often and swing with her to the music. Every sane thought leaves my body.

I nip her ear back before whispering. "That morning was the first time I ever truly wanted to dick punch Dune. The first time I ever regretted meeting Cassie before you. The first time I regretted not claiming you before Dune could just pussyfoot around you."

The only reaction from Summer is a slight hitch to her breath. I had never talked shit about Dune before that moment. Especially in how he dealt with his feelings for Summer. Dune would talk about Summer all the time. He was always watching her longingly. He kept the status quo, never risked anything more. So they just both pined for each other for years.

We dance for a few more minutes before I see Dune starting to cross the dance floor. He shows up a few moments later with every shot glass intact.

"If it isn't Dune Raydn in the flesh."

"Summer." Dune nods. "I bring a peace offering."

Sadly, Summer moves away from me to grab her shots. The space in front of me feels too cold, too empty. I take my two shots from him. We clink them together before each swallowing one whole. Dune is inspecting me. I cannot tell if he is looking for mortal wounds or hickies.

"Alrighty boys. Since I am pretty positive I bought these shots, *your* peace offering to me will be two dances - one for each shot. Then we can all go back to hunting down some fun for the night." The grin on her face is sinful and I want to die. She will absolutely not be going home with anyone other than me tonight.

Summer's shot is in the middle of our trio, waiting for two more to join. Dune's eyes are dark and unreadable. They are clouded with disbelief, lust, or both frankly. My shot glass joins Summer's, my arm loops back around her again, and finally Dune's clinks in.

Shots swallowed, glasses placed on the nearest table, Summer grabs both of our collars and pulls us into the middle of the floor. It was Dune, surprisingly, that spoke first.

"Just remember, Summer, two dances." Dune holds up two fingers as if to hammer the point in.

"While I am very excited to be smashed between you two beautiful men, I won't let myself get carried away and forget to grab my snack tonight."

"That's good. Koda, remember the last girl that danced the night away between us and lost track of time?" A glint of mischief plays across his eyes.

"Oh yes I do." I lean into Summer's ear and whisper, "We kept up that dance through the sheets that night." Summer whirls around to look at me.

"You never told me THAT story!"

Dune smirks, putting an arm fully across her stomach to pull her those final steps into a spot on a dance floor.

"Lucky lady…" is all Summer can get out before we all start dancing. That comment alone chokes my inner leash. Just as quickly, Summer switches into info gathering mode as she circles her hips between us.

"So Dune, welcome back. I hear you moved back last week?"

Hands are everywhere.

"You aren't wrong." Dune grits out.

"No girlfriend?" Summer chokes out the question as Dune is pulling her into him by the waist.

"Clearly."

"Pets?"

"Nope."

I don't think that Dune is breathing. His jaw is clenching so hard despite his hands crawling all over her. It is as if the moment he isn't actively chasing her, he's finally allowing himself to touch her. Anger roars through me. Is this what Dune felt all those years as she gave me playful touches that meant nothing?

"So Star sent you back to Lyra after all these years?"

Dune twists Summer and pulls her into him. "What the fuck is this, Summer? Twenty questions? You going to ask me how many people I've fucked next? Or how many I've fucked over? I don't remember you talking so much when we used to go out dancing. "

From where I am standing, I barely see the slight flicker of Dune's eyes at Summer's lips and back to her eyes. Summer's hand rubs up Dune's chest until she grips his chin between her fingers.

The air is sucked out of my lungs. If I was doubting my feelings for Summer, I definitely would know now. How the hell did Dune hold back for so many years? Watching what could be such an intimate moment makes my chest roar. Dune doesn't get to come back after ten years and think he can kiss her.

I put a hand out towards her hip ready to pull her back into me. Summer is already pushing him away by the chin as she takes a step back towards me.

"Sorry, Dune. It isn't every day I am trying to catch up with someone who shows back up after ten years. Just trying to make small talk is all."

The song transitions into a new one. The second and last song she will give us tonight.

All I know is Summer's hips swaying under my hands. Her ass on my front. A quick twist and her breasts sitting on my chest.

Without fully claiming my spot with Summer in this weird ass dancing trip, I do allow myself to grab her ass, her thighs whenever I can. Dune isn't holding back. Why should I?

I do keep myself from sinking my face into her neck, or nipping her ear whenever she is turned away from me. This slit in her dress is the best kind of temptation.

Two songs go quickly.

Too quickly.

We keep dancing into a third song before Summer extracts herself. Hands from both Dune and myself follow after her, willing her not to leave.

Summer looks exhilarated, high. As we both unashamedly grab at her not to leave, she takes one more step back. "Best not to keep this up. See you around Dune. See you tomorrow Koda."

Her eyes flare, I swear they actually turn orange like a fire, before she turns and sashays over to find the next man to dance with.

"I need another fucking drink." Dune sighs.

CHAPTER 25
SUMMER

can feel Dune and Koda's eyes follow me as I wind through the bar the rest of the night. I meander my way to the bathroom to contemplate, to breathe. I … this … he … isn't what I anticipated.

I've kept tabs on Dune enough from afar. I wasn't nervous about seeing him. I've seen him at conferences, even if we both steered clear of each other. Seeing him here, touching him, smelling him. Fates above, it was almost as intoxicating as all the alcohol I've drank tonight.

Even from across the room when they first arrived, there was a pull to those charcoal eyes that have haunted my dreams and nightmares these last few weeks. The face around those eyes has sharpened its edges, giving Dune the strong jaw to go along with his loud mouth. His black hair is cleanly pulled back into a small bun, but he is not spending his small Fae magic on keeping the gray hairs out. He has kept one large streak of gray. He is probably still maintaining the shoulder length hair based on the size of the bun.

Compared to Koda's lean, functional muscles, Dune has filled out. The broad shoulders match the tightness that stretches across his biceps. His forearms on display should be illegal.

An ache starts forming in my chest as I think about the scar under his left eye. Throughout the night it was as if someone or something was slowly pulling on a rope between us, long covered by years of earth and fallen leaves.

I rub my chest again now, where that pull seemed to stretch and constrict throughout the night. I don't want to think about the meaning behind it. Dune wanted to kiss me earlier. I caught the flicker of his eyes to my lips. The girl of my past that loved him swooned. That girl wanted to let him in. That girl is dead. The woman I am today? She leaned back into Koda.

Sighing, I try not to think of how my skin is red hot, scorched from the path that both Dune and Koda left on my body. Tomorrow will bring a sober Koda. Long gone will be the intoxicated Koda, admitting his visceral feelings. I had been a little extra flirty. Between the alcohol and needing to be a little more fluid around Dune, I figured it would help.

Did I expect a long hidden confession from almost fifteen years ago as the response?

No.

It took every ounce of brainpower to pull myself together to even ask Dune questions after that. He hasn't been shy about what he wants this past week. I did not realize the extent of how long those desires have been there.

My legs are numb. My heart is hurting with the feelings about both men. Maybe I will just take my mind off them both and wait for Stan to get off work. That's what I will do. Stan is always good for a distraction. No strings attached, good fun. Yes.

I emerge from the bathroom, checking my phone for any texts from Koda or Jackie. I start to text Koda when a hand pushes me into the wall of the hallway. My defenses are raised until Koda pinches my chin to look up into his eyes.

The self control I have been keeping reined in all night pulls a little as he purrs into my neck at my shoulder. His other hand grips my thigh, a thumb tracing my hem line. "Oh, Summer. You evil… evil woman."

His thumb slowly runs across my lips. Koda looks crazed with desire as he leans into my ear. "Was this part of your game too? Flirt with me tonight on the dance floor, see what my reaction would be? Grind your ass all over me. See if I lose control? Two can play that game, my love. I already told you, I play to fucking win."

A fog threatens to take over my senses before I grasp at reality. What would it be like to give in to Koda's chase? I feel him smile against my ear, thinking I am already being entranced. He traces my pulse down my neck with his teeth and tongue. He must feel it racing, exposing my thoughts. I bite his thumb and spit out the only thing that I can think of.

"I figured you and Dune would be playing video games or something. Stan is already planning to come back with me."

Koda chuckles against my collarbone before nipping at the small patch of muscle there. He slowly looks back at me, which is when I notice his pupils are blown out. He leans in close now. One hand slowly trails up my thigh, as his other hand at my chin slides to grasp my neck.

"You take anyone into that apartment with you, I will pull them off you myself when I get there." Koda's thumb finds the other side of my neck as he gives the slightest squeeze. The smallest moan sneaks out, killing any pretense. He breathes into my ear, "Now. Be a good girl. Pay your tab. Go home. I'll be there as soon as I lose Dune."

I nod as he releases me from his grip.

"And Summer?"

I turn back to look at him. A damn mistake. He is still leaning over the spot I just left. His forearm is leaning against the wall as he roams my body hungrily.

"Do not touch anything. I want to rip this dress off you myself."

I stride back to him, pushing him against the wall now.

Mirroring him, I hold him by the neck and whisper, "Hurry home then. It won't take long to start taking care of this itch myself." I turn, escaping the dark hall before Koda can grasp my hips and pull me back.

Maneuvering back to the bar, Stan meets me at an emptier corner.

"Out of ignorance, did I just lie to that sucker?"

"You will need to be more explicit than that, Stan." His side eye game is strong as he pulls my tab up on the screen in front of him.

With a huff of a laugh, he comments, "You are a brat when you are drunk, you know?" Passing me my receipt, he continues, "You don't think I remember how Dune Raydn followed you around in college like a lost puppy? Or me making you c-"

"Well clearly you do, sir. Also you only charged me for four shots of that tequila."

"Stop avoiding the question. Think of it as a buy two get one free deal."

"You haven't asked a question." I put the pen down, not with a slam but enough to feign annoyance.

"Dune Raydn shows up at my bar - a man that many of the woman-folk have been fawning over all night. Just like at university, Dune literally had his eyes glued to you all night."

"That -"

"I am not done!" He waves a finger in the air for dramatics. "Then you dance with Koda. He is literally the only person you haven't danced with here. Even though he, too, always has eyes on you. All of that in spite of being Dune Raydn's best friend. I assume you are going home with Koda tonight based on that display by the bathroom. Are you two messing around behind Dune's back?"

I pick up the pen and actually slam it back to the bartop this time. Partially matching the drama, part true annoyance. "He fucked with my brain for years before moving across the country Stan. What was it you said that night, *'I'll worship you like the goddess you are. Maybe it will force Dune to make a move after he's seen you freshly fucked. Don't wait around for him. Show him you are a fucking queen with or without him.'* Puppy dog eyes or not, a lot has changed in ten years. If a couple of dances returns that favor in a small amount, then fine."

"I can't believe he did not recognize me. I mean, I kind of can. I traumatized him the one time we got close." He laughs and puts both hands above his head before I can scourge him with some comment that does not bubble up. "Hey, I am just a glorified people watcher. You asked me to tell you if he asked anything. He asked me if you and Koda had ever fucked. Not in so many words, but he seemed... I don't know. It was like a combination of a student doing research, but there was an edge of personal curiosity. I wasn't sure what to make of it."

"Eh, it doesn't matter anyways. If he wants to fault Koda or myself for it, that is on him. I don't really care."

"Hey," Stan covers my hand. "He does not deserve to eat up any more of your life. Just like I meant it in college. Live your life. I am glad I discounted two of your shots." He gives me a sincere smile.

The smile matches his personality. While he moonlights as a bartender and people watcher at night, he runs a non-profit that provides outreach and after school activities for orphans throughout the inner city. The non-profit that is on my list of large charitable donations every year.

"No one will ever say as sweet of things as you do, dear."

"I live to please."

"Oh. I know."

I slide the pen and paper toward him face down. No need for

him to see my tip in the equal amount of those free shots until I am gone.

"Hey, Summer. One more thing." He straightens, more serious but he is fiddling with his index finger. "When I say live your life, what I mean is … don't let Dune get between you and Koda. I see a lot of nightly pickups. I have seen you and Koda pick up your own various hookups. I *also* know that you two have known each other longer than you have known Dune." Pointing towards the bathroom hall behind him. "That was something more than a hookup. I am pretty sure the temperature in that hallway rose by a couple degrees."

There is a new tug in my chest now. Even when I had circled Dune for all those years, no one had directly said anything about the situation. Except for Stan. He knew even then that my eyes had been set on Dune. He called out the unrequited attention, then spent a night worshipping my body. He was bluntly honest, knowing that there would be nothing serious. Just one night. That morning he heard Dune and Koda barging into my college apartment and did his part to make Dune jealous enough to make a move. The only thing it did was ensure I never went home with a booty call after a night out. Dune never made a move. He also never let anyone else make one.

"You deserve happiness, Summer. I know you are always making sure everyone else is content. You say you are happy and fulfilled. Maybe, just, don't discount that you could be happier."

"You are putting a lot of pressure on my hookup tonight you know?" We are both out of words now. I'll save the emotional barrage of contemplating my future for another day.

"I can*not* believe you actually danced with him." Jackie says from her seat in the round booth. Kyria is leaning up on her, head on Jackie's shoulder.

"I know. I know. I am going to head home. Don't feel like you have to come with."

"You going to be good to get home?"

"Yeah started burning down some of the buzz a bit ago. You?"

Kyria gives a little giggle as my phone buzzes.

KODA

Leave. Faster.

SUMMER

Jackie looks at me curiously, as laughter escapes me. "Yeah I will get us home fine. You…" She bites her lip, as if she is trying hard to not ask who I am texting. I blow her a kiss from across the table and head for the elevator.

As the elevator crawls its way up to the top floor, a shadow comes up behind me.

"I thought -"

That smell of snow creeps into my senses, the tense air that I thought is Koda trying to sneak into the elevator with me was in fact Dune. I turn to face him, flicking my eyes to Koda across the club, his mouth in a firm line. He makes a movement to show him pulling an invisible person away. My eyes happen to also flick to Stan who is switching between watching the elevator and watching Koda. He at least is finding some hilarity in this situation.

"Oh. You. Not your scene?"

Dune is stiff. He keeps making fists at his sides. One arm is crooked enough to hold his blazer over it. He clutches at his pocket at one point. Do I really make him this uncomfortable? Why didn't he just wait for the next elevator?

"I did not want you to walk home alone."

My eyebrows have disappeared into my hair. I am sure of it. There is a flash of memories that scream across my mind. Two college kids drunk supporting themselves back to the girl's apartment. Two kids passed out in each other's arms as soon as they reached the couch those nights.

The elevator reaches in and yanks me back into reality.

"Not necessary. Stay, finish out your night." Despite the dismissal, he trails my steps into the metal box. I stand as close to one wall as I can without hugging it.

"No."

"You are ridiculous."

"This city can be dangerous, Summer."

"Yes. I know Dune. I have lived here for the better part of twenty years. I still run five miles a day and go to a self defense gym. Before you mention the heels, I am not so attached to them that I would not slip out of them before running if I needed to. I am not defenseless. You know *nothing* about me anymore. At least I *tried* to make some conversation with you earlier."

I look at him now, his jaw is sewed so tight his teeth must be grinding to nubs. Waiting for this metal cage to land and release us, I shoot Koda a text to encourage him to still show up later. Surely Dune's endgame tonight is not getting into my bed. Frankly, if it is, that is not the carefree sex I wanted to drown in tonight.

Freedom finally chimes its arrival. The door is held, but as I stride past Dune I feel his fingers brush my back as if to help guide me out before he realizes what he is doing. I march through the lobby, straight into the outside world. The cool early summer air licks my face.

"Goodnight Ms. Chase." Oliver comments as I near, eyeing Dune stalking behind me. The bouncer lets me fast pass on my way in, and watches my back on my way out, keeping stragglers from following.

"You too, Oliver. Broody behind me is fine."

With a nod from Oliver, I cross the street without a second glance behind me. The twenty minutes to my building is filled with the rare patter of other night owls and our own four feet stomping through the streets. The streetlamps leave long shadows, making the path outside of the sidewalks darker than the night surrounding us.

A few stars peek out through the haze of city lights.

Was it nice to not make this walk alone? Yes.

Should I try to make conversation? Probably.

I slow my stride for a moment to give him the okay to catch up. Even though he walks next to me, I keep my eyes set on the sky. If the stars had not been watching closely, would they have caught the change in how we walked each other home tonight? The time that passed since the last rerun of this was just the blink of an eye to those celestial beings. Would they look down and rewind time to see what they had missed? What had changed since that last joy filled walk home? A walk that had been filled with twirls, skips, lingering touches, and so much laughter.

My stomping out of the building turns into a light march then eventually to a normal pace. Contemplating the stars, and three inch heels will take the steam out of any march after a while.

"Remember when we used to do this all the time? Drunk off our asses, insisting on walking home instead of spending the money to call a cab?" I say softly, almost to myself instead of Dune. "Neither one of us would have been any help to each other then." There is a slight stir in my chest at the thought.

Dune's only response is to look at me and huff a small laugh. His face is filled with confusion and hesitancy. I specifically did not bring up the *last* time we took this walk, but it probably doesn't stop either of us from letting that memory float to the top of our minds.

So we walk in silence for the remainder of the trek. It is not until I am on the steps to enter my building that I turn to Dune.

"You have succeeded in your mission, valiant knight. With

that I bid you farewell." I bow my head in mockery and turn to go inside.

"Summer, wait…"

"What?"

"Can I …" He trails off but never drops my eye contact. Oh, no. He can finish that question himself. I cock an eyebrow at him to continue. Coughing he finally does. "Can I come up?"

"No."

The incredulity on his face at being denied sends a blazing flame of anger through my entire body. I stay silent as I tamper down the surge.

"No, sorry, no. I just want to talk."

"Still no."

"Really Summer?"

I am sure my eyes are literally red right now. Based on the step back Dune just took I may need to check my contacts. Somehow I still channel a patient but stern lecturing voice.

"Yes. Really. You had years to *talk*. You walked me home in silence for the last twenty minutes. You already berated me over asking you a couple simple questions. So pardon me, that I do not feel like restarting the conversation. Especially because I thought I'd be going to bed with a good time, not whatever this conversation is going to be. You do not get to just waltz back into this city and expect me to welcome you back into my life, commanding my time as if you are owed it."

"Aren't I, though?" Not a yell, but the raised voice means something in that statement hit just the right nail.

"No. You aren't. Maybe if this was nine years ago. Now though? I owe you nothing. Not my time. Not my personal space."

He pulls me into him, his hand pressing firmly on my back. "I kept your secret for a decade, Summer. Am I not owed anything for that?" Venom laces his tone, although it is hushed as if he doesn't want me to hear it.

"My number never changed, Dune. Plan a coffee date or a

walk around a park for fucks sake. Unless you are going to let me into your own personal space, do not expect me to do the same. I picked up the pieces of my life once before. If I have to do it again, I need a place that won't have memories of you in it."

Pushing him away, I unlock the main door and enter the building. Pulling the door shut between us, we just stare at each other for a single breath before I turn to the elevator without looking back.

My phone immediately starts buzzing at me once I cross the threshold of my apartment.

"That motherfucker."

I don't have time to find the source of the alarm if Koda is anywhere close. I turn on all the jammers after I send Koda a dirty text.

I grab a bottle of wine and pop it open angrily. I do not even bother with a glass, opting to suck a giant sip straight from the bottle. I know Koda would adore it if he found me on my knees waiting for him, but I need to calm down the rage of thoughts in my head.

Dune *knows* about my fire wielding abilities.

Dune *bugged me.*

What the fuck would we have talked about other than rehashing the night he found out about my powers? Why would he want to record it?

Breathing feels like drowning. I steady myself against my kitchen island and start chugging the bottle. I close my eyes and slowly count down from ten. I hear my door click open at three, but I don't open my eyes yet.

That is how Koda finds me, head to toe in my club attire still, leaning against the kitchen island, downing wine straight from the bottle. His eyes turn to a smolder as he watches my lips around the bottle. My brain finally empties out.

No more Dune.

No more pests.

Koda is the only thing taking up my headspace as he stares at me like I am a dessert. He is clocking every movement I make as he takes steady steps towards me. I pull the bottle from my lips slowly, tracing my tongue along my lips to catch the stray wine.

When he is directly in front of me, Koda gently pries the bottle out of my hand. His pupils are still fully black, but there is a crease in his forehead as he swallows the last sip.

"Get up on the island. Show me how wet your panties are." Not looking at me, Koda turns to put the empty bottle in the recycling bin. He watches from across the kitchen as I sit on the edge, letting my feet rest on two stools.

"I can see the wet spot from here." Koda's voice is stern, but as he comes closer his hand trembles slightly as he pushes my knees further open. He traces the line of my thong, leaving me panting on the countertop. I don't dare close my eyes or break eye contact though. Not yet.

We've fucked around. We've played with power dynamics. None of that is new. Even with power dynamics, we discussed it ahead of time. *This* is a night of true seduction. This is not simply finding the comfort or pleasure we needed in that moment. No, this is pure lust for the other person.

He pulls the front panel to the side to slip a single finger into me.

"Fuck," Koda groans, leaning his head into my shoulder. My head hangs back with a sigh. He doesn't move though. "How much of this is for me? Tell me, Summer. How much of this is for me? How much of this is for Dune?"

The words bring my sinking to a halt. I look up again. "Wh-what?"

"You heard me. How much of this is because you were thinking of Dune?"

"I - none of it. It is all for you."

I whine embarrassingly as he pulls his finger out.

He leans over me now, returning with a second finger. "Do

you remember the last time I found you leaning up against a wall, drinking wine from the bottle like a fucking queen?"

My body stiffens under Koda. He coos and turns me back into putty as he keeps his fingers moving inside me. I never told him about that day. I never spoke aloud the reason why I was just chilling outside his room, drumming up the courage to knock on his door.

"I know you were there to make me fuck away the memory of him. He called me right before you showed up. I was heading out to help him drink away the memory of you when you halted me where I stood. I knew what you wanted. I should have been a better friend. Fates above, I was selfish. You were giving me a chance to worship you. Fuck if I wasn't going to take it."

My breath stutters beneath his voice. Between his touch and his words, there are too many feelings clouding my thoughts, clouding my vision. My orgasm starts to build from my toes faster than anticipated. Suddenly I am empty again.

"No, Summer. I know we aren't supposed to change up things on a dopamine high. You need to know - I have been choosing you. Whether it was staying friends after I broke up with Cassie all those years ago, or when Dune left… or when you showed up at my door wanting me to fuck you, while you wished it was him. I am playing to win now, Summer. So tell me now, please. How do I know none of this is for him when I find you in the same state I did eight years ago?"

I stare at him, grasping for an answer that is true. An answer that won't cause this moment to fizzle out. "I - I was jealous." At my words, he teases my entrance again, trying to coax out more. "Of the girl you shared. I could only imagine the fun we missed out on."

His fingers are fully in me again, thrusting and begging for more truth from me. "He asked to come up after he walked me home. I said no."

The air must have been sucked out of the room. Every movement stops until Koda pulls me up and meets my forehead with his.

"You said… no?"

"I said no." I whisper back.

"Do you regret saying no?"

"No."

"Why?"

If a pin dropped in the room across the hall, it would be heard. My answer is clear. I can't tell him in this emotional high. He needs to know about my powers. I will choose him a thousand times over. It needs to wait until the sun is out. He needs to know what he is choosing.

My eyes gloss over at the thought. "Right, no dopamine confessions. What do you need right now, love?"

"I need my head to be quiet." I gasp out. "There is nothing I am trying to forget. I want to be right here, experiencing every moment here with you."

"That I can do." He smiles and plants a kiss on my forehead, before kneeling down between my legs and taking me to the oblivion I've been chasing.

CHAPTER 26
RUNE DARREN

I sip on my whiskey as I stare at my computer screens. I decided to spend my Saturday continuing my hacking of Dune Raydn. From the moment he moved back to Lyra I have been tracking his movements.

It was too easy to get past his out of the box firewalls tonight. There is nothing custom about his technological protection. Dune Raydn is either not actually doing anything suspicious or he is naive to think no one would be watching. If he is working with Ashryn I can see him having false hope that others are turning a blind eye.

I hack into his network from a sandbox virtual machine that I can dump if Dune is just luring me into a trap. So far nothing.

Once in his network, installing my virus onto every device that connects to his internet is easy. I expected this to take more than an hour. With the extra time, I change into some sweats and a hoodie. I grab a book for good measure. While contemplating whether to read in bed or on the couch, my computer dings. I'm not sure how my neck is going to recover from the whiplash.

I roll the chair out from my desk and start navigating around Dune's computer. Part of the virus sets up a synchronization of the files and programs on his computer to my own virtual machine. This way I can choose to just watch him scroll around, or I can rummage through his stuff with him being none the wiser.

The logs indicate that a program called MoschEye updated its program files. Since my task of infiltrating Raydn's computer has not satiated my curiosity, I start poking. Oh am I glad I did. MoschEye is a program that connects to mobile monitoring devices. Who is dear Dune Raydn trying to bug?

There is one bug active currently. I plug the coordinates into a map engine, which spits out an address. Quickly searching for it, the tea just got hotter. The bugs are located at Koda Duran's house. Plugging myself into the nearest street camera to this building, I wait for Dune to emerge. Why would he bug his own friend? I rack my brain for what I know about the man.

He does work for Summer.

Surely that wouldn't cause Dune to bug him.

Before I can dig too deep into that thought, Dune and Koda leave the building. I track them camera by camera through the city until they walk up to a hotel. This hotel has a pretty exclusive club on the top floor. So I have to imagine they will be there for a bit.

Something deep in my gut tells me to stay on top of him tonight. So instead of shutting down with a book I direct my research into Koda and his connection to both Dune and Summer.

He has always been there on the peripherals. I always thought that he was just a loose connection between Dune and Summer. Wow, did I miss the mark here. I have been so invested at looking into Summer, and then Dune, that I missed their friend who posts *everything*. There are no pictures of Summer in recent years. He posts pictures with Dune or while he was out in Lyra or Arcalis. Never Summer. Yet… it feels like some of the photos had her just outside the borders of the camera. Summer places herself just far enough outside his life; her presence equal in visibility as Koda is in her own.

It is an aspect of her life that has been shoved just enough to the side that I cannot control my urge to pick at it. I wanted to see if there was any merit in Dune's actions. I delve through *years* of social media photos before I get to a photo collection that snags my attention.

A younger Koda is tucking the strap of a rainbow colored cardboard hat with a green pom pom under Summer's chin while blowing one of those noise makers. Summer's laugh is frozen in place. The photo feels so alive that I can almost feel it through the screen. If I ever heard her laugh, maybe I could hear it. She is holding a little rumbling shaker.

The date on it matches a timeframe I know from Summer's work history. This was ten years ago - the day she got her first managerial promotion at FaeTech. The picture is grainy, but you can see they are in a bar celebrating Summer. Her face is lit up. She is wearing a cute sky blue dress and silver heels. There is a happiness, a lightness I have never seen before. On her, or really anyone. This is before whatever event caused her to start shutting people out. Whatever caused her to keep her circle of friends small, unnoticeable.

I swipe to the next picture. Summer has slid into a red booth next to Dune. She is smiling at the camera, seeming to not notice the look Dune is giving her. Dune has an arm wrapped behind Summer and his forehead is resting on the side of her head. The feeling of longing is just leaking out of the pixels. The third picture was right after the second and Dune is facing the camera.

If Summer's laugh had shocked me, this picture of Dune rocks the ground beneath me. I've met Dune, seen him at company events; run in similar enough circles around Arcalis. What I thought was his smile, clearly is not. It is the mask of a smile.

Both Summer and Dune are showing their full mouth of teeth. They are grinning ear to ear. You can feel the joy and how utterly at ease they are with each other.

I close my gaping mouth to see what other earth shattering

pictures are in here. For Koda being on the periphery of Summer's visible life - he was one hell of a wing man ten years ago. The next five pictures must have been in fast succession.

The first is the three of them taking a selfie. Summer in the middle, her face and rounded ears squished between Koda on her right, Dune on her left. They must have been a sight to behold. These were three twenty-five year olds ready to take on the world. There is a passion that hasn't been softened or destroyed with the blunt object that corporate jobs are. All they see is a future of possibility, opportunity. The human among the fae just got a promotion - anything was possible!

If you could flip them quickly, the images look almost identical. Dune's eyes slide over to Summer - watching her instead of the camera.

Then Dune is back looking at the camera, and Summer's face is slightly turned toward Dune. Koda's smile is almost a knowing smirk in this frame. The one friend giving the two others a moment to themselves in that crowded bar.

Next, Summer has a pile of icing on her nose. She is squinting her eyes, laughing towards the ceiling as the men on either side of her just smile at her. Looking closely at Koda in this picture, though, you can see the same awe that Dune has.

The last frame is Summer getting the last laugh. She has each of them pressed against her cheeks again. Each hand, full of icing, smashed against each of their outside cheeks.

These photos are ten years old. The web crawl we ran on images of Summer a year ago never returned these. She must have found a way to keep these hidden from the broader world. No one can find these unless they are explicitly looking. From that set of pictures and backwards in time, Summer and Dune fill Koda's social media.

I spin up a script to download these photos into a database on my computer. Out of curiosity, I rerun my web crawler. Maybe luck will grant me something other than FaeTech headshots and marketing photos.

Shimmying my watch around on my wrist, it confirms the late hour. Though it's doubtful I will greet sleep with this web crawler mining for information. Instead I walk into my kitchen to find something to slow my pacing brain. Not caring about how the whiskey is held, a healthy shot is eyeballed into the closest clean coffee mug. The gray slate of my cabinets and walls match the gray of my office. So many dull colors fill all the spaces I go. I don't think this is what my mother had in mind when she made her decision all those years ago. A muted life, staying just under the radar, just out of the limelight. Maybe I should go back out to Lyra. Get some color back in my life.

My computer dings somewhere, I think.

I could just take a walk to the beach. See a sunrise, despite the fact I am in a mood for a sunset. This search just seems fruitless. I wear a mask just like Dune and Summer. Do they feel the weight of their mask like I do?

"I did not want you to walk home alone."

Pondering my glass, I let my mind wander back to something other than my moroseness. *Who would he be bugging at the club?*

There is another ding. Of an elevator maybe? Then the voice that I have listened to for years on end floats through my apartment once more. This sound successfully pulls me out of my thoughts.

"Not necessary. Stay, finish out your night."

Scrambling back to my office, I bring up the camera feed from outside the club. Somewhere in my frenzied movements, Summer is saying "I am not defenseless. You know nothing about me anymore." The words catch a few strings in my brain, lingering, wishing to be understood.

I hear the elevator door chirp again and the whoosh of the doors opening. There is a strange palpitation in my chest as I hear the small clip of what must be Summer's heels on the floor and wait for her to show on the screen.

My stomach drops as she appears in the screen, saying goodbye to the fucking bouncer. I don't know what it is about

Summer Chase. I've always thought she is beautiful. No one can deny that. Watching her strut out of this club in her little black dress and heels would halt me in the streets. She's fucking stunning. She has a glow about her that is different from that aura some of the Fae have. I tug at the point of my ear, but doing so pulls me out of my stupor.

Summer and Dune have walked out of frame. I frantically find the next street camera and follow them. The sound of Summer's strut slowly turning into a light walk echoes across the space. She has her face turned up to the stars.

What are you thinking about?

Do you already know he bugged you?

Did he walk you home the night of those pictures?

As they arrive at her building, I listen to their conversation, watching them from a camera that is close enough to really see their facial expressions. I just want to burrow into their memory banks as they don't exactly yell at each other, but they aren't quiet either.

"You do not get to just waltz back into this city and expect me to welcome you back into my life, commanding my time as if you are owed it."

"Aren't I, though?"

"No. You aren't. Maybe - if this was nine years ago. Now though? I owe you nothing. Not my time. Not my personal space."

From the camera it shows Dune pulling Summer into him. He says something, but it is muffled. Did he purposefully cover up the bug? What could he say to her that would warrant that? Something tugs at my chest to figure out what this conversation is about.

We've always known they went to university, used to work together. They've had a not so friendly rivalry in the workplace for the last ten years. This scene playing out in combination with the pictures found tonight leaves a very large hole. Their story is just fabricated enough to start seeing it.

Summer speaks loudly enough to hear bits, but they are still muffled. "I picked up the pieces of my life once before." Summer pushes Dune off her, and I swear Summer's eyes flash orange for the smallest second before settling back to amber.

No… fucking… way.

I trade windows to go back and look at the pictures of the night of her promotion. Something is buzzing before Summer exclaims "Motherfucker!" Then the bug goes static. I am staring at the picture of her, Dune, and Koda when I realize it isn't Summer's eyes that keeps pulling me to these pictures. It is the lack of scar on Dune's face.

My web crawler does a little jingle to tell me I have another nugget to investigate. I drag my eyes away to look at it. It is a blog post about living in Lyra. This is a picture of one of the main downtown farmers markets right at the beginning. Deep in the background of this picture, though, is Summer. The camera holder is behind but at an angle. You can see Koda's side profile, but the camera happens to be pointed directly at Summer's face. Koda is holding her chin the way a supportive lover would. Summer has a tentative smile, there is a slight tint of pink to the tops of her cheeks.

The camera outside of Summer's house is still up on my other monitor and a movement caught my eye. Koda is striding up to Summer's building, uses a key to get in the front door and disappears. I don't need two guesses to know where he is headed. Are they just lovers? Are they dating? How does she keep so much of her life hidden?

Back to the image in front of me, I zoom in on Summer's eyes. There is usually a tell. You can wear contacts to cover the surge of color and the change in tint from a camera lens. If you don't change them out religiously, or you don't think you are being photographed, someone watching closely could see the flood of color lurking behind someone's irises.

We have never seen orange, though. Blue, yellow, green, white even… orange… orange…

Pulling up a headshot of Dune, I take a closer look at the scar on his face. That *could* be a burn scar.

What if that night, Summer's power surged on accident. That's usually how it happens the first time. It could have been a lover's hold going in for a kiss. Maybe it was a surge of anger as Dune told her he took a job in Arcalis. Either option is plausible.

Either option only leads to one conclusion.

Methodically, I start cleaning up.

I start by wiping the recording of Summer's reaction off Dune's bug. While his reasoning is unknown, I would rather push him back a step. If my theory holds, Dune already knows about Summer's power. This could also explain why he smothered the last bit from the bug. If he is working for Ashryn and she finds out…

Also, why give him the heads up that Summer caught his bug in the first place. If he has her at the mercy of a queen, may as well give her a better level playing field.

I download the picture from the blog post. The timing is pure luck or the Fates giving me a small blessing. Either way, it will probably be gone by tomorrow.

The line on the other side of my phone call picks up.

"Hey. I need you to find me some excuses to get to Lyra."

CHAPTER 27
SUMMER

Stirring from sleep, all my limbs are tangled up in Koda. Letting out a small chuckle , I brush a stray piece of hair from his face. My fingers trail down Koda's face. Inches away, it would take nothing to lean in and kiss him. My luck, that is when he would wake up. His choice taken away. My heart digging itself further into a hole before he has all of the information.

I peel myself out of bed, grab a shirt out of the laundry basket and pad into the kitchen. Yawning, I robotically make my way around the kitchen. Water, coffee grinds, flip switch, let the water start flowing. My eyes blur the white tiled wall as my focus returns inward.

Sometimes I catch myself daydreaming of the two of us growing old together, but also not together. The last week of Koda being extra touchy has lit a fire under those. After last night's adventures would either of us see that future as just a daydream? I'd be lying if I said I didn't miss Koda's flirtatious touches. After we slept together though, the playful touches stopped. Neither of us said anything explicitly. Deep down we must have realized that the playful touches after knowing release in each other's arms could lead right to where we are. Are we really here? After all this time?

Could we ever really make this dream come true though? With Dune back and *bugging* me, I have to tell him about my powers. Maybe he will be so freaked out, he will change his mind. He won't want me as a partner anymore. That would be easiest. It would hurt, but I have survived it once. I could survive it again. Right?

The coffee machine beeps at me, interrupting my internalized pep talk. The warmth in my mug does nothing to stop the downward spiral of thoughts. How do I tell Jackie? How do we deal with our jobs? What do Koda's lips taste like? Will Dune actually care or will he just put up a fuss? Then my eyes find focus on the dress lying on the floor of the living room, halting my train of thought.

Koda sleepily emerges from into the kitchen in a pair of grey sweats. Damn him.

"I smelled coffee," he mumbles as he comes in , crowding me against the counter. He reaches above and behind me to grab another mug. My face is right up on his shirtless chest. It takes all of me not to nuzzle up into it, so I sit my empty hand on his chest. He covers my hand with one of his as he places a mug under the coffee maker and flips it back on.

"Mmmmmh, good morning," he murmurs into my nape as he wraps his now free hand around my back.

"Give a girl some warning next time. Save that magic bean juice." I laugh setting my cup on the counter before looking back up at him. His face is wrought with confusion.

He tugs at the hem of the black shirt I am wearing, brushing his knuckles along my thigh.

"Is this my shirt?"

Fuck.

This must be the shirt Kyria threw at me last night. It was the top shirt on the pile of laundry to put back.

"Uh…well…"

Koda leans his forehead against my own. "Fuck, Summer. I want to see you in more of my shirts." He growls.

The only time we break eye contact is when one of us looks at the other lips. I tug him closer into me by the top of his sweats.

My heart feels like it's about to jump out of my chest.

Why are my fingers tingling?

Fuck. Stop tingling fingers.

Breathe.

Breathe.

Ten. Nine. Eight.

Koda half pushes, half lifts me so I am sitting on the counter now. His forehead never leaves mine. We keep getting closer without actually making contact. He cups the back of my head, his thumb rubbing my cheek.

Koda's breathing is as heavy as my own. I run a hand up his cheek, maintaining just enough control to not tremble. Even without applying any pressure he finally relents and melds closer into me. How is there still any space between us? What if he kisses me and then decides I am not worth the extra drama that comes with my powers? There is no turning back from this.

Control yourself. *Ten.*

Save yourself the pain. *Nine.*

But what if this is my only chance to know what his lips feel like against mine?

No. He needs to know. *Ten.*

"Summer..." he whispers, as if it pains him to talk.

"I ... I will come back."

Everything screeches to a halt.

"Fuck," Koda leans his head onto my shoulder. I peer over him to find the source of the intrusion at my front door.

"It's Jackie isn't it?" He whines.

"Yeah." I whisper.

Jackie is staring at me now, mouth gaping. There was no coming back from this. There is no pretending this was a random dude that I booty called.

Keeping my hand on his back I ask Jackie, "I am assuming we just slept really late and missed the farmers market. Or you are extremely early?"

"I… I mean I am early, but I figured I would just be here once you got back from the market."

I nod my head trying to figure out the best next step here. Caressing his face, I whisper to Koda, "Jackie … will be fine. I'll talk to her. Okay?"

"Okay." He is reliving the lost moment in his eyes, just like I am. His eyebrows scrunch together, probably wondering when we will have another chance like this.

"Give us… a second." I ask Jackie as we walk past her. What a pair we must look like. One of us in just a shirt and panties, the other in just pants. Hesitantly, I emerge back out with a pair of running shorts and large fuzzy socks. Maybe by making myself more comfortable looking, Jackie will take mercy on me.

"We will be talking about this later. You look like a shark tried to eat your neck." Jackie says sternly.

"Yes, mom." I moan. Then halt, slapping a hand to my neck, "What?!" We have a very firm no hickey rule between us. Shit.

"Have you told him?" She reprimands my sass by flicking me in the arm as she whispers her question.

Instead of answering or waiting to see her reaction I grab the dress off the floor and meet Jackie on the couch where she settles herself. Laying the dress face down on the coffee table my fingers start tracing paths along the dress without explanation. Koda bashfully comes out of the room and stops abruptly, staring at us quizzically. He takes the open sofa space next to me before popping the silence.

"So, uh, what did I miss here?"

"Well, I had obviously already planned for Jackie to come over. Mostly, it is to get us all on the same page… and to apologize for the shock of last night. Dune threw us another curveball." As if the Fates love the theatrics by itself, my fingers land on the bug at that moment. Digging it out, I lift it up like a fossil or intriguing specimen to inspect.

"Is that -" Koda is interrupted by Jackie's exclamation.

"He bugged you?!"

Koda goes pale, "When do you think he got it on you?"

Not wanting to talk about the other conversation with Dune, I hope my guess is right. "He pushed me firmly enough into the elevator. I have to assume it was then. My sensors caught it the moment I walked into my flat last night. I turned my jammers on almost immediately, so nothing should have transmitted from that point." Jackie coughs, covering up a mumble. "He probably used the excuse of walking me home to place the tracker. I do want to see how easy this thing would be to hack."

"Why would he have a bug even handy to hide on you anyways?" Koda sputters. "He would have had no idea you were going to be there."

"I am wondering the same. Looking at it now, this is not meant for clothes. It is small enough but too bulky. It easily could have fallen off my dress. That's another reason why it probably wasn't placed before the elevator."

"Thank the Fates," Koda murmurs.

"Would that be concerning?" Jackie asks with enough sass to know she isn't being innocent.

"Yes, and too filthy for your ears Jackie dear." Koda responds in kind.

"Anyways," I interject. "The mic on this thing isn't sophisticated enough to pick up conversations if it is muffled by a laundry basket. My bug wasn't planned. It was haphazard at best." I look at Koda now. "Did he stop by your place before you guys headed to the club?"

"Yeah..." The realization starts to dawn on him. Confusion turns to anger. "He said he wanted to see my place since he hadn't been over yet. 'Pop over then we could just walk to the club together.' Fuck."

"Yeah, he probably bugged your apartment. Maybe it was just an extra."

"Would you happen to be able to scan my apartment tonight?"

"Definitely."

Jackie stands up, angry now. A flip switched somewhere and there are too many secrets for her to not be angry. "No. You aren't going anywhere with him until he tells us *why* he brought Dune to the club he knew we were going to be at. How do you know he's not in on whatever this is?"

"Jackie, stop -"

She raises her palm to my face. "No, Summer. I care about you. And this ...depending on what we find could tank *everything*. Our jobs. Our whole lives. Best case it's a case of corporate espionage. Worst case scenario it is federal treason. Koda never stopped being friends with Dune. So, Koda, I want to know why I should trust you with Summer's life and well-being. And by proxy, mine."

"Jackie, you are out of line -"

I am interrupted again, but this time with Koda's hand on my knee.

"No, Jackie isn't out of line." Koda looks at Jackie and sighs. "I told Summer a part of this last week. I will make this clear right now. My friendship with Dune has been slowly fading for years. We kept up simply out of habit, out of nostalgia. For Dune I believe it became a way to cling to the past. My friendship was a way to ensure that his early years still had a connection to his current life. To Jackie's point - I never needed that extra connection. I had you." He pauses here, looking at me. Koda keeps his focus on me as he continues. "He left us both. That wasn't me choosing you over him. Whatever broke you both, I had the easy job. I simply had to help you hold yourself together long enough to heal the shattered pieces. I never *had to* choose. Just as I promised last week, I will always choose you. Every time."

My chest warms. All of the stress, the guilt, the fear, the lo-

feelings from the last few months threaten to boil over. The threat of turning into a sobbing mess at any second is imminent. Hoping to avoid a complete meltdown, I break eye contact. Koda catches and tips my chin back up before I can look down.

"Please don't shut me out now. Let me choose, finally." He whispers.

A few more moments pass before Jackie fakes a cough, breaking the spell over the room. I turn to her. "I will also admit that I played both of you. Koda doesn't know about the new job function under me. I needed you to be genuine in your anger of Dune *and* Koda for showing up last night. I knew he was coming the whole time."

Jackie sighs. "I thought we were done with secrets. But I get it. I'm making a full pot of coffee. Tell him about the new job function." Jackie waves a hand at Koda. "Next time take it easy on her neck, for fucks sake. That's going to take a pound of coverup tomorrow."

Koda brushes a thumb along my neck. "Sorry, love," he whispers. "It was the closest I could get without …"

"A dopamine confession?" I finish for him.

Koda gives me a small smile. Our own little secret code. "Okay so tell me why work has anything to do with you tricking me into talking to Dune faster."

CHAPTER 28
KODA

"Just so I am clear," I state as Jackie pours all of us another mug of coffee. "There is a new team at FaeTech that is similar to a department at Star Technologies. This department may or may not specialize in putting surveillance technology in devices we provide to government entities. Currently this is just in Arcalis, where humans have been going missing. Summer does not have access to anything regarding this department at Star. If she even goes looking it will be flagged by IT."

Summer nods along with my recap.

"You want to try to befriend Dune again… at least at the surface level… because… why again?"

"You mentioned he had applied for a job within the federal government. A Chief Technology Officer, correct?"

"Yes… Do you think this role would oversee an expansion of the program in Arcalis?"

"That is exactly what I think. Arcalis is a pilot program. Easy to put in place since Dubois is Ashryn's cousin. He can't fight her on it. Why would he? In order for it to expand nationwide you need buy-in from other officials. More importantly, more devices. Most of the government cameras in Lyra are FaeTech devices. Why force governors to spend more budget on new devices, when they can just make a deal with the technology companies themselves?"

"Do you trust Dune enough to just tell him your theory?"

"Not in the slightest. I don't know what his play is. There is a tiny part of me that thought he would have strived to make it less invasive or something with positive intent. The bug on my dress and probably your apartment makes me less convinced.."

"Okay… I'm in. He avoids giving any information on this job so I agree he probably won't be super open about anything unless we trick him into it."

Jackie chimes in now. "Okay great. We are all aligned! I have a wife with an *epic* hangover I need to get back to soon. So Summer, you start hacking that bug. Koda, you and I will brainstorm how to break Dune."

Summer goes into the spare room that stores some spare clothes of mine and comes back out with a *rolling whiteboard.*

"Where the hell do you store that in there?"

"The walk-in closet. Where else?" Summer shrugs.

Summer sits back down on the couch, hacking away at the bug she pulled out of her dress. I watch for just a moment as she carefully connects it to her laptop. My mind instantly takes me back to last night and where that bug was sitting.

I lift Summer up off the island where I had just made her come on my tongue. Wrapping her legs around me, I can't make it to her bedroom before slamming us into a wall trying to rip this dress off her. "You may have worn this to tease him, but fuck if I'm not happy to be the one to tear it off you."

My fingers find purchase on the zipper, but they slip as she whispers in my ear, "The dress was always to drive you wild, Koda. Not him. It was a handy excuse after your post run teasing."

I drop her legs and turn her around. Pressing her chest flush against the wall before biting her neck, I let the dress fall and pool around her heels. "I should fuck you right here, test if you can control yourself enough to not let your heels tear apart that dress. Never let anyone else see you in it." I push two fingers inside her. "The condoms are too fucking far away, so we can test that another time."

The sight of her trembling on my fingers is too much. Spinning her around, I throw her over her shoulder. "The heels are staying on tonight."

"I don't even want to know what is going through your brain right now." Jackie huffs out a laugh, interrupting my thoughts. My face must have lost all its color again. "If she has had the jammer up since last night, nothing is getting out of here. Again, I do *not* want to know. Now let's get to work."

HOW DO WE FIND OUT WHAT DUNE IS UP TO?

Jackie has already written this in big blocky letters at the top of the whiteboard. We ease into troubleshooting the question. I haven't been able to work this smoothly with anyone other than Summer. It is a nice change of pace. The only interruption we have is when Summer asks me for Dune's phone number.

1. BUG HIM BACK

This is the most emphatic of solutions. It could be an easy solution. I helped Dune move, but he hasn't invited me back to his place since. Honestly there wasn't even that much to help settle anyways. The place came furnished and movers were handling anything that was shipped over. Maybe Summer could try to hack into his computer or his phone. It's doubtful he is letting me into his space.

2. DRUM UP THE GOSSIP.
2A. FAE TECH MEET AND GREETS
2B. DINNER AT ANDRE'S
2C. FISHBOWLS

Jackie giggles maniacally as she pulls out her phone. Somehow I think Summer is getting signed up for those meet and greets no matter what.

For any solution to really work Summer is going to have to rebuild a relationship with Dune. The two of them establishing a friendship after a decade of very loud rivalry would reverb through the tech industry. Not only would we have a direct line in with Dune, if we played our cards right with enough gossip, Summer could get some loose tongues in the meet and greets at FaeTech.

Summer will need to break a piece of her soul again. Peel back that layer of insulation around her soul and pluck out a piece just to let enough emotions in to make Dune think this is real. What if she lets in too much history? What if she starts believing the friendship is real again?

I shake away my fears, the risk of losing her. She is coming over tonight. I am not wasting more time.

"Hey…" Jackie nudges me out of thoughts.

"Hmm?" I look down at the silver haired woman who shouldered up next to me.

"We make a good team. And… I'm sorry for hounding you earlier." Her voice is low enough that only I can hear her. With Summer focused on the computer in front of her it would be difficult for her to hear.

"No, you were in the right."

"Has Summer ever told you how she and I met?"

I turn to her and open my mouth to respond that obviously Summer had. My memory is drawing a blank and I am left mouth gaping without an answer. Scanning the photobook in my brain, memories just started including Jackie. There was never really a warm intro. She just slid into our lives.

"I… no. I feel like you met because of the gym you guys go to?"

Jackie keeps an eye trained on Summer as she clarifies. "Yeah. The gym we both go to also has… an aspect of training our mental health, not just our physical health. Training and retraining, especially after some sort of emotional trauma. It could be from anything. I met Summer from the moment she joined. I am one of the specialists that reviews and helps plan through some of the emotional healing and training for new gym members."

I keep myself stock still, eagerly drinking down a new memory of Summer.

"I met her about six months after the Dune incident. I have some of the high level details about Dune leaving, and how it affected her." Jackie waves her hand dismissively to keep me from interrupting. " I remember thinking… whatever glue held her together for those months, this 'Koda', it or they must have been special. I was so glad and eventually thankful to whomever or whatever it was because it meant I was able to meet her. I was able to befriend this amazing woman. Then I met you, Koda, and I knew. You were that glue for her then. You've stuck with her through so much. I believe you when you say you will choose her over Dune. I should not have even interrogated you about it. So for that, I do apologize."

My mouth opens to respond. With what … I don't know. Thankfully I am interrupted when Summer stands up and stretches her arms to the ceiling. We watch her pad over to us.

She eyes the whiteboard with our notes and comments, "I think I may have the easier explanation. First off, everything was strangely easy to hack. It is like he is just being clumsy. Or doesn't think anyone is watching his movements. Anyways, I was able to get into the bug. Nothing has been transmitted due to the jammers. It doesn't look like there is any internal storage. Everything should be all clear on that front. The ones at your place seem to be the same model but we can check it tonight, Koda. I'll bring you over a jammer so that you can still maintain some privacy when you want. It may be more suspicious if your bugs just all die when I come over."

"That… sounds fine. How do you know that I am actually

bugged?" I ask her, trying to connect the dots on those statements.

"Oh, right. So after I hacked this thing. I asked you for Dune's number."

"Yes, but how -"

"I am getting to that," Summer shushes me.

"Yeah, let her talk, Koda. Geez." Jackie jokes but she looks just as intrigued as me.

"Right, so. I dusted off some old code and let it start crawling the web for his phone number on the internet. It only took a few minutes since I guessed that he is a brand loyalist and would use a phone from Star. It isn't jailbroken so anyone that wants to look for it can find it." Summer shakes her head and I swear murmurs "So sloppy," before continuing.

"It found his phone that is conveniently connected to his personal wifi. I planted some spyware on his phone. Then hopped over to his laptop and did the same. I have it running live in a sandbox now. I *should* be able to listen to the program on his computer live so we can test the jamming systems. That way we make sure mine wasn't just a … flawed one."

"Summer, it has only been like twenty-five minutes." I remember to close my jaw this time.

"Yes, I know." She says this almost as if it is a question, or like I have grown three more eyeballs on my face.

"I… well…" Flabbergasted at just how fast she was able to accomplish this with just a phone number.

Jackie saves me. "So I guess we can cross off that action item." She dramatically drags the green marker through "Bug Dune back" to create a giant checkbox.

"Do we need to really involve Dune then?" I ask hopefully. "If we can just spy on him from here, why do we really need to do much else?"

Summer stands there with her hands on her hips as she contemplates the rest of the board in front of us.

"Well… you make a good point about drumming up the gossip. Dune and I being seen together would definitely do that." She drones off as she pinches the bridge of her nose. "I'm assuming you already signed me up for those meet and greets, Jackie?"

Jackie grins maniacally at her.

"Marketing will let you choose who you talk to though. We can pick up the names this week. Remember this the next time you think about pulling more shenanigans like last night on me."

Summer returns to perusing the hodge podge of ideas.

"I like the idea of a dinner at Andre's place. We would need to ask him for two tables so that you can snap some pictures to help with the pot stirring, Koda. I don't want to involve him in this until we have to. He knows enough about Dune to change his mind on it if I give him too much time to think about it. I really don't feel like making up a story to make him go for it."

Summer has her palm curled over her mouth, her thumb pressing against her chin as she takes in the rest of the options.

"Yeah I like this. Maybe after a post-work happy hour with the three of us, I can convince him to go over to Bert & Rocky's. I've been meaning to stop in there anyways. They can have a two for one special."

"Aww, I wanted to go with you. I like Berta. Roy kinda scares me though."

Summer just chuckles as she shakes her head. "Maybe after all of this is done. Can't have her blabbing about how much she loves you. That could definitely make things awkward."

Jackie is looking between Summer and myself now. I realize that Summer has been hiding my flirting for the last week from Jackie. Based on her reaction to walking in on us, she probably also doesn't even know that we sleep together every so often.

"To make this all look real, we need him to *want* to be involved. We need him to actively participate… how do we convince him to do that?" Jackie asks.

"He could still have a weak spot for you. Honestly it could be as simple as just… treating him like any other person that works for you. Kill him with kindness and all that."

"I can't really explain the problem and do that at a happy hour, though."

I chew on my cheek. She's not wrong. Summer leans against the wall as if surrendering to whatever idea she just came up with. With her head up to the ceiling she asks, "Do you think you could wrangle him up to the beach house next weekend?"

"I'll convince him to go for it."

Summer doesn't look at either of us as she just nods. Summer bought the house about two hours north of the city five or six years ago. This apartment may be closer to work, but it is efficient. It is functional. Summer has exactly what she needs here, with a few scattered pieces of art on the wall.

The beach house is where she lets her personality out. It is much like how she used to decorate her dorms and apartments before Dune left. With the exception of probably just Jackie, her wife, and myself, no one else has set foot in there.

The first step back into Summer's reality would crash into him if we do this. It would not just be peeling back one insulated layer. Summer would be pulling off her entire mask for him. Just as I am about to suggest we find a different way she pushes herself off the wall.

"Can you ask Brenda to start cleaning up the place? Check my calendar tomorrow to see if I can work remotely Thursday and Friday?" She asks Jackie.

"I'll handle Dune." I comment.

We each nod and break off for the rest of the day. After Jackie leaves, I stick around for just an extra moment.

"You should make time to talk to her today. She looked hurt as we talked about Bert and Rocky's. I'm sure you tell her basically everything. I assume you haven't told her about …"

"The flirting? The fucking?" She smiles as she finishes the thought.

"All of the above." I place a kiss on her forehead and leave. I should plan how to convince Dune of our weekend retreat. Instead, I spend the afternoon planning for another evening with Summer. I need to find a way to get that stolen moment back.

CHAPTER 29
SUMMER

9.5 YEARS AGO

The handwritten directions lead me to the outskirts of the city. I am met by a woman in black jeans, a black hoodie, but bright purple hair that completely contrasts everything else about her. She emerges from an alleyway. Looking past her, there is definitely someone tailing behind us.

"Hi, I am Summer." I offer up my hand to shake.

"Hey Summer. Nice to meet you."

We walk in general silence as we weave through more side streets. The mystery third person has yet to show their face.

"Is it safe to assume you are not offering up any information, such as your name, because I need to pass a test of sorts?"

"You do assume correctly, Summer."

We end up in a park, strolling past very flammable trees and shrubs until the purple haired woman finds a spot she must deem secluded enough.

"So tell me Summer. How did you find out about your powers?"

"By accident…" Yeah I am not describing that night to a stranger.

The woman sits on a tree stump and huffs out a laugh. "Yeah,

I think most of us did. Okay I'll rephrase. What emotion were you feeling the most when it happened?"

I let out a sigh. "Happiness."

The woman correctly interprets my despondent response and asks, "Think about your accident. What emotion could you feel the strongest of right now?"

It doesn't take long to realize the answer. "Anger."

"Great. I know when you reached out you mentioned you did not have control of your power. Does that mean you have been randomly shooting out spurts of power or pushing those urges down?"

"Pushing them down."

"Okay. You remember as part of this meetup you do need to show us your power? I will show mine in kind afterwards."

I nod.

"Do you need a conduit or is this something you can let out without holding something?"

"Um," looking around there are quite a few options. Although it makes me question if this is a great idea or not. "Everything here is pretty flammable…" I pick up a thick enough branch that looks like it was dragged here by a dog.

"Did you just say…"

"Did she just say…" a new voice comes out from the woods.

"Yes?"

Maybe it was the nerves. Maybe it was the memories I had already dragged up. The branch in my hand immediately lit up.

"Shit."

"She…" The two women look between themselves and me.

"What?" I ask.

"Can you drop the branch Summer?"

I do as I am asked but my hand stays lit. The new woman shoots her hands out and a pile of flowers lands on top of my burning stick. Which turns the stick into a small fire.

The fire in my hand grows taller.

"Kyria, can you loosen up some dirt for me dear? Summer, this is my wife Kyria. My name is Jackie. As you can see her power is earth based. My power is air based. As soon as that dirt is loosened, I will blow it over this now sizable bonfire to stamp it out. So we do not need to worry about that. Clearly my soothing voice is not helping you. So here's what I need from you right now. Steady breathing. Take a deep breath in. A ten count. Ten… Nine… Eight…Seven…"

As Jackie keeps counting down, I begin to see the flame in my hand slowly start getting shorter and shorter. I close my eyes as she tells me to exhale.

"That is it. Keep breathing just like that. Almost there."

I open my eyes to the two women staring at me. Jackie, the original woman, is looking at me not with fear, but with concern. Something about that concern tells me it is not concern for herself. The concern is for me.

Please, please don't ask me about my accident. Please.

My nerves are still feeling like live wires despite the fire in my hands now being extinguished.

"Let us show you the warehouse. I think we have one room we could probably have you test out here. Any room we choose is going to need some major adjustments… fireproofing adjustments."

We meander through some alleyways after we exit the park. Kyria is holding my hand and whispering small comforts.

"Everything is okay."

"I am so glad you found us."

"Just keep breathing steadily, Summer dear."

She weaves flowers in between our fingers. I smile at them and simply murmur quiet thanks. I take this time to really look at the two women. They can't be more than maybe a few years older than me. Their rounded ears give away the fact that they aren't Fae. They have a strange glow to them that I have not seen in other humans like me.

Like me.

I guess I am more like these two than I am my fellow humans.

Kyria must feel something and taps my hand to bring me back outside of my head.

"Breathe. We are here."

In front of me is an actual brick warehouse.

"I was almost expecting a bunker. Not…"

"A building in the middle of the warehouse district of the city?" Jackie finishes my sentence.

"Uh yeah."

"We figured it was a little easier to hide right under the radar rather than deep under. We also wanted to be a bit more accessible than a bunker in the outskirts of the city would be."

"Fair."

"Although a bunker may have been easier if we had known that there are fire wielders."

"You haven't met another person with fire?"

"No, dear. You have taken us quite by surprise."

"What do you do with all the space here?" I ask, trying to change the subject.

"Well, we have renovated some of the space on the middle floors into training rooms. We let people come in and train in a safe space. We are renovating based on powers. The water wielders were the most difficult to renovate before you."

"Mold." Kyria scrunched up her face.

"That… must have been a great feat of engineering."

"Honestly, we over engineered way too many options before we realized we just needed to make it a room sized shower." Jackie laughed. "You, though, I don't think concrete by itself will hold up long against you. Kyria, is anyone watery around?"

"I'll go check."

As Kyria goes off, Jackie explains more about their system.

"We are also boarding people here. We are seeing a lot of people moving out of the eastern districts. They are hearing rumors of people going missing so they are moving west. We mainly treat it as transitional housing until they can get steady on their feet here. Same, though, goes for anyone local. If your accident left you in a bind of living situations we can house you as you need."

"No, thank you, though."

"Definitely. You let me know if that changes. Okay, let's pop in here."

We are on the top floor of the building. The walls here are still lined with brick. The floor is still concrete. There are a few windows here and it has an exposed ceiling.

"I am not sure how resistant that piping and ductwork is going to be…" I murmur.

"Will probably melt honestly. I am going to have you let loose. If we can find someone with water around we will just do a makeshift water and wind layer to keep that protected. You can't hurt us, but I just want to make sure we don't bring down the building from the piping."

I nod, and I can see her decipher something from my lack of surprise from her comment. "Maybe we should just cut off the air conditioning for a few minutes?" I suggest.

"Already did." Kyria cuts in with another person in tow.

The door is closed, and there are three pairs of eyes staring at me. Jackie is explaining to the man what she needs from him while Kyria talks to me calmly.

"We aren't going to ask much of you right now. I realize you probably did not expect to get a training session right as you met us. We do need to test out how stable this room *could* be. So here is what I need *you* to do. Whatever is the source of the anger, I need you to imagine it on that wall right there. Let the anger well up inside of you and literally take aim at the wall."

"Take aim how?"

Kyria lets out a giggle. "It is a little silly at first. All you truly need to do is hold your hands out at the wall. Some people find pointing their fingers in the direction helps, or palms facing that way. Just depends on the preference. I personally like to do a little lunge and pretend I am in an action movie."

I turn to look at her at this, and she is truly in a split stance with a knee bend like she is about to crouch into a roll to escape some gunfire. This finally breaks me out into some laughter.

"There she is." Kyria smiles. "We don't want you to feel uncomfortable. The goal is to get your powers under control. Then we can move further into defensive stances, maybe offensive plays eventually. Ultimately, we need you to be comfortable and feel as safe as possible in this training environment."

"That sounds… fair."

Jackie pinches her lips together as if she is trying to keep from reacting. Have they not talked about offensive training before?

"Okay," Jackie comes over. "I think we are good. The three of us are going to stand back behind you as you aim where Kyria asked you to."

I nod, stamping my heels into the floor. Slowly I put myself into that same crouching lunge position. Shaking my head I grumble, "This feels ridiculous."

I look over my shoulder and Kyria gives me a big grin and two thumbs up. Jackie nods at the dark haired man raising their palms to the ceiling space above us. I get a stray spray or two, but Jackie's wind keeps the majority of it over my head. It protects the ductwork rather than drenching me, thankfully.

I switch from pointy fingers and stretch out my palms towards the wall. Mustering up anger is near impossible while pretending to be pointing gun hands. This allows my soul to turn towards the memory of that night, trying to burn it from my memories.

Suddenly a thick pillar of fire shoots out from my hands directly at the wall "Holy shit!" I exclaim.

The man - who must not have been told why he was coming up - whispers "What the…"

In my excitement a flare shoots out the window to my left, exploding it into millions of shards of glass.

Jackie comments, "Okay that is enough excitement for now. Summer I need you to start suppressing some of that emotion for us now. Try the breathing exercise we did in the park earlier."

I breathe in to her calm counting. Before I even finish that first breath the fire in my soul and fingers is doused. This is controllable. I can actually get this figured out and live a semi normal life.

Over the next two weeks, I integrate myself into the day to day activities of Jackie and Kyria's operation. My daily routine just changes slightly. I still go for my morning runs with Koda. I work eight to ten hours. Then instead of becoming a puddle of emotion on my floor, I go to the warehouse. Koda hasn't asked, and I just mentioned going to a self defense gym. There is still a lingering worry about what his reaction could be if I tell him.

Kyria, Jackie, and I all agree, though, that it is probably for the best to hold off on any more training until we can get a room set up for me.

After some extensive research on fire resistance we end up sticking with the bricks. We fill in the windows. To avoid curious eyes or transactions that would peak interests, we decide to keep the floors as is. If we start seeing divots we may add a layer of bricks there. For now we did not want to buy an actual palette of bricks.

Kyria spends the second week in the roofing to reroute the central air lines, while Jackie and I run down a creative solution for the water line and the sprinkler system.

We line the outside of each segment of piping with concrete before putting it up. We end up using my coding skills to rig a yard sprinkler system to a camera and thermometer. The yard sprinklers have better range and can hit specific angles. The hope is that the camera, thermometer, and my code will see if a fire is uncontrolled and needs to trigger the sprinklers.

"I know we generally try to keep the rest of our lives pretty anonymous… but where did you learn all of this tech stuff?" Jackie asks as she leans over my shoulder one morning.

"Oh, I went to school for computer programming. I work in the application development team at FaeTech."

"Damn girl. That is impressive!"

"Thank you," It has been too long since I was proud of my work.

"Random question for you…" Jackie pauses.

"Yeah?"

"What do you know about hacking security cameras?"

A conniving grin meets me when I look over at Jackie. I can't help but think of the reality of our situations and of the world around us. The grin starts to fall.

"I know a lot, but we should do more."

"Make a plan for us, and let's see what we can do." Jackie says as if it is the most normal conversation in the world. Like this is just another work assignment for me. In reality I would be taking every piece of knowledge that I put into our technologies at work and circumventing them on a large scale. It isn't like I haven't already done all of this to my apartment.

The next day, I show up ready to talk through my technical plan and Jackie puts up a hand, halting me.

"Let's talk tech later. Your room is finally ready to go. Let's get you some hands-on training."

Excitement speeds through me. Between the bricklaying and pipe moving, we haven't done a lot of physical training. Kyria and Jackie have been taking turns helping me with meditations. They talk me through how to keep my emotional responses in check. "We still aren't totally sure how these powers work, but the emotional check is first. You could keep yourself burned down to minimal amounts of power then something exciting happens. Suddenly you are bursting flames in every direction. We will also start teaching you how to burn down some of your energy. You will be able to do that without setting something on fire every day if you aren't a candle person. It's almost like turning your metabolism up full throttle."

Jackie looks down at my hands bringing me back to the present. "Count down from ten, Summer." Looking down, little flames have sparked out of my fingertips. I give Jackie a shy smile.

"At least we know we can get you with other emotions than anger now." Jackie nods as the tiny flames extinguish. We meander through the halls and up the stairs to my room. *My room.*

That is really strange to come to terms with. The handful of people that I have interacted with so far have had other powers. Water, Earth, Wind. No one else with fire. None of us are quite sure what that means. Jackie and Kyria have only been actively searching people out for the last year and a half or so. Maybe it will just take some time.

"Okay, I have put a few scarecrows in the corners of the room. For now you have no barriers or blockers. We will work up to it. If Kyria can direct her vines around walls, and same with my wind, you should be able to bend your fire around things as well."

I nod.

"Today we are going to focus on aiming rather than time to destroy them. We need to get you extremely proficient on the fundamentals. So do not rush. You cannot hurt me. You could leave us both buck ass naked though. That could just be awkward."

I focus on the scarecrow in the back left corner with the number one painted on its chest. I take my stance. Awkward as ever.

"It is going to be expensive to buy all these scarecrows."

"Assuming you hit them." Jackie challenges me.

How have I only known her less than a month and she already knows how to get me riled up? I position myself with more confidence, fueled purely by audacity. Closing my eyes, the excitement that sped through me earlier comes back as a steady flow. Breathe in. Breathe out. The fire starts to tingle in my fingertips before I push it through. The room warms up. Cracking open my eyes, I watch a stream of fire disconnect from my hands and hit the correct scarecrow. There was no instruction on whether to try to just send a fireball, or a constant pillar, so I take it as a win.

Jackie claps me on the shoulder right as the sprinklers go off, dousing us with water. Laughter bubbles up out of me, leaving both of us hunched over still getting drenched in water. Neither of us can move, and my sides are cramping by the time we hear Kyria come over the speaker.

"Are you just going to sit there like psychopaths and drive up our water bill for the rest of the day?!"

"Can you be a dear, Kyria, and hit the sprinkler override so we can keep up Summer's session? Now that the scarecrows are drenched I don't want them molding in here."

"Already done, love."

Jackie turns back to me. "Alright, show off. Let's see what else you can do. Then we will question your tech skills later."

"Fair enough," I chuckle.

"Did you notice how you had your hands stretched in front of you earlier?"

"Um... I think I just kinda pushed outward. Oh I had my index fingers and thumbs touching to make a triangle."

"Interesting. Okay. You seem to be a quick learner. I bought these scarecrows in bulk so let's try repeating that stance on the other three crows. We will replace them and try some more."

"Sounds good."

The next few "throws" are almost exactly the same. As I turn to the last crow, Jackie has changed my stance.

"Lets have less of a hinge. Let's pretend we are superheroes who can push this power out without full body stances. We also aren't witches who need to do full arm motions or hand signals, so take advantage of your mobility."

Repositioning as instructed, keeping my feet apart just enough, I still feel I could be throwing a ball. The stream of fire aims true and hits the fourth crow with ease.

"This is great. You are doing an amazing job, Summer. I think it is fair to say you are going to be one of our biggest prodigies. Before you know it, you are going to be teaching the next round of newbs."

I chuckle to myself as we go out of the room to haul in six more crows and line them up against each corner and at the mid point of the walls.

"Okay, next round. I want you to keep your stance as it was on the last one. No hinging at the waist. I want you to also separate your hands. Have your palms face each other." She moves my hands around to show me.

"Like I am holding a ball?"

"Exactly. What we saw with myself and the water benders, you won't get a fully rounded ball on your first few tries. It helps to keep the shape in your mind's eye as you learn."

Jackie is correct, of course. I am able to concentrate and keep the stream a little more rounded as it moves toward the target. A sphere isn't formed until my final try. It is a crazy sight to see. I am filled with such awe. It isn't even the size of a melon.

I am so distracted by this accomplishment of forming a freaking fireball in my hands that one thought escapes my soul before I can stop it. *Dune would be so proud of you at this moment.*

No. This moment is not for him. This is for me. Being able to control the outbursts may have been for him. Or rather to rectify what I did to him. Dune has not outed my secret to Koda. For that I can ensure to never let another accident happen.

Maybe Dune would be proud. He cannot be the reason I keep up this training.

Jackie notices the wobble in the sphere and brings me back. "Focus, Summer. You are doing great. Now let go."

Let go…

I close my eyes and push the sphere out of my hands. Tears blur my vision as it hits the last target almost in slow motion.

Jackie takes my hand as I let myself fall to my knees. I thought the last of my tears had long since run dry. Tears over the loss of my friendship, the loss of the man I love.

Love.

When will it change to loved?

Fuck.

Finally, after seven months, three weeks, and one day, sitting in the smolders of scare crows that I set aflame, I tell someone my story. And let go.

CHAPTER 30
SUMMER

knock on the door of Kyria and Jackie's apartment thirty minutes after everyone left my place. I hand Kyria a bag with Andre's hangover brunch special that he keeps off menu and only makes when I call.

Kyria dips her whole head into the bag to smell the mix of eggs and bread in sandwich form. "You are a delight."

"In exchange, mind if I steal your wife for a little training?" She doesn't even voice her answer. Kyria starts shoveling food towards her mouth as she shoos us away.

"I cannot believe you bribed her with Andre's. It is like I never even brought her a bloody mary."

I try and fail to hold back my smile. "You know I will go all out when I am asking for forgiveness." We walk the rest of the way to the gym in silence.

We spend a few minutes warming up before sparring. Jackie mixes in some physical punches with her wind powered ones. Unlike many of our recent sparring matches I let her take the offensive. I do not attack with any flames, simply use it as a shield for some of her stronger bursts. I block one of her physical punches to the kidney but miss her leg swipe that takes me to the ground. I cough, trying to gather my breath again, before sitting up.

Jackie is sitting up against the wall next to me. I sit up and look at her. We sit there across from each other in silence for a beat as Jackie chews her lip. "Why didn't you tell me?" The question is asked softer than a whisper out of hurt, not fear.

"To make sure I am on the same page… you are asking about Koda?"

Jackie only responds with the cock of her head that says "Really?"

"There…" I fumble on the right words… "There hasn't been anything *to* tell you."

Jackie gives an indignant snort. "You are going to tell me that the sexual tension this morning was built overnight? Be fucking for real with me."

"No," I moan. "We've had a… friends-with-benefits agreement for a while."

"Define 'a while.'"

"Eight years." I grimace.

"EIGHT YEARS?!"

"I never said anything because early on, it really wasn't something either of us talked about. Later, I couldn't bring it up because he works for me. Then you started work for me. It has always been no strings attached, no drama."

"So what changed?"

I lean my head in her direction. In return she gives me some great side eye. "Do not *even* pretend nothing has changed. Should I just ignore his 'Let me choose you' speech? Or the fact I would have walked in on you two sucking face had I walked in a minute later this morning? Something has changed. This is no longer just a casual arrangement."

"I-" I scoot over next to her so that I can rest my head on the wall with a thunk. "There was a moment… a few months ago. It was right after I figured out that slingshot move. We were at the farmer's market as we normally would be. I was so giddy and proud of what I had done the day before. Even without knowing exactly what I had done, Koda was just so… supportive. He was *present* in the moment. From there we both fell into a couple-y motion. Holding hands as we walked, him keeping his hand on my back. It felt like the most normal thing in the world. Like we just slipped into being *more* without realizing it. Rather than slipping back out, we were ripped out and I think it freaked him out."

"And you?"

"I … I wrapped up those feelings in my chest. I've needed him to sort through his feelings on *us* before I tried out my own. I couldn't let myself fall like that again for someone who would stay one step out of reach. So I held myself back too."

"I kept wondering what was up. You two seemed normal enough at work, but there was a stiffness that I couldn't quite put my finger on."

I hum my agreement.

"Is it safe to assume by your lack of answer this morning that he does not know about your fire powers?" She probes.

The torrent of emotions really starts to unravel now. The question, the conversation I have put off. A conversation I never truly thought we would have. I shake my head to avoid my voice cracking, betraying my fears.

"You should tell him, Summer. I know you are freaking out about it. I know you are scared that he will leave. You need to let him choose with *all* of the information. Don't let him hear this massive secret from Dune. With everything going on, I fear that time is no longer on our side. Don't shut this out. You don't want to wake up one morning and it be too late."

A stray tear crawls down my cheek.

"For what it is worth, I saw how he watched you at the club. I *really* saw you two. I have no idea how I missed it before. I don't think that man will leave you over this. Let yourself jump, let yourself be truly loved. You need to let him know you fully. All of those feelings, those emotions that you are damming up within your soul will need a release soon. Just like fires bring new life from their ashes, you need to let loose those emotions. Let them burn through you, reinvigorate your life, give you true happiness or cleansing. If you don't, one day you will break. We all need to meet our fears, our emotions with truth right now. I doubt we will be given opportunities to collapse in the near future."

CHAPTER 31
SUMMER

ater, I let myself into Koda's apartment to test out his bugs after finally finding my courage. The last time I told anyone about my powers was ten years ago when I met Jackie and Kyria. Even after I told them, it took a few months to finally tell them what had happened between Dune and I. During my trip down memory lane, the realization hit me that there was no real explanation needed with Jackie. I just... prematurely lit a stick on fire. I guess that is one way to do it. My mind is spiralling on this when I am halted in my tracks by the change in frames on Koda's wall.

There is a four by four grid of square white photo frames on the wall where his concert photos used to be. A tall frame that splits the grid down the middle. My chest aches as the image processes. This is our most recent selfie from the farmer's market. It is one of those magical moments that Koda always seems to catch. We are staring at each other instead of the camera, a string of hair stretching toward him with the wind. The flowers are barely in the frame as I had been more focused on Koda's words than the photo. I can't help but drag my fingers across more frames. Pictures from university, work parties, morning runs cross my vision. Some are selfies, others are pictures I never knew existed. He caught me dancing in the ocean at sunset one night at the beach house years ago. I had just finished renovations on the house and it was my first weekend spent there. My sweats were hiked up to my knees and I had a glass of wine in my hand. My hair strewn about as it followed my movements. I knew then that house would be my safe haven, a place where I could breathe without a care.

My nerves poke a hole in the balloon building in my chest, slowly letting out the confidence I was building. Could I bear to see him take our pictures off the wall after I have seen just how right they are?

The smell of food wafts toward me at the door, pulling me from those nerves. I usually expect pizza whenever I come over. I follow the distinctly, not-pizza smell down the entryway into the kitchen, to find Koda hovering over a saucepan. As quietly as possibly, I lean against the archway, watching him toss onions and garlic into the heated olive oil.

Not only is he cooking, but he is also less casual than our normal sweats and a t-shirt. Koda is in jeans - nice jeans at that - and a tight black v-neck. The shirt is not doing anything to hide the biceps chopping up more vegetables. Gazing down at my own attire, my clothes betray how underdressed I am. The apron helps alleviate the discord between our choices thankfully.

He is hopping around the kitchen, listening to some jazzy playlist as he goes around. The music was loud enough to cover my entrance. As creepy as it would be for anyone else, I continue to watch him. I drink in every moment, committing them to memory.

Cooking sausage.

Tossing in the tomatoes with the onions.

Starting a pot of boiling water.

Koda is also *making* garlic bread, not the frozen toast I normally buy myself, or the ready-for-baking one either. He is most of the way done with the meal now. Koda is still dancing with himself but is tasting his sauce.

"Can I try it?" I ask to announce my presence. Koda swirls around his eyes wide before he cools them back down to a simmer.

"Of course." His voice is strangely low. I stride over, and Koda holds me by the hips, pulling me closer to him and the spoon. Tenderly, he feeds me some of the sauce. Of course it is delicious. A small moan escapes me at the taste of it. Koda holds me close now, swaying us around the kitchen, intoxicated with the music.

"Can I help you with anything?"

"I have seen your attempts at cooking, Summer." He smirks at me without letting go.

I let out a mocking gasp. "I will have you know - I am an expert bread cutter."

Koda plants a kiss on the forehead, smiling. "I have wine chilling on the table for you, but all of this should be done in just a few minutes." Then lowering his voice, as if remembering the real reason I am here, "Stay here. Dance with me. *Then* you can cut up the bread."

It was not a question, and he did not loosen his grip. We hum to the music, both lost in thought. How easy would it be to just fall into him? Unfurl those feelings where they are being held tight. Not before he knows everything.

I've been running away. Away from relationships, opportunities with other companies, friendships. I've always been afraid to let anyone not like me into my soul again. Now all I want is him.

Naming that feeling sinks into my whole body. I settle my head into his chest, hoping the sinking emotion is not visible on my face. Neither of us dare to voice our thoughts out loud. Koda's chin rests on the top of my head. His hands hold me tight to him, as if willing me not to run.

I need to make peace with whatever the fates have for me... The premonition of change has kept its grip on my soul. Even if we only have a few years together... That will be enough. I will make it enough. It has to be. The running needs to stop here.

And he needs to understand everything. He needs to find a way to be okay if a time comes for me to yield to my fate. If he changes his mind after tonight, I can at least find solace in the fact that I saved him a bit of heartbreak later. He keeps talking about playing to win now. But what if me loving him, him loving me is a losing game? Fates above I still want to play that game, if it means having him for just a bit longer.

Luckily my thoughts are interrupted by the oven timer. Koda's fingers flex on my back, crinkling to not let go. We have to get the food out, but I do not release him.

"Summer, are you okay?"

"Can we go for a walk or something after we eat?"

He pulls my chin up to look at him. In his eyes all I can find is sparkling hope mixed with a tinge of concern. My face is surely showing all of my thoughts and fears.

"Of course, I know just the place."

We set up to eat dinner at the rarely used dining room table. I slice up the bread while Koda readies the plates. At the table there is indeed a bottle of wine chilling. It is a bottle from Andre's. I pour the two of us glasses as Koda brings out the food. Koda doesn't normally keep a stockpile like me. Odd that he would go all the way to Bocelli's just for a couple bottles of wine.

We settle into our normal conversations about work and other ongoings throughout our meal. At one point I pull out my laptop and a couple earbuds to see if we can hear ourselves live on the bugs.

"I see you changed out your wall of photos." I probe.

I swear Koda's eyes twinkle as he slides his fork out of his mouth. "It was time for a change. Those feel more inline with life currently. You like them?"

To keep the blush from creeping up my neck, I take a moment to peek at the computer to confirm the audio transmitted. When I look back at Koda he has his chin cradled in his hands, waiting patiently for my answer. I press the jammer on.

"I think they fit well."

Koda sways his head back and forth as I press the jammer back off. "You always amaze me with what you capture with that camera of yours." Confirming the test on the monitor, I turn the jammer back on quickly. "With a lack of local storage, if the jammer is live the bug never transmits. But we probably shouldn't turn a jammer on too often when I come over. He may get suspicious."

Koda rests his hand on mine, pressing the jammer back off for me. "You know I love capturing powerful moments and beautiful people." He presses our hands back down again before adding, "The most beautiful person I've ever captured is you."

Before I can find words to respond, Koda leans across the table to press a kiss to my forehead, then disables the jammer. "Dessert now or when we get back?"

"Hmmm. How good is the dessert?"

"Oh, it is good. There is extra if you want another serving later."

"Well then, now, of course."

A sneaky grin spreads across his face before disappearing into the kitchen with all of our dishes in hand. There is a clanking of dishes in the sink and doors opening and closing before he walks back out with a tray. There is a ridiculously proud skip to his step. He lowers the tray to the table where two ramekins sit, a hand held blow torch and …

"Creme brulee?"

"Only the best for the best, dear."

He must see concern etched across my eyebrows. "Oh don't worry. I got this from Andre. I wouldn't even dare to set a home-made creme brulee in front of you. Not without a decade of practice."

I huff out a laugh at that. Koda takes this as a positive signal and lights the torch, crystalizing the sugar on top. "I was wondering about the wine. Andre is going to be all up in my business now. Nosy bastard. I swear he keeps his restaurant open just for gossip." Koda's gaze is directly focused on me, lips pursed. He flicks his eyes in the direction of the bug before deciding to let his response stay a secret.

Hooked together arm in arm, Koda silently leads the way to a spot he knows. The silence leaves the gates in my mind ready to release a river of memories. This is not the same situation that happened with Dune. I should just be glad with Koda. There is time to bring this up before an accident happens. The decade of practiced control helps my confidence levels.

Letting the floodgates fling open this one time, the scene paints itself in my mind. The night that broke us. I had just been promoted and the three of us along with other team members went out to celebrate. There is a picture Koda had taken that night that is superglued to any memory of Dune. Dune and I sat so close in that old maroon booth. Dune is giving me a celebratory hug so close before he had let go when Koda had screamed "Say Cheese!" My hand was raised with a glass but my head leaned into Dune's shoulder with laughter. Koda had broken what was sure to be another awkward moment between the two weird kids. Dune never wavered. His soft, charcoal eyes remained locked on my face.

The rest of the memories of that night play across my mind. *Dune walks me home as he has any other time we go out. He leans down and whispers in my ear, "We have to make sure the queen gets home safely." His arm brushes against my own, gooseflesh follows the trail. Feeling confident, I grab his wrist and wrap his arm around my shoulder, allowing myself to snuggle closer. He seems so stiff. Normally even a small amount of drinking will have Dune being more playful, more flirty than his sober self. I would not have had to do this for him. He does pull me in closer now, his arm lowering to grip me by my waist instead.*

"You are so warm." I say as I bury my face into his shoulder.

He lets us in with the key I had made for him years ago. I plop down on the couch, pulling off my shoes obnoxiously. Sitting down next to me, it is as if he is taking measure of the space between us. He is trying to figure out how to say something. Finally, he quietly blurts out, "When I found out you were getting promoted I went searching for just the right gift. A local jewelry store had just acquired this, and I thought it would be perfect for you. I didn't want the others to feel left out for not getting you anything." He hands me the small box he pulled out of his pocket. A silver oval locket with an enamel tiara sits on a cushion. It has a burnt orange, almost fiery background.

"It's beautiful, Dune. Thank you so much." I bring my hand up to his cheek to look up at him. "I love it. I really do."

His eyes glitter with joy, transforming doubt into courage. "Summer, I, I have to tell you -" Courage morphs into confusion in his eyes. His hand touches my own and he pulls back in pain. Shock runs through the apartment as neither of us understand what just happened. All we know is that a line of my fingertips runs down the back of his cheek. Our lives are about to be forever changed.

"Summer, come back to me."

Refocusing on the present, we stand in front of a small pond surrounded by trees. Koda could have transported us to a different planet. I would have believed that more than the fact that this tiny haven exists within walking distance of the city.

"What is this place?"

"I found it on a walk one day. I was meandering, thinking about life. It is so well tucked away. There aren't many people here in the evenings when I am usually here."

"You come to contemplate life often?"

"Lately, yes." He twines our fingers together as we walk towards a small pocket of sand near the water line. "So let's contemplate together tonight?"

I can already feel the color draining from my face. Koda pulls my hand to his mouth, kissing my knuckles. "Summer, you are my best friend. No matter what. Nothing you tell me will change that."

I laugh out a sob at this. This will change everything. It will be hard for any positive feelings to overwhelm the sense of dread I already feel. So I lean into my nerves, my anxiety. Anything to feed the power within me. Slowly as my fingers start to tingle, I remove my hand from his. "I am going to need this."

I look at him one more time. Taking in every crinkle at his eyes as he watches me, the quip of his chin. The sparkle in his face when he sees me walk into a room. Even the glint of that earring as he tilts his face at me.

Just in case this is the last time. Just in case he changes his mind.

Closing my eyes, I take a deep breath. The anxiety is released to my blood, my willpower is given over to simply containing the release.

I open my palm.

CHAPTER 32
KODA

Summer is on fire. Like literally on fire.

The fire on her hands forms into a small little fireball hovering over her palms.

"Wh - what …"

Summer sighs in relief. Closing her palm extinguishes the flame that was just there. I grasp at her hands to inspect the palms.

No burns.

Nothing.

I look up to her eyes. "How?" I cannot let go of her hands.

She scrunches her face, debating with herself on it. "I don't think anyone really knows 'the how' outside of some old lore after the Fae-human wars from like fifteen hundred years ago."

Summer continues to explain that when the Fae-human wars ended, the Fae promised peace eternal. Should the Fae try to break the peace whether through oppression or violence, that humans would be gifted the powers of the Fae. This way they could protect themselves from another massacre.

What would happen if the humans actually banded together if a rebellion actually happened? Most of the Fae had such watered down powers they never used it, saved it for those extra few years of life. How many humans have this power? Is it passed on to their children? How have there not been more accidents? More news coverage?

There has, though, hasn't there? All over Alnitak, people go missing in mysterious ways. That region has had more infrastructure damage in the last five years than reasonably imaginable. Are the Fae trying to keep this quiet? Hiding it? Scaring citizens enough in one region so people, people like Summer, remain quiet and in hiding?

"This… this is why you are so big on security. Also, why you have signal jammers and such?"

"Yes…"

I stare at her hands, "It doesn't hurt?"

"No. Interestingly, I have… met others, trained with them. I don't think we can really hurt each other. Like, I could have someone tie me up with some vines, or get knocked over by a gust of wind, but from what I can tell we cannot do any real harm to each other. I could make a room go up in flames and the only thing we would lose would be our clothes."

I play with her fingers a little bit. Touching the pad of each finger is my only attempt to avoid my last question. I find another one instead. "You know the history books talk about how Fae power was like a well. Back before powers started fading, it would fill up to the top. Now depending on the person the well could be deep or shallow, but either way if they did not use their magic enough, the well would fill up, overflow. To avoid an explosion or outburst they would do random spurts of magic here or there. Things that seemed trivial. Is it similar for you?"

She almost looks sad at the question. Summer purses her lips to the side, as if trying to find the right wording. "Yes and no. There is definitely an aspect of using my powers every so often. Something about this magic is different. Like it… I don't know how to explain." Pausing just for a moment she folds our hands together before continuing.

"It's actually a pain in the ass for most people to train. Unless they are constantly living life - feeling everything that life gives to them. Or someone like me who is just perpetually stressed. Our well of power can fill up quickly with an event that causes enough of an emotional response. Probably built out of the rapid response your heart has when something scares you. So I found creative outlets for the power. Lots of meditation, yoga. Part of my cool calm demeanor at work is out of necessity. When I feel like I am getting close to topping out, I have a place I can go to burn it down to the bottom. After a lot of training and pure luck, we found I have a unique ability to burn alcohol out of my system."

Our laughter joins the chirping of crickets surrounding us. "No wonder I could never outdrink you!" Pulling her into my side, she rests her head on my shoulder. We sit in silence for a moment. Summer isn't necessarily relaxed. She has kept this a secret for a while. I don't blame her. Especially with everything going on right now. The country is on the verge of turmoil due to all of the people going missing. Based on how they have gone missing, they must be other humans like her. Murmuring to myself, half joking "Outside of hiding from the current govern-ment, it doesn't sound like a bad gig."

She stiffens in my arms before looking up at me. Then my entire stomach bottoms out as Summer leans up close and cups my cheek. Her lips are mere millimeters from mine. I cannot move. I do not even dare. All I risk is gripping her hip. A drum is beating so loudly in my ears. Her fingers shake a moment before she all but grips my cheek.

Breathing into me Summer whispers, "I think the thing they forgot when making our magic surge with a fear response is that it is so similar to moments like this. The moment when the person you've been chasing or been chased by moves in for that first kiss. That grand professment of love. Those seconds that feel like eons. The anticipation that brings fear along. Sometimes it's just simple as 'How does my breath smell?' to 'What if I fuck this up?' What if by doing this everything changes? What happens if he breaks my heart? What happens when I break his?"

I lean my forehead against hers without losing any space between us. Her statements no longer sound hypothetical. She must be talking about what happened with Dune. He broke her heart, though. Not the other way around. What does she mean by *when*?

I pull her other hand up to my heart where it is pounding. I breathe out, "I can see how that would be very similar to a fear response." For a moment I think Summer moves just the slightest in towards me before she closes her eyes.

"Without training, depending on the person, this moment could bring an explosion of flower petals. Making it more romantic. For others … it turns into a horror show." Removing her hand from my cheek, she shoots a fireball at the pond.

Forehead to forehead we watch it coast a few feet from us and plop into the water with a hiss. The scars on Dune's face appear in my mind, morphing into the shape of fingerprints. It's as if, as soon as she showed me her powers, the scars never could have been anything else. I press my forehead to hers, whispering, "I am so sorry Summer."

I pull myself behind her, settling her between my legs to hold her tight. This is the second time in two days I must promise myself we will find our way back to this moment again.

"Did you and Dune ever talk about what happened?"

"No, he walked out that night and never looked back. Never answered my calls, eventually blocked my number. It was so stupid. He was just trying to tell me he was leaving."

She couldn't actually believe that. I remember Dune excitedly showing me the necklace he planned on giving her. It was beautiful. He had heart eyes for her all night - more so than usual which was saying a lot at that time. He was going to *finally* close the deal with her. We could all move on without the weird tension of neither of them ever admitting their feelings. I never saw that necklace again. He did not even tell me about his job at Star until a week later when he gave his notice and bounced.

"Was that the first time it ever happened?"

"Yeah…" Then I remember her right afterwards. Summer was a mess. She made it through the work day… barely. The three weeks between the event and Dune leaving she tried holding it together. As soon as Dune was gone though, she was a shell of herself for a couple months. Her couch had disappeared. She refused to stay at my place, so I camped out on her living room floor until she would force me out. The puzzle is finally complete. The love of her life had left without a trace. Add in the layer of having just found out she had Fae powers as a human. A power she found out about by accidentally burning said love of her life. No wonder she was a mess.

If they had just been acquaintances, I could understand Dune's reaction. I would have been scared shitless. But for her best friend to hightail it and run? Annoyance at his initial reaction, quickly transforms into a surge of anger at the realization of where he ran.

"Summer, you don't think he…"

"Told anyone? No. I think I would have been kidnapped by now if he had. Though, there is obviously more at play than what we have seen so far. I just… I need him to trust me enough to let us figure it out. Who are the good guys in this scenario, and does Dune know which side he is on?"

I plant a kiss on her forehead. Fates, I want to kiss her, hold her face in mine. But she needs more than just physical reassurance right now. She needs to feel confident that I will stay. That running away didn't even cross my mind.

"I needed you to know. Before you choose. You deserve to make this choice with every bit of knowledge about me. I am sorry I never told you before now. It's just… I don't know. There was never a great way for it to come up. Eventually I just became okay with you not knowing. You not knowing was never hard. A little lonely sometimes, but not hard."

"This changes nothing for me Summer. Outside of not letting you con me out of fifty bucks in drinking competitions."

We sit like that for a while longer, contemplating our words, our lives while fireflies dance and crickets chirp around us.

CHAPTER 33
SUMMER

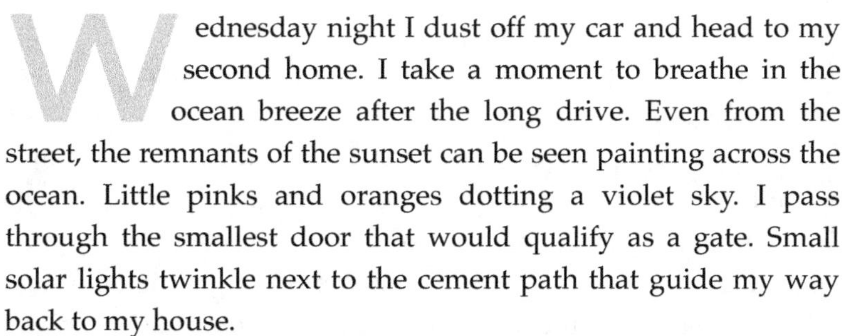

Wednesday night I dust off my car and head to my second home. I take a moment to breathe in the ocean breeze after the long drive. Even from the street, the remnants of the sunset can be seen painting across the ocean. Little pinks and oranges dotting a violet sky. I pass through the smallest door that would qualify as a gate. Small solar lights twinkle next to the cement path that guide my way back to my house.

Once inside, my giant lounger couch is calling my name, but I don't give into it yet. My first order of business is letting the house breathe. I open up the large doors that lead out to my little piece of paradise in the sand. There is a small alcove that's barely walled off before the beach takes over. It has a grill, firepit, and a small table. I'll check all of the appliances tomorrow. With doors and windows open, I roll my suitcase back to my room.

That may have been a mistake. Shadow boxes filled with memories from the last ten years pull at me. They remind me that I have a few more to create. Boxes that will be filled with memories that have been tucked away. Set aside but never truly forgotten. I throw on a shawl, and stroll down to the ocean barefoot. The image of Dune's dimpled smile crawls out of a deep hole somewhere inside me. The first time he ever flashed that at me left me speechless. At the time, I never thought there would be a "last" time. The water laps at my feet now as I hear the tide moving in and out, coaxing memories of a time long past out of my soul.

The next morning I still get up to go for a run. It's strange running alone, though. I watch as the sky turns from dark blues to hues of pinks and yellows and oranges as the day starts anew. A fresh start. Koda will be here tomorrow. My heart still leaps at the reminder that he is still here. He didn't leave after hearing my secrets.

A day of working passes by. The house stays bright with the sun that passes through all the open doors and windows. I've never been quite sure which has the most calming effect for me - the ocean breeze or just being able to hear the steady beat of the waves outside. Either way, by the time evening comes, I am not as anxious as I could be.

I take a large swig of wine before sitting down on my couch as far away as possible from the shoebox on the coffee table.

Unwrapping three shadow boxes, I reflect on the best years I had with Koda and Dune. Thumbing through digital photo albums, I settle on the year we graduated from university and the year before Dune left. Somewhere deep in a server farm, a machine just woke up out of a deep sleep of cold storage. The memories crash into me like the waves outside my door as I look through these old pictures. Moments large and small interweave together.

Spring break where we finally scrounged enough money to take a vacation. The three of us had to share the smallest hotel room and take turns cramming in and out of a tiny bathroom.

The three of us standing on the quad, our blue graduation gowns unzipped, ready to go to the after parties. We attempted the cap toss and all failed to catch them.

Our work desks crammed together in basically a server room where FaeTech used to put all of the new grads that they hired.

All of our snacks piled where our desks touched so we could all steal from each other. There are plenty of moments where we cleared everything off the desks and huddled on top of them to troubleshoot work assignments.

Koda taking a selfie as Dune and I stare at the instructions for a "super simple, build-it-yourself" storage shelf.

Our first adult money dinner out where we tried the fancy burger place and immediately regretted it.

The sound of my laughter pulls me out of my trance. I stare at a picture of the three of us in our dress attire for the company holiday party. The party itself wasn't a huge event, but the free bottles of champagne sure were. The picture is taken by the reflection in the elevator doors. Each of us carried out an obnoxious level of champagne before anyone could stop us. Dune had three bottles in each hand. I had three in one hand, the phone in the other. The only reason Koda was not the picture taker was because he also had three bottles of champagne in one hand, aaaaaaand a jar of cookies in the other.

I send the pictures over to my photo printer. The horrible quality of my photography skills and shitty phones at the time make me nostalgic. Those years weren't always the easiest. But I was happy. I did not feel perpetually lonely. There was no doubt in the support and trust I had in our small trio.

When I decided to make a third shadow box that was basically an ode to our old trio, I thought it would be fine. I am fine. Everything is fine. Even if I procrastinated pulling this box out of the closet it typically hides in until everything else was packed in the car.

The printed photos are separated out into three piles. Staring at a few that are just Koda and myself, I have to wonder if either of us thought we would end up where we are now. Just like how Dune and I always used to just… fit, Koda and I do as well.

No other obstacles blocking me, I finish my glass of wine, then just grab the bottle to bring back with me before sliding the shoebox towards me. There is still a slight film of dust on top. I close my eyes, take a breath, and lift the edges of cardboard. Not a single image was ever burned. They were just hidden away in this box along with every other memory Dune left me. I know exactly which photo is waiting on top for me because of that. Koda had gone home and unknowingly printed these out as little polaroids while my life was imploding. He gave them to me later with a weak smile. Images of our last night together out at that bar stare back at me.

My chest starts to clog. None of us could have predicted the outcome of that night. Dune leaving had been devastating...

Dune left me alone at a time I desperately needed a friend. My friend, even without the weight of what we could have been. The pictures punch me with the reminder that for so long I thought our trust in each other was invincible. That our trio would persist until time itself ended. The reality was that it had never been truly tested. *I* had been tested. Time and time again, my strength and resolve had been poked at by those around me. Those Fae that didn't think a human girl should or could succeed in their space.

It was easy to support each other, to support me, when I was the only one in danger.

I push through the anger and sadness just to continue ripping apart the bandaid on my soul. Selfies as we walk home intoxicated, the only times we would let ourselves touch the other. Holiday party pictures where we look like a bonafide couple. Assortments of birthday party celebrations in pointy rainbow hats or cake smashed in one of our faces. The New Years Eve party where I was in a short little silver tassel dress. Dune had pulled me in by the waist for a picture, and never let go. At least not until fifteen minutes to midnight when he conveniently disappeared. Notes upon notes upon notes that he would leave me hide between pictures of us picnicking on the quad or lunches in the cafeteria. Whether hidden in binders at school or among the stray papers at my desk, I could find a note once a week. Before I know it, I am back to the beginning. Letter tiles spelling each of our names, crossing at the "U". Our first ice cream outing at Bert and Rocky's when Dune suggested we should come back every week, to try out the new flavors.

Fates above, I was so naive. I loved him so much. Deep down I always knew he would never risk our friendship for anything more. There was that nugget of hope that always dug into my soul whenever I would reflect on these moments. The rumble in my chest that I alone felt. He cherished our lives, our memories together. Rather than risk it for more, he threw it away and left us both with nothing but loss and heartbreak.

I start placing photos into all of the shadow boxes. My chest continues to beat heavily as I stare at the final one that contains our first and our last picture together. As of right now, a person could see the full life of our friendship in this box. A clear beginning, a clear end. Tearing my eyes away, I stare at my purse. Taking the last sip of wine out of the bottle, I set it in my lap and pull out one last item. Dune's locket.

Every pebble of hope I ever had exploded out of me that final night leaving a crater in its wake. I am unsure of what would happen if I looked inside the locket. I'm not ready for the ramifications of pulling back the final layer protecting my soul. So committing to never know, I take the necklace and place it in the shadow box where it will stay.

CHAPTER 34
DUNE

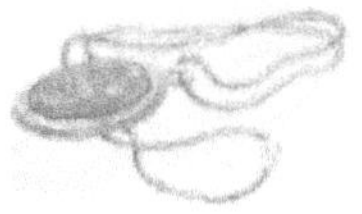

"So how did you find this place?" I ask Koda as we pass through the small driftwood fence.

"What do you mean?" Koda responds, distracted.

"Dude, we just got here. Who are you texting? And I asked how you found this place. Seems really lucky that it was available so last minute to book. It is off the beaten path so it is plausible."

He stops and mumbles something that sounds like, *"shit"* before turning to me. "Oh, this isn't a rental. It's Summer's beach house. I just borrow it from time to time when I need to get away."

We slow down as we reach the door. "Is … wait. This is Summer's beach house?"

"Yes… that is what I just said."

"Don't you think she might mind me being here?"

Koda pauses as he is fumbling for the right key on the ring. "No, I don't think she would honestly. Normally I just give her a heads up that I am coming up. Although this time I only let her housekeeper know. Which…" He trails off as he unlocks the door and pushes it open. The house is cute. It looks like it could have been a surf shack in a former life. This entry hallway is the only set of walls with no windows.

Walking into the main area the first thing I notice are all of the frames. Art and pictures litter the wall space. This place feels like more of a home than I personally have ever had. It floats up memories of Summer's college dorms, pictures pinned up to every square inch she could get to. The jolt of that memory forces me to register the rest of my surroundings. All of the lights are on. The door to the outside is half open. It is like a little barn door that splits in half. The outdoor market lights are also on. Through one of the windows I see a woman in a lounge chair in front of a firepit. Of course it is Summer, book in hand sipping out of a glass of wine.

"Hey Koda, I just saw your text. Did you eat already? I can order pizza!" She doesn't move from her spot.

Koda is stock still beside me.

"I … definitely didn't realize she was going to be here. It was her car that I parked next to. I was hoping I was wrong… fuck."

"Huh?!" Summer gets up and treads towards the door. She has an incredibly oversized sweater that just about reached the bottom of what looks like bike shorts. Her caramel hair is in a loose braid hanging to one side of her face. Koda and I both just stand in our spots like idiots. I can't move, my chest is filled with a flood of images of us in moments like this for years. This cozy outfit cut straight through my soul more than her club attire ever could have. Doing homework, working late, catching up on a tv series. "What did you -"

"Hey…" Koda drags.

"Hey…" Summer switches her gaze between me and Koda. "I… I understand now why Brenda set up both rooms. Um… well." Summer flips into fixit mode. She sets down her wine glass before hopping around the room. "Hey Dune. Nice to see you again so soon. Welcome to my second home. Never in my life would I have guessed this would happen."

Summer yanks open a closet door and is trying to find a step ladder in there.

"What are you trying to grab?" I ask. She's talking to me like an acquaintance. She may not be the center of my world anymore, but something strikes a match in me that hates the fact she's uncomfortable at this moment. So is it an olive branch? A stupid one, but it's all I can offer.

"That top cloth looking container with the handle."

I reach up for it, facing her the whole time. Why is she not freaking out? Why is she not trying to kick us both out the front door? Why am I so angry that she rightfully is uncomfortable? I look at the lump of material in my hands and realize it is an air mattress.

"Wait, how many rooms does this place have?" I ask.

"Two. And I will be keeping mine. So you boys can fight over who will take Koda's bed, the sofa, or this air mattress. Dune, if you want to put your stuff in a room either way, it is down the hall and on the right. Each room has its own bathroom."

"Are you sure it is okay for us to stay, Summer? I don't want to impose on your alone time." I poke, unsure if I want an easy out or not.

"Nah, it is fine. I need to get a little work done tomorrow, but it is nothing confidential. Otherwise there is plenty of space for us all."

Koda takes the air mattress. "I'm gonna hole up in your room. Keep either of you from trying to murder the other or anything crazy. You mentioned pizza?"

"Yeah, I've got your order. Dune, are you still an every-topping-available person?"

I stare at her. The normalcy of it all. After ten years she still remembers my damned pizza order? There is no fight. No push back. What the fuck is happening?

"I ...am..." I hesitate and can't help the words that spill out next. "Are you seriously going to just brush this aside like this is just another vacation among friends?"

Summer stops dialing.

"And what reaction would suffice for you Dune? Obviously it won't be ecstatic happiness. Would you rather me quietly cry from frustration or explode with anger?" Koda even flinches back at the force of her words as she stares me down.

"I know this just plays into that nickname your peers over at Star have for me. Ice queen, isn't it? Just because I am not losing control of my emotions does not mean I don't have them!" There is a prick of guilt in my stomach. I don't know how she found that out. I don't encourage the use, but it is part of the unfortunate reality of the mask I still wear.

"Fuck," she murmurs. "I'm going to order the pizzas. I'll leave cash on the island. Koda, can you show Dune where everything is?"

"Yeah. Set it up for pickup. I assume you are ordering from Joe's?" Koda is shaking his head at me with disappointment.

Summer nods as she puts the phone on speaker. Without another word, she simply grabs her glass of wine, and heads out towards the ocean.

"The ice queen comment - what is she talking about?"

"They, uh, I mean it's just a nickname, Koda. To the outside world she seems so cold. Emotionless."

Koda just turns and flicks his finger to follow him. "And you never thought to discourage that? As a respected leader within your organization? Here is your room."

"What about Summer, huh? A respected leader playing house with one of her employees? Would you also tell me to discourage that?"

Koda steps into my face now. "You and I both know if the situation was flipped, no one would blink a fucking eye. She would never even give it a second thought if it was anyone else. It would be an automatic no. Hell, I was about to move into her apartment to save some money on my own rent. A few months before my lease was up the company reorganized and suddenly she was my boss. We both knew what it would look like, no matter how innocent it was. So we kept our living situations the same. But us sharing a beach house isn't harming anything."

Koda sighs, "Stay here. Unpack. Mosey around. Beers are probably in the fridge. Better yet - you've been bringing up Summer all week. Go fucking talk to her." Before I can get a word in, Koda storms out of the room leaving me alone.

My brain is still buffering on each random tidbit of information Koda gave me. Whether it is the innocence of it. Or the fact that I had no idea Koda had almost moved in with Summer. I open my bag, but just stare at it until I hear Koda leave with a slam of the door. I stare at the bag that contains a couple more bugs. Koda never told me exactly where we were going. I thought maybe I could get one into a bag or something. It is pure luck that we ended up in one of Summer's homes. It will come in handy that Koda is sleeping in Summer's room as much as it pains me to admit it. I don't want to be setting these up and Summer comes back in from the dark and catches me. Even if it is luck, my stomach goes sour at the thought.

I let my curiosity get the better of me and explore the small house. My eyes are drawn to shadow boxes Summer has lining the hallway. She looks ... happy in most of these. Content in the rest. Most of them have pictures of her, Koda, Jackie, and Jackie's wife. There are a few of just her and Koda, smiling, giddy.

The last time I truly saw Summer for who she is would have been eight years ago. She strutted past me at that conference and never even looked at me. I was still angry then. Sometime between then and now Summer learned how to be happy again. She had grown. In my mind she stayed stagnant. She would be wallowing in her anger and pain. Instead she is living.

I need to change my plan. I am not going to be able to get close to her by poking at her and trying to get her to rise to anger. The last box on the wall is dated from nine years ago. She is smiling in all of the photos, but there is an element of sadness. Loss.

Koda's command rings in my ears as the open door to

Summer calls my name. She won't want to talk to me. We really should just go back home tomorrow. I search the fridge for a beer of my liking. It is lucky that Koda and I have similar tastes in beer. I lean against the counter and take a sip. As the bottle reaches my mouth I am distracted by the frames on the wall across from me.

Even from here I can tell these are old, just by their graininess. Pictures from vacations, parties, nights out. In every one I only had eyes for Summer. The two on the outside are dated but the one in the middle isn't. Taking a closer look, these are just pictures of all three of us. Every picture brings with it a memory that bubbles to the surface of my soul, trying to bring it to a boil. The boy I locked down long ago starts rattling my lungs, pounding to be released. Fuck if only I could. The drumming gets louder as my eyes land on the locket.

Unable to decipher the feelings rushing through me at the sight of our ending, I snatch my beer and rush to find her.

She's sitting on the beach just out of reach of the waves. The moon is full and bright so it isn't too hard to see her once my eyes adjust.

"Do you mind if I sit?" I almost whisper to her. She simply waves her hand to the spot next to her. I leave enough space between us but still stay close enough. Just as she sucks in a breath to say something I interject. "I am sorry. I pop up into your home unannounced and was really fucking rude. You had every right to tell us both to turn around and go home. I think I was just so shocked, I immediately chose to try to pick a fight."

"Thank you. I am sorry also for reacting the way I did."

We sit in silence for a few moments, each of us sipping on our drinks. I pull my shoes off to match Summer's bare feet in the sand.

"This is a really nice place. I like what you've done with it."

"Thanks. It was a nice passion project to put some time into. This place was an old run down surf shack when I bought it. Fixed it all up and made it something I would want to come home to. It brings me a lot of peace. I just wish I could get up here more."

"And then jackasses like me invade it." This gets a chuckle from her so I probe. "Can I ask you how you are doing? I know the Emily Turner case is top of mind for a lot of people. And there are a lot of protests going on. You holding up okay?"

Summer turns and looks at me with a question in her eye.

"What?"

"That's not… exactly a small talk question. Do you actually want a real answer to that?"

"Y-Yes?"

She chuckles before continuing. "I am doing … okay. There is a strange relief that it isn't me. Then an immediate bout of guilt for not doing more. I try to maintain my webinars to help people maintain their security without raising too many questions. Really though, everything I have done has been done with my own safety in mind. Just trying to keep eyes off of me long enough to do my part in the best ways I know how."

When Summer doesn't continue I gently probe. "Does Koda know?"

"About this?" She opens her palm in front of me and flagrantly summons a small fireball before tossing it at the waves. It takes all of me not to flinch. "Sorry, that was an asshole move. Just breaking the ice poorly I suppose. Anyways, to answer your question. Yes. I told him pretty recently actually. So I guess thank you for not telling him." She takes a gulp from her glass this time. "I was gifted a new department at work." I remain as chill as I can, unsure of how this connects. "It is under extreme discretion to not be reported on. I am really just in the org structure for it on paper. I have to assume that this is similar to the program that Dubois contracted Star to create for Alnitak. So I finally told Koda. It directly affects me, so I am trying to dig up as much information as I can. For me, for others like me. If I go missing because of it, he deserves to know why. There is too much going on now for him not to know. The others like me shouldn't put themselves at risk should anything happen. If there was one Fae close enough to me to know, it is Koda. You are back here now, I suppose. Though I was not expecting us to become close enough friends to think you'd really take up a mantle for me or anything. Frankly I am surprised at how often we've run into each other since you moved back."

I don't need to ask her about Koda's reaction. The answer is clear. He is still here. He didn't run.

"That must have been lonely."

Summer puts the back of her hand to my forehead, checking for a fever. Her hand is soft. It doesn't scorch like her touches did as we danced with each other last week. As she pulls her hand away, it feels like a rubber band is stretching between us.

"It was lonely, Dune. Very lonely."

"Summer, I –"

She holds up her hand, "I will tell you I am sorry for hurting you. I hope you know it was an accident." I simply nod my head. "I lived with my guilt for a long time. Mostly in the form of loneliness. That was my choice. I didn't tell Koda at first because frankly there was a valid fear he would leave. After some time, I found others like me. I learned how to deal with this new found power. It was a secret, but something I could now control. I wasn't putting Koda at risk every day any more. You both were still friends. And … with all the nasty rumors about me going around I… " She looks at me now, keeping it trained on my scar. "Even ten years later it didn't take Koda more than a few minutes to piece it together. All those years ago, I did not want any rash anger to get back to you. Or frankly to the fiends of the fishbowls. I would have been labeled a selfish bitch if I stole your best friend from you."

She gives me a soft smile before looking back to the waves. It is the parts left unsaid that weigh heavy in my gut. The nasty rumors that were mainly started by me in those early years. The gross people that fed off of my anger have continued it ever since. She had already been lonely before then. She is a human woman trying to make it in a Fae world and the male-dominated field of tech.

Summer doesn't say anything more. I don't have anything to add so we sit in silence. She is leaning back and her face up to the moon. With her eyes closed, I take a moment to take her in. This is the first soft moment we've had in ten years. All of those hard edges and stiff postures are gone. The face that is normally so strong, is soft. The light breeze tries to take some of her hair with it across her face. A younger version of Summer flashes across my mind. Summer was taking a bite of my ice cream cone and the wind kicked up and took a couple strands of hair across her face. Just like it's sitting now. She had the smallest little giggle. It was the first time I almost threw caution out the door, and kissed her. I was a split second from knocking that cone out of her hand when her hair was then strewn *into* the ice cream. Everything was so chaotic. I will forever have the image of streaks of ice cream across Summer's face in my memory.

I chuckle to myself, causing Summer to peek open an eye. And now I've been caught staring at her.

"Should I even ask?"

The softness of the last few minutes must have seeped into my bones. I lean over to tuck her hair behind her ear. "I was remembering that time at Bert and Rocky's when my ice cream got tangled up in your hair."

At that she laughs with a bellow and falls back into the sand. Luckily the movement breaks me of whatever enchantment had led to my hand resting on her cheek. I lie down but prop myself up by the elbow.

"Fates above, that was so long ago."

"A whole different time." I murmur. "I know… I know me being back is weird. But maybe…" Fuck this is hard. I needed her to keep her edges. I have no right to ask her for a friendship back. Especially since I am going to abuse it. I am selfish. So incredibly selfish. Because if she would let me I would make more memories like that one. Like this one. Cherish them. Then crush whatever friendship grows out of this when I take that federal job.

"Dune?"

I blink out of my thoughts and realize I've been staring at her silently for probably a full minute now.

"Sorry. I, uh, just. I … wow. Do you think we will ever get back to that point? That friendship I mean?"

Summer chews on my words. Fuck, I did not phrase that sentence well enough. The answer to that question - will we open our souls to each other again? That is the reality of what I let go of. She was my everything. The pause in response makes me think that maybe it was the same for her.

"I … think I can try. To be friendly again at least. I won't promise we can get back to what we were before."

"That's fair."

Before we can say much more the lights start flickering on and off from the kitchen. I help Summer up and we head back to her house where Koda and pizza waits for us.

CHAPTER 35
SUMMER

After a run and breakfast this morning, I spend most of the day on the beach lounging. I've been laying here reading for a couple hours now with no interruptions surprisingly. That also means it is time to put more sunscreen on. Pushing myself up, I turn to grab the sunscreen. The view of the two men staying at my house pauses my movements. Both of them are in their swim trunks tossing a frisbee back and forth. I grab my phone and discreetly steal a photo.

Shamelessly I take in both sets of chests and abs while applying my sunscreen. I had not noticed last night in the dark, but the daylight has confirmed that, yes, Dune's biceps do look incredible outside of that blazer. Dune's hair is also in a loose ponytail, little strands flowing wherever they want instead of up in his normal bun. Koda's hair is also flowing wherever he moves. My eyes glaze over as I recall licking his abs. In the haze, my sight lands on his calves.

Every time they toss that blessed frisbee, their calves on the sand have a nice tight strain to them. How have I never taken the moment to appreciate those calves on any of my runs with Koda?

I look up from said calves to find both men staring at me.

They only break eye contact to toss the frisbee. Dune just puffed up his chest a little bit. At my chuckle, Koda squints his eyes at me. Oh he definitely doesn't like me playing into that peacocking. Unfortunately for him, the reaction makes me want to push it a little bit more. Just to see what he does.

I start rubbing my own calves and legs down with sunscreen. Do I add a bit of unnecessary movement to it to really rub in the lotion? Yes.

I am poking a bear. Koda is already upset. Last night, we watched new bugs activate in Dune's tracking application. This morning as I walked out of my bedroom in my bikini he immediately pushed me back in. "He does *not* get to be rewarded for whatever bullshit he's doing, Summer."

"It's not like he hasn't seen me in a bikini, Koda. It would look much weirder if I went out there fully covered up." He rested his forehead against mine and sighed.

"Your boobs are so much nicer now though," he practically whined.

"KODA!" I pushed him out of the way, grabbed all my stuff and walked out to the beach. Dune seemed to still be waking up. I only saw him long enough to see the pause of the coffee mug before walking out the door.

Dune's phone ringing brings us out of the haze I am conjuring. He indicates to Koda that he needs to take it and heads back towards the house. Koda waves him off and turns to me with darkened eyes. Sitting down in front of me he just twirls his finger and snatches the sunscreen bottle.

"Who do you think he is on the phone with?" Koda asks like he did not come over here with ulterior motives.

"I… have no idea. We can go back and check the recordings later tonight. If he went close enough to the house I should be able to pick it up."

At this, Koda hums and puts his hand to the back of my neck and pushes me down flush with the towel. Straddling me, he leans into my ear and growls, "I have much better plans for us later tonight, love. And none of them have to do with Dune."

Then as if it was any other day, he scooches back, basically sitting on my ass, and starts rubbing sunscreen on my back.

"You were both preening. Are you going to tell me you guys stayed behind me and didn't check out my ass the whole time?"

To this he simply slides down a little farther and massages up from my knee to my ass on both sides. He gives each side a small tap before just saying "Up."

When I meet his gaze sitting in front of him now he grits out. "Keep an eye out for him."

As I nod he squeezes another small dollop of sunscreen. My eyes over his shoulder I don't notice his hand going for my collarbone. My immediate reaction is to arch my back. He drifts up and squeezes my neck slightly. "Pay attention."

His hand rubs down to my breast. I am trying not to breathe or moan as I watch the door subtly. I am concentrating so much that I don't notice Koda's hand slip under my top. With a smirk, I comment "You know the sun isn't getting there, right?"

He simply glares in response as he switches sides. Finished with his fondling, he turns around and hands the bottle to me.

"I could probably use some on my back too."

Dune crosses the threshold of the house again. I check my watch as discreetly as possible while he watches me rub lotion all over Koda.

"Sure you don't need any on your chest? It is much more visible than my own."

Koda lets out a scoff that turns into a deep laugh. I give his hair a playful tug and shoo him away.

Groggily, I wake with a start from my sun induced nap. I groan, checking my watch. It has been at least an hour since I last checked. My book is face down on my towel. I must have used it as a pillow. Even though I am still a little out of it, something has jolted me out of sleep. My ears listen for noises or signs of a struggle in the house. All I hear is the deep whispers of the other two men. There is a soft chuckle before a pair of feet walks in front of my face. Internal alarm bells start to go off as I realize there should be two pairs of feet.

Suddenly Dune's face is right in front of mine as he grabs my wrists. Koda must grab my ankles, as I am now being lifted into the air. Years of being tossed into pools on a whim floods my brain and my legs start kicking as they start jogging. Koda hangs on for an admirable amount of time. Eventually the kicking and jogging gets the better of him. Dune doesn't miss a beat. My heels have barely hit the sand before he turns and lifts me over his shoulder like a fucking fireman. They just laugh and laugh as they jog closer to the waves. I half heartedly pound on Dune's back, knowing it won't stop him.

The splashing of the water under their feet trips a wire in my brain. Both of them even curse, hopefully rethinking their plan. This beach - lovely. The sun - not too demanding. The actual ocean water? Frigid. Wetsuit-only type of water. This is the type of water that neither Koda or Dune would submerge themselves in willingly. They must have decided that for old time's sake the frigid cold would be worth it. I bet Dune is planning to just launch me off his shoulder once he gets far enough.

Nope. Not happening. If I am going in, he is going in too. Instinct takes over. I need to get a lock on Dune. I swing my legs around him, but I can't lock my ankles without sliding down his chest. I practically put him in a chokehold for good measure. I am not being peeled off Dune unless I am clearly about to land on sand.

"I can throw fireballs goddammit. Why are neither of you scared of me enacting my revenge on you?" I whined.

Koda had just chuckled but stopped once the waves were lapping at his knees. Dune keeps as much of a light jog as you can through ocean water. I just flip Koda off as I watch the dry shore slowly get farther away. I catch the slightest glimpse of regret on his face. Once Dune gets waist deep he slides me farther down so I am basically straddling him now. I keep my arms locked around his neck for leverage. I jump because the water is caressing my ass at this point. I gave one more whine. "You *really* don't have to. Aren't you cold?"

Dune just gave me a half smile. "We said we were trying to be friends again? This feels like a solid new memory to start that off. Right?"

This is all he says before taking two more steps and dipping us fully into the ocean water. In the five seconds we were under water he pulled me closer to him by my hips, and cups the back of my head. Emerging from the water, I keep my forehead pressed to his shoulder. He wades through the water back towards the coast. As soon as my skin hits the sea breeze the uncontrollable shaking starts. Underneath all of that though, the ropelike tension I felt last weekend shoves its way to the surface again. Despite the cold, this tension causes me to feel the heat scorching through me wherever Dune is touching me. One hand is still on the back of my neck, the other is supporting me under my right thigh. His hand is way too close to my ass. Closer than he ever let it go before. My whole front is burning from the touch of his chest to mine.

I push down these feelings. The girl that loved this man died a long time ago. She is not allowed to come back, she is not allowed a say here. The heat subsides and the shivers start again.

"Can you please stop that? Or like start a fire. Or something. Please." Dune's voice sounds like his control is on edge.

"Excuse me? You are the one that *plunged* me into that icy ass water! What do you think I -" Then I feel the reason why he was gritting his teeth. I guess it is good to know that if I need to pull the sex card to get info from him I still have that effect on him.

"*Seriously*? Isn't ice cold water supposed to cause shrinkage?"

"It clearly doesn't care about the fucking cold when there is a very beautiful woman straddling me. The shivering is causing a great amount of friction."

"Fates above." I look down to see the depth of the water. The water looks ankle deep now, so I push myself from Dune's body and stomp all the way back to my house. Koda's face is unreadable. He wraps my towel around me as I walk past him, but he's looking behind me. I don't stop as I rub my chest and will the girl I once was back into the grave I dug for her.

CHAPTER 36
DUNE

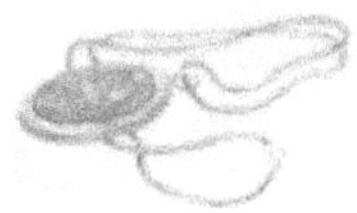

Koda puts a hand to my chest before I can follow Summer into the house. "You need to wipe that look off your face. Now."

I physically take a step back at Koda's bluntness. "What the hell are you talking about, Koda?"

"You. Left. Her. Now take that look of longing and put it back in whatever box you need to."

"Koda, what is this about? So what if I realize how much I missed her? Am I not allowed to regret my choices?" Why am I fighting him? I need to use her for information. That does not require me to fight him on ... whatever this is.

"You *broke* her when you left. I had to pick up the pieces and glue her back together. If you think I am going to give you the chance to break her again... you are severely mistaken. I am glad you both are open to trying to be friends again. But lock that shit down because you are not hurting her again." Koda punctuates the last six words to hammer in his point.

I rub at my chest. The words clang around my soul. Not that I hurt her by leaving. Not that she missed me. That I *broke* her. I stare at my friend, wondering what he saw and how he stayed friends with me after. I push the boy that loved Summer back into the box I try to keep him in.

Koda clocks the motion of my hand and I stop. He walks ahead of me into the house. Summer is locked away in her room as I find my way to my own. I suck in deep breaths to calm the erratic beating of my heart. Something is wrong with all of this. I should not be having this sort of reaction to Summer. My whole soul seems to reorient to face her whenever she is around.

We both need to find out what Aaron Dubois is doing in Arcalis. We both need to figure out why humans are disappearing. I just can't tell her *why* I am. I have a whole day left with her and Koda. I need to find a way to stay in her life. *For the next couple months, not forever.*

After a cold shower, I emerge back into the living room to find Summer curled up on her couch in front of a pile of files. She is in a white tank top that forms to her curves and oversized sweats with fuzzy socks. Her hair is still damp and twisted over her shoulder. When I meet her eyes, Summer glares at me and chomps angrily on her pizza.

I chuckle softly, "Keep telling yourself that you hate me for that." I grab a beer out of the fridge before coming up behind her. In an act to try to soften her a bit, I lean over the back of the couch and take my own bite of her pizza. Her eyes widen, but before they can revert back to anger I shrug. "Friends remember?"

I could have mistaken the flash across her face for my own. Memories of stealing each other's food off plates. Taking my seat next to her on the couch, I toy with the idea that maybe I should let my past self out a little more, melt her into trusting me. Looking at the files, I probe, "Can I be sitting here with you?"

"Oh yeah. I would actually love to hear your opinion on some of these people." She shifts a handful of folders over to me. Koda is drying his hair with a towel as he returns to the living room. Summer does not seem to see the flare of Koda's nose as he takes in the scene. Some caveman part of me puts my arm behind Summer on the couch and scoot closer without breaking eye contact with him. Koda simply shakes his head and heads to the kitchen.

"Are you listening?" Summer's voice cuts into my haze of brutishness.

"Sorry, tell me again what or why you need my opinion?"

Koda returns, sidling in on the other side of Summer with a plate of pizza slices.

"Did you actually get roped into those meet and greets?" Koda scoffs as he tosses a slice of pizza onto Summer's plate. His knee rests against hers.

"At FaeTech next month?" I probe, ignoring the pang of domesticity.

"Well… I actually volunteered myself this year."

"I bet Mark thought he was hallucinating." Koda chuckled.

"Why did you volunteer for these? I don't even do these for Star." I am curious about why, but I have a hunch. This is almost too easy.

"I'm trying to drum up any gossip. You both know about my new department and my lack of access to anything. Normally, I would at least have access to the network drive. There is nothing. My computer is being watched, so any official ticket I put into IT is going to be flagged. Brad from IT has been replaced by a major prick who will not give me the time of day. He is definitely not someone I could sweet talk into giving me access without a paper trail. So with no help from IT, my boss, or my own damn employee, I decided I would try to see what lies in the rumor mill."

"But if no one knows your department exists, how do you expect to gather rumors from these contacts?" I ask as I pause on a folder in the pile. Wendy Cranst. Why does that name sound familiar? I dig through some of the papers as Koda and Summer keep flipping through papers. I flip through pages of discussions in my mind trying to place her.

Koda probes, "Have you thought about trying to get people talking before the conference?"

"I mean… I created an anonymous Fishbowl account to try to gather intel from there. But that is it. Which by the way - I had no idea there was a whole damn section dedicated to just Dune and I."

I peer up from the folder in my hand. "I will have you know I have not contributed to that in …. A long time." I almost drop my head before sharply turning back to Koda. "Are you saying she should go stir up her own drama?" This could actually work in my favor. I just need to find a way to convince them I should be part of the drama.

"Hell yes!" Koda hops up to put his feet under his butt on the couch, finally removing his knee from Summer's. "Think about it. We all agree we think Aaron Dubois is doing something shady with Star and that it is spreading to FaeTech, yes?"

Summer and I nod in agreement.

"How would I stir up that drama?" Summer asks.

"Use me." Summer and Koda swing to face me. "Think about it. The department is more established at Star, you still have to be hiring some folks at FaeTech for roles. There have got to be people who interviewed for the lead role and didn't get it. If *we* are seen together, it would definitely get people talking."

Summer does not look convinced, so I push a little more, "We could fake most of it if we need to. Post a few pictures a week on social media until the conference. We could use your anonymous account, Summer, and post the pictures in the Fishbowls too."

Koda has moved from bouncing in the seat next Summer to pacing in front of us. "Do you think you could get a reservation at Bocelli's?"

"I mean, yeah, Andre's been begging me to eat at the restaurant for ages now." She turns to me again. There is no trust on her face, just questions. There shouldn't be since I am using her to get information I need. "But would you really be willing to? I know we just agreed to try to be friends again. This would definitely force the proximity. You want to take some time to think about it?"

"No, I don't need time. I will help." I point down. "Wendy Cranst in your list is going to be your best bet for info. She is also why we should definitely be as social or whatever as possible."

"Her folder seemed so bland, though."

"That is on purpose. On paper she is the..." I shuffle the folder over to show her as I continue. "... Scheduling Director, Office of the CTO, for the Government of Alnitak."

"Yes, a CTO that does not actually exist -"

"That is because she *is* the CTO. She reports directly to Aaron Dubois."

"How do you know this?" Shock is leaking out of her face. That job role has been buried for as long as I have been looking into all of the things that happen in the Alnitak region. I am sure Summer has done plenty of research on regional politics.

"I have... sources."

"Do you trust those sources?" she scoffs.

"Yes." I change the subject quickly. "So you mentioned Bocelli's... Doesn't that place have a waitlist that is like three years long?"

Summer waves me off. "It is a long story. I'll call Andre and get it squared up. Have any bars you have been wanting to test out?"

"I do..." Dune chews on his lip. "Come to my office next week. Tuesday. I hear Dubois is supposed to be there. Maybe we can snag a photo of him walking in the front door. Koda, maybe you can take one of the two of us walking in together?"

"Eh, I do *not* want to be pinned with corporate espionage that easily. Maybe we should just take a picture at a bar later. Let others put their own story together."

"Fair enough."

We sit with our thoughts for a small moment before Koda plops back down on the couch with phone in hand. "Smile!"

We do as we are told, but when Koda inspects the photo he shakes his head. "You two are going to have to do better than that if we are going to try to sell this. Try again."

It takes three more shots before Koda is finally satisfied. He posts this picture along with one that Summer took earlier. I had not realized she had been watching us enough to sneak a picture of us tossing the frisbee. There is a selfie of Koda and Summer on the beach that I don't get a good look at as he quickly swipes past it.

There is a surge of jealousy that I tamp down with the reminder that they probably took it while I was on the phone with Ashryn earlier. Koda texts the first two pictures to Summer and myself in a group chat.

"Thank you for eliminating the awkward question of getting phone numbers again after all this time." I jest.

We all look at the new post Koda tagged us in. *The gang's back together at last! #bestfriendsforever #bff*

"You are so weird." Summer shuffles Koda's hair as she gets up. I ignore the pounding in my chest from this and the last photo slide of just Koda and Summer cozy on the beach. "I need to call Jackie about clearing my schedule Tuesday."

I nod, trying to not think about the fact I haven't seen her smile like that in a decade. Or that when she did, it was at me.

CHAPTER 37
SUMMER

I know it is Dune walking up behind me on the beach. I sip on my wine, willing myself to *not* turn around. I tell myself I only know it is him because Koda is attempting to sound-proof my room. It isn't the waft of his smell. It isn't the tension in my chest that eases as he gets closer.

It would figure that the moment I allow myself to be happy and fall for Koda, Dune would just walk back in and wreck it.

"Is this what you do every night you are here? Come out in the dark and sit in the sand?"

"How do you know I wasn't trying to lure you out here with malicious intent?"

Dune's eyes widen so I back track. "This is far enough away from neighboring houses, phones, and street cameras. I don't really have to risk spilling any state secrets this far out in the sand. I actually wanted to ask you a question about something you said last night."

Dune's eyes scan my face before he nods.

"You mentioned something about the protests in Arcalis after Emily Turner's disappearance. There haven't been any reports of protests here...We get the news articles on the buildings exploding but that is it."

"You know … the lack of news coverage on it is interesting. Right before I moved out here, there was a protest right down the street from me. It caused chaos. Smashing cameras, everyone was in masks and there was confetti everywhere. They are happening almost every day. Something about this disappearance changed the game."

I stare out at the ocean, letting the sound of the waves calm my heart. If there is actual movement in Arcalis it is time to start really thinking about making a call. Do we start sending people back? Start a rebellion there?

We still don't know what the surveillance technology is that the Alnitak government is using.

"I need to figure out what Dubois is doing out there." It is more of a murmur to myself. I had almost forgotten Dune was there until he rests his hand on mine.

"We will figure it out."

As soon as I am back from the beach house I walk over to the warehouse. I roam the hallways of the gym, not finding anyone. Neither Kyria or Jackie has returned my text. Unease climbs up my back as I take the stairs to the second floor. I follow the voices as they get louder and louder down the hall.

I sneak into the training room meant for the earth and air wielders. It is brick similar to my own training room, but the windows are not filled in. Instead they are covered with a film that blocks anyone from seeing into this room. I close the door quietly. Kyria is waving her hands down as if she is trying to calm an unruly crowd instead of coaching powers.

Wait… is that what is happening here? Emily is pointing at a smartphone and shouting about "Missing the beginning." Jackie is leaning against the wall and silently shakes her head. She even nods at me to walk back out. It is time though.

I am sidled up next to Jackie for five seconds before Emily spots me. The arguing she had been doing with Kyria converts to blind rage.

"YOU!"

The twelve or so other wielders take a step back at this. No one knows my gift, my curse, my power. They only have their suspicions.

Emily stomps over to me. "You are supposed to be helping! My best friend is running protests and you are playing housewife with your little boyfriends! I cannot believe you were an icon to me for so long. You talk all of this talk about security. You give housing to people that need it. But you are not willing to walk alongside those starting to light the fire of rebellion. How dare you come in here and even pretend that you are working toward any cause?"

Jackie is pushing off the wall next to me before I put up a hand to stop her. I push myself off the wall instead. "Phone?"

Emily puts the phone in my waiting hand tentatively. Her eyes never leave my face, trying to read it. I look at the images she was showing Kyria. Sure enough there are pictures of dumpsters on fire; molotov cocktails being thrown at surveillance cameras; humans masked in balaclavas linked arm in arm as they march down streets.

I look at Kyria and Jackie, "I was actually trying to find you two." I squint my eyes before pushing on. "One of my *little boyfriends* let slip the fact that protests have been happening almost daily since Emily's disappearance. It isn't showing up on our socials which means the algorithm is suppressing it from reaching outside of the Arcalis region. It must be sophisticated if people's lives and stories are not reaching people on the other side of the country. Which means we cannot rely on just social media anymore. We've been watching the wrong spots."

"What are you suggesting?" Kyria asks.

"Send us back to Arcalis." Emily stares me down. It isn't a bad idea - for most of the people in this room. Emily is too well known.

"Is that why you were getting in Kyria's face when I walked in? You want to go back?"

"Yes!! I am not content to sit here while my friends fight my battles for me. I came here looking for a fire wielder to take back with me. I never intended to stay. I just needed to regroup." She pins me with a look that tells me she knows exactly what I am. She probably has not questioned that since the day I met her.

"Prove that you are ready to go back." I power down her phone. "If anyone else has a phone in here, turn it off or get out." No one moves. "Now."

"Summer..." Jackie starts.

"Will the room be okay?" I ask as I toss Emily's phone to her.

Jackie looks at the exposed ductwork. "I'll watch it. The floor can be replaced." I forgot about that fun feature. Foam and bouncy since wind wielders like to knock each other off their feet.

I turn back to Emily, a feral smile spreading now. For every sure step I take towards her she falters back a step. "Show me, Emily. What will you do if someone recognizes you? What if someone tries to kidnap you?"

This is why she can't leave yet. The confidence that was there just a moment ago is sucked out as soon as anyone challenges her. I want her to go. I need her to understand what is at stake when I ask for my favor later.

I start walking backwards, still facing her. I take a moment to tie my hair up in a ponytail as she and the others in the room try to gauge what is about to happen. The dozen of other wielders in the room are all water, earth, or wind wielders. Teival starts moving back towards Emily. Before he can make it to her side I charge. Teival immediately reacts, sending a powerful stream of water right at me. Despite now having water logged jeans, socks, and a t-shirt, I do not slow. I simply change my course just slightly.

Before anyone else reacts I tackle Teival to the ground. It is not the easiest feat since he is pretty fit and a few inches taller than me. But momentum and surprise can give you the power to do many things.

No one in this room has moved. Teival is gaping at me. I point at him as I shake some loose droplets off and say, "You are the only one to pass that test. Good job."

"I just… I thought …" Emily stutters.

"You thought what Emily? That a Fae officer is going to do what? The Fae are dangerous right now because they are *weak* and *losing power*. They are not going to hit you with a magic power. It will be physical. So stop acting surprised and *show me* what you will do with someone chasing you."

I have wrung out my hair and turned back around on the other side of the room. I sprint at her again. This time she starts moving around, shooting vines in my direction. I easily dodge her attempts. "Try harder, Emily. I've been training for this for ten years. You can imagine anyone dispatched to kidnap you will have similar training."

Angry tears start to well up in her eyes. I notice that no one else has moved. The only person who even made a move was Teival. She cannot break.

"The face of your rebellion is about to be kidnapped and you all are just standing around? You want to go back to Arcalis? This will fail before it even begins!"

This gets them moving. Now I am avoiding dirt clods, hurricane force winds and even tidal waves. Much better. After evading most of the blows sent my way, I finally trip over a fucking boulder.

I hear Kyria yell, "You need to get her tied up while she is on the ground." The wind wielders are covering me from all sides, preventing me from moving without it feeling like molasses. Emily stands in front of me, wrapping vines around my body, holding my arms into my body. She then ties my wrists together. The leverage allows her to pull me to the center of the room. I shuffle my hands around so I can grasp the vines closest.

"Did we pass your test?" Emily sneers.

I smile at her genuinely before pulling her to me by her own vines. "Not yet. But you are close." Craning my head to Kyria and Jackie I finally do what they've asked me to do for years. Lead.

"For the next month, their training becomes more aggressive. They need to know how to work together and avoid being captured. Start prepping caravans and landing zones. I know we have mapped it out, but double and triple check timings and checkpoints. Jackie, I need someone starting to find as many cameras they can hack. In Arcalis and outside of the country. Finding the cameras should be easier once we have people in the city."

"Outside of the country?" someone probes.

"If they are hiding protests from within our own borders, what are they hiding from across the oceans?"

A brunette man chimes in now. "Why should we trust your judgement? You don't even help us with our training outside of technology. You come in here and judge the training we've been given. How can we even trust you to lead us?"

I let my fire burn through the vines in my hands and travel through everything holding me back. Ash sits at the floor by my feet to the sounds of small gasps. "I am not asking you to trust me. I am asking you to follow her." I point my finger at Emily. "I have been training in secret for years. I never knew that I was the only fire wielder. Every time someone new walked through these doors and they were not like me, deep down I knew. I would be chased down the moment anyone knew of my existence. So asking you to wait for a month is for your safety and mine. We still don't know what we are up against in terms of surveillance in Arcalis. I need at least a month. Let me do what I do best and finish the job before taking any light away from those who truly deserve it."

I stride towards the door, but turn before exiting. "Take a month, confirm your counts. What happened here today is not spoken of after this moment. No one knows I exist."

Maybe it is more to just make progress, to know that *something* is within my control. I am just putting off admitting the truth about my situation. I open up the bug out bag packed in the closet. I check anything that could expire, make note of those things to replace. After Koda and Dune left, I printed out some more pictures to add to the bag. I chose a few pictures mainly with Jackie, Kyria, and Koda.

At least Koda knows now. I won't tell him about this new "chosen one" status. At least not until I absolutely have to. I cannot have him freaking out about me while I am trying to calmly leave. Now we can continue onwards. My anxiety may flare but Koda can think it is only about the situation at work. Or with Dune.

I pull out my will from the file in the office. It needs to be updated and finalized. Kyria enters the office and sits across from me without a word. All of my possessions to Koda. Kyria helps me write the language to ensure Koda does not flounder. Whether I disappear, or die, I cannot have him not moving on. All of the possessions will be out of my name and in Koda's within six weeks of my death.

Kyria pulls out all of the paperwork and files on all of the side businesses and ghost companies we have put together over the years. There is only one that explicitly has my name as a co-owner. She starts the process to remove my name from it. I adjust my web crawler to remove the evidence of this in any and every database it can find. Some of these companies are just covers to hide transactions with the gym. Others are legitimate but used as ghost accounts to send charitable donations to various organizations. Sometimes we use those to sign for my part in co-ownership of other businesses.

Kyria does not bother me with small talk. We have known each other for too long to know this is work that needs to be done. I do not ask Kyria to keep this info from Jackie. I won't ask them to keep secrets from each other. Jackie will understand why I am putting things in order now. What neither of us know is what the trigger will be. We never explicitly planned to really start or join a rebellion. We just knew something like this would happen to me eventually.

I start clearing anything that could be suspicious off of hard drives, shredding anything physical. I keep only what is relevant to our current situation. I have already done the same at the beach house; my apartment will be next.

Kyria and I finish our unspoken to-do list and I return to my room. I sit on the edge of the bed and stare at the selfies taken just yesterday. In one of the pictures he had not posted, Koda had kissed my temple as I leaned into him. The happiness from the picture crept straight into my heart and soul, trying to make me break. Then there is the picture of the three of us.

It is a ghost of pictures we had taken a decade ago. Yet, looking at Dune's tentative smile, an ache starts to build in my chest. It beats against the wall that I am building around my soul. The soul that is looking at this bug out bag and seeing the finality of my situation. This is the path that I willfully ignored for all of these years finally calling in its debt. I still have some final choice in all of this though.

Gaining the courage to voice my question, I walk into Emily's room with a soft knock. Teival looks up from the book in his hand. "Can I have a few minutes please?"

Teival leaves after Emily gives a nod.

"Summer, I am sorry for -"

"There is no need to. I think it was time for a shake up. It is truly needed."

Emily sighs. "So if you aren't looking for an apology… why are you here? I haven't seen you since I showed up."

I sit in the chair Teival just vacated. "I have one more reason why I need you to stick around for a month. Call it a favor. Realistically though, if this does what you think it will, it could change the tides."

CHAPTER 38
SUMMER

I do not normally pass the Star Technologies headquarters despite it only being a few blocks away from FaeTech. Star is located in one of the taller, more imperious looking buildings. Windows reach for the sky, mirroring it back. Others call it beautiful, but I know what goes on within ten of those floors.

Dune suddenly appears next to me, placing a hand to my back to urge me inside. He leans down a tiny bit to whisper next to my ear. "I wasn't sure if it was going to be better or worse to put your name down on the official guest list. So we are going to take a different route."

We pass the main elevators used for visitors to the floors. The elevator we take is around the corner. It could be a service elevator, although it does require badging to get to the floor you want. "Sneaking in does make it look like corporate espionage, you know."

He gives me a light push into the elevator and scowls at me. "I have my assistant picking up a friend around lunch time and he will put a name on the sign in sheet."

"It is still a *paper sign in?*" I look at him wide-eyed.

"Yup. Which is why this is so damn easy."

Sure enough it is. Once we enter the floor all I have to do is walk around like I belong. Either people don't realize who I am or don't believe their eyes as we walk past.

Once we reach Dune's office, he lets me in before frosting the glass and closing the door. His office is about as plain as my own. A white board behind his desk for his notes, a couple of gray chairs for guests, a coat hanger, a gray sofa. And that… is it. With the windows frosted it feels dark, almost small due to all of the gray in the room. I settle onto the couch.

"So what now?"

We stare at each other blankly, realizing that we could be stuck alone with each other for hours. We haven't spent that much time alone in over a decade. Dune picks up his phone "Hey, can you come in here for a second?"

A tall, gangly Fae man opens the door hesitantly a moment later. His sandy brown hair is short enough for his pointed ears to be very visible. He stares at me and then looks at Dune.

"You needed something, Mr. Raydn?"

A snort escapes me before I can stop it.

"Sorry, sorry. I've just never heard anyone call him that before. *Mr. Raydn.*"

Dune glares at me before continuing, "My friend *Sarah* here… see I'll cut the chase. Sarah here is from our Arcalis office. She has a huge crush on Aaron Dubois. Changed that virtual working session I had to be in person and came all the way out here for it. While we work, would you mind moseying around the office? See where he's at. As one of my *best friends*, I really would love to give Sarah here a chance to at least see her crush."

I put my hand over my mouth to keep from spitting an angry retort. The man must think I am trying to cover up a blush. His face goes from pity to bewilderment as he looks from my ruddy cheeks to my rounded ears. Then there is a moment that with anyone else it would be recognition.

"Yeah I will keep an eye out and let you know!" As quickly as he came in, he left.

"Had to lay it on thick there, eh?" Dune simply shrugs.

The seconds pass like hours as we sit silently. Neither of us can take any video calls. Both of us just started clearing out our mailboxes. This weekend at the beach didn't contain this much silence. Koda was always there to break it. The quiet allows so many reminders of the past to leak through. It's as if they play out on my laptop screen in front of me. Dune and I huddled together in the stacks of the library doing homework. Dune sending me glances and winks over his laptop from across the room in class. I refuse to acknowledge the tightening in my chest as anything other than that nostalgia.

My brain is pulled back to focus on the Dune in front of me when he says something I don't quite catch.

"Sorry, come again?"

"How was your run this morning?"

I must be looking at him like he has four heads because he continues, "Koda mentioned you run together every morning. You still got up and ran even at the beach house… I just …"

"Oh, yeah." I wave away the awkwardness. "The run was fine. Are you still swimming?"

"When I can, yeah." Dune pauses before continuing. We didn't really try to catch up this weekend on the small things. "How many books have you read so far this year?"

I smirk at him. "Forty-two. How many non-fiction bores have you read?"

"Two." He genuinely smiles.

"Boyfriend?"

"Asking for personal reasons or for a friend?" The snarky retort takes us both aback. "Anyways, what is this? Twenty questions?" I mock his reaction to my same questions from the club a few weeks ago, trying to steer us to safer ground. "You going to ask me how many people I've fucked next? Or how many I've fucked over?" I chuckle at him chewing his pen.

His eyes darken before answering the very question I tried to distract him away from. "Yes, I have a personal interest in that. All of that actually."

"I've lost count of how many people I've fucked. I am not sure I have fucked over anybody. I am sure if I did, they probably deserved it."

"You didn't answer the question."

"I didn't?"

"No. You didn't."

Cooly, "Well, I figured with all of your questions to Stan, you would have the answer to that already."

"What's the deal with Stan?" Good. *That* misdirect worked.

"Stan volunteered to let me use him to make a guy jealous. It didn't work. But we've been decent enough friends since."

Before he can find another response, I stand. The room is closing in on me. That twinge in my chest desperately wants to be let out.

"I just need to go to the restroom. Will be right back."

On my way to the bathroom, Dune's assistant almost runs into me.

"Hey I didn't get your name earlier."

The young Fae man looks at me with a question in his eye. He can't be more than twenty-five. "It's... Mark. I ... thank you for asking, Ms. Chase."

We both go stock still as he stutters, trying to find some way to cover it up. "Dune, er, Mr. Raydn didn't exactly choose a great cover name for me." I laugh it off. "Were you off somewhere fun at least? You seemed to be in a hurry."

"Oh, I was actually coming to find you. I know which meeting room Governor Dubois is in." We start walking in the direction he came from before he realizes, "Should we go get Mr. Raydn?"

Still needing space for a few minutes longer I answer, "Nah. Why don't you walk me over there. I was just heading to the restroom anyway. Then I'll go back and tell him." Blasting him my best smile, I wait for him to crack.

"Sure, okay." Mark's shoulders seem to lose their tension as he turns around to lead me to a separate wing of this building.

"So Mark, tell me. How is it working for Dune? Did you move from Arcalis?"

Warily he looks back at me. "Yeah, it was very sudden. I actually just moved this weekend."

"Geez, he didn't even give you some time off to get settled?"

Mark gives me a soft smile, "He is a busy man. Working for him… it is what I expected. I am just trying to pay my dues and get through these first few years here."

"What's at the next rung of that career ladder for you?"

"I actually want to get into software development. That is what I have my degree in. When I applied there were no open roles. It still doesn't seem like there are any." He frowns at this. "Would you -" He cuts himself off with a shake of a head.

"We have a few openings. I'll send Dune an email. Feel free to snag it and send me over your resume if you ever want. He may hate me later if you ever tell him, but that wouldn't be anything new."

"Thank you. I will do that. And Mr. Raydn doesn't hate you." He pauses with a little smile. "He is actually the reason I knew exactly who you were earlier."

"Is there a shrine to me hidden in his desk drawer or something?" I joke.

Not catching my sarcasm, Mark responds, "No, but he keeps that magazine article from a few years ago there. When it first came out, he wouldn't put it down. Day after day after day that magazine sat open on his desk. One day I snuck a look at the issue and grabbed my own copy. Read up on all of your accomplishments." Mark stops and then realizes just which article that was. I am assuming it was BusinessSociety's "Most Eligible Executive" issue.

One day I will find out who nominated me for that stupid ass award and will wring their neck. I was the only woman nominated. The magazine editors liked my accomplishments. Sure. They mainly liked the unicorn of having a woman win it. Even if I was human.

"Shit." Mark murmurs.

"It is fine Mark. Mr. Raydn and I have a long past. Maybe he likes to see pretty pictures of me to make up for our not-so-pretty past." This isn't exactly where I thought my leading questions would go. Info is info, though.

"Well, um, we are here. He is in that conference room over there. If you are trying to catch the Governor, the nearest snack room is right around the corner." As if remembering the excuse Dune gave earlier, he puffs up his chest. "I could go get him for you. You want to meet him? I can just knock on the door. You don't need to hang around waiting for him to come out."

I hold up my hand to stop him. "Thank you, Mark. I will be fine. I am just going to hop into the closest bathroom first, okay? Go ahead back to your desk. I'll be right behind you."

With a nod, Mark turns and leaves. I watch as he keeps a slower pace than before. I am about to go find that bathroom when I hear, "Fifteen minutes, boys. Be prompt."

I look back and forth to find a place to hide for a moment. Out of the paths to the kitchen and the restrooms. *Quick. Quick. Quick.* Finally finding a spot I calm my breathing just enough as the door to the room we had been watching opens. Aaron Dubois glides out. I flatten myself against the wall before he can see me.

If I can actually get into that room and see what's in there… *Shit.* This was *not* part of the plan. I can't let this chance go. Get in, get as much information as possible, and get out. I email Dune a quick "I'm going in!" knowing he will have to wait for Mark to get back to his desk.

I set my alarm on my phone for thirteen minutes from now. As the last person leaves the room, he pats his pocket before locking the door. *Double shit.* I pat my head. Thank the Fates I put a couple bobby pins in my hair today. I stroll across the hall, pulling the pins out of my hair.

Discreetly, I attempt to let myself in. And fail. Shit. Books and the movies make this look extremely simple. I jiggle the pins around for another moment before trying to find another way. What is the point of being a special fucking chosen one if I can't even pick a damn door lock? This is a real chance to get into this room. Stop freaking out. Just think.

Actually… let those nerves loose. I jam a bobby pin back into the lock and do an even stupider thing. Come on, come on, come on.

Finally, the well tips over and my flame coats the bobby pin. One hand still on the lock, keeping a handle on the fire, I start jiggling the door handle until the pins inside become malleable enough for me to get it pried open.

I let out a breath, pulling the molten flame back into me. A small trickle of metal attempts to drip out of the key hole. Jiggling the door handle a couple more times to make sure it doesn't stick, I wipe anything visible away with my shirt before entering the room.

I leave the door slightly cracked to hear any movement. As soon as I turn around, my senses are overloaded. It is like a tornado went off of papers on tables, whiteboards full of scribbles. A shredder in the corner to clean up the mess. Nothing is leaving this room.

Words confirming my fears are sprawled across this room. It is in the ugly handwriting of men willing to do whatever it takes for power, no matter the cost; because as with most things - they won't be affected by that cost. This won't hurt them. So why should they care?

MACHINE LEARNING
SENTIMENT ANALYSIS
SCROLL OF PEACE
FIRE + WIELDER / -ING / -S

A little too late I hope there are no cameras in this room. It is used for ultra secret meetings, surely it isn't a recorded space.

Too much time has already been wasted. I pull my phone out

and start recording everything, careful not to touch or shuffle anything.

A step outside the door causes a pause, but it passes.

Could this table be *any longer?* I never thought a twenty seater table would be *so long.*

I make it to the end of the table and start back.

Just this side of the table.

Then the whiteboard.

Do not rush. The camera stabilizer is only so good. It cannot unblur.

Another set of feet pass.

This was so stupid. What the fuck was I thinking?!

I am going to get caught and fired. With great prejudice. Star will also find a way to fire me. Dubois will also find a way to fire me. Then throw me in jail. That is if they don't notice what I did to the door.

CALM THE FUCK DOWN SUMMER.

Just the whiteboard is left. *Keep your head on Summer. Just get this DONE.*

My alarm shakes me out of my doom scrolling of scenarios. There is so little left, I risk it to get the last seven feet of the whiteboard.

Six feet.

Five feet.

A few more shuffles outside of the door.

Four feet.

Three feet.

This is for everyone like me. Just. Keep. Going.

Two feet.

"Hey!" A voice calls. My arm drops to my side. As soon as the panic dissipates, Dune's smell of pine and snow overtake my senses, calming my erratic heart. "Did you get your drink?"

I breathe, stop recording. *My drink?* There's a fridge in the farthest corner of the room. Dune is white as snow, his head on a swivel.

I head over to this half size fridge and lower down to take a look at the drink options. Searching through it, I attempt to find the fanciest drink I would actually drink. Time is running short, whoever needs to unlock the door is probably on his way back before the rest of the group. Suddenly, I am very grateful that Dune read my email and sprinted over here. Hopefully, he doesn't give Mark too much trouble over it.

"Mr. Raydn, are you lost? Can I help you with something?"

This voice ping pongs around the empty conference room. It could have been echoing for all I could tell. If Dune's voice had calmed my inner soul, this one causes it to scream, to bolt. There is a disgust in Aaron Dubois' voice as he speaks to Dune.

"Oh, uh, no sir. Is this your conference room? So sorry. Ms. Chase really wanted one of the good drinks. This room always has a few of those hidden away."

Slowly, confidently, I raise myself from the fridge. *Don't let the nerves show.* Aaron Dubois is already halfway across the room. His blue eyes sear into me as he strides to me. His blonde hair bounces just a smidge as he continues his path to me.

"*Ms. Chase.* So *very* nice to finally meet you. I never thought the Fates would grant me such luck." The fact that there are secrets written on every inch of this room is forgotten behind the sensual voice of the predatory man in my path.

Then, this man who is big as a tree, extends his arm. Not his hand for a shake. No, an arm. He loops my arm into his, and walks me out of the room. Everything I have read about Aaron Dubois suggests that he loves a chase. If I need to get him off my tail, I need to let loose an obnoxious giggle. Right. Now. He cannot set his sights on me. Those blue eyes are alive, almost dancing. This is a *very* dangerous game. This is a man who would order my disappearance the first chance he found out what I am.

"I never thought you'd be so lucky either, *Governor*." The wide grin confirms that my normal sass is exactly what would egg this man.

"Oh such formalities," he hisses. "Please just call me Aaron. May I call you Summer?"

"I suppose that will be okay."

We stop just short of the doorway. "I am a collector of information, as you must already know. Let's check out this drink of yours. This way I can stock my fridge with it should you ever make it out to Arcalis."

I can see Dune out of the corner of my eye, glaring at us. Glaring at me to cut this game. Now.

I let a chuckle out while extricating my arm, "Well, *Aaron*, I haven't been to Arcalis in thirty-five years. Not sure if much could convince me to visit at this point. Your fridge should be safe."

I swear an actual glint of light just shuttered across Aaron Dubois' eyes. He hands me back the cherry drink. "I fear the rest of the day is going to be such a bore now. Or just distracted as I attempt to find a way to meet the challenge. Feel free to come back and find me again."

Striding out of the room to Dune, I look over my shoulder and just comment, "Good luck with that." The face of a hungry wolf reappeared as Dune places a hand too low for business associates. The wolf's eyes flick down and back up with a smirk. Dune was trying to stake a claim, but it seems to have the opposite effect - stoking the flames of Aaron Dubois' interest.

"I will see you soon enough, dear."

Back in the relative safety of Dune's office, I plug my phone into the wall to ensure it stays charged. Then I immediately start ensuring the video gets uploaded and then backed up to multiple cloud systems.

"What the fuck, Summer? You couldn't just let out one

teensy, tiny fucking giggle? Or look less…?" He waves his hands up and down at me. "You were practically in slow motion coming up from the fridge. He is going to track your every movement until he goes back to Arcalis. This wasn't even part of the plan. What. The. Fuck."

"I am pretty sure I am the only woman on this floor. Whatever this means," I wave my hands, mirroring his movement. "I would look *like that* in a potato sack. " Dune actually turns a light shade of pink at this comment. "And yes. I've read all the stories and the gossip about Aaron Dubois. I couldn't do it, Dune. It would be like asking you to be less fucking bull-headed. When you are genetically wired to be the way you are, it is difficult to fake not being that way."

"Bull headed?!" Dune sputters as he spins back at me.

"YES, DUNE. That man never would believe a fake giggle out of me. A fake giggle would probably have fanned the flame. Then you had to go and basically grab my ass in an attempt to shield me, which really just came off as an act of pissing on your territory."

"Oh."

"Yeah. Oh. Speaking of which. All the nerves have reminded me that I still need to use the bathroom. I'll be right back."

Dune rises to follow me. I raise a hand to stop him. "Don't worry, I am actually going to the restroom this time."

Within thirty seconds, I am in the closest bathroom, puking up my nerves. That is a first. I don't even care about who the next person to enter the bathroom behind me is. Let them think their poor stall mate just had a bad lunch.

Spitting the last bit out I slowly raise myself, then straighten out my blouse before emerging. Only to find my bathroom buddy is none other than Aaron Dubois. Dubois is leaned up lazily against my exit, door locked behind him. His arms are crossed in front of him with his head cocked to the right as he stares at me.

"You get lost?"

"A theme today it would seem, *Ms. Chase.*"

"Back to formalities I see. Can I just settle with *Dubois?*"

"Certainly. I really just wanted to get a rise out of your Dune Raydn. I like the way calling you Ms. Chase sounds more."

"I see. Bad blood between the two of you?" I poke.

"You could say that. I thought we had that in common, frankly. That little show the two of you just put on does make me wonder."

"Care to talk about it?" I attempt to get his attention away from my intentions.

"Maybe another time. Unless you want to tell me what he did to make you trust him again?"

"Maybe another time." I shrug back, ready to play his game.

Aaron Dubois watches me like he is taking in a painting at a museum. Watching the flicks on my face. Every tiny movement. Then he does something unexpected, he relents an inch.

"Raydn has been attempting to join the team I work with here at Star for years. It was like his next obsession after he stopped slandering you on the internet. I couldn't quite pin down what it was that gave me pause on bringing him on. Maybe it was his eagerness. Possibly it was how he treated you. I hear you were friends long before you turned workplace nemesis. None of it has ever quite sat well with me. So I never let him on the team. I do not trust him. I am curious, would you like to put in a referral for him? "

I cannot make my mouth move to lie. I walk towards the sink instead. When I do not give another inch, Dubois nods at the stall behind me.

"Bad lunch or accidental love child?"

"Are you always so..."

"Intrigued? Enthralled? Curious?

"I was going to go with 'cavalier'. Maybe blunt?"

Aaron is still leaning up against the door, a smirk growing on his face. He has yet to bring up the room of secrets. He is a collector of information, and as he tilts his head at me I know he is waiting for an answer. He gave me information, it is my turn.

"I would have some doctors to sue if it was the latter."

"I see." There is a look I am not sure how to decipher on his face at that answer. I take the opportunity to watch him as I wash my hands, knowing he is pocketing that information in some box in his mind.

From here, the pictures really do not do him justice. Aaron Dubois is hardly ever photographed with others. If he is, everyone is usually sitting. You only see the top half of him. The side swooped blonde locks, dark blue eyes, chiseled chin and cheekbones. Walking side by side earlier, he has to have a solid six inches of height over me even in heels. His pointed ears are there, but just seem less vibrant than the rest of him.

"I would hope you of all people would know it is rude to stare, Ms. Chase." Dubois states so nonchalantly as if he has not been doing the same. Granted he wasn't staring at my ears.

"Can you blame me for my fascination? Seeing you in person seems incredibly different from what the public eye typically sees."

"Ah, yes, the height." Dubois takes the opportunity to come up behind me now. We watch each other in the mirror. His arms cage me in. He leaves a very precise and measured distance between us. He leans down closer so we sit cheek to cheek without any friction. Still, it causes gooseflesh to crawl down my neck. "Some say, Ms Chase, that I have giant's blood. All bullshit of course since the magic of giants has been drowned out for a millennia now."

"The height was surprising, yes. There are other things. You are also brighter in the pictures. Your hair blonder, the blue of your eyes the color of the skies. Reality gives you more darkness, brown mixed into the blonde, storm clouds mixed into the sky." Suddenly I have an urge to reach up and sift through that hair as if I could split the brown from the rest.

"Fascinating observations. No one is ever as bright as the

pictures portray. Darkness swims beneath the surface of most of us, it is just a matter of who notices. Usually those are the ones who have come to terms with their own darkness. So, *Ms Chase,* what darkness lies hidden under those cheery bright blazers you so often wear?"

A finger slowly twirls a piece of my hair, an action that probably sends most girls into a tizzy. I can definitely imagine how easy it would be to melt into the deep dulcet tones of Aaron Dubois. But what game is Dubois playing? Just like our darknesses, this game is not surface level. He stops playing with my hair. It is the only time he actually touches me, and he shocks my shoulder. If it wasn't crazy to admit, I swear I could see the electricity pass between his hand and my shoulder in the mirror.

"Nothing so interesting to even warrant conversation on it."

"You know… I find that difficult to believe. Especially based on finding you in my conference room filled with deep dark secrets. Have you asked yourself the question yet?"

"Which question?"

"How did you know I would be here? This meeting was *extremely* underwraps. Who wants you here so badly that they convinced you to risk your life's work to show up here today?"

Pulling a paper towel from the roll, I slide out from his cage of arms. "Purely coincidence. Although now you have piqued my curiosity. I will have to ask Ed to let me consult on whatever work my new department is working on. Especially since, from what I understand, you personally advocated for me to own that team anyways. Why shouldn't I know?"

Aaron is sitting up against the sink, and my comment transforms him into something truly feral. "Oh this is going to be so much fun. Find your way to me again, Summer Chase. I'll make sure you get anything you want. You won't even have to use Dune Raydn to get it."

I flip the lock on the door and with a grip on the handle I shrug and toss out, "Who knows, maybe that would finally convince me to take that trip to Arcalis."

"You'll have to tell me your actual drink of choice before you come out. Fridge will be stocked for you."

The "mission" complete, I leave the Star office without another word to either man. Dune and I need the space whether he realizes it or not.

Once home, I do the only thing to make the feeling of being trapped dissipate. I go for a nice long run.

CHAPTER 39
SUMMER

I t's been four days since my first and hopefully last interaction with Aaron Dubois. As I walk to Koda's apartment the events of the week whirl together in my mind. The kind words from Mark at Dune's office as I left. The vague words from Aaron Dubois that instill doubt and fear. The selfies Dune and I took at the bar. That feeling of sinking right into my past self as we sat there chatting with Koda. You could have overlaid that night with any other from our past and the only difference would have been our age. It had been too easy to forget everything I had done. To almost forgive everything he had done.

It is our first date night since I told Koda about my powers. The first one since our trajectory started turning, starting changing. Like any of our previous ones, we stick with pizza and a movie. Neither of us had talked about it since our night at the pond, but Koda already has the jammer I gave him enabled upon my arrival. He pulls me into him on the couch without a word like it was the most normal thing in the world. Not like we are two friends who have gone from friends, to friends-with-benefits, to friends that are somewhat really dating. All while also pretending to create a friendship with the man I always thought I would be dating. The ridiculousness of the whole thing almost makes me laugh. But I don't dare break the moment. His fingers swirl along my shoulder. The feeling blazes itself into my soul. The soft movement finds a way to calm me. It finds a way to finally allow myself a moment to relax after this week. A moment to not think about all of the potential futures that lay ahead of me.

Once the credits started rolling, Koda wordlessly takes my hand and walks me out the door. We walk in silence for the stroll to the nearby pond. The pond where I told him about my powers. It means he wants to talk about something without the possibility of Dune overhearing. I wonder if I could distract him? I could kiss him. No, I don't want to diminish our first kiss into a distraction tactic. No matter how much I want to do it anyways.

"Are you going to tell me what is wrong, Summer?"

"How could you tell?" I sigh.

Koda whips around and arches his brow. He pulls me down with him as he sits up against a tree. "How could I not? You've been my closest friend for years. I have watched you break and rebuild." He cups my cheek. "You put on a good front like nothing is wrong. You have been distant all week. The other night at the bar you loosened up a bit. But it was like as soon as you realized it, you clamped back down. So tell me. If it is Dune we can call this plan off. We will find another way."

I shudder with the thought of dumping all of these anxious feelings on him. "Dubois was at the office on Thursday." I search his face before amending. "Our office."

Shock ripples across his face before anger. "Did he approach you? We were at the bar that night. Why didn't you tell us then?"

"No, he... he did not approach me. He had someone hand deliver flowers to my desk though. They would not leave them with Jackie or the front desk. I personally had to get them."

"The lilies from Linda's place that you lugged home?"

"The very same." I thought I kept enough of my life under

wraps. For Aaron Dubois to take the time to track down my favorite flowers from my regular local shop... It leaves a lot of room for doubt. I have read his note so many times I can recite it by memory.

> INTERESTING THAT YOU KNEW ABOUT MY MEETING AT STAR. BUT I COULDN'T GET ANYONE TO LET ME NEAR YOU WHILE I WAS JUST TWO FLOORS AWAY. SO I ASK AGAIN, WHAT DOES DR WANT TO KNOW SO BAD THAT HE WOULD RISK YOUR REPUTATION TO FIND OUT? OR BETTER YET, WHO IS HE GETTING THAT INFORMATION FOR? ARE YOU SURE HE IS LOOKING OUT FOR YOU AND THE OTHERS LIKE YOU?
>
> – A.D.

"Others like you. Do you think he knows about your powers?"

"If he did I doubt I would be sitting here with you right now. What if..." My throat dries up. "What if our theory about Dune working with or for the Queen is right - but..."

"We are wrong about who the bad guy is?"

"Yeah. I just can't understand why Dubois would care that I know. Why didn't he send me straight to prison for espionage after he caught me in a room full of his secrets?"

Koda hums in thought. "The flowers weren't tapped?"

"Nope, there was nothing. I've checked all of my firewalls, there is nothing new outside of the bugs Dune planted at the beach house."

"If you get any inkling that Dune will throw you under the bus or to the pits of this country's worst nightmare - we call it. We find another way to figure it out. Maybe we even take that gamble and see if Dubois would give us any leads at that point. We aren't risking you."

My heart cracks with the extra bits I haven't told him. That bit that has now defined my life. Correction, it has defined the life I will have to live. My life is no longer my own. Not with what I know now. All I can do now is hold it off as long as I can. So I do what I have been for months and push the feeling down.

"Stay with me tonight?" I whisper.

Koda presses his lips to my fingers twined in his. "Of course."

CHAPTER 40
DUNE

Summer meets me after work today for this week's edition of fake dates. We agreed to meet around the corner from my office so people don't catch her *right* outside my building. She hasn't mentioned where we are going so I am reliant on her navigation.

I watch as she maneuvers around other pedestrians until we find a less crowded sidewalk where we can walk side by side. After the mundane questions about the day she asks, "Happen to find anything about Star's contract with Alnitak?"

I hadn't. I know enough without it, though. The program seems to be doing exactly what it intends. It is processing video and microphone footage to try to locate humans like Summer. Humans with earthly powers that the Fae could only dream of. What I still haven't quite cracked is why Ashryn is assuming the program is not working. I called her after I had gone through the footage Summer had shot and given her my recap. She simply told me to keep digging. People are disappearing across Alnitak, which all things considered would point to the program working. Something isn't adding up. Emily Turner. Emily Turner's parents conducted a press conference and implied Emily had almost been kidnapped by terrorists - not the government.

So is the program just not working faster than this terrorist group? And if not… I cannot imagine what any of our governments would do if they actually got ahold of someone with powers like Summer's. They could easily use the cover of "protecting innocents from a terrorist organization." I never breathed a word about Summer's unique abilities. Even when I was drunk and angry and spiteful in those early years. I never wanted to risk that. Whatever *that* was. That doesn't mean there hasn't been whispering.

Summer is blinking at me, waiting for my response.

"Unfortunately, no."

"Hmm," is her only response.

This walk is too quiet. Walking alongside her right now, it gives me a moment to appreciate how much I've missed her. I rub my chest without realizing it as her hair plays with the wind. A moment of our past lays itself over my eyes. *A Summer ten years younger, dancing along with her hair. One of my hands twirling her, the other on her hips to keep her going in the right direction.*

"Reading anything good?" I choke out, attempting to create a distraction for myself.

"Actually I am. It's about a werewolf shifter who mates with a human girl -"

I huff out a laugh, "Please forget I asked."

"But it is just so cute and filled with the best drama." This does actually make her spin around. I pull my phone out to snap a picture of her, hair whipping around her face from the wind more than her speed. As if she pulled the memory right from my brain, I can't help but walk up and hold her hand up for another twirl. After her third spin, I grab her hips stopping her in front of my face.

"You can spin and dance all you want, but you have to tell me where we are going first so we make it in one piece."

Summer gives me a smirk over her shoulder as we round a corner to a very familiar sight.

"Is that -"

"Bert and Rocky's. I've owed them a visit for a few weeks now. Figured if I brought you along it would serve me well."

"How so?" I try not to stutter. The well of nostalgia in this almost keels me over where I stand. Bert and Rocky's is the first place Summer and I ever visited on our own. In my eagerness, I practically asked her to come to this place every weekend for the rest of our college years. She heartily agreed. We were here every Friday night, just the two of us. Sharing ice cream, stories, and touches. It is tucked away on a corner, a small shop with a surprising amount of fortitude to still be here.

"We can get our pictures for the week. You can serve as my distraction for missing the last few of my weekly visits."

"You still come every week?" My shock must be written across my face.

"They still have flavors I haven't tried," she murmurs as we walk through the door. A small bell jingles at our entrance. A teenage human boy walks out of the back room to wait for us behind the ice cream.

The store has not changed a bit. Outside there are still a couple of benches for people to enjoy their treats when the weather is nice like today. Inside, the whole left wall is filled with stools and a small counter. The remaining two walls are filled with glass cases of treats. To even get to the buckets of daily made gallons of ice cream, you have to pass an explosion of chocolate covered snacks and candies.

Memories unbidden spill to the surface of my mind, almost if Summer had purposely planned this. These assorted baskets of chocolate covered pretzels, cookies, and marshmallow rice cakes used to sit on desks between Summer and I at work. Fall usually brought an assortment of chocolate or caramel covered apples. She nudges me by the hip as if to respond *"Yeah this was on purpose."*

"I will take a small cone of the flavor of the week." Summer tells the young cashier. He gives her a knowing look before stopping. Is this Berta and Roy's son? The small child Berta was pregnant with the first time we walked into this place? The vertigo this realization gives me distracts me from Summer giving her order.

"A cone?"

"Yup a cone."

Summer always got bowls. She would always get so nervous taking my cone for a taste of my flavor. The first time Summer ever ordered her own cone, she dropped it within five minutes. Roy refused after some time to give her cones no matter how much she argued it.

I sidle up next to her, careful to press against her slightly. I let the boy of my past out of his cage and wrap my arm around Summer. "You do *not* have to prove to me that you can hold an ice cream cone, Summer. That time has come and gone."

"What are you talking about? Of course I get cones. Waffle cones are my favorite."

I look between her and the boy behind the counter.

"Do not bullshit me. That boy looks scared shitless to hand you a cone." I look at him now to say, "I'll take the same - except a large please. Fates know I'm going to need it."

Summer guffaws and says "No! I need you to try last week's flavor and share it!"

A booming voice calls out from the back. "She is absolutely not getting a cone, son. Summer did you finally decide to -"

Roy stops in the doorway, and cocks his head at me. I hear Berta before I see her. "Did she bring him? He's a cutie." She pops her head around Roy's arm. "Dune?"

Berta and Roy walk out of the back room. It has been ten years since I last saw them. They are both in their mid-fifties now, Berta is bouncing on her toes now excited by the new visitors. Excited with an air of confusion. Her husband has to be at least a foot and a half taller than her and three times her weight, but they are a most exuberant pair of humans. Summer on the other hand goes stock still and takes the full weight of Roy's stare.

"Dune Raydn! It has been a long time." The small woman squeals.

Roy at the same time deadpans, "Back in town I see." He eyeballs the two of us. Fates above, compared to when we were shy college kids, this must be a drastic change.

I slowly peel myself off Summer to go give the small woman a hug. Roy watches the whole extraction, then keeps his gaze on Summer. It is a fatherly inquisitive gaze. Before either of them say anything to each other, Berta cannot stop squealing.

"Summer, you did not tell us Dune was back in town!" There was an edge to it that I couldn't quite put a finger on it.

"Yes, Summer, do tell." He is trying to be jovial like his wife, though the flat tone makes me wonder how much Roy knows. Is it the surface level knowledge of our fallout or the following years of antagonistic behaviors? Or does he know more than just the surface level? Apparently the owner of Bocelli's - a man who does not even know me - has all but banned me from his restaurant because of his love for Summer. It would not be too hard to imagine that Roy is at least weary of me popping back up after all this time.

"There is nothing to tell. Dune moved back. I decided to be kind and bring him back with me this week."

"Why don't you bring your friend from the farmer's market?" The memory of Koda informing me that Sunday's were off limits due to the farmer's market rings in my brain. So even after all of this time, she never brought Koda here. This stayed *our place*. An anvil sinks in my stomach.

"He - he doesn't like ice cream, Berta."

"We have other things than ice cream!" Berta scoffs.

"Koda, that is his name correct?" Summer simply nods. "Koda doesn't like ice cream, so you don't bring him here. But Dune comes back into town and now he's here." Roy huffs.

"Yes?" Summer squints and grits her teeth. Every person in this shop can tell she is not telling the truth. What that truth is though is a complete mystery.

"So which one of these cute men are you dating, Summer? I just would like to clear up all of my confusion." Berta asks.

"What?" Summer gapes. "Neither of them, Berta. I am dating neither of them. Fates above! I just wanted some ice cream."

Roy keeps a calculated eye on both of us.

"Summer, we just want you to be happy. I thought after seeing you at the farmer's market with Koda, you had finally moved on!"

Summer pinches the bridge of her nose as Berta realizes that I am in fact still standing here.

"Henry, for the love of the Fates, please make me my ice cream. In a bowl, please, since your father won't let you give me a cone."

"Summer, just date one of them! Try them out for a ride. Dune even filled out. He'd probably be a good ride. Although the other one looks spritely too."

A cacophony of "MOM!" and "BERTA!" breaks out.

In an attempt to salvage something, I stutter, "We - Summer and I - there was never…" The lie dies on my tongue. Especially when Roy lets loose with that boisterous laugh of his.

"Don't even try to pretend, Dune. We watched you two for what, eight, no, nine years. The way you watched her was like you were looking at a goddess. She was on a pedestal of unattainable heights. She would just giggle behind that ice cream cone and blush herself silly. She is already out of your league without that pedestal." Then he looks at his wife, "Don't fault the woman for moving on with her life in the way she wanted to."

Now it is my turn to gape at Roy.

"Hey, we see a lot more than either of you realize." Roy shrugs. "But to quell my dear wife's curiosity. I can tell she is itching to ask. Did you *ever* make a move after all those years, Dune?"

"Of course I fucking made - " I stop myself. This path would lead to too many questions. Questions I still have about that night that shouldn't be hashed out here. I am not sure what the point of this visit was, but surely this is not it. Roy, Berta, and Summer all have one eyebrow raised in my direction now. Summer though looks like she's seen a ghost.

I can tell Roy is about to push our buttons again. He's going to dig into that stupid statement I blurted out.

Fuck it.

Fuck Koda and telling me not to break her. *She broke me first.*

Fuck *Roy* and whatever he is trying to tell me. Taunting me with my previous failures. So I take four strides back to Summer to do something even stupider. I have one hand reaching for her elbow before her hand on my chest forcefully stops me.

"Whatever it is you are thinking of doing, Dune Raydn. You better the fuck not."

Henry, the teenage boy who has aged ten years in my absence, coughs behind Summer with her monstrosity of a bowl of ice cream.

Summer slaps down cash on the counter. "I am going to go sit outside. This should be enough to cover us both. Thank *you* for making this really fucking weird." She removes herself from my grasp, pointing a finger into my chest as she does. Then she looks at Berta and Roy. "Last time I bring you two a surprise gift." There is no malice or spite to her words. Roy chuckles as she walks out the door.

Roy pats his wife on the shoulder and follows Summer out to one of the tables. I ask Henry to scoop me out last week's flavor while I watch Roy and Summer. If you didn't know them, you might think he is her father. Not scolding her, but definitely trying to figure out what is going on.

"He cares about her. Don't mind him."

Berta leans in for another hug before moving back behind the counter. The splinter in my heart itches to ask her. "Berta, what did you mean earlier? When you said you thought she had finally moved on."

Berta chews on her lip and watches the door before shaking

her head. "No, Dune. I - I don't think that is my story to tell you." Before I can push further, she pushes the door to the back and walks away.

The sigh I let loose must have been louder than I planned because Henry speaks up as he scoops my ice cream, "Who are you?"

"You won't remember me. I used to come here with Summer. A long time ago. You were very young."

The boy, almost man, pauses scooping and squints at me. His eyes keep flicking across my face as if he is trying to place me.

"A long time ago… like ten years ago?"

"What?"

He almost stabs the ice cream for the last scoop.

"Summer is basically a big sister to me. I've known her my whole life. I guess that means I must have known you for a bit." I don't dare speak or interrupt him. "Based on the reactions from my parents, I am going to assume you are the reason she was sad for so long. She would try to hide her tears from my parents, but never from me. I think my parents knew that she just needed someone to sit with her. So they would send me out to that table there. I would sit with her as only a small little nine year boy could. And she would silently cry into her ice cream."

The temperature in the room seems to drop as Henry looks back at me with ice in his eyes. "Fates, I hope she's moved on. I hope it hurts you so much to watch her just be happy with another man. I had never seen her look so happy, so free, than that day we ran into her with Koda. I hope you realize how much you fucked up when you walked away from her."

Henry dumps my cone into a waffle bowl and extends it out to me, practically begging me to say something. The door swings open and Roy strolls back in, but halts suddenly. Looking around he sees the two of us staring at the bowl of ice cream. "I see you've put two and two together, son. Go on to the back for a minute. Calm down." Roy settles himself behind the counter and simply says, "If you break her again, I will pummel you into the ground."

I sag and nod at Roy, knowing it was time to go. I grab my ice cream and go back to Summer. She is still pinching the bridge of her nose when I get to her.

"That was a cluster. I'm sorry, Dune. I truly did not anticipate… that."

She takes a bite of her ice cream, then holds out her spoon to me.

"Ha, I am pretty sure Henry would have spit in my bowl had Roy not stomped back in. Roy seems …"

"Overprotective? Pissed off? Probably all of the above. You aren't the only one who can hold a grudge, you know."

I give her my spoon now, letting her try this cherry ice cream concoction from last week.

"Should we snag a couple pictures?" She nods and we take turns on our phones. I take a picture of her eating her flavor, then stealing my spoon again. We take a couple selfies while I do my best not to look at her. Not liking any of them, I set the phone against a napkin container on the table in front of us and set it up to snap a few timed pictures. I pull her in to my side, and we both smile, ice cream in hand. I don't show her the one that caught me staring at her again.

"Did you really never bring Koda here?"

Summer stiffens at the question but just whispers, "This was our place. It just … never felt right."

"Summer …" I have to stop, before my voice cracks. I press a finger to her chin, willing her to look at me. I need her to look at me. I need her to yell at me. I need her to rage. Anything to replace the images of her sitting here on this same bench with tears in her eyes. Tears caused by my pride, my stupidity. I need that wave of anger to flow from her, otherwise the boy that escaped his cage in me is going to revolt. He heard the words "she moved on" has been causing a hurricane in my chest ever since. I also hadn't truly comprehended what Koda had meant all those weeks ago - about holding the pieces of her together. Hearing Henry reflect on tears that impacted his own growing up. Tears that stayed with him ten years later. That is also rankling chains in my chest.

Suddenly Summer sits up, still not looking me in the eyes. "Probably for the best anyways. Berta would have been hounding me way sooner about my love life. Let's go."

I take a deep breath, trying to keep my voice steady. "Summer, please. Look at me. Talk to me. I can't... I can't change what happened. But we will never be able to move past it if we don't talk about it."

"I don't want to talk about this right now. After everything that just happened, I just... I am too emotionally raw to talk about it."

"Wasn't that your whole point in bringing us here? To break down my walls. See how I react to real nostalgia? Well congratulations. That worked!"

Summer finally glares at me. "You -"

Whatever she was going to say is lost to the wind. Sirens blare from our phones interrupting the conversation. Frowning at her phone she murmurs, "What the fuck?"

She pulls up a feed from the national news station on her phone as we walk.

Aaron Dubois takes the stage, standing behind the podium. The blue wall behind him is meant to brighten the blues of his eyes. But even the backdrop cannot hide the exhaustion written over every other part of his face.

The smile is short. His blonde hair just put together enough for appearances. The short brunette clutching a portfolio behind his right shoulder gives Aaron a once over, probably checking for wrinkles based on the rest of his appearance.

Aaron taps the mic on the podium until the *thump, thump, thump* brings the room to a silence. A few flashes snap the moment into a history page somewhere, causing a slight flinch from the man at the podium.

"Thank you all for coming today, and watching for those virtually." Looking down, Aaron adjusts the notecards on his podium before facing the crowd and continuing.

"There are two matters that require updates and therefore this press conference. First, we are continuing our search for Emily Turner. We maintain hope that Miss Turner is still alive. We do not believe she has left the region. We are taking every measure to find her. Additionally, our neighbors in Alnilam have committed resources to keep eyes open at our mutual borders. We will work together should Miss Turner be found.

"With that said, we have redirected the resources from looking for the group responsible for the building destruction in order to continue the search for Miss Turner." Muffled shock inches through the crowd in the room. "Once Miss Turner is found those resources can be redirected back. The reality is that the trail for the group has gone cold. Any surfaces that could be checked for fingerprints have been and resulted in only matching Miss Turner's. The only lead we have *is* Miss Turner. So the case is on hold until we can speak with her."

Aaron shuffles the cards in front of him again before sighing and looking back up.

"While all of this has been occurring, we contracted a private non-partisan investigation firm to review the allegations made that the government of Alnitak has been responsible for exten-sive monitoring and subsequent kidnapping of its citizens. The initial results of the probe has found no indication of any segment of the government that has even spoken ideas of this nature out loud or taken action on it. Details on the probe will be released and made available on our public website."

In a shift from slight exhaustion to protectiveness, Aaron continues, "As Governor of this great region of Elinder, I take allegations of this nature incredibly seriously. Should any group choose to flaunt their rights or abuse their privilege in this way, I assure you the full weight of the law will be used against them."

He gathers all of the note cards together, tapping them against the podium. "With that, I will turn it over to -"

Summer and I do not hear who Aaron Dubois is turning to as their screen and millions across the nation go snow gray, then black. A booming distorted voice echoes across the room.

"WE ARE INTERRUPTING THIS BROADCAST TO BRING JUSTICE FOR EMILY TURNER. YOU WILL NEVER FIND US. WE ARE TOO MANY AND IN EVERY PLACE. EMILY TURNER WAS TARGETED FOR BEING A HUMAN WITH POWERS OF THE FAE. WE WILL FIND HER BEFORE OUR GOVERNMENT. THE SEAL ON THE SCROLL OF PEACE HAS BEEN BROKEN. OUR CHOSEN ONE HAS BEEN FOUND. SHE WILL LEAD OUR PEOPLE TO A NEW FUTURE. SHE WILL CLEANSE THIS WORLD WITH HER FLAMES. THE TIME FOR HUMANS TO CREATE A THRIVING WORLD IS NOW!!!"

A white circle with the silhouette of a flame of fire flashes on to a background of black and ten seconds later flashes back to the news conference where reporters unfazed continue tossing questions out at the private investigator on the stand.

CHAPTER 41
KYRIA
DAY 0

Jackie and I are rewatching the interrupted news conference, trying to dissect the meaning of it. We know from Emily that this rebel group knows she does not have fire wielding powers. Do they know who the actual fire wielder is? Or are they just pushing Emily to truly be the face of a rebellion and fake her power? Emily's disappearance has already created a movement. Maybe they don't actually need Summer. They just need the idea of a fire wielder.

"This is random. Did we ever track down that webinar attendee - the 'Rune' alias?" I ask Jackie.

She leans back, surprised at the question. "No. We kept trying to track them after the last webinar. We just kept popping to different IP addresses. I think it eventually cycled back somehow and started over. So we stopped spending resources on it. It was a dead end."

"They dumped Summer into a server to talk to her in that last class, right? So they *wanted* to talk to her."

"I'm not sure I understand where you are going with this."

"Do you think they would talk to us if we went looking again? It's been weeks since we last tried. Maybe they would see us trying to find them again as a way to simply talk. Maybe we can do our own info finding. See if we can trick them into trusting us."

Jackie presses a kiss to my lips. "You are a genius. I am going to go ask one of the surveillance guys to start that up now."

As she stands to go to the door, she pauses. A door slamming downstairs echoes all the way to our second floor office. If the building could shiver, it would with the overwhelming presence of anger wafting from Summer. It is as if everyone could feel the moment she walked through the doors.

When she crosses the threshold for the office I can see from her face that it isn't just anger, but agony competing for space. Summer doesn't speak a word. She simply puts her phone on the desk in front of me, shrugs her backpack into place again before turning and marching back out of the room.

I place a hand on Jackie's shoulder before she can follow her. "Give her the night."

"But -"

I shuffle around one of the junk drawers for a phone charger to plug in Summer's phone. I know she wants me to leave it off, but we will need to keep an eye on who is trying to call her.

"No buts. She's angry and upset. Even if this group doesn't know that she is the fire wielder specifically, they just outed her 'chosen one' status to anyone who knows her."

"Realistically though, who wouldn't know that?"

As if hearing the question, Summer's phone starts buzzing. A picture of Koda and Summer flashes on the screen, Koda's name bold at the top.

"Oh, shit." Jackie murmurs to herself.

"Exactly. Right as she was finally letting herself love him too. Go get someone running down 'Rune' again. I'll try talking to Summer tomorrow morning.

CHAPTER 42
KYRIA
DAY 1

"Summer, please call me. Please let me know if you are okay."

"Jackie, call me. Tell me you know where she is."

"Thank you for tuning into Lyra News42 this morning! I am your host Susan Steele."

"And I am Chad Newsman. What a day we have in store for you."

"That we do, Chad! You viewers have sent us so many pictures for our Sunrise Spotlight and our Pet of the Week that we will be expanding these segments to be daily."

"Wow! And it is Motivation Monday, Susan. Our local entrepreneur Walter Strongjaw will be bringing us a story of grit and inspiration."

"That is going to be great to hear, Chad. We will also hear from our Station 194 Fire Chief as our local heroes tell us about their record number of cat rescues this year."

"What an amazing newsday we have, Susan. Shall we get this party started?"

Silence greets my knock at Summer's door. It is typically only used for changing outfits between classes or training. The door is unlocked, so I take a chance but find the room empty. Climbing the stairs, I can hear her from the moment I open the door to the top floor.

The raw screams halt me in my place. She really hadn't told Koda then. I listened to Koda's voicemail to try to understand what I am about to walk into. I don't feel too bad since he had also left one for Jackie.

Should I really go talk to her now? This feels like more of an intrusion than listening to her personal messages. There is a thumping of fists against a punching bag, echoed with her yells. She never wanted to lead. She never wanted to be alone at the top. Summer hasn't let herself realize that we will all still be there to support her.

As silently as I can, I click the door to her training room open just enough to slip inside.

"Go. Away." Summer grits out with the beat on her punches. I remember when we first met Summer, it had taken time for her to finally open up. When she did, stories of how Koda was simply there were replayed. Based on the force in those punches, I would say she is not in a broken phase yet. What could it hurt to just stay?

"I thought I would come sit in here for a bit, see if you wanted to spar."

"I. Said. Go. Away."

"I heard you. But I won't bother you."

Summer turns where she stands, about twenty feet away from me. Her eyes are not puffy, reinforcing my theory that she has not let herself break yet. I wonder how long it will take. Summer holds her hands out wide to both sides, palms up, flames rising from both.

"Are you going to spar sitting down? Let's get this over with."

I place her phone and my own in the protected cubby and start putting my hair up in a ponytail. "Should have thought of that before you came in."

Summer goes on the offense and whips fireball after fireball in my direction. I dance around the room as I get my hair up and finally able to take a stand. Jackie usually is the one to spar with Summer. I forgot how damn quick she is. A few weeks ago she had slowed it down with Emily and Teival.

I bounce around the room, watching her as I go, trying to find the best move. Then she sends three fireballs at me in quick succession. The last one skims over my right bicep. We may not be able to severely damage each other, but this doesn't stop my shirt sleeve from disintegrating or the hairs on my arm from singing off.

That's it.

I start pitching clods of dirt at her. She dodges one, then explodes the next. Dirt flies everywhere, including into her face. If I could cloud her vision long enough…

Any onlooker might think we are playing dodgeball or tossing snowballs. We keep circling each other, hurling projectiles of fire and dirt at each other. Summer only blocks a dirt clod with a fireball when she can't avoid it. After three explosions back to back I take a play out of the protestors playbook and turn my arms into confetti cannons. Confetti of petals that is. These shoot straight into Summer's face before she sends a wall of flames out as a shield.

I just need her other hand out close enough to get them at the same time. If I have to wrangle one wrist at a time this will fail. I pause my stream of petals, which also pauses her fire shield. I hit her with a large clod of dirt from one hand and a stream of dirt dust from the other.

Both of her arms are reaching out now attempting to block the attacks. I sprint to the side and send out ropes of the thickest vines I can conjure. I am able to connect to both forearms and the vines twist downwards along Summer's arms until she is flush together from elbow to wrist. Before she can attempt to burn through my hold I fling the vines up to one of the hooks in the ceiling and then back down to me. I pull hard to get Summer off the ground. She is only a few feet off the ground before she starts swinging herself to find a grip on the vine. The knot from the side really did the trick.

She lands back on the ground with a thump. Our heavy breaths echo across the training area. There is the slightest twitch of Summer's mouth as if she is trying not to smile. It truly has been a long time since we sparred one on one. As a plant wielder, my powers are typically used in conjunction with another. The dirt getting swirled into a tornado of sorts by a wind wielder, or a mud cannon by a water wielder. It is nice to see I could still *almost* best Summer on my own.

"That was fun." I say, just a second too late. The moment is lost. Summer's face hardens, reminding herself that she needs to show no emotion. If she cannot feel, she cannot hurt. If she cannot hurt, she cannot break. I take a mental note and move to the cubby to grab my things.

"Get out. Don't come back." Summer raises up a wall of fire again, using it to usher me out the door.

I am less than a third of the way down the hall when Emily emerges from the stairwell with a manilla envelope in hand.

"Hey Kyria, I hear Summer is around. Is she in her training room?"

"She is, but it is probably best if you don't go in there right now. What do you need?"

She nods, but lowers her eyes with a sigh. "Summer asked me to do some research for her before I left. It did not sound like a 'Get it done or you can't leave,' request. Though, I do imagine she would be pissed if I didn't get it done. Now that it's done, and almost delivered, I won't feel bad about bugging you. Can we talk about plans to head back to Arcalis?"

My head is swimming. Emily had been so adamant about going back, and yet hadn't pushed for details on the planning since that day. What had Summer asked her to research? Does Jackie know?

"Let's go back to my office to discuss details. We should be good for you all to start heading out in the next week or so."

"Oh good! Can I leave this folder with you in your office?"

I stare at it, wishing it would spill its contents. Summer hardly kept anything from us. If she asked Emily to research something, but didn't mention it could mean one of two things. It is either not super important to us, or it is so important that she doesn't want too many people knowing about it.

Either way, I should stay far away from that folder until we become desperate to bring our friend back from the brinks of oblivion.

"No, you should give it to her before you leave."

CHAPTER 43
JACKIE
DAY 2

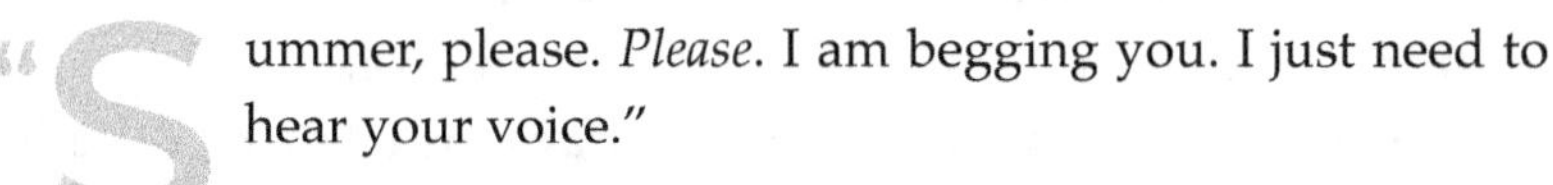

"Summer, please. *Please.* I am begging you. I just need to hear your voice."

"Jackie. Call. Me."

"Aaron Dubois keeps telling us everything is fine, nothing is wrong. But there are people destroying our buildings! Just because some humans are going missing doesn't mean they need to cause so much damage! That isn't the way to protest the government."

"I agree. Clearly if it was the government doing something wrong, they would stop this right?"

Kyria and I have been sitting at our computer for hours now. First thing this morning, I restarted our hunt for "Rune Darren". We had hoped that if we restarted the IP address jumping again that this Rune character would drop us into a chat room immediately. The computer ran all day yesterday before we killed it. Maybe it will be better to restart the process each day. Use the starting and stopping as a smoke signal to this person.

It's still visible, running on a third monitor, while we prep the final logistics for the people going back to Arcalis. Emily, it turns out, is full of surprises. Secret research and apparently secret recruitment. After weeks of silence from Emily she finally starts asking about the plans. The original caravan is being drastically upgraded. We initially thought the plan needed to account for twenty-five people. She informs us that she has over a hundred people that have volunteered to go. I don't even know how she got the word out to that many people.

The best place to house them all is going to be our warehouse that Emily's friend is currently staying in. It will look suspicious as hell if there are a hundred or so people coming out of that building on any given protest day, though.

Emily, Teival and ten others are going to leave next week. All of them have very specific tasks and duties once they get there - like starting to clean up and re-open the old unused safe houses. Sarah doesn't know any of us so Emily and Teival have to go, despite my own concerns about it. We do not know the status of her phones so we don't want to risk any digital communications to tell her we are coming. We thought about logging into her social media account again and messaging her from that, but the risk is too high. Who knows if she would even believe the words came from Emily or us.

Once we have details from that team, we will start sending

more caravans of humans there. Luckily Emily gave us a prioritized list of those looking to leave. Some people do have lives here that they need to put in order.

I scrub at my eyes with the heels of my hand as Kyria walks back in from getting coffee and a snack.

"Get out of here."

"I can't -"

"I'll watch the computer scrolling through IP addresses," she interrupts, knowing my excuse. "Go spar with Summer for a bit. It will get you moving, probably get your blood boiling."

Kyria gives me a light kiss on the forehead before shoving me out of my chair and then the door. After changing outfits, I hesitate outside of Summer's door. We've been friends for almost ten years and we've never experienced anything like this. I don't know what she needs in this moment, and she is very unwilling to tell us.

Taking a deep breath, I open the door. Immediately, I am greeted with a fireball exploding on the wall to my left.

"I told Kyria yesterday. Get out. I don't want to talk."

"Good. Neither do I. I just want to spar."

"No." Summer turns back to her punching bag. I look around the room, remnants of another punching bag sit on the floor below the new one. Some of the props around the room look singed. Others are dust on the floor. Many still are untouched. I make a mental tally of things I should rush order for her. The longer I can keep her distracted here, at least she is here. Not making drastic decisions that she may come to regret.

"Come on. I've been staring at a computer all day and just need to get my blood pumping."

Summer stills at my words for just a moment before returning her attention to the punching bag. Fuck it.

I conjure up some wind to pick up remnants of one of the scarecrows and sling it at her back. I can almost hear her angry breathing over my current, but she still doesn't turn around. I keep a river of air swarming around the training room. It picks up every small piece of destroyed targets and pummels them at her back. She wants to ignore me? Fine. I am just going to be her biggest nuisance. Wind currents are circling in two directions. One to scoop up debris at her feet, one to take that debris and fling it right back to her again.

Finally, I have pissed her off enough to get a reaction. "Shit," I have to jump out of the way as a pillar of fire shoots directly at me. I hold a wall of wind in front of me when Summer follows me, but she gives no pause in the steady stream of heat pouring out of her. I shuffle, one step at a time as I keep watch for any hint that this stream may slow down. Her fire is so powerful it is starting to climb *over* the wall of air protecting me. My visibility is slowly being crowded by a wall of orange and red. For her to be able to pull this much of her power after two days straight… She is letting her anger consume her.

Out of the corner of my eye I spy a small box. I use my right hand to build up enough air to lift it up. I keep it on the air current until it has had enough momentum to become a projectile. Summer sees it hurling at her just in time to spin a fireball at it, turning it to ash before it can reach her.

I start gathering more lighter weight props into a fast moving river of air to create a continuous cannon of objects. After destroying a pile of green army men figurines, five aluminum pie tins, and a scarecrow, Summer finally called back her fire.

She said nothing except, "I expect you to get replacements for my target practice," before turning back around to the punching bag.

CHAPTER 44
JACKIE
DAY 3

"This isn't the Summer I know. The Summer I know doesn't run from something that scares her. She stands up. She fights. Stop running! Tell me where I can find you."

"Fuck you too, Jackie."

"Hey Summer, it's Dune. I don't know why I thought you might answer my call. I saw Koda this morning, he said you were fine. But I could tell he was lying. Is this about that terrorist group? I can't – nevermind. Can you just let either of us know you are okay? Will you be back before we are supposed to have dinner next week? "

"Why can't they just protest in a less violent way? It is just going to hit the taxpayers when the city needs to replace all those cameras they are smashing."

"Ugh - and the *street cleaning*. They are leaving confetti and flower petals *everywhere*. And the street cleaners have to come out more often. I can't even park on the streets most days."

I trudge up the steps to the top floor for the second time today. Last night, we had one of the guys go to the local shooting range and department stores to pick up random things for target practice. You can get paper targets and silicone men from the shooting range, but nothing creates more joy than watching someone take out green army men one by one from across a room. We also get a variety of clay disks, tin pans, and cheap stuffed animals from five dollar bins. Usually we do an online order to avoid any recognition but we don't want to risk Summer running out of things to destroy. The supplies dropped off early this morning.

It seems she accepted those gifts. Not only do I see the pile of goodies gone, but Emily is standing in my path to Summer's door.

"Are you looking for me or for Summer?"

"Summer."

We stare at the heavy, metal door to our side. At least the screaming seemed to have stopped today.

"But you were waiting on me?"

"You know her better than I do. And..."

I take a guess. "Whatever it is she asked you to give her... you are not sure if you should give it to her in this state?"

Emily nods her head with a breath of relief.

"I am not going to ask you what it is. If it were you, in this current state of mind - would you do something rash with this information and regret it later?"

"Absolutely."

"Then wait. Please." I try not to beg her.

"What if she isn't ready for the information before I leave in five days?"

I look between her and the door. "I will make her break before then, or I will give it to her myself next week."

"What makes you so confident that she will come out of this?"

I don't have an answer. She is clearly in agony that this choice has been taken away from her. No one has come knocking on our doors, so I don't think anyone outside of these walls truly knows *she* is the fire wielder. She was finally starting to open up about her powers to others, but not the chosen one status. Her ability to be unique but not alone has been stripped away. Now anyone who knows her powers will know this status.

All I know is she cannot let her soul harden. She deserves to share her emotions with others. If it takes the next two weeks before FaeCon to break her, then so be it.

"I have to hope."

Emily simply nods and walks away. I wait until she crosses the threshold to the stairway before I head into Summer's training room. After yesterday's immediate offensive attack, I spread a wind layer between me and the room. I don't feel like losing my hair today.

Summer glances my way before turning to a militia of army men spread across one half of the room. I drop my barrier as I watch bolts of fire ping through the figurines. Summer takes each one out with precision. Even though these are two inch models, each hit intentionally hits a specific mark. Headshot to the marked general. Taking out the plastic weapons on clusters of them.

It is as if she is building a scenario from her own mind. Which is when I notice that the army men were not just randomly scattered across the room. There are chalk boundaries around each grouping. She really is creating battles in her head.

"What did Emily want?" Summer asks, pulling me from my thoughts.

"To see you, but I told her to wait."

Summer chuffs out a laugh. "Didn't want her to see *the chosen one* in such a state, eh?"

"No, she's idolized you before she ever knew you were the fire wielder. I didn't want you to regret anything you might say to her."

"And yet you still come to see me." She sends what could be called a waterfall of fire down on a figurine near the front of the pack.

"I've known you much longer than her. And have much tougher skin to deal with you right now." I move a row of figurines closer with a stream of air pushing them. Summer glares at the movement and then me. "I was also hoping to clear out some of your voicemails. You have about ten from Koda so far." Summer's face flinches at the sound of his name.

"I have gotten four. You also have one from Dune today. Which is why I think it is time to start clearing them out."

"I don't want to hear them." Summer grits out.

I move another row of army figurines as I say, "They deserve to be heard."

"Stop moving shit!"

"What? They are going to move in real life, not just stand there waiting."

"Are you sure about that?" She asks with a glint in her eye. It's then that I smell the burning rubber. A normal human would have noticed the heat licking the soles of their feet. In my distracted state I assumed it was just nerves. No. Summer had created a river of fire that started behind me and had been slowly creeping toward me ever since.

"Fuck," I grunt as I pull up my pant legs before turning to leave the room. I can't help but turn and watch as every single army man melts from the bottom up as Summer's river of fire engulfs them all.

CHAPTER 45
RUNE DARREN
DAY 4

Five days ago, I lost eyes on Summer Chase. I watched Summer go to a lovely ice cream shop with Dune. She returned to her apartment in a hurry. She never left, at least not where cameras would pick her up. Looking at the blueprints of the building, there are fire escapes around the perimeter. Conveniently, the one that would be closest to Summer's place is the only one without a camera pointed in its direction.

We have kept surveillance on Koda and Dune instead. Some people have a theory that she is just holed up in her apartment. It is a valid theory. No one has seen her leave. Koda has a key and access to the building. My theory is that he simply wants to make sure he is there if or when she does return. He has the look of a man trying to hold it together. The bags under his eyes can be seen through cameras a street away. If Summer was hiding in her apartment, Koda's demeanor would be more protective rather than the look of almost losing it.

For someone that he hadn't seen in ten years, Dune also seems worried. A little on edge, but worried all the same. He posted his pictures with Summer at the ice cream parlor that same night. He may not have even realized she had already disappeared by that point.

Even I have had to mask my concern. I am the only one of our group that has had a slight obsession with Summer Chase for years. This does not match her normal ways of tackling issues. Half of the people I interact with don't know I even keep tabs on Summer.

The other half just think it's a weird crush. That word obsession gets thrown around. So no one in my life is bothered by the fact that Summer is missing. I cannot help but feel responsible for this disappearance. So when I am not at my main office, or my second office, I am here at home, scanning troves of surveillance flags trying to see if any of them are actually Summer. There are *a lot* of people walking the streets of Lyra that look like Summer.

My third monitor glares at me. I sip on my fifth cup of coffee for the day as I decide my next course of action. Three days ago someone started trying to track our IP addresses again. With my current sleep schedule being overrun by searches for Summer, I was the first to see this notification in the dark of night. I suppressed the notifications so I am the only one that has seen it. The program has been doing what it was intended to do - loop and redirect, loop and redirect.

The callers on the other end have not stopped. It cannot be a coincidence that a day after Summer disappeared, this search started again. Do they suspect us of foul play? Or do they understand that we were responsible for Emily Turner's disappearance, raising her up as the face of a rebellion?

I thread my hands through my blonde hair before making the decision to talk to them. Maybe it is Summer trying to find a way to talk. I dump them into a virtual machine and make the first move.

>> **Meeting you was everything I thought it would be.**

Surely that by itself would be enough to tell her who I am

right? Shit, what if it does and she kills the connection based on my public persona? I would.

The minutes I wait for a response feels like eons. This was a mistake. I start pacing the room wishing I could take it back. Finally the screen moves out of the corner of my eye with a response. I rush back to my chair attempting to not fall while finding my seat.

>> Unknown: We've met?

>> Are you Summer?

>> Unknown: Yes.

The answer came back too quickly.

>> Then you did what I asked. You found me.

>> But it doesn't sound like you know that yet.

>> Why did you come back looking for me?

>> Unknown: I want to know about the rebel cause. How you are doing it all.

>> I can't tell you any of that without you coming to Arcalis. I have a refrigerator full of cherry sodas with your name on it.

>>Unknown: Weird, but okay.

>>Unknown: Emily Turner ran from something. Was that you?

Okay this is definitely not Summer then.

>> Unfortunately yes.

>> Unknown: How do you know she is the fire wielder? You claim she is your chosen one, how do you know?

This is… an interesting line of questioning. Perhaps she is just trying to see how much I really know.

>> As claimed, she burned a building down as she left it, leaving us to deal with it.

>>Unknown: That didn't answer the question.

>>Unknown: I would like to work together.

>> Unknown: But I need to trust you.

>> And I need to trust you. Where is Summer?

>>Unknown: She's … fuck. She isn't here.

>> Unknown: I would like to send a… let's say an ambassador of sorts. To Arcalis. Can we have them meet you? Or your own ambassador?

>> Only if I can speak to Summer first.

>> Unknown: How can she reach you?

>> She found me last time. I will find her this time.

>> I will dump you out of this server in twelve hours. Copy this transcript. Give it to Summer when you see her.

CHAPTER 46
JACKIE
DAY 5

"If you aren't listening to my voicemails, I have to guess this could be one of my last messages before your box gets full. I am so fucking mad at you. But I miss you so much. I miss that smirk you give me over your shoulder as we run. I miss going to get coffee together in the mornings. Kristyn is also worried about you, by the way. I've been reading your gross ass monster romances. And yes, I took note of your annotations. Please call me back. Please let me know you are okay. Please let me know where I can find you. I will keep texting you every day."

"Welcome back to today's panel on recent events and news. If you are just joining us, we have been discussing the recent protests happening across the city everyday. Why do we think Governor Dubois is doing nothing to stop this reckless behavior?"

"I think the better question is why is Queen Ashryn

suppressing the coverage? These protests aren't new. They've been happening since Emily Turner disappeared. You want to tell me that suddenly they've started flaring up? The reality is we are finally starting to report on them. Why aren't these conversations happening on national news? Why is this coverage not making it out of Arcalis?"

When I am not trying to convince Summer to talk, I am scouring through the news. Emily has been logging into her friend's social media account to watch the footage of protests. The news coverage is spread far and wide. We are still trying to figure out if we are missing news coverage internationally. So far everyone outside of Arcalis seems … unaware of what is happening in the city. There has not been any mention of humans with supernatural or Fae like powers either. We still haven't pinpointed where the gap in coverage is coming from. Content and coverage does seem blissfully ignorant unless you know exactly where to look.

The conversation with Rune Darren yesterday was a bust. After the initial excitement of them finally "picking up the phone", it devolved. If she has met this person before, they found out we weren't Summer by some weird clue in the conversation. They did not confirm if they know *she* is the fire wielder, though. I printed out the transcript to see Summer's reaction. The cherry soda comment claws at my mind, but Summer doesn't even drink sodas.

I check with the surveillance guy who is trailing Koda. Every day, the pictures come back worse. He leaves Summer's flat. Goes to Starstruck. Goes to Work. Goes back to Summer's flat. Each day, the bags under his eyes are darker. His hair is a little less tidy. Today, he is just standing outside of the office, staring at the sky. His eyes are pleading with whatever Fate he sees above.

Having put it off as long as I can, I head to the top floor to try once again to get Summer to talk to me.

Summer's responses have escalated whenever someone enters that Fates forsaken room. Every day, we try to talk to her. We try to make her see reason. To stop pushing us away. Every day she throws one of those crazy fire skills back.

When she did not immediately launch an attack, yesterday, I tried a new tactic. "It is time for you to hear your voicemails."

Koda's voice echoes across the room. "Summer, please call me. Please let me know if you are okay."

"Summer, please. Please. I am begging you. I just need to hear your voice."

Summer's face hardens at the voice. I don't think I have gone too far... yet. The third voicemail begins but it is overrun with Summer's screams.

"When will you all stop coming back?" Then with hands lifted to the ceiling, fire licks the air above us and starts loosing droplets of fire on top of me. I cocoon myself in a ball of wind. Protected, but it is a nuisance. I can even see her flinching as drops bounce off my protective bubble, ping ponging around the room. Then I see her clawing at the air harder. I don't quite understand until a lick of fire falls into my wind, streaking around me now. More and more fire drops poke into the barrier and I can no longer see the rest of the room clearly.

I backed up the way I came in and pushed the fiery wind to the floor as I left.

"And don't come back!"

I take two breaths before stomping into Summer's pit now.

"What, no protective barrier today?" Summer remarks without even looking over her shoulder.

I shoot wind to pull her back by the hair to face me. "You can talk shit to my face, Summer. You want to fight it out? Let's do it."

"Why not make it a fair fight and bring in Kyria, too?"

"No, we are going to get this out. You and me. You have already hurt my wife enough with this tantrum you are throwing." I wave my fingers between us to make a point while releasing my grip on her hair.

Summer's fists light up. "Tantrum? TANTRUM?!"

Her right hand flings out to her side before swinging back in. The warmth of a spritz of fire blows past my back. I momentarily regret working with her on keeping that sort of directional control. It takes all of my concentration to watch where her attacks are going to land from. The sheer concentration it takes removes my ability to form words to react.

"You want to call this a tantrum? Of course you both do. You have wanted me to lead. To *be more*." Spite coats her words. "I am sure you both couldn't be happier about the fact that I am actually the chosen one. That you groomed me into the monster that I am going to have to be. You may have let me train with anonymity. But you have been waiting for this. Waiting for my life to fall apart."

An arrow of fire hits me square in the back as my defenses drop at her words. Could she actually believe we wanted this for her? Does she not know that we only want what is best for her? Another flame hits me on the left side, recentering my focus on her fire.

I throw a wall of air pushing her into the wall. "You think I chose to be your friend to groom you? Do you really think we see you as a monster?"

Summer's arms are flames as she pushes herself through my wall of air to lunge at me. Splaying her hands around the room. "If you didn't think I was a monster, Kyria would be here at your side." Embers of flames climb up the wall surrounding us.

"I have *tried* being just and fair to everyone. To be a better person than those that would want me dead. That has only led to people being captured or worse killed. This 'chosen one' nonsense. I am going to have to be ruthless. Whoever this enemy is will not give a shit about taking someone I love to get to me. Maybe it's Andre, first. Or Henry or Berta. But what if it's you?

What if it's Koda? *I couldn't live with myself if something happened to you. Any of you.*"

"So what is the answer? Do you become a lone ranger? Do you shut down so much that you no longer care?"

"It didn't take much for people to nickname me an ice queen. I can't imagine it would take much for people to believe I am actually cold and dead on the inside."

"That's a bunch of bullshit, Summer. What about those of us that know you? That will follow you, support you…Oh."

Once again, I fall distracted by her words. I am surrounded by dozens of flaming arrows pointed in my direction. "That's new."

Summer stays still as a statue. The flames inching closer.

"Is this the plan then? Push away every person that cares about you, that fights for you until it is only you left? Then do it. Show me that the mask is fully glued on now." I raise my hands in the air, summoning the blows.

I wait a few moments before turning and walking out of the room. A single arrow hits the wall to my right as I shut the door.

CHAPTER 47
JACKIE
DAY 6

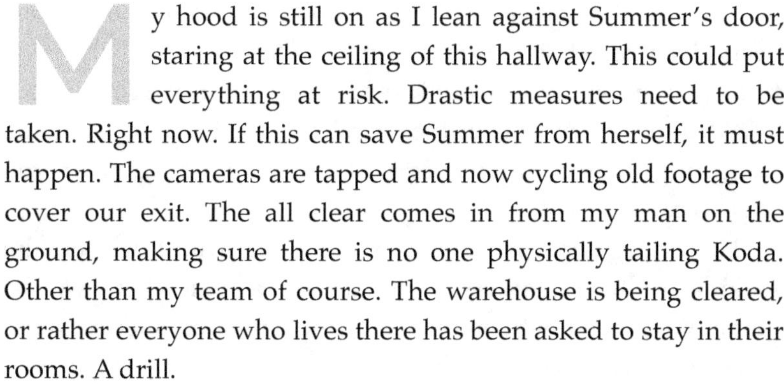

My hood is still on as I lean against Summer's door, staring at the ceiling of this hallway. This could put everything at risk. Drastic measures need to be taken. Right now. If this can save Summer from herself, it must happen. The cameras are tapped and now cycling old footage to cover our exit. The all clear comes in from my man on the ground, making sure there is no one physically tailing Koda. Other than my team of course. The warehouse is being cleared, or rather everyone who lives there has been asked to stay in their rooms. A drill.

I sigh before slipping the key into the lock. When the door opens, Koda is scrambling across the room. Seeing me, instead of Summer, makes him crumble. He is on his knees in gray sweats and a very wrinkly black t-shirt. The bags under his eyes are so much worse in person.

"Where is she, Jackie?! Where is she?!"

Koda's voice cracks as the tears start to flow. With it, my own heart also cracks. It's been six days. I, at least, have known Summer is safe. That she is okay. Koda has had six days of silence. Dropping to my knees in front of him, my tears greet his own.

Quietly I tell him, "I am going to take you to her. I am so sorry it took me this long." Koda chokes on a sob as I take his hand. "She's trying to push away everyone that loves her. We need her to break. You need to be there when she does. I won't lie to you and say that she is going to welcome you with open arms."

He bows his head to our hands that are trembling.

"Can I… have a moment to pull myself together?"

"Take fifteen. You need a shower." I lift him up and give him the lightest push towards the bathroom.

Fifteen minutes later, I adjust the beanie and hood on Koda before we leave Summer's apartment. As we start meandering the streets, I take Koda's arm. In an effort, I assume, to not break down, his hands start to tremble again.

"I am really sorry, Koda." I barely whisper. "You should have been given the choice to talk to her. Instead I stole that option from you, hoping you would understand when we finally told you. I didn't want you in the literal line of fire and her doing something she would later regret. I still should have given you the choice."

He simply nods. We continue along our path. I can see him looking at street markers, trying to figure out where we are going. When we finally make it to our destination, I let us in but pause just inside. The door locked, Kyria greets us quickly before telling us she will inform security. They need to kill the surveillance loops.

"There is one more thing I should have told you sooner." I step between Koda and the stairs that will lead us to Summer. "Kyria and I met Summer because of all of our abilities. We had been trying to find others like us."

Koda's face hardens momentarily, but then seems to understand. "It isn't fully her secret to tell. I understand why she didn't say anything at the time. Are you truly like Summer then?"

Treading lightly, I guess that he is trying to gauge how many other secrets Summer has been keeping. He just barely got the tip of the iceberg - it is a large tip certainly - but it is one of many he has been kept unaware of. "I have the power to wield air." I answer cautiously. "Kyria has the power to wield um… earth. Wow, I have never had to phrase it that way before." I let out a small chuckle.

Koda arches an eyebrow at me. "Vines, plants, dirt, you name it."

"But fire?" His face is filled with distraught hope. Hope that the secrets did not go that deep.

"We have always kept up the hope that we would find another fire wielder. In ten years we haven't found one." I take his arm back in mine to walk him up the stairs. I am not sure if his stony silence will be what she needs or not. We need her back, though. So I push.

"I have an idea why she did not tell you. But that is not my story to tell. I know she had her reasons, even if it was more to protect herself. Hopefully you can get her to talk. You can stay here or keep coming back until we can get her to come out."

He simply nods. When we emerge on the fourth floor, we are both surprised to hear the click of a door at the end of the hall. Koda seemed ready to jolt straight down the hall but we are met with Emily Turner's blonde hair instead of Summer's caramel.

"You are supposed to be in your room!" Kyria scolds her before Koda audibly gasps.

"Fuck," is all I can get out before Koda turns to me, anger seething out of his pores. Before I can stop him, he marches down the hall to the door that will take him to Summer. He grips the handle before turning to me, silently confirming it is okay to go in. "Be on your toes. She has not hesitated to throw fireballs at the door without looking."

He nods before pulling the door open and disappearing behind it.

"Wait, no. No, no, no, no. Do not send him in there." Emily is visibly nervous. "Go get him! NOW!"

Kyria scrunches her face, "Why?"

"I just… shit." Emily looks at the door, shakes her head as she sprints out of the hall. Kyria and I go to the surveillance room on this floor to make sure we can pull the sprinkler system at a moment's notice.

CHAPTER 48
SUMMER

Emily's research results are better than I expected them to be. When I tasked her to track this down a few weeks ago, there was a part of me that thought it would be impossible. She would give it a shot, come up empty, and then wave goodbye as she left for Arcalis. Instead, she kept her word, found an answer, and did not tell another soul about this either.

I have my answer. I know what it could cost me if we are wrong. Am I willing to follow through on it?

The door behind me clicks open. The tightness in my chest loosens. Every day, Jackie and Kyria try to pull me out of my anger. This spiral. Every day I curse my decision to not have an extra house that no one knew about. Up until the last few weeks, I imagined if I needed to leave, my friends would have been by my side. I was not prepared to leave and land somewhere they wouldn't find me. Every safe house we own would have had the camera tapped to find me the moment I didn't show up here.

Jackie wasn't totally wrong that I have essentially been throwing a tantrum. The world is expecting a fire wielding leader. I cannot let my friends follow me into whatever hells await me because of that. I have caused so much pain already and I am not even leading anything. I was only trying to help them.

So every time my friends come to reason with me, to calm me, to pull me back, I push. I throw fire at them, knowing it won't hurt them, but it will certainly inconvenience them. And no matter how hard I fight, they keep fighting to get to me. Why can't they just let me go? Why can't they let me do this without endangering them? With the knowledge I have now, it will be so much easier if they would just stop.

I sling a fireball towards the door without looking behind me. My body stills when I realize the fire exploded on the wall behind me. Not to either side wall. There was no burst of wind to move it out of their path.

It has only been six days.

They stopped fighting.

My eyes start to water.

This is what I want. I have to keep telling myself this. This mantra does not stop the tears from forming. I may as well get used to being cold. Nine years of friendship, and it took less than a week to stop fighting. They've stopped fighting for it. For me. How could I expect anything more? Dune wiped nine years of friendship away in a night. I want to be surprised they lasted this long. The only person who ever stayed -

No. Do not think about him.

The ice cracked with the thought. I can't even form his name. He will shatter me. He doesn't even know where I am. If I am going to have a clean break it has to stay this way.

The footsteps are getting closer, I close my eyes. I wish I had that preternatural ability to tell who it was by their gait, but I don't. I just need to give the final blow. Then I can leave. Figure out this chosen one shit without anyone following. Without me putting any of them into harm's way.

I turn, my hand readying to land my final fiery blow. But the glacier forming on my soul cracks, and the flame on my fist winks out as Koda catches it.

"I would rather you not, please." Koda says gruffly, like I didn't just shoot a fireball *at* him. Every single flame in the room is doused as Koda and I stare at each other. The momentary flash of horror transforms into anger.

They hadn't given up, yet.

No. Jackie and Kyria just brought in the person that could slice through the wall I've been building. They risked all of our secrets, our building location, everything... to bring me back. But to put him at so much risk. If anyone knew how much he meant to me, and now how much he knows... I yank my fist out from his hand.

The embers around the room start to spark again.

How *dare* they put him at risk? How dare *he* put himself at risk?

How dare they take away my need to leave without this goodbye? That primal part of me that deep down knew Koda would never let me leave without a fight. He didn't ten years ago. He isn't going to now. I do not want to fight him. I do not want to lace my words with lies to get him to let me go.

I push at his shoulders. Hard. "Get the fuck out, Koda."

"Oh is this how we are going to do this?" He meets me at eye level and gives me a light shove of the shoulders back. "You throw a fucking fireball at me, then shove me out the door?"

I pause, which is a mistake. Koda takes a couple steps around me, blocking me from being able to simply push him back out through the door.

"I don't want you here!" I scream.

"Ah so we are just going to yell while circling around each other." Koda isn't smirking like he normally would. He almost looks... angry. He's never been angry with me before. Good. Anger I can work with.

I shove him again, trapping him against the wall. "I cannot believe Jackie wouldn't let Kyria near me. I've become so much of a monster to her that she won't let her wife in. But *you?!* I could destroy you with a thought, Koda. I cannot *believe* you would agree to come in here."

"Then show me, Summer! You already threw a ball of fire at me. Show me! Do it, Summer!" He taunts.

I shove him again while my flames creep to the ceiling out of the scatter pile of ash and punching bag carcasses. "Why can't you all just leave me alone? Let me leave?!"

Koda grabs my arms, shaking me. "When are you going to realize Summer? You are fucking stuck with me."

"No!" This time I put a little more strength into the next shove.

"No?! Who said you had a choice in that?" Koda grips my arm again as he gets in my face to yell right back at me.

"Me, Koda! I get that choice!" I pound my fists against his chest.

Suddenly, Koda spins us, pinning me to the spot he was just in.

"And what, Summer? Are you just going to punch all of your friends until they leave you? Throw your rage and fear at them until you are left alone? Is that what you want? Don't you remember we have done this song and dance before? It didn't work then. It. Isn't. Going. To. Work. Now."

"I don't want to hurt you!" I choke back my tears as I scream in his face. "I don't want to hurt you. I don't want someone else knowing how much you mean to me and them hurting you to get to me!"

"Look at me, Summer. You already hurt me." He pauses and I can see the tears starting to spring from his own eyes. He grasps my cheek with one hand. "I've been worried fucking sick trying to find you. Trying to figure out where you would be. But you are too fucking good at hiding. You hurt me. By running. By not coming to me. By not bringing me with you. Tell me you don't want me around. Tell me you don't want *me*. But don't fucking lie to me. Don't tell me you don't want to hurt me. You can keep trying to convince me to leave you. Sling your pain at me. I. Am. Still. Here. I will keep coming back no matter how much you hurt me."

I feel the tremble of my lower lip, the tears now streaming silently down my face as I take him in. Despite the freshly clean smell and damp hair, he looks tired. He has dark bags under his eyes. Those bags barely cover how puffy his eyes are. His clothes are wrinkly. I did this to him. That was my fault. No one else's fault. Mine.

The wall finally disintegrates in me. Koda catches me as I try to crumble to the floor along with it. He has smothered me in a hug as my sob escapes my soul.

Koda's hand is tangled in my hair, but he pulls back just enough to look at me. "I want to know everything. I need you to tell me. First I need to tell you this." He scans my face. "I thought I lost you. I thought you had left. That you left me behind. I've been going out of my mind trying to act like everything was fine. I seriously expected Jackie to show up at work on Monday with a resignation letter." He pauses and takes a deep breath.

"You are my best friend. You are my *everything*. I should have realized it months ago, years ago. I was trying to sort through my feelings, but couldn't stand the thought of missing the farmers market, or coffee, or date night. Even our morning runs. And now… Now I just know if you leave, whether it is to start a rebellion or to hide in an underground bunker, I am coming with you. I'll make myself worthy of you in any and every way you need. You are stuck with me until the day I leave this world. If you leave it before me I will hunt down your soul because I won't believe it."

He swipes a thumb at the tears now freely falling down my cheek. "I promised myself ten years ago that I would never be the reason you cried." Leaning his forehead against mine, he whispers, "I should have done this the day you showed up to my room needing comfort eight years ago. And every day since.

Thank you for waiting for me. Please, please don't leave me again."

Before I can find a response, Koda has leaned us back into the wall, his lips brushing against mine. This building could be lit up and I would only notice the feel of Koda's lips against mine. He is soft, tentative at first. It is as if he is waiting for me to truly give in. To really show him that I feel the same. I wrap my arms around him, pulling him closer. There is a hint of a growl, as Koda lifts me up, wrapping my legs around him. Still pinned to the wall, we explore each other with our tongues. Tasting, feeling. Every fear, every worry is wiped away. Twenty years of friendship, and finally, *finally*, I can know that taste of his lips on my own.

This is the happiness I stole from myself for years.

His hands cup my face, my tears of joy meeting his thumb. "You are perfect, and I am so grateful you are mine." He smirks as I scoff and push his arm. He just swipes his thumb over my cheek, removing my tears. "No? Not the right time? You'll get there eventually." He pulls me back in for another kiss while pulling us away from the wall. "Now direct me to your room, woman."

CHAPTER 49
SUMMER

Kyria and Jackie walk out of the room down the hall. They must have been monitoring to make sure I did not actually hurt Koda. *Fuck.* I had been so close. After the information Emily brought me I was ready to really hurt someone. Cut ties and leave. Deep down I knew I wouldn't have brought real harm to either Jackie or Kyria. *But Koda?* An *accident* left me unable to forgive myself for years. How much would I have punished myself if I had landed that hit on Koda? I shiver at the thought. Koda's hand on my waist grips me tighter. Jackie opens her mouth, but Koda simply says, "No."

"Go down the stairs one floor. My room is all the way at the other end from the stairs on the left." I murmur against his lips. He groans and tugs me by hair back to fully pressing his lips into mine. Once we enter the staircase, Koda pushes my back up to the entryway door. His kisses turn from exploratory to something more. Hungry. Angry. He is consuming me from the inside out. I grind him the best I can pinned to the door. His sweat pants are doing nothing to hide his erection.

"*Fuck.*" His voice is gravelly. "I don't know how to stop." He presses his lips to mine again before quickly turning us away from the door. He keeps one hand on my ass, the other on the railing as he attempts to get down the stairs quickly.

Out of the stairs, Koda's hand grips the side of my neck as he commands, "Key. Now." Somehow I pull the key out of my front pocket and hand it to him as he is marching us down the hall. He pins me against the inside of my door the moment we cross the threshold.

"I want to keep kissing you. Fates knows I want to fuck you slowly, drawing out your pleasure while I get to taste your lips on mine." Koda grips my hair, not letting me roll my head back with the thought of that. "But I am still so mad at you. I need to fuck you. Hard. Make sure you don't forget the pain I went through." I can only nod. "And don't be a brat and do this again for the fucking. You have me, anytime, anywhere, however you want."

I can't help but smile and he grips my chin hard. "Even the chosen one needs someone to keep her grounded." He drops me out of his arms and takes two steps back, looking around the room. "Now strip."

I do as he demands, the leggings, tanktop and sports bra shed quickly. His hands are trembling. I know I fucked up trying to disappear without telling him. I could quietly submit to whatever he needs to do to get this out of his system. That just isn't my style. He needs me to still give him some bite. "How are you going to fuck me with all those clothes on?"

He smirks, and instead of lunging at me like I expect, he walks over to my bathroom door. My mouth goes dry as he pulls my robe tie out of its loops. Striding back to me, he wraps the silk around his right hand. My eyes on the motion, he's on me before I can take a step back. He devours me as he pushes me back towards my bed. Tracing his fingers across my mouth he whispers against them, "You kept your mouth shut for almost a week. Now the only noise I want coming out of your mouth is the sound of you choking on my cock." He lightly pushes me down to the bed. My hands gravitate to his pants but he grunts a

"No." Turning me around, he lays me across the bed, my head hanging off the end.

I watch as he does that sexy one handed shirt pull over his head before dropping his sweats and black boxer briefs to the floor. He steps back to me. "Open that pretty little mouth for me, love."

I do as he asks and he slides his hard cock across my tongue. He gives me a few shallow thrusts. He groans as he finally pushes further, my throat opening for him. My back arches off the bed as he finds a rhythm, taking his pleasure. I'm losing myself to the ecstasy of it, when he spits on my entrance from above me. Koda hooks two fingers into me, drawing out a moan.

"Fuck, baby. I want you moaning on my cock every day. You don't get to disappear again. This mouth -" He thrusts for emphasis. "This mouth is mine. This pussy is mine. You go out there. Save the fucking world. People may think your powers belong to the world. But you - you belong with me. I will drag you back to me every single time the world tries to take you away. Every time you try to run."

His words and his fingers build towards my climax. I am just barely aware enough to keep my fire tamped down. His fingers are continuing their rhythm with his hips. I let myself sink into the feeling of him, ready to find my release. His fingers and his dick stop moving. I whimper around him, squirming on his fingers. He pulls his fingers out and I can feel him leaning over me. His breath skitters across every nerve, lighting them up without letting them blow.

It could have been a few seconds or a few eons, Koda hovering over my clit with me wrestling for his touch under him. He chuckles before pressing a light kiss to that bundle, already knowing that I have another mountain to climb before I find my orgasm.

"Remember how you left me … no note… no phone call… no text?" He says, his lips teasing mine. I can only whine around his cock still in my mouth.

"How many days did you leave me for?" He pulls himself out for my answer.

Trembling at the thought of where this is going, "S-six."

Grunting, Koda slips himself back into my mouth, all the way to the base. "Six. Consider that your payment for day one."

He starts thrusting again as the reality of what he just said hits. One orgasm denied for every day I was gone. My mind and my body are already warring with each other as my fire is filling my veins again. My body must go tense with my focus on draining the fire because Koda's tongue flicks at me before he says, "Oh, baby, don't try to fight it. I'll know just when to stop to give you the most torture."

I have no time to digest that thought before he sucks on that bundle of nerves. Hard. My body arches once more, Koda somehow getting deeper inside my throat. The torture continues as Koda strums his fingers inside me in time with his tongue now. In a flash, I have the idea to trap him. Just hurl that leg over his neck, keep that tongue flush against me until I come. Before my leg can make it far enough, Koda pulls his fingers out of me to hold my legs down by the thighs. Without a word, Koda starts feasting on me relentlessly. My whole body is trembling, begging him to let me fly.

Instead, Koda drags himself out of my mouth. My high subsiding, my eyes coming back into focus, Koda pulls me back towards the headboard.

"I figured you would need this." Koda laughs gruffly. Silk caresses my skin as Koda binds my wrists together. Fuck. If he had found anything else, I would just burn my way through it if I really couldn't hold back a fiery reaction. But that's my favorite fucking robe. I can do it. I can make it through this.

Once the other end of the sash is tied to a rung on the headboard, Koda slides himself on top of me. He presses kisses down and up my chest, before finding my lips again. We let our tongues slowly explore the other. We nip at each other, our tongues tasting what we've never had before tonight. I don't even realize Koda isn't inside of me until he groans into my mouth as he slots himself in.

"Shit. Do you have condoms here?" He halts his movement as we both realize there is no barrier between us.

"No," I can barely get out, "But it's okay. I'm clean… you…?"

"The only woman I've touched in a year has been you, Summer." The admission drops between us. Sadness at the time we've lost tries to creep in before he kisses me again and starts pulling in and out of me. He leans down, kissing me fiercely as he keeps an infuriating cadence. I barely make it through my third denial. All the while, Koda pulls his pleasure from me, kissing and tasting every inch of me. My nerves are on fire. As he brings me closer to the edge once more, I hook a leg around his waist. Another attempt to keep him close, to force him to push me over that cliff.

He chuckles against my collarbone. "Do I need to go find something to restrain your ankles, love?" It feels as if my brain is hovering above my physical body at this point. I cannot even move my head, whether that was to shake or nod I don't know. Koda could remove my restraints and my body would still be a limp noodle. Every final crumb of my consciousness is focused on not exploding anymore. Even if it comes at the cost of not getting my orgasm in the end. Koda switches back to his fingers, one hand inside me, one caressing my face.

"You are so fucking beautiful," he whispers, almost reverently.

Grounding myself back to reality, I huff out, "I am a sweaty wreck."

Koda gives me a soft smile, "My beautiful wreck. My amazing chosen one." He cups my cheek, "My best friend." Blame it on the multiple denied orgasms, or all the events of the day, but the tears come unbidden and I can't stop them.

"Baby, you are almost there. I've got you." The flush of emotions brings me to the brink faster than I can stop the fire from rising within me. Koda stops his ministrations and is still wiping away my endless tears when he looks at my hands. Still tied back above my head, he climbs back on top of me, with a furrowed brow. The silk falls away, but Koda's thumb rubs against my palm.

"Your fingertips are burning." He says quietly, his face draining slightly. "No more secrets. I'm a pretty confident man, but... does... you mentioned all that time ago. Your well of power can surge with heightened emotions? Have you been... faking your orgasms?"

That question slams my brain back into my body. Does he really think I would purposefully sleep with men if I had to fake my orgasms every time? "No, Koda. I swear. I can usually keep my powers locked down and still come. We've just had a lot of emotional energy spent tonight on top of your edging. It's just getting a little harder to hold back."

The reality that had surged through me has apparently calmed my powers down as Koda presses each of my fingers to his lips. "I'll make a deal with you. Give me everything, don't hold back on me. I'll let you come this time. But I mean it when I tell you I want it all."

"I don't want to hurt you. At this rate, I don't think I'll be able to come without burning something."

A feral smile crosses his face. "Perfect."

"Koda -"

He puts a finger to my mouth to shush me before spearing back into me hard. "Don't you dare hold yourself back now. Let me have every bit of you. I don't mind a little burn. If I make you come so hard you lose control it would be a scar well earned."

Pounding into me now at a punishing rate, Koda is serious. He wraps his hand around my throat as he bites my lips. I pull at his hair, scrape my nails up his back. Both of us, fighting for more pain. My head is still spinning. Despite his words, I try to keep one last brain cell focused on the fire screaming through me now. My hands fling around, trying to find a pillow to hold on to.

Koda sits up enough so he can watch me thrash under him. He takes the hand not on my throat and runs circles along my clit, sending me deeper into my pleasure. Sending me closer and closer to the edge. Koda's breathing quickens, maybe I can hold out. Maybe I can make it.

Leaning back down, Koda consumes my mouth before saying. "I'm not coming until you do. That's always the rule, babe. Now fucking let go and come for me." Sitting back up he keeps one hand holding me down, and uses his other to grab one of mind, placing it over his heart. His pace speeds up, pulling my climax closer and closer to the surface.

"I've got you, Summer. I'm not running away. I will run through fire to get back to you. Now let go."

After hours of being brought closer and closer, I finally release my last anchor and explode.

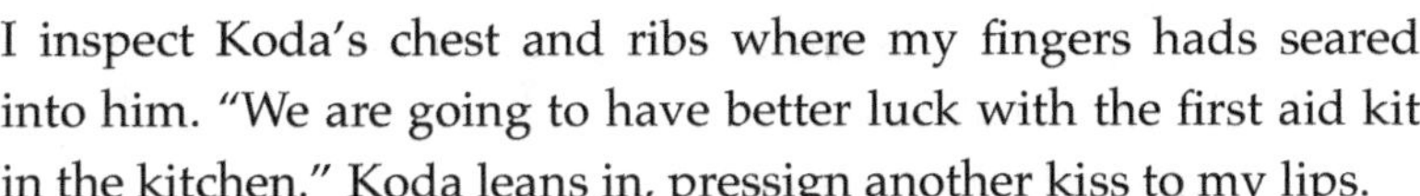

I inspect Koda's chest and ribs where my fingers hads seared into him. "We are going to have better luck with the first aid kit in the kitchen." Koda leans in, pressign another kiss to my lips.

"Stay here, I'll find it." He hops back into his sweatpants and walks out the door without a second glance. I can't help but stare at my fingers as the minutes tick past. He didn't leave. Once again, Koda is the reason my mind and my soul are back to this reality. A life that almost slipped through these fingertips.

The smirk on Koda's face as the door clicks open means he probably ran into Jackie or Kyria along the way. His grin falls when he takes me in. He's back on the bed in an instant, thumbs cradling my face, wiping away tears that were silently falling.

"I'm still here, love. I am here, not in pain. I even grabbed an extra tube of burn cream in case I can't help myself later."

Choking out a laugh, I grab one of the tubes out of his lap where they landed. "I am so incredibly sorry for putting you through the last week." Lightly, my fingers spread the burn cream on the five small circles over his left side. "These should be fine, shouldn't scar."

Koda lifts my chin to force me to meet his eyes. "The moment these start to fade I am getting them tattooed to my chest."

Moving to the spots on his opposite ribcage, I inspect those marks before covering them. I am barely finished before Koda pops back up and pulls us over to the bathroom. He cleans my fingertips with a warm damp towel one by one before pressing his lips to each one. "Don't put your clothes back on, but I figure you may want to clean up. I'll be just outside waiting for you." He presses one more kiss to my lips before he pulls himself away.

Throughout the night we rotate between falling asleep, being nudged awake by Koda hardening between my legs, and talking ourselves back to sleep. I am pressed into his chest now, his hands tracing circles along my back. His fingers coax story after story out of me. I tell him about Emily Turner. The surprise she gave us, showing up on our doorsteps all those weeks ago. Her decision to go back to Arcalis.

"She sounds like a firecracker."

I chuckle, "She certainly is."

I reminisce on memories of how Jackie, Kyria, and I met; how we built up this system to be what it is today. How we crafted all the training rooms. "I'll show you the room for the water wielders tomorrow. It's a trip."

Koda digs in deep with the security and surveillance items. It is his actual background, after all. It will be really great to have him on board with everything here now that I think about it. I know a lot about surveillance and maintaining secure devices to the extent that helps me. We are quite proud of how we were able to soundproof the building just enough, without making it a dead zone on a technological map. He is already talking about secure ways to ensure the building blends in more than it does.

Koda is twirling a tendril of hair in his finger as he nuzzles into my neck. He pushes me onto my back and wedges himself between my legs once more.

"How are you still going?" I huff out a laugh that turns into a groan as he hooks his fingers into me. He presses a kiss to my lips and any complaints are lost.

"I never knew how much I really wanted to kiss you while being inside you. Now that I have… I don't know if I will ever be able to stop." He cups my face with one hand and slides himself into me. We both groan with the movement. Koda kisses me once more before whispering the question I know he has been waiting to ask. "Will you tell me how you found out you are the chosen one?"

One tear escapes as I nod my head, thinking about the last few months. Koda keeps a steady pace between us. "I found out a little over a week before I told you about my powers. Right before you told me Dune had moved back to Lyra. I think… I think I always knew. There was always that tiny kernel of hope that I would find another person like me. I …torched my entire training room after I found out."

Koda leans down to kiss along my neck, my collarbone. A reward for my vulnerability. "My own experience was already tough, confusing for myself. The thought of having to tell another person that - let alone you - made me want to puke. And…" I hesitate to tell him this next part.

"Tell me, love," Koda whispers. "I can handle it. I promise."

"I was scared…" My lip trembles with the truth spoken. "The circumstances are different but… There was still a fear you might change your mind. I was still grappling with that news. I didn't want to push you away, encourage you to run." Koda stills, hovering above me, watching me. "We could have had a few months, or a couple of years. Then that rebel group … you would put the facts together. I was so worried about you running, that I never stopped to consider it might have been me. I thought… maybe it would be easier. If they already know who I am… I couldn't bear it if they ever hurt you."

Koda devours me as my words come to a stop. I cannot believe I almost let myself walk away from this. From him. Any remnants of the ice I had been building over the last week have long since melted. "I want every jagged piece of you, Summer. Every fiery piece. Every chosen piece. Give it all to me. I will always come back to you. I will always chase you down to bring you back to me. Chosen one or not, you are mine. I am not letting you walk away now that I have you."

CHAPTER 50
KODA

Summer convinces me to finally let us leave her room. She does make a solid point that her bed at home is much more comfortable. We take a shower to clean up. Of course, I took the opportunity to kiss her in the shower. We will have so many firsts. If kissing her in the shower already gives me butterflies, kissing her in the rain might send me to my knees. Thank goodness we really only need to keep up this charade with Dune for another couple weeks. I am not Summer with all of these epic secrets she has held close. I don't think I will make it long without slipping up and kissing her in public.

"I just need to get something out of my training room. On the way back down, I will give you a tour of the training rooms. I just need to check if there are people in them first."

When we enter her training room, Summer marches across the space where some cubbies sit. Not very fireproof, but I suppose it works. I take a moment to take in this room. Yesterday, I was focused completely on Summer and did not take in my surroundings. I run my hands across a path of scorched bricks. The path continues across the room. The floor is filled with the ash remnants of whatever was used for target practice.

I'm inspecting the pond of green plastic in a far corner when Summer comes up next to me.

"I melted a battalion's worth of green plastic army men." I look over to see Summer attempting to hold in a laugh.

"Only a battalion's worth?"

This makes the laugh escape. "I was being *extremely* dramatic. I will have to ask Kyria if she has that recording." Nodding at the door and adjusting the straps on her backpack Summer leads us back the way we came. I follow down two flights of stairs and out into a hallway. Summer lets me into the first room.

"This one is for wind wielders." The floor is covered in that soft, squishy rubber. It goes up the walls also.

"It's like a giant playground."

"Yeah we figured even if we can't hurt ourselves, a bone may still break if you hit a wall or the ground hard enough. Where else do you find something so fall proof?"

The next room has a floor that is entirely made of compacted dirt. Scattered along the walls are various outcroppings. Brackets, shelves, steel piping, stone ledges and other various props jutting out of the walls. "Jackie said that Kyria is… an earth wielder. I get the dirt…"

"Vine ropes. Sometimes you will walk in to see three or five people just swinging around this room." We chuckle as we leave.

"You weren't kidding, your room is the most boring of the bunch." I elbow her in the side.

As we come up to the last room in the hall, Summer doesn't enter. She just pops her head in and I can hear her talking to someone inside. After a moment, Summer opens the door fully allowing me to follow in behind her.

"Water," I murmur as we enter the room. It really does look like a giant white bathtub. The smooth surface goes halfway up the walls before it turns into bathroom tiles. Drains line the middle of the floor. I look up to find Summer putting her hair up in a ponytail.

"There's a watch room right over there. I have been challenged to one final sparring match before Emily and Teival head to Arcalis tomorrow." Summer is handing me her backpack, but Emily is eyeing me warily. The man next to her must be Teival and he looks as confused as I feel. Summer pulls me to her and presses a quick peck to my lips before whispering, "Go, be safe, dear."

As Summer passes by Emily to find a corner, she must say something to Emily. She visibly drops her shoulder as if in relief. Odd.

I settle down to watch this sparring session. As it starts the five of them seem to split up one on one. It is crazy to watch balls of water, dirt, fire, and wind colliding with each other around the room. Soon they team up - everyone against Summer.

No one can say it is an unfair fight. Summer holds her own. Eventually though she is overtaken. Enough dirt turns into mud, slowing down her movements. This allows Kyria and Emily to get Summer wrapped up in vines.

Everyone is soaked in sweat or steam from Teival's water spouts being evaporated. They have collapsed on the floor, leaning up against the far wall. There's a mini fridge filled with water bottles. Now that I can no longer be accidentally murdered, I bring a few out for them. Sitting down on the wall next to Summer, I pull her into my side.

"Ew, no I am gross."

Sneaking a kiss, "I don't care. Remind me to never get on your bad side." I pull her face to mine for another kiss. "Mmmmh, salty." I smack my lips as she pushes against my chest.

"I told you!"

Not caring about the salt or sweat, I pull her into my lap and kiss her collarbone as she squirms.

Groaning reaches my ears, reminding both of us that we are in fact not alone in this room.

"Y'all are cute," Jackie says, "But I am almost missing it when you two were hiding the fact you were sleeping together." She pushes herself up and waves off Kyria. "I'll be right back."

"Even Emily and Teival aren't out here making out on every surface possible." Kyria comments.

"Please pardon the fact, I only *just* pulled my head out of my ass and expressed my undying affection for Summer. Every second and surface counts. You know I am dating a chosen one. Every moment should be cherished."

I can't help the wide grin on my face. *Dating.* I kiss Summer again, deepening it, trying to slip my tongue into her mouth. Summer shakes her head, laughing.

Jackie comes back and plops a couple sheets of paper on Summer's lap. "Before you two go off and we can't get ahold of you until Monday…" Snorts echo around the room interrupting Jackie. "We tried getting in touch with our friend 'Rune'. He answered after letting us run in circles for a few days. Somehow, he knew we were not you. He made it sound like you would know him though."

I lean over her shoulder to read the chat conversation. As we both read, Summer starts to stiffen. Summer's voice when she answers is just light, "No, nothing about this seems familiar." It is enough that Kyria and Jackie seem convinced that Summer is unaffected. The stillness in her body remains, though. She is not even using my body to support her. She just sits on my lap like a doll on a ventriloquist.

She recognizes something in the papers, but before either of them can figure out she is lying, I cause a distraction. I turn her, forcing her to straddle me. "You don't even drink cherry sodas."

"Exactly." She scrunches her eyebrows before I lean in and capture her lips in mine.

"No more talking to strange men on the internet. You are all mine."

Groans erupt around the room.

"Please leave. I'll ask surveillance to cycle the camera footage on your route home. See you Monday. Do *not* ask me to come over into your hormone filled apartment at all this weekend."

CHAPTER 51
SUMMER

Taking a week of work off a couple weeks before the biggest industry conference of the year is a mistake. I have never given that idea any thought before. I definitely will not now. Tech conferences are brutal and wait for no one. Even if you are having a mental breakdown over your chosen one status. There is all of my actual work to catch up on. Then finishing my official prep for the conference, the meet and greets, and harassing sales reps for their meeting briefs. My normal day to day work. Then my extra credit, non-official prep for the meet and greets.

Days are long. Work comes home with me. Koda comes home with me too. He does not help with making the work at home go any faster. Foot rubs turn into getting pulled under him on the couch. Shoulder rubs turn into Koda kissing my neck and collarbone. Which turn into makeout sessions.

Koda has practically moved in. After having to leave to go get work clothes from his own place, Koda came back with a giant suitcase. Neither one of us brings up the fact that Dune will definitely know that Koda is not going home every night. The thought of wasting another day not waking up in Koda's arms is absurd. Every day with him is more precious than the last.

On Wednesday, we both agree that we should keep up the facade with Dune through FaeTech. After that, we will tell him. Probably. We have one last thing to get done before we get too far ahead of ourselves. I text Andre first. He should be the least complex of the conversations.

Once he confirms that he can join us for a late lunch tomorrow, I decide it is time to call Dune.

Koda was not the only person I completely disappeared on. I did practically run away from Dune right as the news conference ended. He did not leave me as many voicemails as Koda, but a couple of voicemails and text messages is no small thing after ten years of silence. The irony is not lost on me that I did to Koda what Dune did to me all those years ago.

That's when I realize I never looked to see if Dune had posted anything from our trip to Bert & Rocky's. Putting off the call, I open up my socials instead. Looking at the pictures feels like more of a flashback. I scroll through the selfies we had taken slowly. The first is normal enough - sitting on the bench, eyes on the camera. The next picture I am still looking at the camera but Dune is tilted just slightly towards me. He must have set the phone up to take multiple timed selfies. Scrolling again, is a picture from when I had turned to face him. The picture tells a story that is not real.

I thought the pictures would stop there, but I see a couple more dots to flip to. This is just me. I am frozen in a spin. Based on the frame, he had snuck this in while we were walking there. The last slide is another casual - just me eating my ice cream.

This is still fake. *To me.* One interrupted comment floats to the front of my mind.

"Did you ever make a move after all those years, Dune?"

"Of course I fucking made - "

There is no need to go down this path. The hole in my chest aches louder than normal. I have my answer. I just need to make it through a couple more weeks. I can do this.

Jabbing Dune's number on my phone before I can change my

mind, I put the call on speaker phone. At least that way I cannot do something rash like hang up from nerves if it's sitting on the island.

"Summer?" Dune picks up on the first ring, breathless like he had run to the phone.

"Hey Dune."

"Thank the Fates. Are you okay? Where are you?"

"I - " I pause, not sure how to take this line of questioning. "I am fine. At home. Sorry about … you know… disappearing on ya." I try to laugh but it gets caught in my throat.

"It's fine. I'm just glad you are okay."

"Yeah…"

"Can I come see you?"

I physically flinch at the question. Koda pops his head out from my room at the question and must see my face scrunched up.

"I - I am just really busy trying to catch up. I took a whole week off work and it's all catching up."

"Summer - "

"I am actually just calling to ask if you are still up for dinner at Bocelli's next week."

"Yes. Yeah of course."

"Okay. Okay, great. I am going to see Andre tomorrow. I will let you know the reservation time and all that after I talk to him."

"Summer, we - " Sighing, Dune must stop his train of thought. When he starts talking again it seems to be in a different direction. "I posted pictures from Bert & Rocky's."

"I - Thank you."

"You should know, with you … going silent on us … I forgot to post the pictures into the fishbowls."

"Shit," I murmur.

"No, no. It was only a couple of days. By the time I went in to post though, someone else already had. If you haven't looked you should go take a peek. There is some interesting commentary."

"Okay, I'll go take a look at it. Thanks, Dune."

There is a pause before Dune simply says. "I'm glad you are okay. Let me know the details for dinner."

Koda and I lean over my phone as I pull up my fishbowl account. Although the post is over a week old at this point, it is still at the top of the feed due to activity on it.

Most of the comments have some theory about why Dune and I are talking to each other. Every comment has something to say about how we could be dating. Or re-igniting a friendship. Most of them just think we are probably just sleeping with each other.

I am about to get to the juicy tech world gossip when a hand slides the phone across the island. Koda spins me to face him. He lifts my chin by his index finger before leaning in to kiss me. We stay like that for a few moments. Slow moments, memorizing the feel of the other. Koda pulls away just slightly before pressing his forehead to mine.

"Sorry. The caveman in me had to be reminded that you are mine." Koda whispers so softly.

I press a hand to his cheek. "I am yours, Koda. It's just a couple of weeks."

"That's good. Because I have a couple job interviews next week while at the conference."

I whip back at this. "What?!"

Koda pecks me on the lips. "I want to be able to do this outside of these four walls. To hold your hand as we walk to work or coffee or through the farmer's market. I don't want us to be a secret. So I will give you my notice as soon as I land another job. It would help if I had a letter of recommendation from *the* Summer Chase."

"I'll get right to work on that."

I break out in giggles as he picks me up, kissing me and

walking us to my room. "It can wait a little longer. I have better plans for our immediate future."

The walk to Bocelli's is difficult. Not because of my work heels. The light breeze keeps me from sweating in my blazer as we walk. No. It is actually the first time Koda and I are together, outside of my apartment, alone. No colleagues. No all-knowing baristas. No Jackie. There are plenty of cameras though.

Koda walks by my side, closer than a friend would. He keeps his hands in his pockets though. Every so often he bumps his hip against mine. Each time I roll my eyes at him, his grin gets wider.

"This is your rule, love. Not mine."

"For good reason!"

"Yes, yes. The webinar stalker who may or may not be the current leader of the rebellion or helping to really kidnap people in Arcalis. I know."

Knowing that my webinar stalker is the one and only Aaron Dubois, I would not put it past him to have me on his facial recognition alert list. Until I can find out what his actual play is, Aaron Dubois goes nowhere near Koda. No one will touch him if it is the last thing I do.

Caught up in my thoughts of stabbing and setting a certain blonde ablaze, I don't notice the Koda has steered me practically into the wall. Koda walks us into the alley that breaks a path between the buildings.

"Here is the thing. Stalker man is just using maps of cameras and can hack them. Great. I can also use the same digital map to find paths *without* cameras."

I look up at him as he takes my hand in his and continues walking. Like this is the most normal thing in the world. He deserves so much more than this. Fates above, though, I am selfish and will take anything he will give me. Halfway between the entrance and exit, I pull him to me for a quick kiss. "Maybe we should take up hiking or something." I whisper against his lips.

"Be careful what you ask for," he chuckles before pressing his lips to mine once more.

This alley spits us out half a block from Bocelli's so I do not have a lot of time to tuck all of my emotions back into the flimsy box I am trying to keep them in. With the lunch rush done, Andre meets us at the entrance. The silver haired man is propped up against the door. His chef's coat is nowhere to be seen. His black button down is almost ready for the dinner rush to start. He will spend almost as much time in the front of house with customers as he will in the back directing his kitchen staff. Those that don't know Andre think he must love the energy of dinner hour. He likes quiet lunches more. Andre takes Koda's hand with a firm shake.

"Koda, good to see you."

"You too, Andre." Koda's eyes flick over to me with a smirk on his face. "Save the paper today, I am paying for lunch."

"Mmmmh, you make me wonder about this visit even more." Andre comments with a slight frown on his face before he turns back to me.

"Summer, my dear. Always lovely to see you." He holds my arms and gives me a peck on each cheek before leaning back.

I pluck at the *three* open buttons on his shirt with one hand, tapping a rolled up sleeve with my other. "Who is coming to dinner tonight, sir? Gotta put some of this away, the patrons may combust when they catch sight of you!"

There is just the slightest tinge of pink on his olive cheeks before he chuckles and pushes us inside. Koda and I look at each other, eyes wide as we are guided to our table. As we sit down in the booth Andre nods to one of the few tables with people at this hour. "That handsome young man's name is Kenneth. We've been dating for about six weeks."

"What?!?" I exclaim without meaning to.

Kenneth, turns around now, smirking at Andre. "Told you," Andre calls his way. Turning back to me he simply says, "It is not *my* fault you haven't been by to see me in ages." Tapping the table, he continues, "I'll be back with wine and appetizers. I hope you are hungry. I've got a new meal I want you to try."

Koda and I scooch in closer to get a better look at Kenneth. Andre sends the wine and appetizers with a waiter.

"Kenneth!" I call over to him. "Come sit with us."

He is hesitant at first but gives in after just a moment. Koda and I pepper him with questions. Turns out he has been to a couple of my webinars which gives me pause. The three of us have now gone through our second bottle of wine when Andre finally returns with three plates of food.

"Oh lords," he says as he realizes we roped Kenneth over to our booth. "Scootch." A plate is given to each of us before Andre sits down in the booth facing us. His eyes glitter with mischief as he temples his hands. "You called this meeting to order, Summer, dear. What is it that you wanted to tell me?"

His demeanor goes from smiling and mischievous to confused as I tell him what I need.

"So, let me get this straight. You and Dune are going to have dinner here, as a sort of fake outing to rouse up rumors about your work. Koda is going to take pictures from another table as some sort of plant. You are all in league with each other, although I feel like I am missing an element. Probably better off not knowing."

I look at Koda, who shrugs a nod. "Yeah, that's about the gist of it. I am sorry to do this to you on a Friday night. We just don't want to bring any doubt by staging it on a less busy night."

"Okay, now to what I thought you were here to tell me..." Andre pauses as he is trying and failing to keep a smile off of his stoic face. Sternly he flicks his finger at us and continues, "Does Dune Raydn know about this?"

I scrunch my face, "Wh-what?"

Kenneth starts laughing. "They don't even realize they did it. That's not good."

I look at Koda to see if he understands. Both of our eyes go wide when we realize just how close our faces are. Koda's arm is slung over my shoulder. I am wrapped snuggling into him. We look like a certified couple.

With a smile filling his face, Andre comments, "Better make sure to keep that under wraps then, you two." Andre stands, pulling Kenneth out of the booth. "I'll make sure your tables are ready on Friday. Enjoy the rest of your lunch my two little lovebirds."

CHAPTER 52
SUMMER

The rest of the week passes in general normalcy. Well… for the most part. There is a certain normalcy mixed with irony. Like the Fates are laughing at me. I keep avoiding Dune's texts or requests to talk. For all my attempts, though, Dune apparently now knows my schedule well enough to just show up. He shows up for coffee every morning, making Koda increasingly more grumpy.

I slip out of the corners he tries to trap me in, both literally and figuratively. The pull in my chest tightens every time he chases me. I escape before we can ever have any sort of heartfelt conversation.

The unfortunate part of our relationship, even with ten years apart, I know exactly what Dune needs. He wants to talk about that night. He needs to truly apologize for his sudden disappearance. I wish I could congratulate myself. Part of the goal of this charade was to break down Dune's defenses. Make him trust me enough to work with me, maybe even give me insight into what *he* is doing. Peeling away the layers of calcified hurt, though, brought more than anticipated.

I refuse to name it. Not until it is time to break it.

Every time a layer gets removed in the name of rebuilding

our friendship, we get a layer closer to it. That thing I thought was just a college crush. I don't even know if Dune realizes this is more than just my crush or perhaps his lingering feelings. If he even had feelings. Based on his insistence on talking, he must feel something.

Which means I am running out of time.

The knock at the door brings me back to the present. Right. Dinner. *Just make it through dinner.* Game face. I open the door to find Dune leaning in the doorway waiting. His hair is pulled back nicely and he is donning a pair of black jeans with a baby blue button down and sport coat. I will match him almost perfectly with my black cocktail dress. There is no way anyone will believe this is not actually a date.

The look he gives me though almost looks nostalgic. The acid creeps up my throat realizing that he may also end up falling for our own tricks. I take a step back to let him into my apartment.

My phone starts buzzing on the counter. I pretend to check it, knowing that it is just my monitoring system letting me know about the bug or bugs in Dune's pocket.

"I just need to grab shoes and then I will be ready to go."

The bug that most likely will be left under a countertop or on a lamp as soon as I go to my room. It is a reminder. No matter what there is between us, he still doesn't trust me fully. And he truly does not know if he is working on behalf of the good guys or the bad. I close my bedroom door.

Breathe in.

Breathe out.

Harden my soul.

You still have a choice.

I slip on my shoes that are sitting within seconds reach of my door.

Breathe in.

Breathe out.

Sending off a text, I let Koda know not to come over tonight until after I figure out what type of bug Dune left for me.

Breathe in.

Breathe out.

I give myself one last look in the mirror before opening the door.

"Ready?" He murmurs.

"As I will ever be."

"You are missing one thing, though."

Patting myself down. Purse, wallet, keys, shoes, excessive makeup. Dune smiles at me softly, that damn dimple making an appearance after all this time. The sinking feeling in my stomach is definitely nausea at whatever he has planned. Not butterflies.

"Turn around."

Gently, he brushes my hair onto one shoulder before reaching around in front of me. A weight hits my chest. I look down to see my locket, his locket, being clasped around my neck. My gasp escapes before I can smother my reaction.

"Did you steal this from my house?" I demand.

"Yes."

"That is all you have to say for yourself?"

Dune delicately holds the locket, his hand barely brushing my sternum but it sends fireworks through me. Quietly he simply says, "I wanted to see you wear it. At least once. With or without it…You look beautiful. Thank you for letting me see you in it. Maybe it can be a new beginning, instead of an ending."

He is so sincere about this, it almost makes me forget that he bugged my apartment. He does not wait for a response. He simply pulls my arm into his and walks us out the door.

The walk to the Bocelli's only feels long because of the silence between us. Instead of focusing on keeping my heart cold, I am eyes to the sky, looking at the clouds starting to form. Rain isn't in the forecast, but perhaps the Fates know something I don't.

"You good?"

"Yup," I pop. "Just hoping the rain doesn't ruin my dress on the way home."

Dune raises an eyebrow at me. I have been straight up

avoiding him, so it is fair for him to question it. I give him another, more believable excuse. "Andre is… Andre means a lot to me. I met him ten years ago. When I ate his food, it was the only time I allowed myself to truly heal. He saw a lot of tears." Careful to choose my words, I do not mention Koda. Bocelli's was my safe haven, the one day a week Koda would leave me to myself in those early weeks after Dune left. After our lunch with Andre the other day, I don't want to breathe his name or think about Koda in Andre's presence.

Andre greets us at the door when we arrive, letting us avoid the ever growing line outside his door. That alone should be enough to start spreading some rumors, as scowls turn to curiosity as bystanders take in our trio.

"Summer, dear." He presses a kiss on both cheeks before taking my hands in his. "Koda is already here and seated."

He turns and gives Dune a small frown, the slightest disapproval he would ever show a customer. Honestly no one but myself would even notice. "Mr. Raydn. Welcome to Bocelli's. You both will follow me. Summer, I have your table ready." Andre leans in to whisper, "And some wine is being poured for you as we speak."

Dune's hand presses to my lower back to usher me forward, then lets it crawl to grasp my waist as Andre leads us to my table. This is good for the show, but hard for my soul right now, knowing Koda is watching. This needs to look real. Dune's eyes widen a bit as he takes in the table. It is a corner table, rounded into the wall, and is well lit when sitting forward and eating. But should the lucky couple sitting there lean back they would be all but blacked out from most onlookers. It keeps those that are watching curious. Andre only opens it up to VIPs, otherwise it remains empty.

The eyes of the human and Fae at the tables we pass graze over our trio. Recognition of Andre gets people stirring, even if they do not recognize Dune or myself. Every step of this plan continues to work in our favor.

As we each slide into the booth, Dune closes the space between us. Shrugging at my questioning glance his only response is, "What? We need to make this look real enough, right? That means you can't sit so far away. We are actually going to have to *talk*."

"Talking. Ew." I mock like a child while I pick up my pre-poured glass of wine.

I pause with the glass midway to my mouth as Dune squeezes my thigh. With his other hand he reaches for my glass. "You are going to have to not chug this glass of wine looking like you want to be anywhere but here." He takes a sip of my wine. "Damn this stuff is really good."

Pouring himself a glass, he remarks, "It is still mind boggling that you have bottles of this on retainer. Then again, he likes you so much he made sure *your* glass was poured by the time you sat down."

"How would he know that you also liked his wine?" I muse. "For all he knows this is the first time you are trying it. Or that you are biased against sweet wines."

I lift my glass to his own. "To keeping a lifetime supply of Andre's sweet wines."

"To overcoming my transgressions so I can maybe get a couple bottles."

We move into some colorful and increasingly obnoxious commentary on shared appetizers over personal salads when our waiter came over to ask our preference. I keep my mind off of Dune's thumb that is rubbing circles on my thigh.

"Sharing is caring, Summer. I haven't been here before. So think of it like our ice cream pact. Instead of tasting every flavor of ice cream, we are just sharing all the options there are." When I am not buying it, Dune leans in to whisper in my ear, "It will also help sell the fact that we like each other."

Once the appetizers come out, Dune picks up a piece of bruschetta and leans over to feed it to me. His hand on my leg has moved to being stretched behind me. I try to hide my shock as I take a bite. Dune takes the rest of it in one bite. I grab an oyster for myself before he can try to feed me that.

"At least your hand is visible now. No one can even see your hand if it's under the table."

I shoot the oyster and Dune takes the empty shell from my hand, his face close to mine. "You have been avoiding me for the better part of a week. We could have created a game plan for this. But you wouldn't talk to me. So. You wanted this to look like a date. A date is what you are fucking getting. Thigh caresses, cuddles, getting fed your food."

He must see me swallow my nerves. It's as if he sees the dreams that used to float through my head. Dreams of exactly what he is describing. Smiling - the second time this dimple has emerged - Dune reaches up to cup my cheek. "I can't let my reputation be ruined with a fake date."

"Here I thought your only reputation was that you didn't go on dates."

Luckily Dune simply chuckles as he turns to grab the next appetizer to try. "Oh Summer, if you only knew. Most women by this point would have melted into my arms at those caresses. At minimum would have attempted to pull me in for a kiss."

Before he can try to make *that* a reality I spit out, "Here, try the garlic bread. It's delicious." Then I attempt to not shove said garlic bread down his throat.

In between Dune practically shoving food to try in my face, we talk about safer topics. Particularly the restaurant scene in Aetherium. Every company there takes this opportunity to throw the flashiest party we can for our customers and partners. Clearly we must decide which of ours is better.

I lean in closer to see the images on Dune's phone of their location. "I mean…" I hum. "It looks nice in terms of the rooftop bar. But it looks incredibly cramped."

"Right?" Dune laughs. "Like why is there a couch set in the middle of the main area. Hopefully they take it out, otherwise the bar is going to be incredibly cramped."

"Yeah you better grab two drinks on the first round and make those last the night. You aren't getting back to the bar." I jab him in the side with my elbow.

"Okay, okay. Show me yours then."

I pull up the website for our location and Dune sighs. "See those seating areas are much better placed. Out of the way of the bar. Looking out to the skyline."

"I definitely won't have to drink a watered down cocktail throughout the night."

"Think you can sneak me into yours?"

"Not a chance. We use actual technology, Dune. Not paper sign-ins. We have a QR code and waitlist just as big as the number of people confirmed to get in."

He elbows me back as we both laugh at how ridiculous the last few weeks have been. Without consciously doing it, we've both fallen comfortable with each other. It reminds me of how quickly he started stealing my food again at the beach house. My phone buzzes and a text from Koda flashes up on the screen.

"Looks like Koda went home. Got some good pictures, apparently." I click my screen off and flip over my phone in case Koda sends another text outside of the group one.

"With our chaperone gone, then, are you going to close off again?"

Conveniently, our waiter comes over to take away our empty dinner plates. "We will be back with dessert shortly." With a nod they are gone. He knows he has me trapped here. There is nowhere to run, and I cannot afford for Dune to start bringing more emotional revelations into this dinner.

"Well, Dune, seeing as *you* coined my lovely industry nickname, I do like to keep you on your toes. Hot, cold, hot, cold." I take a sip of my wine and look back at him. No wonder Aaron Dubois collects secrets. They are a great distraction tactic.

Blanching more every second, "H- how did you know that? Why did you never tell Koda?"

"Is that remorse for the name or guilt for getting caught?" I tease before continuing. "I went looking for you that year at FaeCon. I had snuck over to Star's booth. You hadn't seen me, but I heard you talking. I had been pumping myself up to come around the corner to say hi. Then I heard what... or rather who you were talking about. So instead of saying hi, I just marched right past you without a word. I never told Koda because as mentioned before... I was short on friends at the time. Having been abandoned by one of my closest ones fairly recently."

"I - *fuck* - There is no excuse. Anger was controlling all of my actions back then. And no one was around to stop me from digging myself into a hole because of it. I will always regret my actions during that time. Most of all leaving you." Dune takes my hand in his, sincerity pouring through his words. The pang in my chest signals my mistake. Dune is leaning in towards me "Summer, I - I never should have left. I never told you -"

"You can make it up to me if you tell me a secret." Dune's face transforms from shock of the interruption to stern to a soft hesitant look. The tension is coiling in my chest. He needs to stop thinking about what we could have been. I need to distract him. I bring my drink up to my lips and flash him the most innocent smile before asking, "How long did it take you to buy the magazine?"

His eyes flash as I take another sip of my wine. "How do you know about *that*?"

"*That* wasn't the question."

Dune scrapes a hand down his face and leans back into the booth. Space enough now that I can breathe. "There's no reason to be embarrassed, Dune. Just tell me." I let out a laugh.

"The issue is I have to tell you the whole story then."

"Now I am even more invested."

He groans and mutters, "Fuck," before taking a breath. Then he has a look of clarity before smirking. "I know what you are doing, Summer. But, I think this is about to backfire on you." He doesn't let me respond before saying. "The editor for the article is a friend."

"Ah…Jackson Hightower."

"Yup. The asshole has been trying to get someone to nominate me for years. One night we are out at the bar and he mentions to me that the winner of most eligible executive that year was not only a woman but also not even technically an executive. He told me as a joke that it meant now I could be nominated next year since they bent the rule for another vice president. I'll admit, I immediately asked if it was you. He, of course, then wouldn't stop needling me with questions about you, how we knew each other, what you were like, all of that. I answered some of the questions in exchange for one thing. That he would let me know when you would be in town for the photoshoot."

I remember Jackson asking me about how I knew Dune at the tail end of the shoot. I thought it was strange at the time. I brushed it off and told him the same vague story I tell anyone that happens to ask. We went to college together and drifted apart when he left for Arcalis. End of story.

"I didn't have the shoot in Arcalis."

"I know. Jackson told me that you requested it be in Lyra."

"What was your plan? Try to sabotage the shoot? Make me look like an angry bitch in all my photos?" I chuckle at the thought.

"No, I was going to apologize. You never would have answered a phone call from me. You deserved more than a text message from me. I wanted to see you. Clearly, I had underestimated your ability to stay away from me.

"Dune, I am now only partially aware of how people in Arcalis are disappearing. Back then, we had no clue. I wasn't risking walking into that city willingly."

Dune's eyes flick across my face, looking for the lie. "That shoot was almost three years ago."

"Yes, and I've been watching the missing person's pages for five years."

A dawning realization crosses his features. "I am a fucking idiot. I thought you had requested the change because of me."

"You are an idiot." I jab as our waiter brings over our bill.

"I could never seem to track you down at conferences though." Dune goes to hand the waiter his card without looking at the tab when I interject. The young man cringes as I open the book, find two tabs, and leave the full tab in the billfold. "Please make sure that is the one you run please."

He gives a nod as he takes Dune's card.

"You know how you always would tell Koda where you were going in terms of after parties? He would go with you to those parties." Dune gapes at me. "I just never perused the same happy hour circuit as him. I wasn't looking to start a riot."

Dune shakes his head before changing the subject. "Should I ask about the check thing?"

"Andre is a master at holding a grudge. He ran two tabs." I show him the discounted one. "One if I paid, one if you paid. I told him it was a fake date. He should have just assumed *your reputation* would be tarnished if you were seen not paying."

Dune laughs so hard. "Holy shit. That is honestly, pretty fucking awesome."

"Back to the question at hand, you never finished your story. What did Jackson Hightower have to do with you having a copy of my magazine?"

"Jackson left a copy at my office a week before it went out."

Eight years ago I would have desperately wanted to know why. Right now, though, Dune is right. This has backfired on me. I desperately want to be alone, to allow my soul to stop racing. It does not matter that he wanted to apologize. He could have made more of an effort. He did not. He made his choice. Now I need to make mine before he changes his mind.

Luckily a response isn't required as the check comes back for Dune to sign. Before I can slide out of my side of the table, he grabs my hand and pulls me after him. Every cell in me is electrified as he twines his fingers in mine to walk us out. We don't make it far. We are halted at the front door where it is now pouring rain.

"Shit." We both curse.

"Want to call a cab?" Dune murmurs.

"It is so close, most cabbies aren't going to take that short of a drive."

Andre comes sprinting from the back. "You didn't stop in to say goodbye." He leans in to give me a peck on the cheek as he hands Dune an umbrella.

"Thank you for the umbrella, Andre. I'll be back again soon."

"Give Koda my regards."

Dune walks out into the rain, opening up the umbrella to give me a dry path. Dune's outstretched hand feels as if the world is watching. The forks of my fate lay there, waiting for my fingers to link with his once more. He's staring at me confused. It's just his hand. It's just the rain. A breeze picks up, blowing droplets in his direction. My chest is pounding underneath the locket that ended us.

Do I take his hand, let the locket really be a new beginning? We run through the rain like giddy teenagers, dropping the umbrella along the way. I will buy Andre another one. Skipping and twirling and dancing. Dune would pick me up at one point. He would finally kiss me after all these years. We could go back to my place and let this thing between us finally, *finally* become reality.

Or do I let it stay what it is - an ending. Build those moments with Koda. Koda who has been there for me at my lowest. I am tired of running away from the things I want most. While Dune used to be that, he isn't anymore. Maybe if there was more time. Maybe if I hadn't fallen for Koda. If I only have so much time left, I know who I want it to be with.

Breaking the spell between us, I grab Dune's forearm for balance before pulling one heel off.

"What the hell are you doing?"

"I don't want to ruin my shoes."

"You are not walking barefoot back."

I expect to have to put up a fight about the quality of the shoe, but instead he sighs and crouches down.

"You…"

"Jump on, let's go. I either carry you, or you ruin your shoes. Pick."

I chose my shoes over my pride and climbed onto Dune's back. I take the umbrella as he carefully and very intentionally holds my legs right where my thigh meets the knee. After Dune finds a good pace, I rest my chin on his head.

"Comfortable back there?" I can hear the smile in his voice.

"Quite comfortable actually. I should pay people to do this for me more often."

He chuckles, "Well since you're so comfortable, can I ask *you* a question?"

"Have at it, chariot."

He gives my thigh a slight pinch before he asks, "Does Andre also do the two check thing with Koda? I feel like there is more to this story."

Swinging my head side to side, the truth wins out. "He does. Although Koda caught on fast enough that he just started letting the waiter know when he was paying."

"Okay… don't hate me. After seeing Andre, he is a well fit man. I know some women have a thing for silver hair."

"Are you asking me if I slept with Andre?"

"More thinking maybe you dated for a bit and it ended amicably. It was the only logical thing I could think of that explained the whole paying situation."

"No. Fates, no. Yeah, Andre is a silver fox. But no. When Bocelli's was struggling a few years ago, I sold off some of my vested FaeTech shares and infused Bocelli's with enough cash to keep the doors open and then flourish. I am technically now just a minority owner. Forty-nine percent. Andre wanted to keep it fifty-fifty, but I insisted that he buy in on the last one percent. In exchange, I don't pay for my own food. I am allowed to pay for other people's food though."

"That is a huge risk. Why take it? I haven't done too much research on Bocelli's. I just know there was a huge revamp a few years ago and ever since it's been hugely successful."

"I wanted to see someone follow their dreams and really make it. Andre's food has always been good, but the restaurant had been bogged down by poor decisions from his grandfather. He only told me he was close to shutting down so that I could buy up some of his wine. Instead I asked him what he would do, what would his business plan be if he had the capital. The timing was perfect to allow me to sell my shares and pull the funds."

I can tell he is about to dig deeper into that, so I pull my phone out to take a selfie. We take a couple with my head still on top of his. He's rolling his eyes with a smile on the screen.

"You are so weird." He says, shaking his head. Then Dune reaches a hand up to softly guide my head down to his shoulder. We snap a few more photos that way. I catch him trying to sneak a look at me from the corner of his eyes. Holding the phone out in front of him, we flip through the photos before he tells me to just send them all to him.

"Summer… why? You can't go around just funding everybody's dreams. What made Andre so special?"

My building is in sight, my escape is close. I can show him a piece of what he did. My time has already run out. There is no more shoving this thing down. It is rearing its ugly head whether I like it or not. If all of my plans are about to be ruined, I may as well give him a piece of me as they do. I sigh before whispering the piece of my soul back into the open.

"Andre sat with a young girl who showed up one day and came back every week to try his new food. He sat there, contemplating his life while she cried over hers. He didn't know that it was one of the only times a week she would openly cry in front of another person. She had assured her best friend that enough time had gone by. She was fine. Everything was fine. She only cried in front of a nine year old boy at an ice cream parlor, and Andre. He gave her the freedom of release while he cooked a new meal for her every week."

I still remember the first meal I didn't cry through. *"You can finally taste my food without bits of your own soul mixed in. Only mine now."*

Dune walks us all the way up the steps to the awning in front of my building. He ensures I land on my feet before he turns around and pulls me into a hug. I am suddenly struck clueless on what to do. I wrap my arms around him as he rests his chin on my head.

The familiarity of the whole night kicks me in the stomach. The severity of what I am about to do. It takes all of me to not sink into the feeling. To grasp onto Dune's shirt and not let him go. I didn't just lose a lover all those years ago, I lost a friend. A friendship that was so deep that it would be so easy to pretend all of this is real. He and I are just ripping our souls apart to make us trust each other to meet the other's needs. So instead of gripping on to something I lost, I leave my arms simply resting on his back. I let myself freeze over. With that one slice of my soul, I have cemented my fate.

Breathe in.

Breathe out.

Stop the racehorse in your chest.

In. Out. In. Out.

Cold.

Still.

Koda.

Koda.

Koda.

I still have my choice.

"Jackson left me a note with the magazine."

I don't dare to breathe or speak.

"All it said was, *'For all the time you lost.'"*

Steadying my breath, I close my eyes for one last moment

before patting his shoulder, pulling back from our embrace. I cannot accept this mirrored shard of his soul. Handing him the umbrella, I simply look at him and say, "Thank you for dinner, Dune."

His eyes gleam as he whispers, his grip on me tightening. "Summer…"

"Dune, I will always cherish the time, the moments we had. And I really did enjoy dinner. But …" I shake my head at a loss for words. Our friendship and my love for him were so entwined that I can't find the words to make him understand how hard this is for me. Our time, our moments, were important to me. Now though, I don't want words from someone who already chose to walk away from me once.

I shake my head, before turning to my building entrance. "I'll talk to you later. Text me when you get home."

CHAPTER 53
AARON DUBOIS

Summer Chase and Dune Raydn leave her apartment. I try to ignore my feelings around Dune bugging her. Mostly I am just annoyed. Perturbed that *he* was able to finally get it done. Impressed that Summer has pretty much kept everyone out with the exception of brute force. Curious because she is so locked down, she must know. Although she may not know yet that these have cameras, unlike the bugs at their friend Koda's. Then I cycle back to annoyance because I cannot wipe these bugs out without suspicion from *both* parties.

If Summer is leaving them on knowingly, what is she playing at? How much does she know?

I follow the pair on street cameras as they walk, finally ending up at Bocelli's. That is a very nice restaurant to go to on a Friday night. It is very hard to get reservations there - even as the governor of an entire province. There is no way they were able to get reservations in such a short amount of time.

What am I missing?

I run another internet scrape on Summer. Links to Dune and Koda's social media accounts are returned along with links to discussion forums. I peruse the pictures. Some are just of the trio.

Others are of just Dune and Summer. There is the rare posting of candid photos of Summer now also. What are they doing?

Some of the pictures are on a beach. Are the bugs north of the city at this beach house? Maybe I should go back and listen to those conversations if they are in the archives. More curious about the forums, I click one open.

Someone had posted one of Dune's photos with the caption "What do we think this means?!?!?!"

What is this hell hole?

I scour through hundreds of anonymous comments across multiple posts all surrounding Dune and Summer being seen together.

Consultant 1: *Are they dating?!*

Developer 1: *It looks like they are just working together.*

Architect 2: *Maybe it's both! Did you see the picture where it looked like they were at the beach together? I heard they used to be friends in college!!*

Director 1: *Could this mean FaeTech and Star are merging? Why reignite a friendship after so long without being forced? Maybe they are starting their own company?*

Developer 1: *I hope they wouldn't date each other if that is the case. Dating and starting a business together is just bad news for us all.*

Consultant 1: *I want to know how much groveling he had to do to even get back in her presence. He has been such an asshole to her for years.*

Architect 2: *I wonder how that all works. She is super security focused. Have you attended any of her security webinars? I bet she has her shit locked down completely. And he works for a company that helps a government spy on its citizens.*

Now that catches my attention. There are hundreds of comments discussing the theories on what is happening here in Arcalis. People are starting to track the missing persons and dig deep. Really deep. Some theories come extremely close to the truth. Especially after the interruption during my last press conference. It seems as if Emily Turner was not actually the start of my visibility issues. Emily Turner lit a flame. Emily's roommate started destroying my city. Summer and Dune have turned it into a maelstrom with these rumors.

I hustle through tabs to start searching for recordings from the bugs I never checked. That was the weekend I was playing governor instead of super stalker. There were reports of Emily Turner being sighted at the border. Turns out those videos were a few weeks old. The video quality had been grimy but on the off chance it had been her, I spent that weekend scrubbing the evidence myself from anywhere I could find.

Listening to these recordings now, I regret not having gone back through the footage. I could have had a much more productive time while at the Star offices in Lyra. Just like everything else, Summer had somehow managed to obfuscate the fact that she owns a whole house north of the city from the internet.

It is helpful to find out a bit of the plans being laid out for drumming up gossip. I've already got a nice surprise for Summer lined up. I need to make a move next week. I need to know how much Summer knows and figure out the best path to take. My thoughts are cut off watching Dune carry Summer home from dinner. I can't see everything super clearly, but based on Summer's face once she makes it back to her apartment, the two clearly had a moment. Her face switches between relief, distraught, and sad.

She must shoot off a text before going into her room and emerging moments later in running clothes. Within ten minutes of arriving, she is back out the door and jogging out the front door of her building.

Don't break yet, Summer Chase. I am coming for you. Don't break yet.

CHAPTER 54
SUMMER

I text Koda to let him know I am going out for a run but quickly put my phone away to ignore his response. It's a shitty thing to do. Having to watch Dune and I on a fake date couldn't have been a joy ride. I need to empty my brain of any thoughts and just run. There is a slight tremor in my hand that I push from my mind. *Find a place of heightened emotions* the instructions simply said.

For twenty minutes, the beat of my feet as they pound the sidewalk is all my ears hear. Before I know it, the trail entrance is ahead of me. It's the running loop near my old apartment. I keep jogging for another mile and a half, the distance marked by the only bench on this trail. Before Koda and I had our little pond, Dune and I had this bench. This trail. Some days we would jog it, others we would just mosey around. You can still see the drunken carvings of our initials into the tree next to the bench.

I start pacing to subdue the tremor as it kicks back into gear. Just like running to this spot, the picture I took with Dune under the umbrella felt like second nature. It didn't feel forced. Ten years or just a few days could have passed. We slid right back into our old selves.

Hundreds of photos just like that one already exist. Even

from the quick glance at the pictures from Koda, we had fallen into a comfortability I had not thought possible. But how real is this?

Asking him about the magazine was supposed to be a small jab. It was not supposed to result in a soul opening confession. The theorized instructions from Emily float to the top of my brain again. "In order to keep your soul from turning to stone, the breaker must maintain thoughts on selfless reasons why they are taking such steps."

What will happen if he is actually working with Ashryn? We still do not know if Ashryn is actually doing anything malicious. The rumors we've stirred give me pause. Any person under her employment, from legislators to the cleaning crews are all Fae. Despite how she started her reign, she has not made any meaningful changes since that time for the humans in her realm. In fact, one of the threads has a theory that Queen Ashryn commanded Dubois trial out this technology in his province. Even with the technology, the government hasn't filed any paperwork to warrant the disappearances. Someone else must be hacked into the system and they are getting to the humans first. This tracks with what we found out from Emily. But one comment snags my thoughts, again. *For a government funded and owned initiative, it sure is insecure if you think someone hacked into it before it could really go into production.*

What if every piece of this lines up? Ashryn ordered the technology to be built. Dubois had it built, but gave it a back door for someone else to get in. A rebel group of power wielders if their story for Emily is to be believed. Ashryn is not seeing the results she wants. She expands the initiative to FaeTech. Now she needs someone to oversee both firms. A mole in the system to make sure the holes are plugged. Who better than the VP of Technology for the company building the technology into their devices?

Acid creeps up from my stomach to my chest. Lingering there, it feels like someone is sitting on me, each breath gets harder and harder. After ten years, *ten years*, Dune could be putting everything at risk. Does he just not know what she is doing? Or is all of this an elaborate lie just like my own?

If it is all a lie, if Dune is using me to get to Dubois… Why is he rekindling the friendship? I already know the answer. We both needed to make the other person trust just enough to open up and share the knowledge. I just never anticipated this level of betrayal laid side by side with the friendship he keeps offering up. *And the -*

The weight in my chest expands, my whole upper torso feels like it is on fire now. Memories of our friendship bubble up through the pain. From the moment we met, to the one where he left, images splash across my mind. All the sticky notes he left me; the time he punched my machine learning professor after he humiliated me in class one day; the first time he choked on his words after I walked out of my room in a shimmering dress for the club; spring afternoons laid out on the quad; the walks among these very trees.

No. No. No. No.

The memories are leaking through urgently. Pushing this cord up from the ash and dirt I keep trying to pile on top of it. I cannot risk losing Koda. I cannot risk this choice being taken away.

This is supposed to wait until next week. There is supposed to be more time. I focus on the days and nights I've spent with Koda this last week. It may be seen as selfish in the eyes of whatever Fate is about to judge my action. I cannot help it.

I see the pure joy in Berta's face as she formally meets Koda at the ice cream shop. Even Roy looks happy. The walks around the pond - the only place where we can safely act like a couple. Holding hands, falling into the grass, lips on each other. Picnics with our feet in the beach sand.

Koda's eyes flash before me as the morning sun peeks through my window. The grumbling as he pulls me back to him when I try to make us coffee.

The small interrupted whisper, "Summer, I - " My finger pressed to his lips. Unable to hear those three enormous words with this bond still here. Unwilling to tie him to me if this act goes wrong.

Now that it's been acknowledged, I can feel it. It starts to run taut in my soul. It's as if Dune is getting closer. As if he knows what I am about to do. Closing my eyes, something lifts it into my hands in my soul. The tears run steadily down my cheek.

I think of everything this world can have when this is done. They can have a chosen one. They can use me as their figure head. I will be the country's most wanted and most revered.

I can have Koda. His brown eyes glitter in my mind. *"I want every jagged piece of you, Summer. Every fiery piece. Every chosen piece. Give it all to me. I will always come back to you. I will always chase you down to bring you back to me. Chosen one or not, you are mine. I am not letting you walk away now that I have you."*

I close my eyes, content. The buzzing that had taken over my body ebbs as if relaxing to my decision. "Please forgive me if this doesn't work," I whisper to him in my mind.

I hear Dune from somewhere, yelling my name. It cannot stop me. I tear at the bond in my soul. Ripping it, shredding it.

This is my choice.

This is my choice.

This is my choice.

Dune runs into the clearing right as everything around me explodes.

CHAPTER 55
DUNE

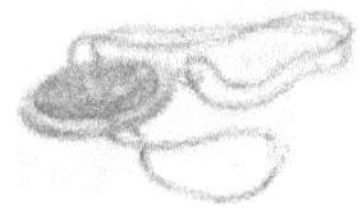

After I get back to my apartment and change into some comfier clothes, I pull up Summer's feed. It's just to make sure they are actually working is my excuse. My hand can't help but rub my chest as I replay Summer arriving back at her flat and then leave not too long after. There is a moment of sadness in her eyes that tears at the ache in my soul. There was no way after all this time I could fall into an easy friendship with her. She was supposed to hate me. She was supposed to be reluctant to work with me. And in spite of it all, I keep finding my way back to her.

My hand still feels the loss of her not taking it.

I snatch up my headphones and go out for a walk, hoping the movement will quell this pain. The pounding in my chest gets louder. Heavier. It's as if my body is trying to tell me to go faster. Unbidden, memories start flooding my mind. I should not be surprised. This whole city is filled with memories of Summer. I swear sometimes I see ghosts of our younger selves giggling in the elevator of my building.

The rain has turned into a torrent. It hits my back as if pushing me further along the path I am walking. Despite looking like a sad fucker walking through the park, in the rain, by myself, my soul is frantic. Why won't Summer let me in? Why does she keep pushing me away?

Just like when I recklessly stole back her locket, my feelings for her keep steering my decisions. That's it. I am going to tell her. Everything. How I fucked up for so long never telling her how I truly felt for her. Those feelings are re-emerging with or without my permission now. I am going to tell her the truth about why I am helping her. How I can help be a mole for whoever is actually the good guy. Or just sabotage everything if Ashryn and Dubois are in it together.

But I just can't walk away from her again.

There is a drumming in my chest. Heavier than before. Physically pounding into me. I pull my headphones out, listening for any loud music that could be the source.

I only hear *screaming*. Summer.

It feels like there is a cranking in my chest. I cannot breathe. Is she…

All those years ago, I went looking for lore on mating bonds. Summer and I were so drawn to each other, nothing could tell me that wasn't a mate bond. Simply put, though, Fae powers were so drained at that point, even if there was a bond, a Fae more than likely would not feel it. Moreover, there was no case for a Fae - Human bond.

But she's not technically human… she has a well of power so strong, a bond would be uncovered at some point.

This thought sears through me, forcing my legs into a run now. For the place we carved our names into nature. The place that holds so many memories of us being pulled closer together and yet never uniting. "Summer!" I yell for her.

The drumming is growing painful. It's as if every beat is shattering my chest open, cracking it bit by bit.

"Summer! Summer!" I see her around a bend right before I double over. It feels like someone punched me so hard that a scan would show a few broken ribs. I find Summer staring at her fire covered hands, trembling.

"Summer, what ..." I cough, still trying to suck air into my lungs while crawling to her. My hands are caked in mud as I struggle through it. It will not stop me from getting to her.

She throws a hand up, "STOP!" shooting a bolt of lightning out.

"Fuck!" She yells as she swings her arm to the side as I duck out of its path.

"What did you do?" I cry out.

"Please. Shut. Up." She grits out.

Staring at the sky above us, water falls down her face, I cannot tell if it is rain or tears. At the same time, a large stream of water starts flowing out of her palms.

"Have you always -"

Flames encircling her wrists, blooming out as lightning shoots out of her fingers to the ground below her.

"Dune. Stop. Talking. Now."

She closes her eyes and starts taking deep breaths. Each breath seems to calm her, the trembling slows, the fire starts to subside. Struggling to my feet, the pain is still there but starting to dull in the same rhythm of Summer's counting. Looking around, that is when I notice that a couple trees took the brunt of whatever explosion happened. This was a direct hit...

That's our tree.

The thought slices through my brain. A crater sits in the wood where our names used to be carved. I swing around to ask what she did, but stop abruptly when I see Summer. She is staring at the sky still, but she no longer seems to be leaking random energies. That's when I finally feel it.

There is a hole in my chest matching that tree. I stumble a few steps, unsure if I want to close the distance between us or create more. Unbidden, I start to hyperventilate. Everything *hurts*. The pain in my chest is back and radiating through all of my limbs.

"How did you know?" I whisper.

"What?" Summer swings to face me fully now.

"How did you know?" This time I yell it, fueled by anger filling in the cracks of my pain.

Taken aback, Summer stutters, "I... I found someone who had high research credentials. She found out how to do it."

"No, Summer. How did you know I was your -"

"Do not say it."

"I will *fucking say it.* You are my *mate.*" I growl out. I march over to her. Trapping her against the tree behind her. "How did you know? How did you not tell me?"

"How could you not?!" She exclaims. "How did you not feel this every time we were together? Every time we ever got close. But you never wanted me. You made that clear when you left me broken on the floor of my apartment. You *made your choice.*"

I grasp her face with my hands. "I never wanted you? Summer I loved you from the moment I set eyes on you." Summer sucks in a breath, shaking her head.

"How can you even expect me to believe that?!" Summer thrashes in my arms.

"How could I not? You are beautiful, exuberant, kind, so fucking smart you ran laps around us all. And it scared the living shit out of me."

"*You. Left. Me.*" If words could slice me open, those would have.

"I will regret that for the rest of my life."

Summer pushes me away with more force than humanly possible. "You will continue to regret that choice, Dune. Because I made mine."

Trying desperately to keep the tremble out of my hands, I try to find the words as I pull her back to me. How was I so blind? How did we lose so much time? I can't get enough air into my lungs.

"Tell me... tell me you feel nothing now." I whisper. "Tell me that there is not a chance for us to rebuild what we had. Because Fates above, Summer, you were the center of my universe. I couldn't breathe without thinking of you. Even now, I get lost when I am around you. I don't know who I am supposed to be. I am back in this city for less than three months and I am drowning in your gravity."

"That is just… the bond. That is all that gravity is. You are here, hoping the girl you left is still waiting for you with open arms. That girl, Dune… she's gone. It wasn't an immediate death either. Hope kept her alive, even if just barely… for years. Hope that you would come back. You never did. That girl is never coming back, either."

"You are *right here*, Summer. I am here. What girl are you talking about if not the one right in front of me? The woman who is fated to be with me?"

"The girl that loved you!!" It takes all of me not to release her in shock as my heart finally cracks. The gaping hole she left in my soul is filled now with this ache. "The girl that loved you, pined after you for years. *Years*. Before either of us truly felt this bond. That stupid love is what caused me to burn your face. To talk about that love is to remember that *it wasn't enough to keep you*. It forces me to remember that I poured so much into a person that could leave without a second thought. You left *her*. That girl withered and died. I mourned her. But I learned to be me without loving you. And now… now I don't know how to be your friend. Being your friend was so entwined with loving you… I don't know how to be your …"

"Say it," I curse.

"No." She spits out.

Maybe if she can acknowledge the word, she will come back to me. Maybe she will fill this hole that is growing deeper and deeper inside me. Throwing caution to the wind, I finally do what I should have done that first night. The memory of Summer fidgeting with her keys in front of her dorm after we discovered Bert & Rocky's. Before she can run from me again, I pull her lips to mine.

Electricity courses through me as the rain seems to whirl around us. Every moment I thought about doing this flits through my head at lightning speed. It would have been so easy. It would have saved us so much pain. So much agony. Summer lets me coax her mouth open. I devour her. I want to taste every inch of her. I need to have her. I need to make up for all of those years we lost.

I was content, paying my penance of regret. Never seeing Summer again would have been fine. A just punishment for all I did and did not do. Now though, knowing what she tastes like, knowing how she feels wrapped in my arms... I can never go back. I won't be able to stop loving her. I can feel the chasm in my chest healing slowly, though. Is there a chance ...

Summer gasps. I open my eyes to find literal sparks of lightning skittering across our skin. I raise a hand beside us, seeing but not feeling the jolts. The current passes back and forth between our arms, traveling down one, back up another.

Summer takes the opportunity to pull herself from me. My soul yearns to follow her.

"Summer, come back. Please."

She is shaking her head as she takes steps backwards. Steps that take her away from me. Her eyes watch as the small lightning currents stretch between us until finally they are torn apart. The currents dance across each of our skin as if trying to get back to their other halves.

"I know I fucked up."

"What's done is done, Dune. I wish - " Summer gulps in some air. "I wish it could have been different."

"We can still - "

She takes two more blasted steps back. "No we can't. We are out of time."

"You are my mate!"

"Not anymore."

I watch as Summer Chase runs away from me for the last time.

TO BE CONTINUED...

ACKNOWLEDGMENTS

First and foremost, thank you to my husband, Kyle. You patiently waited for me to not be writing… and will continue to wait. Thank you for supporting me on this journey and being okay with me only showing up for GBBO.

To my bookclub girls, Veronica, Lori, Tami, for specifically not reading my first draft when I thought I was done with this thing two years ago. I shudder to think of it. Thank you for always being supportive when I would randomly pop in and out with updates on this process. Especially since I had no idea what I was doing. (Frankly, lets be real, I still don't know what I'm doing.)

Erica, thank you for being my unofficial alpha, beta, test reader. Your chats as I would give you pages gave me more momentum to finish than you will ever realize. You are stuck with me now though.

Nikki (and by association Sam) I will always love the story of how you came to proofread this thing. Cannot thank you enough for taking me up on Sam volunteering you to proofread and redline the crap out of this thing. The night I got a "OMG" comment from you made my day. (Sam, mission accomplished my taxes will be harder next year).

To anyone that heard I was writing a book and unknowingly held me accountable simply by asking how it was going - thank you for watching me slowly open up more and more over time about this.

Aimee you are the real MVP here - thank you for letting me borrow your Vellum since mine pooped out on the only day I really needed it to work.

ABOUT THE AUTHOR

After being an avid reader through grade school she was able to rediscover her love of all things books while commuting to work on the train. There was always a fascination with writing though. Although she went to college for math, and continued with a career in STEM she always tries to do something right brained to balance out the techie - whether that was creative writing or painting classes.

Her house feels lonely without any animals and is a fur baby mom to two dogs and a cat. They do make appearances in her stories on IG, don't worry.

instagram.com/kwrightwrites